Captive Heart

Elizabeth Bourgeret

DCT Publishing
St. Louis, MO

Copyright ©2012 Elizabeth Bourgeret
All rights reserved.

DCT Publishing
St. Louis, MO
Printed in the United States of America

Cover photo by Elizabeth Bourgeret
Author photo by Bret Harris
Additional artwork by Kylie Prestien

www.elizabethbourgeret.com
Elizabeth Bourgeret-Author on Facebook
@EBourgeret on Twitter & Instagram

ISBN: 9781479174539

This book is a work of fiction. Names, characters, places and incidents are the product of the author's imagination or are used fictitiously. Any resemblance to actual events, locales, or persons living or dead, is coincidental.

1. Women authors- Fiction 2. American Indians- Fiction 3. Strong female leads- Fiction 4. Midwest America- Fiction 5. St. Louis- Fiction 6. Forgiveness- Fiction 7. Christian Faith- Fiction 8. Prejudice- Fiction

Captive Heart

In memory of Mrs. Joan Caldwell (1940-2010) She was the epitome of kindness and goodness. She lived, walked and breathed the meaning of forgiveness and friendship.

And for my mother, Barbara Bourgeret who taught me the meaning of unconditional love and who is and always has been, the wind beneath my wings.

Elizabeth Bourgeret

Chapter One

Her dirt-covered lashes fluttered against her cheeks, before her dry swollen eyes opened to let in the dim light. She glanced around and saw the smoldering embers providing heat to her right. Her eyes followed the flimsy angled walls to the opening at the top. The sun was shining through the escaping smoke, but she had no idea what time it was. Fear engulfed her, but she did not move to escape.

Sarah Dobson raised her arm to remove her hair from her face. Her muscles ached. Her hair was a tangled mess. There was dried blood on her face and arms. Tears overflowed her eyes again and slowly spilled from the corners. She brought her hands in front of her face and looked over the wounds she had sustained. She gently touched her wrists where the ropes had dug into her skin. Her hands have not been bound for two, maybe three days.

Sarah looked around her and struggled to sit up. The fur beneath her was warm and soft and beckoned her to stay. Every muscle in her body screamed out in pain, but she made no sound. She used her scraped hands for leverage as the tears silently rolled down her face. The bottoms of her feet still burned. She didn't remember exactly where she lost her shoes. Her stomach ached from lack of food and days of sobbing.

What now? What is to become of her? Her back was to the tent's opening. She turned to see if the older dark skinned woman was watching her. Always watching but never speaking. She was alone. What did that mean? Could they have left her?

She strained to hear beyond her deer skinned prison walls. Suddenly the noises of a community came to her attention. Baby cries, dogs barking...conversations. Life, going on without her.

Sarah shifted her position to try and keep her back muscles from burning from lack of support with nothing to lean against. That was when she saw it. Her breath caught in her throat and a sob escaped her lips. She quickly covered her chapped lips and looked to the opening, hoping that her sobs had not called attention to herself. Nothing.

Her eyes came back and focused on the small rectangular, cherry wood box that was resting by her pallet. She reached out and gently stroked the delicate carvings of roses and the inlaid butterflies. It was a gift from her husband. One of the dainty feet was broken off and the corner was chipped.... her box. The tears flowed freely and she wondered if she would ever run out. Would she ever feel any other emotions besides grief and sadness ... and fear? No. She would never feel happiness again.

She looked around her again. How did it get here? She lifted the box onto her lap, afraid to open the lid. Would all of her letters still be there? Oh, Katherine...

Her body wracked with sobs again. Her fingers found the clasp in the front and she flipped up the latch. The lid opened easily on its hinges and inside lay stacks of letters. She shook her head, not wanting to believe all that had happened in the last few days. She wiped the tears from her eyes and picked up the letter that lay on top. The letters were from her sister who lived in the growing town of St. Louis in the state of Missouri. She was on her way to be with her when... when...

She ran her fingers over the stack of letters. Some were frayed with age and wear. There was dust and dirt among them showing that they were probably scattered and returned to the box after the ... She furrowed her brow wondering again how the box came back to be with her. Surely the savages couldn't have...

She didn't know how much time she had alone before someone returned, but took full advantage by opening the first letter. Its edges were still crisp and the fold was not yet creased. She wiped her cheeks and her eyes with the sleeve of her blouse and read:

My Dearest Sarah~

I can't tell you how happy I am that in about a month's time, you will be sitting here with me having tea. I can barely contain myself! I know I will scarcely be able to sleep until I can hold you once more my dear, dear sister.

James has taken care of all the details for your journey. You are scheduled to leave early Spring. He assures me that Captain Pike is an honorable man and will make every effort to make the journey comfortable for you and young Thomas.

In your last letter, you were concerned how

Elizabeth Bourgeret

Thomas would make the trip. I would not worry. He is a strong young man. I know that he and I have not met, but what else could he be with such wonderful parents as yourself and Frank. And you have mentioned time and again that even as young as five, he is quite the young man.

Enclosed you'll find a more detailed itinerary that will explain your stops and what opportunities you'll have to purchase supplies. You are much luckier than James and I! You'll be able to ride the train for a good portion of the trip!

We have found a cottage where you and Thomas could stay until you find something more suitable. Although I do wish you would stay with us. The cousins have so much to catch up on, as do we. Well, you have a month or so to think on it. Please do not think on it as pity. I am sure you would insist on it for me if, God forbid, James would pass away.

Oh sister, I look forward to your arrival. Even as I write this my stomach quivers with excitement. This should be our last correspondence! How I love you dear Sarah.

Safe journey. God bless your every move.

Your sister~
Katherine

Sarah could no longer control her sobs. She clutched the letter to her breast.

"Oh, Katherine!" she wailed, "Oh, my Thomas!" Anger washed over her and she squeezed the letter into a ball in her hands but thought better of it. She looked down at the crumpled pages and smoothed out their creases. "Our last correspondence..." she cried into the paper. Sarah pressed it to her heart and rocked back and forth. Her breath caught in her chest and she struggled to swallow the lump that had settled in her tight throat. The pain stabbed at her insides and her throat was dry. But the tears would not stop. She looked down with blurred vision at the box nestled between her folded legs. She kissed the letter before she re-folded it and set it gently on the stack. She fingered the lid ready to close it but then against her better judgment, she picked up the next letter.

My Dear Sarah~

Oh my sister, how my heart breaks for you! I could hardly read you letter for the tears I shed. I wish I could have been there for your comfort.

I don't recall your mentioning his being ill in your past correspondence. It must have come upon him so quickly. I am so very sorry for your loss. Sarah, truly, Frank was like a brother to me.

Sister, allow me to plant a seed in your thoughts. In this time of grief and loss, James and I would like to be with you. We would like for you to consider moving here, to St. Louis, with us. With mother and father gone, and now Frank... I can honestly see no reason for you to stay there.

You and young Thomas would be most welcome here. We would love it if you...

Sarah's reading was interrupted when the flap of the tent opened. The Indian squaw that shared the tent with her entered and held a shallow bowl filled with water. The flap closed behind her and she stood up straight from her bent position and looked at Sarah.

Sarah drew back and clutched her letter box close to her for fear of having it taken away. The Indian woman placed the bowl of water close to Sarah's pallet and knelt down beside her. She made no sound, and her face revealed no emotion. Sarah, too, remained silent wondering what was to happen next. The Indian woman's face was deeply creased and tan. Her eyes were a light hazel color but looked cold and unfeeling. Her dress was very simple. There was hardly any decoration or fringe of any kind. This time she wore no shoes. She sat back on her feet, still kneeling and rested her hands on her thighs. It appeared that she was waiting for some response from Sarah, who only looked back at her holding her box tightly.

At a length of a few moments, the Indian woman inched closer to Sarah. She paused waiting for Sarah's reaction. When Sarah gave none, she placed a cloth in the water and wrung the access out.

"Denda tae," she spoke softly with a raspy voice. She brought the warm wet cloth to Sarah's face and Sarah allowed her to run it across her forehead.

"Denda tae," she said again and gently continued to wash her face and neck but did not attempt to remove Sarah's tattered clothing.

The squaw reached out and softly touched Sarah's hand. Sarah's knuckles were white from squeezing the box. She hadn't realized her grip and relaxed it at the woman's prompting. The Indian's hands were calloused but her touch was very gentle. She slowly removed Sarah's hand from the box and washed it with her cloth. Sarah jerked and pulled back when the cloth hit her scrapes and open wounds. The woman nodded and waited for Sarah to give her hand back. The right sleeve of Sarah's blouse was missing completely and most of the left sleeve. The woman washed the exposed portion of her arms. Sarah was surprised at how grateful she was at this simple gesture.

The squaw sat back on her heels and returned the cloth to the water. She sat silent for another moment and then pointed at Sarah's feet. Sarah looked down at her blanket covered feet and then back to the woman. The squaw pulled the cloth from the water and pointed toward her feet again. Sarah nodded and pulled the cover off exposing her scraped and scratched legs and feet. Self-concious, she attempted to cover her legs with what was left of her tattered skirt.

The Indian shook the cloth at Sarah. Sarah understood and took the cloth. Sarah put her head down, embarrassed to wash herself in front of the stranger, but when she pointed to her feet again, Sarah reluctantly obliged. This must have been exactly what she wanted because she nodded again and left the tent.

Grateful for the time alone, Sarah breathed a sigh of relief and began washing her body before the squaw returned. Her feet were so tender; it hurt to brush the cloth along the bottoms. She dabbed the cloth up her limbs trying to clean the caked dirt and blood from her torn legs. The pain was terrible, but she felt so much better getting the filth off of her skin and infected wounds.

The squaw returned moments later with a smaller bowl. She set the bowl on the ground beside Sarah and picked up the water bowl and cloth. She said nothing but stepped back outside.

Sarah leaned over and looked at the thick, green paste in the bowl. Curious, she picked it up to smell it. The smell was pungent. Sarah recoiled and set the bowl back down.

Outside the tent, she heard the woman's voice. She didn't sound happy. There was a man's voice as well. Her stomach tightened and her hands trembled. She covered herself with the blanket and prayed, "Please, God, not that. I could not survive such abuse."

The woman's voice raised an octave to a shout. She stomped her foot and said a final word before stepping back inside. Her face frowned, but as usual, she said nothing. She carried two other bowls. One was fragrant. Sarah's empty stomach responded with a loud growl to which the Indian woman smiled. Sarah, embarrassed, held her stomach as if that would be able to control its volume.

The woman knelt down beside her again and handed her the bowl with water and nodded for her to drink. She drank heartily not caring that some spilled from the corners of her lips. Her mouth was so dry it felt as if she would never be able to quench her thirst. She drank until its contents were empty. She looked at the bowl's bottom and realized that it was a gourd of sorts. Sarah was impressed that these crude and uneducated savages were so ingenious. She took in the aroma of the food. The other bowl held a stew of some kind. The Indian woman showed her to make a spoon of sorts with her fingers. Sarah made a face but her hunger won out over manners. Sarah tentatively took a small bite. It wasn't unpleasant, but definitely different from anything that she had ever eaten before. Her stomach reminded her not to be picky and to eat what she was given. And the food gave her comfort. The Indian woman was next to her and chewing on something too, but she had no bowl. As Sarah finished off her stew she watched the woman spit the contents of her mouth into the other bowl. Sarah grimaced in disgust. The woman stirred the contents with her finger and pointed at Sarah's hands.

"No... No thank you. This... was plenty..." she muttered shaking her head and holding up her empty bowl. The Indian woman took the bowl and grabbed Sarah's hand. Instinctively Sarah tried to pull away, feeling tricked and deceived. The woman held firm to Sarah's hand and scooped a finger full of the poultice onto her wrists. "No, ow!" Sarah said and she pulled back. But then the cool mush began to ease the pain of her cuts. Sarah relaxed.

The Indian woman nodded and sighed. "Sorry," Sarah said humbled. She pointed to Sarah's other hand, which she happily placed in front of the Indian.

The Indian crawled down and threw off the blanket exposing Sarah's legs and feet. Sarah gasped and tried to cover herself again. The Indian woman tugged at the blanket and spoke something while holding up the medicine bowl.

"Oh. Sorry." Sarah pulled the blanket back off of her feet and lower legs, still keeping her knees and above covered. She tried to relax and let the poor woman do the job she came in to do. She had to admit that her wounds felt so much better once the medicine was applied. Her feet and legs were so sore, that even though the Indian woman used such care, Sarah flinched at every touch. By the time she was finished, Sarah was covered with drying clumps of green mash. The Indian woman spoke to her again, but Sarah did not understand. She gave Sarah a smaller bowl of liquid to drink. She was still so dehydrated that she drank it down without noticing the bitter taste. The woman pointed to her pillow and to the opening of the tent. Sarah followed her fingers but not their meaning. The Indian applied pressure to Sarah's shoulders to get her to lay back. The dark skinned woman nodded and ran her hands down over her own eyes, then pointed to Sarah.

Sarah lay back on her pillow and watched the squaw take the bowls from the room. She lay very still not wanting to disturb the drying medicine. She watched the smoke from the small fire wind its way through the top of the tent. Her head felt light and the smoke seemed to wind around her and lift her. Was she really floating? She watched the smoke climb up and mingle with the trees branches. She was happy. The walls of her prison seemed to disappear. When she opened her eyes again she was in a familiar place. She looked around and saw that Frank was smiling down at her. Both of their ice skates were draped over his shoulder. *I remember this,* she thought. The iced over lake was just behind her and a fire was blazing away in the barrel directly in front of her. The smoke drifted up. She followed it with her eyes. He had just asked her to marry him. She said "Yes," much to his relief.

He had been courting her most of her life. He would walk her home from church ever since she had turned twelve. Other men simply did not have a chance because he was always there. Sarah really didn't know other boys. She didn't even know if she loved Frank the way he loved her, but her mother always said that it would come. It never really came. She cared for him and esteemed him greatly, but loved him? Her memories flashed to Frank lying in their bed. His face was covered in sweat. His dark brown curls wet and pressed against his head.

Sarah sat at his bedside and held his hand. The doctor said he should get over it in a day or two. No need to panic. The next morning, he was gone.

Sarah didn't know what to do. There was no panic, no tears, just... a loss. "I am alone," she said to herself. Their son Thomas had turned five only a few months ago, and now there was no man to make the decisions. No man to walk them to and from church, no man to lie beside her. What was she to do?

When Katherine's letter arrived, at first it filled her with fear, but then second, a little glimmer of excitement ran through her. An adventure, she thought. She had never had adventure in her life. All of her decisions were made for her, but today was a new day. She would write to her sister and accept their offer.

Her eyelids fluttered and her body quivered as her mind flashed again to still another scene. The ground around her was covered with pools of blood. Her skirt and petticoat were soaked as well. She felt the weight on her lap and shifted her eyes to her arms. She sat on the ground rocking her bleeding son back and forth.

Sarah gasped and woke with a start. Her body was shaking. The Indian woman sat across the tent on her own set of furs watching her. A low fire separated them. Sarah tried to catch her breath and calm her pounding heart.

The woman came over to wipe her face with a cool cloth. She muttered something and even smiled while she tended to her. Sarah wondered how long she slept. It felt like days.

The woman continued to talk softly while wiping the sweat from Sarah's face and arms. Sarah deduced that her fever must have broken because of her drenched clothes.

"Thank you," Sarah spoke softly to her, but the words obviously made no connection.

Sarah jumped suddenly and looked to her left and then to her right. Her hands patted down the blankets frantically. Her panicked eyes looked to the squaw. The Indian reached above her head where her pillow lay, and grabbed the cherry wood box, then handed it to Sarah.

"Oh, thank you. Thank you," she cried, and held the box close to her chest. "It's all that I have left." Sarah was sure she saw sympathy in the old woman's hazel eyes.

They were silent until a great commotion startled them from outside the tent. The Indian woman smiled at the sounds of whooping and shouting. She got up quickly and went outside. Sarah hadn't realized how quiet it was before, but now all the new noises were deafening.

She was curious to see, but at the same time she was terrified that it was similar to the scene and fanfare that brought her here. She thinks she remembers this much shouting, but can't be sure.

Perhaps it was all in her head.

Curiosity getting the better of her, she struggled to get to her feet. Her muscles screamed out at her every movement. She rolled over to her hands and knees to help her to stand, but even then had to pause to deal with the pain. She felt dizzy and light headed, but pushed back to stand on her feet, convinced that it would help. She noticed that she was wearing a shoe of sorts. She paused for a moment to get a closer look. They were made of leather that formed to her feet. There was something inside them as well. Sarah assumed it was the poultice and it felt like fur also. A most comfortable feeling.

The whooping continued with the sounds of many horses. She stood up all the way and grimaced at all the weight on her feet and her skin falling back in place from lying on her back for so long. She sucked air in through clenched teeth, and hobbled over to the tent's opening before she changed her mind.

She gingerly walked over to the door of the tent and tried to peek out of a small opening, but could barely see anything but the backs of a crowd of half naked savages. She took a deep breath and straightened out her clothing as much as possible to make herself feel more presentable, should she get caught sneaking out. She opened the door of the tent and quickly stepped out, with the flap falling closed behind her. She was amazed at the sight.

An Indian city was spread out before her. Rows of tipis were evenly spaced, all facing the same direction as far as the eye could see. There were Indians of all ages gathered together directly in front of her. No one seemed to notice her standing there pressing as close to the tipi she emerged from as possible. There were mostly women gathered together in front of her with children running in all directions. The excitement made the air electrified. To the left of the crowd, a long procession of men on elaborately dressed horses was riding into the village. They were greeted with cheers and applause in addition to the celebratory noise made from different percussion instruments.

The horses were decorated with feathers and paint. Some had elegant drapes across their backs and necks. Some had braids in their manes and tails. It was quite a spectacular sight.

The first group of men to come into view was decorated much like their horses. They had headdresses made of feathers that were as short as just past their shoulder blades to as long as to their heels. They looked very regal as they came. They carried staffs decorated, too, with feathers.

The children ran up to the procession and touched the men's feet and legs, or would pat the horses as they walked past. The older ones would walk alongside proudly as if they were part of the party all along.

Behind this first set were more men, not so elaborate as the first, but still sat just as tall and proud as the first group. Bringing up the rear, younger boys that didn't look much older than twelve. They were waving and yelling at the crowd. They had huge smiles on their faces as they whooped and waved their staffs in the air. Their horses pulled travois, loaded down with fur-covered mounds. The crowd was smiling and cheering all the more as the parade got closer and made its way

Captive Heart

through the center of the tipi city.

Small children ran about in circles wagging noisy toys in the air. A pair of young Indian children stopped in front of Sarah and stared. Sarah tried to smile but as she leaned forward to reach out to them, one of them screamed.

Sarah stood erect and slid along the tipi wall looking again for the entrance to get back inside before they came after her with ropes. *"Oh, why didn't I just stay still?"* she thought to herself.

She found the entrance and was struggling with sneaking back in while the children ran off to snitch no doubt, then, she saw him. And he saw her. The look of surprise shown immediately on his face. Sarah was filled with a panic and she tried to disappear into the tipi again, but not before she tripped over backwards on the tent's entrance flap.

She crawled over to her pallet ignoring the sharp twinges of pain and drew her knees up to her chest hoping to shrink away to nothing. Her heart raced with anger and fear. "Oh Lord, Oh Lord, why have you spared me?" Sarah cried into her hands. "Am I to live as a prisoner all the rest of my days? Will this fear ever leave me? I cannot bear the sight of that... that... savage! I hate him! I hate him!" She cried out through gritted teeth, shaking with anger and fear. When her tears calmed and she regained control she whispered into the night knowing that her Father would be listening, "I know that I am supposed to forgive... but it is I who ask your forgiveness Lord, for I am so filled with grief and hate. How do I forgive?" Sarah dropped her head to her knees and spoke into what was left of her skirt, "Why didn't you take me too, Lord? Why?" She wept again; heavy grief-stricken sobs.

The celebration continued into the night but Sarah did not venture out again. She could smell the feasts being prepared and her stomach growled. "What kind of people are these? How could they just leave me here with no food and no water?" Sarah complained. She sat on her bearskin bed and decided to comfort herself with her letters. She found one that was very old and had been read many times. Sarah knew most of it by heart but went through the motions of reading it anyway:

My dearest Sarah~
I am so homesick. I know that this is a wretched way to begin a letter, but there it is. I long for your company dear sister.
I am trying not to be downhearted for James' sake, he is working so hard, but I do admit that at times I am not a very supportive helpmate! There's nothing like a six month journey to get newlyweds better acquainted!!
The store is doing well, and James has been well received with the other merchants. And you might not believe it, but there are some that are leaving the town of St. Louis and traveling even further west! Into the unknown! I have heard that the land is so beautiful and fertile they believe that new cities will sprout up from one ocean to the other. I, for one, have had enough travel. The good news is, sister, that they come into James' store for all of their supplies. So he is very pleased. And with the money that Frank invested, my husband thinks that he will double the size of the store within the next year! Isn't that wonderful?
But sister, I will be much too busy on my

own to deal with that, for I have some exciting news of my own to share. James and I are expecting!! How I wish we could be together. You are the first I have shared this news with, except for James, of course! I am so happy with this news and yet so saddened at the same time wondering when we will ever see each other again. Will you ever get to meet this new little angel? I do believe that God has sent us a child so soon so that I will not be so lonely without you, my sister, and best friend.

Well, I must think positively and pray that the good Lord will bring us together again. Please feel free to share this good news with all, and as always, I look forward to your next letter.

Sarah folded the letter again, carefully so as not to rip it. "Will we ever be together again? Oh, sister, now I am not so sure, for surely I am to die a horrible death here." Sarah cried out loud.

These letters would not bring her joy as they once had before, but remind her of all that she had lost. But it was her only tie to her world and she never knew if the next moment was to be her last... so she picked up another letter. They were no longer in any order, so she just read on...

Is it true? Did I read correctly? Did Frank Dobson finally propose? I know he is quite a bit older than you, but I'm sure that he will make you a fine husband. I was beginning to wonder if he would ever overcome his shyness to actually ask! And you will make a beautiful bride, sister. Know that I will be there in spirit. And you and Frank are always in my prayers.

Sarah paused to reminisce. How long ago was that proposal? Her mind began calculating.

"Katherine was 18 when she married and left with James to St. Louis. I was 18 when I married Frank…" she sighed, "Poor Frank."

Frank was older than Sarah by almost ten years. He was more her father's choice than her own. It was Frank's gentle persistence and kind manner that finally won her over. She knew that he would never harm her and always take care of her.

He would sit on her parent's front porch and sip lemonade for hours barely uttering a word.

"The weather has been w-w-warm for this time of year," he would stutter.

"Yes. Yes it has."

"The p-p-pastor gave a good sermon this week."

"Yes. Yes he did."

Sarah would giggle with her sister later as they lay in the bed they shared about how shy he was. "We sat there for hours and he barely said two words, Katherine!" she whispered.

"Perhaps you have just charmed him with your beauty and rendered him speechless!"

"Every Sunday??" The girls giggled into the night.

And every Sunday evening would end the same. He would set his half empty glass of lemonade down on the table and break out into a sweat before he built up the courage to ask if he could walk her home again next week.

He was a good man. A merchant like her father; like her brother-in-law. He was tall, and his brown hair was curly. The top he would press to the side with so much oil trying to keep it straight, that he developed a nervous habit of smoothing it down again and again throughout the day to keep it that way. A smile escaped Sarah's lips as she remembered.

And how proud he was of his son. Thomas was born with the same brown curly hair as his father. Frank passed out cigars to everyone he met for a full week. What a proud father. He fought against the pneumonia before it took his life. He was barely skin and bones at the time he took his last breath.

Before she knew it, she and Thomas were packed and on their way to St. Louis. She didn't want to give herself the chance to change her mind. Their house was closed up and put on the market. Her lawyer knew how to get hold of her through her sister.

Katherine's letters assured her that the Indians would not be a threat because the Army had supposedly "cleaned out" the area for travelers.

"I guessed they missed a few." Sarah growled under her breath. She closed her eyes tightly trying not to allow the visions of that fateful day slip into her thoughts. "No... no, please. I don't want to remember." Her prayer was answered when the flap of the tipi opened and startled her.

The Indian woman came in and smiled at her. She was chattering excitedly. It was a side of her that Sarah had never seen. She couldn't help but smile as a giggle escaped her lips at the woman's animation.

She held out a plate with a piece of rawhide folded over its contents. She pulled the top back to release the decadent aroma of two thick strips of meat next to a mound of prairie vegetables. She talked and pointed to the food and nudged Sarah to eat.

Sarah took the plate responding to the tightness in her stomach. The Indian watched until Sarah reached out with her fingers and brought the strip of meat to her mouth. The squaw jumped up and danced around their tiny fire and sang in a language Sarah did not understand. The Indian woman put her fingers on both sides of her head to show horns. Even as Sarah was trying to figure out exactly what she was eating, the dance told her.

"Oh! Buffalo! They were hunting buffalo!" Sarah said out loud with a smile, which quickly turned to disgust... "I'm eating buffalo?"

The Indian woman stopped in front of Sarah and smiled. She nudged Sarah to take another bite. She put her fingers to her head again and said, "Danka."

Sarah sat up straighter, actually thrilled to have made a connection with this woman. She tried to repeat the word, but must have done a terrible job, as she was corrected several times.

"Danka," Sarah finally said and put a greasy finger to her head for the horn.

"Danka," the Indian woman nodded. Then she rattled off again as if that was the key that unlocked the whole language. Sarah could only smile back and continue to eat the uniquely flavored meat that was brought to her in her deerskin prison.

The Indian put a few more sticks on the fire followed by a heavier log and rubbed her arms and pointed to Sarah's blanket. Sarah nodded and pulled her fur blanket closer to her with her free hand.

The Indian woman went to her pallet and lay down, wrapping her thick blanket over her covering all but her eyes and nose. She closed her eyes, but the corners of her eyes wrinkled up betraying the smile that lingered on her face.

Sarah, amazed by the simplicity of this woman, sat quietly and ate her "danka" and whatever vegetables these happen to be. Thankful to be fed and intrigued to see another side of these blood thirsty savages. She finished her meal, and lay down staring at the fire, allowing it to lull her to sleep.

Elizabeth Bourgeret

Chapter Two

In the still of the night, the visions she had feared came back to her in her sleep. The scenes were vivid and the screams were as haunting as the day that it happened. Her closed eyelids fluttered and her muscles twitched as she unwillingly went back to that fateful day that changed her life.

The wagon train had stopped for the day even though there was plenty of light left. The captain was going from wagon to wagon as he usually did to check on everyone.

Mary was a young bride already heavy with child. Her husband and Captain Pike were hoping she would make it to the next town. It was difficult travel with a baby as Clara daily proved. Her baby was not quite a year old, but was the cause of many problems that slowed the wagon train down.

Sarah's sister, Katherine was right; Captain Pike was very attentive and knowledgeable. He took extra care of Sarah and her son, Thomas by always building a fire for them and sleeping close by in the night. Sarah's maidservant took care of the cooking and cleaning and mending so there were some days that Sarah felt useless. But she couldn't do the things that Millie could do, and it didn't dawn on her to want to learn.

Sarah spent her time with Thomas and his lessons, when he wasn't following Captain Pike around or playing with some of the other children. Some days, she would sew tiny, intricate designs on handkerchiefs and other fabrics or write to her sister.

The men would sometimes make a large fire in the center of the wagon train circle, and entertain with their banjos and guitars. The music made Sarah happy for her decision to come. This would be an excellent experience for herself and her son. Today looked to be one of those times, as the men were bustling about gathering wood for the center of the circle.

Sarah was cutting up the cooked meat that Millie had prepared and was putting it on her son's plate. She saw some of the uniformed men come up to the captain and whisper to him. He looked behind him, but did not seem to be concerned. The officer spoke to him with great animation, but the captain just put his hands up in front of him and nodded, as if to say he would take care of things. Thomas was hopping after a grasshopper trying to catch it. Sarah smiled at her son and he caught her eye and smiled back. What a beautiful boy, she thought.

The dream moved to slow motion from that point on.

Sarah looked around to the rest of the families preparing their individual meals. One woman, about her age, Nelly, caught her eye. They smiled at each other. It was their sons running after the wildlife. They spoke to each other without words by looking at their children and shrugging their shoulders and laughing.

Gunshots interrupted the pleasant evening's natural noises. Sarah turned to see Captain Pike running in the direction of the sound shouting, "Stop shooting! Stop shooting!"

Sarah blinked again and the entire circle of wagons was swarmed with savage, barely clothed Indian men. The ground shook from dozens of horses that raced between the wagons. The dust raised and clouded the view. Gunshots were being fired; Indians fell in mid-stride. The Indians in turn effortlessly slaughtered men and women in every direction.

Sarah heard Mary cry out and looked up in time to see an Indian puncture the throat of a horse carrying an officer, which fell on top of Mary, crushing her and her baby. Mary struggled to free herself from the weight of the horse. Sarah's eyes burned from the dust as she looked around for her son. "Thomas?" Sarah heard her voice echo in her head as the nightmare continued.

"Mama!" Thomas called out running toward her. Sarah reached out and grabbed him and put him under the wagon.

"You stay there with Millie. I'll be right back." Sarah turned to run towards Mary but only got a few steps when Captain Pike was in front of her blocking her and covering her eyes. "Don't look, Sarah, don't look. Go back and hide with your son."

Sarah looked into his eyes and nodded ready to obey. His body suddenly convulsed and blood dripped from his mouth. "Run, Sarah, run!" he gurgled as an arrow pierced through the front of his shoulder. Sarah screamed as the captain slid down in front of her, his back littered with arrows. She turned back toward Thomas. She could see him under the wagon looking at her. Millie was screaming and rolled up in a ball by the back wheel. Another Indian grabbed a man standing beside

Sarah. She saw the Indian take his knife and slice it along the forehead of the white man. He stood there screaming. Blood poured from the wound and ran down his face. The savage turned the man loose who fell to the ground, still screaming, while the savage whooped and yelled, waving his bloody human pelt in the air. Sarah turned away from the gruesome scene and made her way back towards Thomas. She was almost there. The massacre went on around her but she kept her eyes on her son. Her feet felt weighted, and heavy. Each step took a great deal of effort. "I must protect my son." She heard screams all around her and tried to block out the sound.

A man in uniform stepped in front of Sarah and tried to change her direction.

"No! No!" she screamed. "Let me go!" She looked past him at her son crawling out from under the wagon.

"Mama! I'm coming!" he shouted.

"No! Thomas, NO!" Sarah screamed as she tried to pry loose from the soldiers grip. Her words were slow and her movements were weighted. He held her tight. He was screaming something but she couldn't hear. She had to reach her son. She pushed him off of her as hard as she could. When she did he was shot with arrows across his chest. His body jolted and his arm reached for his gun. He shot off a couple rounds haphazardly, but the damage was done. The Indians drew back and shot off again. But the soldier had already fallen to the ground.

Sarah turned back to see two Indian men behind her following the course of their loose arrows. The other round of arrows had missed their original mark. Sarah watched horrified as they passed the fallen man and then penetrated her son's chest and stomach.

"Thomas!" she screamed. The boy's name came out slow and her voice did not sound like her own. She ran towards her son. Sarah fell to her knees and he fell onto her lap. She looked back. The Indian who shot the fatal arrow still stood there watching her. He did not draw a weapon against her, but his face was forever burned into her mind.

"Thomas... Thomas," she said gently stroking his hair. He coughed and blood spilled from the corners of his mouth.

"Mamma...." he gasped, "Mamma, I save you, Mamma."

"I know, baby, I know. Shh, rest now... don't talk... Please God, please, not my baby. Please, God, save my baby."

"Mamma..."

"Yes, baby, I'm here," she looked down at his limp blood-covered body.

"Mamma..."

"Shh, honey, I'm here. I'm right here."

"I see Jesus, mamma."

Sarah's eyes closed tight and the tears poured down her cheeks. She held him tighter trying to keep him with her a little longer.

"Oh, my baby... please don't leave me...please, please don't leave me."

"It's okay, mamma. I don't hurt any more," he hiccupped and drew in his last breath.

"Thomas?" Sarah brought his face up to her and kissed his forehead. "Thomas?" she kissed his cheeks and nose and eyes. "THOMAS!!" she yelled. "No, Thomas! Come back! Come back to mamma!" She sucked in gulps of air and pulled his still body close to her own, rocking back and forth willing life back into him. She knew nothing of what went on around her but when she released the wail of a broken hearted mother, one man heard her. The one who took her son's life.

Sarah's real tears and grief woke her from her memories. "Thomas," she whispered. The small fire that still burned lighted up the tipi. The woman was across from her, sleeping still bundled up. She was right. It was an especially cold night. Sarah sat up and wrapped the heavy buffalo robe around her shoulders. The tears flowed freely and she stared into the fire remembering what happened next.

Her curly auburn hair fell loose from its bun hours before and hung in a tangled mess down her back. Her head was tipped down as she stared at the dry dirt passing underneath her. Her face was dust-covered and tear-streaked, but she had no more tears.

She attempted to turn her head back to look behind her but a man pulled at the rope that bound her wrists. The woman that was tied in front of her fell to her knees. The rope was tugged again. Sarah helped her to her feet. It was Nelly. She was suffering the same loss as herself. Her son was also killed. Sarah wiped away her tears and tried to give her strength through her looks and her touch, but she had none to give. Nelly's face was bruised and scraped. Her dark brown hair fell into her eyes, and Sarah pushed it away and attempted to tuck it behind her ears. The rope was tugged again.

Somewhere behind her another woman, bound to the same line was crying and talking nonsense. Sarah would catch glimpses of Millie, her maidservant ahead of her. She was quiet and fearful but walked obediently onward. If Sarah had to guess, there were about nine women survivors out of the fifty or more travelers from the wagon train. So many men, women and children lay dead... unburied... out there, alone on the vast prairie.

They were all tied to a horse that was ridden by a very unkind and brutal Indian savage. He laughed and taunted them. The other Indians did not participate. It was clear that his actions were unpopular.

At length, he dismounted and untied the women from his horse. He slapped his horse and it took off running. He screamed out alerting the rest of the village to their arrival. Soaking up all the glory and applause that was ringing out due to their coming into the village, he paraded his prisoners around behind him like trophies.

The men and women stepped forward and greeted the returning warriors. The man holding the rope lined the women up side by side as they were set out for display.

A group of men surrounded the women prisoners, their tan skin exposed from the waist up. They murmured amongst themselves, but Sarah heard nothing. The ropes that tied them together were cut. The men went up to the women and pulled their lips back to examine their teeth. Sarah only slightly pulled away. They lifted her head and tried to look into her eyes. The men laughed and talked as they poked and prodded the women as if they were horses.

The woman that was crying and talking

wildly was slapped until she went quiet. Sarah did her best to stay still and quiet while she attempted to take in her surroundings. She heard the deep male voices all around her.

One of the Indians cut the ropes that bound Sarah's wrists together. She numbly massaged them. She looked down at her blood stained hands. The dried blood creased into her palms and around her nail beds. Her eyes shifted to her clothes and she saw the dried blood down the front of her skirt that got caked with dust from walking the beaten path. Her eyes were dry, burning with every blink. She kept still, watching… wondering what was to become of her.

The other women that were brought in with her were taken, still tied together to the other end of the village. Sarah followed them with her eyes, realizing that her death was soon to come. Her eyes caught with Nelly's for the last time as she looked over her shoulder back at Sarah. The woman who had been crying was drug silently at the end of the row. Sarah blinked and a single tear made its way down her dirt-caked face. She looked after them until they were no longer in view.

The men were talking and there were Indian women standing behind them. The Indian women looked on but did not interfere with the men's business. Every once in a while, they would steal a glance towards Sarah. Was it pity in their eyes or were they as blood thirsty as the men?

A man who stood very tall was before Sarah. His face was weathered and deeply creased, but there could have been softness in his eyes, if Sarah would have looked. His skin was a darker shade of copper. He raised his hand and spoke to the others around him, commanding their attention. Their conversation sounded like it was taking place a million miles away.

A woman screamed in the distance. Sarah chose not to hear it. The muffled voices continued. They could all be talking at once for all she knew. Until... one voice raised above all the others.

She recognized this voice, but not its language. Her eyes followed in the direction of the sound and then she saw him. When their eyes met, he stopped talking. She held his gaze and could feel the rage build up inside her.

Before she knew what was happening, and in a voice that did not sound like her own she screamed out, "YOU! You killed my son!" Her feet moved automatically as she rushed at him and no one tried to stop her. "You killed my son! My only son!! You took him from me!"

She stood before this young Indian brave and beat with closed fists on his smooth bare chest. She was so weak that the impact barely made him blink but he made no move to escape her wrath or try to restrain her.

Tears blinded her vision as she yelled over and over and struck him again and again. "You took my baby... my only son." She gasped for breath and she was running low on strength as she dropped her head against his chest. The Indian stood patiently and quietly while she released her anger and pain upon him.

She cried into his chest and limply brought her tired fist down upon him again and again. Two other men moved forward to remove her but he raised his hand to have them hold their ground.

Barely above a whisper she cried, "How am

I supposed to forgive you?" As she slid down his body in a faint, his strong arms reached out to catch her. He scooped her up and took her inside a tent.

Sarah woke up in a sweat. Her face was wet with tears. She had fallen back to sleep while staring at the fire. She gasped, remembering where she was and looked around her. Her heart was pounding within the confines of her chest. The Indian woman was gone, but food lay beside her bed.

She closed her eyes again. "Lord..." she whispered. "I know that I have neglected you, and I am sorry. Please don't leave me alone. I cannot deal with this on my own. I am so broken and empty, yet filled with so much rage. My son, Lord, is he there with you? Yes. I know he is. That is my only comfort. I don't know why you have left me here, but I am praying for the strength to be able to endure it."

Chapter Three

The flap opened and the Indian woman came in with an arm full of smelly fur. Three other women followed her in and stared at Sarah with wonder. They smiled timidly. Sarah felt uncomfortable, as they made no attempt to hide their curiosity. She felt like a caged animal under scientific scrutiny. One woman, young, probably in her teens was bold enough to walk over and touch Sarah's hair. She said something to the other woman, but Sarah did not understand. Sarah didn't know whether to smile, to be friendly, or frown to show intimidation. So she tried her best to smile. This was her first encounter with anyone other than her dark skinned guardian.

The fire in the center of the tipi was completely out and the women had erected a frame around it. It took up most of the space. The women squeezed their way around the frame.

The guardian Indian went to the doorway and unfurled the fur across the frame. The smell made Sarah's stomach lurch. Each of the women grabbed an end and rolled it onto their edge. Every one did their part with the exception of the youngest one who was still fascinated with Sarah's hair.

Sarah watched with amazement, as each woman went about doing her own specific job. The teenager's mother said something to her daughter that made her prop open the flap allowing fresh air and a bit of sunshine in. The young girl then smiled and spoke to Sarah until her mother prompted her to get to her place and start in with her duties.

Sarah strained to see a glimpse of the blue sky but it was blocked when a younger woman, perhaps Sarah's age, maybe a little younger came through the flap and sat beside Sarah. She handed her a flat stone with ridges cut from its edges. Sarah took the stone but didn't know what to do with it. She looked about the room and saw the other women scraping off the thin layer of fat and membrane that was still attached to the fur.

Sarah wrinkled her nose and stared, but realized that the woman sitting next to her was encouraging her to join in. Sarah watched for a few more minutes then tried it herself. Her first swipe made her gag again. She picked up the stone, looking at it and then looked at her neighbor wondering what to do with the fat that was collected on it. The woman showed her a gourd that was being used as a fat container setting between them. Sarah scraped her knife along the edge and the woman smiled at her nodding. Sarah took a moment to look at her. She seemed very pleasant while she worked. She chatted with the other women across the smelly fur. Her skin was a warm, copper color and looked smooth. Her hair was long and shiny, braided on both sides of her head. She smiled a lot and seemed to be the one to carry the conversations or start new ones. Sarah concentrated on her task, but was fascinated by their camaraderie. It was almost like the quiltings that Sarah attended at her church back home. They seemed almost... human. Not like animals as she was led to believe.

They worked for hours scraping and re-scraping the thick fur. The more they would scrape, the tighter they would pull on its edges. They would roll it tighter and tighter around the wooden frame pieces to make it smaller so they could reach the center. They worked quickly and fluently. Sarah was just an extra. She could tell that she slowed down their regular flow, but they were patient with her.

When they were happy with the final product, they unrolled the fur and painted it with a clear, and equally smelly solution then they took it from the tipi.

Sarah watched them go; knowing without being told that she was not allowed to follow. The young woman who sat beside her stayed behind. She sat where the guardian usually sat. She smiled as she sat. She attempted to speak to Sarah. She tried again, only slower and louder. Sarah could only shrug her shoulders. "I'm sorry. I… I don't understand." She offered knowing that it probably sounded the same to this woman as her attempts sounded to Sarah. She wanted to know what the Indian woman was saying but didn't know how to make the connection. It was then that a thought came to her.

Sarah held up her hand to tell her to stop. Then she pointed to herself, and said her name. "Saarraah." She said slowly and pointed to herself.

It was the Indian's turn to look puzzled. Sarah tried again. "Saarraah" and pointed to herself. This time she looked and pointed at the young Indian with a questioning look. She caught on immediately and nodded. "Saaarrrrr" the young woman stuttered, and pointed to Sarah.

Sarah nodded and repeated the syllables of

her name again. The Indian smiled and tried again. "Saaarraah." Both women smiled. Sarah pointed to herself and said quickly, "Sarah…" she pointed again to her.

"Shhhebennnaa- Heeennepinnnn," she said, and pointed to herself and smiled broadly, enjoying the game.

Sarah tried to repeat it. It sounded funny to her and apparently to the Indian as well, because she began laughing. Sarah tried again, determined to make the connection. Better…

Shebenna- Hennepin made movements with her hands indicating the opening and closing of the mouth, and then flapped her arms like a bird's wings. Sarah looked confused. Shebenna-Hennepin pointed to herself and tried again.

The light went on. Sarah translated her Indian name to her own familiar English words. Talking Bird. "Talking Bird?" Sarah said in their language. "Shebenna-Hennepin?" Sarah said again.

She shook her head and smiled. Sarah breathed a sigh of relief. It was so nice to know someone by name.

Sarah pointed to the mat where Talking Bird sat. She pointed out the door. Talking Bird shook her head from side to side, not understanding. Then suddenly, by the grace of God, the woman came in the door. Sarah pointed to her and then placed the hand on her chest. Talking Bird understood. She pointed to the woman and called her, Kiswahkee, which means Grieving Mother.

Grieving Mother smiled shyly hearing her name and giggled at the sound of it from the lips of a white woman.

It was a good day. She'd done something

useful and she didn't feel so alone *and* she knew the names of two other women.

The days passed and Sarah's wounds healed more quickly. She was still not allowed out of the tipi, but Talking Bird came to visit often. They would spend the afternoons breaking down the language barrier between them. Talking Bird patiently taught Sarah more and more words, and Sarah was getting so she could put a few sentences together.

Later, when Talking Bird would come to visit, she would bring in a task they could accomplish while they were learning. Sarah learned to braid rope from the sinew of a buffalo and strips from young trees. She ground up hooves of buffalo into a powder to be used for a type of glue. For what purpose, Sarah did not know. They even had her scrape hair from hides. This was her least favorite task thus far. It was messy, and it would stink up the tipi for hours. She assumed that this is a task that would usually take place outside, but they were bringing it indoors, for her. They would spread the skin out and tack it to the floor. Then they would spread a thick, black tar-like substance on it. Sarah did not know what was in the mixture, but she had her suspicions. After the mixture was rubbed in, they would pull the hair out in handfuls. Sarah fought the urge to throw up.

There was one afternoon that Grieving Mother brought in a soft piece of leather, and was stitching a design onto it that piqued Sarah's interest. She was amazed at how soft and supple the leather was and was most impressed at Grieving Mother's handiwork.

"Beautiful." she managed to say in their language. Sarah held her hand out and struggled for the right words... "Can.... Me?"

Grieving Mother gave Sarah a smaller piece of scrap, some sinew and a needle. Sarah sat down on the pallet next to Grieving Mother and tried to situate herself. She struggled at first with the larger needle made of bone but it was carved down so smooth that soon, it was comfortable in her hands. Sarah made a few stitches as Grieving Mother looked on instructing her to keep them tight and close. Sarah nodded and improved. Sarah asked for a few of Grieving Mother's beads to see if she could add those to her line. They were loose and she used too much thread, but not bad for a first time.

Sarah worked on Grieving Mother's type of stitches until they flowed smooth and tight on her fabric, then she tried a few of her embroidery stitches that her mother taught her.

They sat in silence and stitched. Sarah could see the pattern emerging on Grieving Mother's cloth and she herself was content to experiment with the different styles and stitches. She was going to have to get used to supporting her back herself. There is no furniture here and everyone sits cross-legged or on his or her knees. Sarah's back muscles burned from not having a chair back to lean against. But she was learning.

When Sarah's scrap was as full as it could be, she showed her work to Grieving Mother, whose expression was one of great surprise. She started talking but it was too overwhelming for Sarah to understand. She shook her head and said, "Slow... more, slow."

Grieving Mother smiled at her and said, "Beautiful." She thought for a moment about her words then asked, "How do you know this?" Of course, Sarah could only pick out the words "how" and "know" so she placed her hand on her chest for "My" and answered with, "mother." Even as it escaped Sarah's lips in slaughtered Indian dialect, she had to swallow hard to keep her sudden grief in check.

Grieving Mother patted Sarah's leg with a heavy hand and nodded, "Beautiful."

The days passed and Sarah prayed to be content, and to make the best of the situation. She prayed to understand their language, and to try to see them, not the way the pastor in her church described them, but as people. Just people. People who haven't killed her or brought her harm and have kept her alive... for some purpose. She prayed that the purpose was wholesome and in His will. She would constantly repeat the verse of Matthew, "And lo, I am with you always, even unto the end of the world," in her head when she would get anxious. For tomorrow could be her last day.

Some days, she would wish for the end to come; to be reunited with her son. Others, she was anxious to see what awaited her when the sun came up again. "I put my trust in You, oh, Lord," she would sing to herself.

She was happy to discover that her captives were musical people. They would sing as they completed tasks and they would sing as they were walking about. When they would catch Sarah singing, they would encourage her to continue while they sat and listened. At first it made Sarah uncomfortable, but then she warmed to the idea.

She even picked up a few of the tunes she had heard from them and joined in occasionally.

And so it went on until, one evening, Talking Bird brought Sarah's dinner meal to her. "Grieving Mother has been showing your sewing to the other women and it has been greatly admired," Talking Bird said.

Sarah, struggling to understand, asked, "Other women?"

Talking Bird smiled and curved her hands to form a silhouette of a female figure. "Women," she laughed.

Sarah laughed easily with Talking Bird. She honestly liked Talking Bird. It was so nice to have someone near her own age to talk to. Sarah nodded then furrowed her brow as another thought passed through her mind.

Sarah stammered, "I understand word… woman. Are… are there other women…"she paused thinking of the words. She wiped her finger across her cheek… "like me?… here?"

The smile faded from Talking Bird's face, as she looked down at her feet. "Cannot say."

Sarah nodded in understanding and decided to change the subject. "Why are you called a talking bird?"

"I talk too much in high voice!" Talking Bird laughed.

"I am… happy you do. You teach me much."

"I am happy too. You are learning so fast. Must mean that I am a good teacher!"

"What means Kiswahkee?" Sarah asked.

Talking Bird thought about how to put it

Captive Heart

into words that Sarah would understand. "She has lost many sons and a husband to war or hunts or... or white man. Ummm...your people. She has only one son left and a daughter, me."

"You are Grieving Mother's daughter? I thought you belonged to..." Not being able to find the right words, Sarah pointed across from her and made the scraping motions from the buffalo hide cleaning.

"Oh." Talking Bird understood. "That is my husband's mother, and her youngest daughter. She never smiles."

"You have a husband?"

"Yes. A good, brave man. I have two strong sons. She pantomimed as she spoke to help Sarah understand. Sarah's eyes filled with tears. She looked off into the distance and struggled to say, "I had a son."

"Yes. I know," Talking Bird said, placing a gentle hand on Sarah's. She tried to comfort her. "That is another reason why you are here with my mother. You are grieving. She will help you through it."

"I do not know if there is a way," Sarah said, "I am so..." she searched for a word in her new Indian language but knew none so she used her own English word, "hurt." She placed her hand on her heart as the tears rolled down her cheeks. No translation was necessary.

"I am sorry for your... 'hurt'." Talking Bird said trying to mimic the Eniglish word that would be familiar to Sarah.

A flash of anger rushed through Sarah's veins as she stood. "It's your people who did it!" She switched over to her own language not having

41

the words to express her pain, "You took away my son! You hold me prisoner here, against my will! All of my things... my belongings are left somewhere out there, scattered among the corpses of good people! Good people whose lives were taken for no reason." Her breath was coming in gulps and the lump in her throat tightened. "I will probably never see my sister again... Why are you keeping me here?" She was screaming now. "Why won't you just let me go home?" She crumbled to the ground, spent and crying.

Talking Bird came over to her and wrapped her arms around her. The young woman's words were like a song as she cooed them over and over while stroking Sarah's hair or back. "I am sorry for your loss. I am sorry for your pain. I pray you will have many more sons. They will be strong and brave. Let time heal your heart... I am sorry for your pain..." Sarah did not understand most of what she was saying just as Talking Bird could not understand Sarah's ranting words, but words were not necessary to convey the emotions.

Sarah let Talking Bird comfort her as she cried into the night.

Sarah had no idea how long she had been a captive with this tribe. She had never attempted to escape because she had been too weak and with her one and only glimpse of the outside, she was overwhelmed at the amount of Indian people she saw. There was no escaping.

And, she was convinced that she heard screams in the night. If they were from her dreams, or actually within the village, she was not sure. But she recognized her own language. No one would give her any information of the other women that came in with her. She was almost thankful that she was unconscious for her first few days here, or was it weeks?

Sarah longed for the sunshine on her face, even though her skin and lips were still healing from the severe sunburn due to the long walk to the camp. Her delicate white skin was freckle covered with a light shade of pink between.

She had thought to starve herself to death; anything to end this miserable heartache and terrible fear that grew in her each day the sun went down. *Why do they keep me? Why are they getting me healthy? Am I meant to be a slave all the rest of my days?"* Sarah whispered into the night. She prayed and prayed but can't hear God respond to her cries. Why does He keep her here? Why did He make her so strong willed that she can't take her own life?

"Oh, Father in heaven, are you there? Your word tells us that you will never leave nor forsake us. But Lord, I feel so lonely, so empty. I don't know if I can handle all of these things happening to me. Am I to trust these people? I can barely stand my own memories much less the images my imagination comes up with. I am so fearful. Please, please, give me strength to endure."

She sat alone in the tent. She almost preferred it when they would give her tasks to do. It would help to keep her mind busy. She was just getting ready to pick up another letter from her precious box when Talking Bird came in.

"I have a gift for you," she smiled. Sarah's face questioned the new word. "Gift... when you give someone something that they are not expecting."

"Why?" she asked.

"It is from my brother." Talking Bird pulled out a small bundle from behind her back. "It is deer skin. So you can make some new shoes. Talking Bird made hand motions so that Sarah could follow along.

Sarah was flattered with the gift and tried to smile but her heart was anxious. She reached up to Talking Bird's hand and pulled it gently to coerce her to sit down beside her. Talking Bird showed a look of concern.

"Do you not like the gift?" she asked.

"It is... happy... no, I... like gift, but..." Sarah not only looked for a translation of her English thoughts, but also did not want to offend Talking Bird, who had become as close of a friend in a situation such as this.

"What..." Sarah began, "What is..." Sarah shook her head in frustration. She furrowed her brow trying to think of words that would express her thoughts. Talking Bird sat patiently resting back on her feet. "Do you... kill... me?" Sarah swallowed hard, bracing herself for an answer, not even sure if Talking Bird understood what she wanted to know.

Talking Bird's face looked almost sad realizing what Sarah had needed to know. But how much should she tell her? Not only was there a language barrier, but also there were some things that she was just not ready to know yet. She reached up and placed her hand on Sarah's cheek. "No harm will come to you. Be at peace ... here." She put her hand over her own heart and placed Sarah's hand on hers. Sarah calmed instantly. Sarah saw Talking Bird still looking at her as if trying to read her thoughts. Sarah dropped her hand to her lap and looked around for distraction. She was grateful for the answer. She spoke nervously in English, "That is comforting. Thank you... I must... look a fright." She pulled her tangled hair away from her face and tried to bind it in the back with a knot, but to no avail.

Talking Bird took her hand and gave her the deerskin. "Let us make some moccasins." Sarah smiled and nodded.

As they worked, Grieving Mother came and went keeping busy with her own tasks. She would smile at them every so often, but spoke little. Talking Bird had to leave a few times to tend to her boys who were ages three and five. Sarah wanted to meet her sons, but knew that her own heart was still too tender. She would let them decide when they wanted her to meet them. Before Talking Bird had to leave for the evening, they had made a fine pair of moccasins that fit Sarah better than any shoe she had ever bought from any store.

"Good night, my friend. Sleep peacefully. I will see you tomorrow." Talking Bird said as she stood.

Sarah smiled and stuck out her feet to wiggle her toes in her new shoes. "Thank you... helping," she stammered, "and thank you... brother for leather?"

"I will." She smiled and slipped from the room.

Elizabeth Bourgeret

Chapter Four

Sarah was beginning to get restless being cooped up in the tipi for who knows how long. "What I wouldn't give for a bath," Sarah whispered aloud. She couldn't even get her fingers through her hair. It was so caked with dirt and knots; Sarah shuddered at how she must look and smell.

Grieving Mother allowed her to clean with a cloth and water and removed the "chamber pot" regularly, but it just wasn't enough. "I suppose it could have been worse. They have not beaten me, nor starved me, nor used me in… in… other ways. Lord, I am thankful of that." She recalls hearing stories of the Savages of the West that would scalp men and rape women by the dozens. They would burn and pillage entire towns. But the soldiers assured her that the plains were "cleared out." The Indians were to be taken to a fort and a community built for them so they can learn farming, reading and writing.

It was this information that helped her make her decision to go to Missouri. How had things gone wrong? *"Why did the Indians attack the wagon train? We were not hurting anyone. Why all the killing?"* she thought. Sarah set her handiwork in her lap and closed her eyes. How long would her yesterdays haunt her?

"Mamma?" She heard it as clear as day. Her

eyes flashed open and she looked around the tent. Was he still alive? Could he be elsewhere in this village? No, they couldn't be so good to her only to be so cruel. *"Am I going crazy?"* she thought. She closed her eyes again, hoping the voice would come back to her.

"Mamma?" Why did God make it so hot today?" There he was. He was sitting right beside her. She reached out to touch him. Her fingers ran through his curly brown hair. They were on the train. She put his wide-brimmed hat back on his head, which was a little too big and covered most of his curls. He subconsciously brushed his hair from his eyes as he looked out the train's window.

"Just like your father," she thought.

"Mamma? Why is smoke coming out of the train? We sure are going fast, aren't we?" Thomas' hands clung to the window frame as he climbed up onto the seat to sit on his knees for a better view. "Can a horse go faster than a train?" He wasn't really looking for answers. He was just talking. Trying to take everything in. So many new experiences.

"I can run fast, can't I mamma? Can I run as fast as a train?" Thomas turned away from the window to look at Sarah. His eyes twinkled in the sunshine. Sarah's heart skipped a beat when he smiled... she couldn't breath. She reached out to touch him again, she wanted to pull him onto her lap; change the past, but he faded away.

"Oh no...no, no... no, no, I can't do this," she whispered. She opened her eyes and her cheeks were wet with tears. She wiped her face with the palm of her hand. "He's gone, Sarah. It's time to move on," she spoke sternly to herself, but knew,

Captive Heart

even as it passed her lips, there was much healing to do.

Talking Bird came in bright and early the next morning and found Sarah mindlessly working on her sewing. Sarah smiled but her thoughts were a million miles away.

"You are day dreaming?" Talking Bird asked.

Sarah smiled before answering. "My sister." She said with the faraway look still in her eyes.

"I have never had a sister. And my brother's wives were not very sisterly. When my brothers died, they went back with their mothers. So I am without a sister."

"I only have the one. I do not have any brothers."

"Be thankful. They are mean." Talking Bird laughed. Sarah nodded not wanting to go any further. Talking Bird was silent for a moment sensing that Sarah had something else to say. Before too long, Sarah worked up enough courage to say it. "Talking Bird, I ... feel... not clean. When... umm... when... I bathe?"

Talking Bird smiled, "Yes, you do have an odor," she teased.

Sarah laughed and said in English while holding her nose, "Are you saying I stink?"

Both women pinched their noses and made faces. When they realized that they did the same thing at the same time they both burst out with laughter.

Sarah sent up a silent prayer, "Thank you, Lord, for Talking Bird, she is my only shining light."

49

"I will see," Talking Bird said patting Sarah's leg.

"Thank you." Sarah smiled.

As Sarah lay beside the low crackling fire feeling restless she could see across to Grieving Mother. She thought about her situation and how she could make it better. Yes, she was a prisoner, and yes, she has suffered great losses, but what about those around her. There were actually days that she didn't feel like a captive, but as a guest. She certainly did not pull her own weight, and according to the other women, that was frowned upon.

Clearly, the others were making sacrifices for her. She accepted their offers of friendship but never extended any of her own. Grieving Mother is being kept away from her family to tend to Sarah's needs. And she looks after all of them. Her food, and she is tending to her wounds, which have healed, save for the scars that will forever remain. And she has had to listen to her hours and hours of crying and nightmares that still come too frequently.

"Grieving Mother?" Sarah asked softly.

Her eyes opened at the sound of her name, but she made no sound. She lay in the opposite direction of Sarah so she sat up on her elbow and asked, "How many sons have you lost?"

Grieving Mother closed her eyes again and lay still for a moment. Sarah thought she did not want to answer so did not press the issue. Then, Grieving Mother opened her eyes and sat up on her pallet. She rolled her sleeve, to her shoulder and there, on her left arm were scars. Five of them. All straight lines, one below the other.

She pointed to each one and said a name.

"Five? Five sons?"

She counted off the marks, then pointed to the one in the center and said, "pentae" the Indian word for husband. Grieving Mother rolled her sleeve down and lay back on her pallet turning away from Sarah. Sarah's eyes filled with tears as she thought of the pain she felt in losing a husband and a son. Grieving Mother's pain is many times that amount.

It was in that moment she realized that she would probably never see her sister again and that these were to become her people. She allowed herself some time to grieve over that, but decided in the morning that there would be a shift in her attitude. She was not familiar with all of the Indian ways and she would have to eventually release the anger that she felt for them taking her son. But they didn't seem to be hateful people. They appeared to be very family oriented. Perhaps something happened that caused them to attack that Sarah didn't see. Whatever the reason, this is where God had placed her. Whether they are savages or not, she is a Christian and God says to forgive and live in harmony with all men. She prayed for Grieving Mother and she prayed that God would change her into the person she would need to be. These were all fine words, but actions are what count.

"Thank you, Lord, for not leaving me," she whispered aloud. She closed her eyes and slept with great peace that night. The first night in many.

Still another day passed and Sarah was not permitted to leave the tent. Her comprehension of the Indian language amazed even herself for the relatively short amount of time she has spent attempting to converse with them. She knew that it was God's hand helping her to adjust to her new surroundings since she was willing to submit to His will.

The day finally came. Talking Bird came into the tipi, smiling from ear to ear. She carried a bowl that was filled with a foul smelling lard-like substance.

"My brother thinks it should be safe for you to come out today."

"Safe?" Sarah laughed, "I was kept in here for *my* safety?"

"Yes. Others sometimes watch our camps and they sometimes steal our women. Especially one as beautiful as you." Talking Bird tried to explain, "And your people... if they see one of their own, they would kill us all to get you back," she said somberly.

"Oh, no, I'm sure they wouldn't do that," Sarah said. "Perhaps I could be sold or traded back and..."

"No. That will not happen." The immediate silence felt heavy.

Sarah tried to change the subject. "What is in the bowl?

"Yes!" Talking Bird happy for the change, continued, "This is for your hair."

"That is going in my hair? What is it?"

"It the fat from a buffalo and some oil and herbs. It will soften your hair and take the tangles out."

Sarah was reluctant so Talking Bird encouraged her, "Let me do it for you."

Sarah took a deep breath and sat where she was told. Talking Bird draped a woven woolen blanket over Sarah's shoulders. Talking Bird put her hands into the fat and scooped some out and landed it on Sarah's head. "Oh! That smell!" Sarah laughed to keep from getting nauseous.

"You will get used to it. You will smell buffalo a lot!" Talking Bird teased her.

Talking Bird caked it onto Sarah's hair in thick globs and then squeezed it onto each curl. Talking Bird tenderly but firmly massaged the greasy substance into Sarah's scalp.

"That would feel good if it didn't smell so bad!" Sarah laughed.

"There. Leave that on for a few minutes to kill all the bugs," Talking Bird instructed as she wiped her hands off on the blanket around Sarah's shoulders.

"Bugs?" Sarah reached up for her hair in a panic.

"Yes, bugs." Talking Bird reached out to put Sarah's hand back down. "Just a minute or two and we will take you to the sunshine."

Sarah sighed, "I am looking forward to that."

After the right amount of time had lapsed, Talking Bird instructed Sarah to bring the blanket up and over her head.

Sarah stood up on her scarred feet. She told her to keep her head covered and not to make eye contact with anyone. "The others will pretend that they don't see you but some will glance your way," she explained. "I will take you to the river close to the women's tent. There we can bathe."

"We?"

53

"Yes, I would not be allowed to let you out of my sight," Talking Bird warned. "Sometimes you cannot hear a predator until he is very close and it is too late. But since you are new and not used to our ways, it will be just you and I and my brother will keep watch."

"Your brother? Oh no, I just… I cannot." Sarah brought her hand up to her neck and fingered her buttons nervously. "I have never…"

Talking Bird smiled. "He will not watch us; he is just there to stand guard. It is dishonorable to see a woman unclothed if she is not his wife. It is our way."

"But… I thought most of your people went without clothes."

"No. Once our children reach the age of around six years, they must separate and be clothed. Our men do not wear shirts when it is hot, but our women are clothed, always."

"I am sorry. I did not know." Sarah apologized.

"It is alright. I am sure there are things that we have heard about your people that are wrong." Talking Bird adjusted the blanket over Sarah's head, then guided her by her elbow to the tent's opening. "Are you ready?"

"Yes. Yes."

Sarah kept her head down as she was told but listened intently as Talking Bird lead her through the village. The conversations changed to a whisper as she passed and some people moved out of her way as they approached. Sarah noticed that there were not many who wore shoes.

The grass felt good on her feet. Talking Bird was patient and walked at a slow pace knowing the condition of Sarah's feet. Sarah saw trees and a gentle sloping hill then a shallow river. She could hear the water ripple over the rocks before she could see it. It was a calming sound to her.

Talking Bird spoke, "Thank you, brother, for being here. We will not be long." He must not have replied because Sarah did not hear anything, but saw his moccasin covered feet step out of her way. There was a clearing next to the water, where the grasses and flowers did not grow.

The mud was cool against her feet and her toes sunk in. It felt uncomfortable at first, but then it felt soothing. Talking Bird led her all the way to the water's edge and she willingly put her feet into the cool water.

Talking Bird took the blanket off of Sarah's head and placed it on the ground. Sarah stretched up to her full height and let the sun shine down on her face. The sun. How she had missed its warm and soothing glow.

"Here. Sit here." Talking Bird motioned to the blanket, which Talking Bird placed close enough to the water's edge that Sarah could still keep her feet in. Sarah's hair hung down her back in one balled up greasy lump. Talking Bird knelt behind Sarah and tried to get through Sarah's hair with a sharp tool. Sarah cringed and when she could take no more, she asked, "What are you using? That is killing me!"

Talking Bird reached around her so she could see it. It had a handle made of wood and porcupine needles stitched to it. Now that Sarah saw it, she could show Talking Bird how to better use it on her hair. "Here," Sarah said grabbing a handful of her own hair and pulling it over her shoulders, "if you start from the bottom, the tangles come out easier." Sarah worked on her hair and was surprised to see how quickly the knots seemed to slip from her hair because of the buffalo grease concoction.

"Let me." Talking Bird took the comb back from Sarah. "It's almost as if we were sisters…"

Talking Bird chatted on about her sisters-in-law but in Sarah's mind, she went back to her only sister. Her best friend and childhood roommate.

She saw the image of them sitting on their bed. "Oh, these curls, Sarah, what am I to do with them?"

Sarah would just laugh, "I did not make them, sister. Besides, we can't all be as pretty as you."

"Do you want one braid or two for bed?" Katherine asked as she ran the soft brush over Sarah's waist length red hair.

"Just one, thank you. Then I will do yours."

Katherine agreed and as they brushed and plaited each other's hair, they giggled and chatted about their futures. "James is awfully handsome, don't you think? And he is very ambitious. Papa likes that about him. I hope that we will be married someday."

"Has he even asked you?" Sarah teased.

"No, but he and father spend a great deal of time together down at father's store."

"Yes, that's because he works for papa." Sarah giggled as she wound Katherine's thick blond hair around her fingers to form the braid.

"Oh you!" Katherine spun around and knocked Sarah on her side with a soft feather pillow.

"Are you ready?" Talking Bird asked again nudging Sarah's shoulder.

"Oh... yes, I suppose. Are you sure we are alone?" Sarah stuttered coming back from her daydream.

"You see? There stands my brother." She pointed up the hill to a man standing with his back to them. "He will make sure that no one comes near."

Sarah's eyes lingered on him a moment more. His black hair shone in the sun and fell smooth and straight past his shoulders. He stood with his feet spread apart with his shoulders squared and his arms crossed. A weapon of sorts was angled across his chest and he barely moved a muscle.

"He is a good man." Talking Bird came alongside her, "He is in his 28th year and has not taken a wife. Our mother worries for him. She thinks that he will not take a wife because he feels that he needs to care for his mother."

"That is very thoughtful," Sarah commented. "What does your brother say to that?"

"He says that he has not found the right someone to love. He thinks the Great Spirit will bring the right someone to him."

"That's very romantic," she said in English.

Talking Bird took Sarah's hand and they ventured into the water. "His friends tease him that he will be too old to make children."

Sarah blushed but laughed, not knowing how to respond.

As they immersed in the water, Talking Bird removed her clothing and threw it onto the banks.

57

Talking Bird was amazed at how many layers that Sarah was wearing. "Do all the women of your kind wear your kind of clothes?"

"These clothes hardly look like the ones I usually wear, but yes, we dress a lot alike."

"Why do you have so many clothes on top of clothes?"

"I... do not know how to explain. It makes us look... like... women. It gives us... umm..." she made the silhouette of a woman with her hands, "shape."

"I do not understand. It does not look very comfortable."

"You get used to it. It feels... not right... without it."

"We use clothes just to cover us up... and to keep us warm."

"It makes sense. Your way does look more comfortable." Sarah would wring out her clothes before she would throw them onto the beach. She decided to keep her white, cotton bodice on that covered her from her shoulders to her knees.

"What about that piece?" Talking Bird asked.

"I think I will keep this layer on... for now."

Talking Bird shrugged and flipped on to her back and floated down the river. She would reach a certain point and swim back up to check on Sarah, then float down again. Sarah stayed under the water so no one would see her wet bodice and tried rinsing and rinsing her hair. Talking Bird moved to the opposite side of the river and scanned the edge. She stepped out and reached for a plant and snapped it close to its base. She brought the green stalk back over to Sarah.

Sarah was embarrassed for Talking Bird and her lack of modesty, but perhaps just a little jealous that she felt comfortable enough in her own skin not to feel embarrassed for herself.

Talking Bird split the end of the stalk and peeled away the outer edges. She rubbed the exposed plant against Sarah's scalp. She rubbed her long strands of hair between her hands and the stalk, then piled all of Sarah's hair on top of her head and rubbed everything together. Sarah caught on and began washing her own hair. Talking Bird swam off to the other side again to grab another stalk for herself. She washed her hair with Sarah. "Your hair is so beautiful," Talking Bird told her.

"I think yours is," Sarah complimented back. "I have always wanted straight hair."

"I have never seen anyone with your color hair before. I have not seen very many white people and even fewer women. Are there many with your color?"

Sarah thought for a moment. "Not too many, I guess. But a lot of yellow, and brown and black."

"The Indian men like the yellow hair. I think because it is so different from their own women." Talking Bird laughed. She dipped her head back into the water and Sarah did the same.

"I feel so much better!" Sarah said.

"Wait, I have more for you." Talking Bird said as she swam back to the edge of the river and snapped a thin, long dark green stem of a plant and brought it back over to Sarah. She broke the stem in half and gave one piece to Sarah.

"Chew on this." Talking Bird said as she began chewing on her half.

"It tastes like..." Sarah did not know the

word.

"Mint," Talking Bird answered for her. "It is for your teeth. Rub it on your teeth."

"Oh. Thank you. I am so lost without my… my…" she could not think of a word to describe her cleaning regime. "Shampoo, and tooth powder," she said finally in English.

Talking Bird frowned at the odd sounding words, but seemed to understand what Sarah meant. Sarah rubbed the spongy, onion-minty flavored stalk against her teeth, running her tongue over the smooth cleaned areas. Talking Bird pushed off the bank lay back in the water and Sarah joined her. She was enjoying the water making its way around her not minding one bit that she was in its path. Sarah ran her fingers through her hair and was amazed at how soft it was. The combination of the grease and the soap root made her hair clean and soft.

"My hair! It feels so good, I cannot thank you enough!"

"I will think of some way for you to repay me. Perhaps you could teach me to make your stitches."

"Talking Bird, I would love to. It is not hard at all."

"Good." Talking Bird smiled a mischievous grin and sent a small wave of water at Sarah. Sarah responded with a splash. The two women laughed and splashed like children. When Sarah looked up at "big brother" he still remained unmoved and two women laughing and carrying on could not entice him.

"You see? I told you he was an honorable man," Talking Bird smiled. "He is handsome, too."

"He is maybe sleeping!" Sarah teased.

With one final splash, Talking Bird climbed from the water and lay down on the blanket to dry in the sun. Sarah could only drop her gaze and blush for her lack of inhibitions.

"Are you coming out or are you staying in there forever?" Talking Bird called out, never opening her eyes.

"I cannot," Sarah called back.

"Come and dry in the sun." Talking Bird told her.

"I cannot. It is not ... 'decent'." Her English word made Talking Bird laugh. "Talking Bird, my clothes are…"

Talking Bird stood up and nimbly ran over to a fallen tree that lay on the beach. Behind the tree was a dry deerskin dress that she promptly slipped over her head and still-wet body. She leaned forward and pulled her hair from the neck and wrung it out.

Sarah drew in a deep breath, thinking she was stuck in the water until sundown, or her clothes dried, whichever came first. Talking Bird reached back behind the log again and pulled out a second dress.

"See? I made this for you!" Talking Bird smiled broadly as she brought the dress closer to Sarah.

"I kept it plain so you can put some of your beautiful stitching on it. I hope you like the fringe on the top and the edge." Sarah said nothing. "It matches the moccasins you made." Still no response. "My brother killed this deer as a gift for you," Talking Bird paused, "Do you not like it?"

Sarah rubbed her burning eyes and pulled

her hair back off of her shoulder allowing the water fall down her back. "I am sorry. Yes, I love it. It is beautiful, how could I not love it?" Sarah looked at her pruning fingers, as Talking Bird remained silent. Sarah came out of the water with her arms covering herself. She walked over to Talking Bird and accepted the dress. "It is very well made," she said as she fingered the seams, and then slipped it over her head. "It fits perfectly, too. How did you know?" Sarah tried to smile but her emotions were feuding inside her.

"I measured it to myself since we are so close in size. You are a bit taller, so I added more length." Talking Bird smiled humbly at her handiwork. "It looks very nice on you." Talking Bird stood back looking her over and waiting for the reply that looked to be close to the surface.

Sarah looked down at herself. Her legs were still dripping with water and the leather stuck to her arms and chest. It felt peculiar over her sopping wet bodice, but there was no way, she was going to take it off. "Talking Bird, it is beautiful. I say that with honest heart." She looked down at the dress again and ran her fingers through the fringe. "It is hard to accept..." Sarah began again, "that I will never be with my own people again. Not wear my own clothes, sleep in my own bed or embrace my own family..." Her words drifted off and Talking Bird felt horrible.

"Please forget. I rush things. I want you to feel at home here and I..."

"Forget? You think that I could ever forget? This is NOT my home!" Sarah looked as if she had been punched in the stomach. "I am a prisoner here! The reason I am here is because your people killed the hundreds that I was traveling with, including my son!" Sarah paced back and forth along the edge of the water shaking her head. "What have I done to deserve this?" Her voice rose with anger and remorse. "Why could they not have just left me out there to die with the others... with my son?" Sarah choked down a sob. "Please do not misunderstand me." Sarah touched Talking Bird on her shoulders. "I am grateful for you. You have taken me in and have been teaching me your beautiful ways and your beautiful language... I am honored that you would want to consider me a sister, but..." she gasped for air, "But... I already *HAVE* a sister. One whom I shall never see again, and it is by no choice of my own. My choices have been robbed from me. I find it easy to love you but I am still so angry and hurt." Her voice drifted up the hill and even though he fought every urge to turn around he never did... but his heart went out to her.

They walked back up to the tipi in silence. As Talking Bird turned to leave, Sarah reached out and took her hand. "I am sorry." She spoke in English not knowing the proper phrase.

Talking Bird's eyes glistened with tears but they did not fall. "I know." Talking Bird wrapped her other hand around their clasped hands. "I do wish that you have not had such pain, and I am sad that it will always be between us." Talking Bird turned and walked away leaving Sarah standing outside her tipi.

While Sarah stood outside the doorway, she hoped she wasn't taking advantage of Talking Bird's kindness by standing outside a little longer. Sarah did not want to go back inside. Not just yet.

She felt the sun on her face and closed her eyes to take it in, but only for a moment, for there was so much to see.

Sarah guessed that it was probably early summer. The flowers were all in bloom and the blossoms of the trees were beginning to fade and fall off the branches.

The village, as large as it was, was neatly placed. The openings of the tipis all faced the same direction, the rising of the sun. They spread out along the tree line and made a circle within a circle. In the very center, Sarah could see there was a huge fire pit dug into the ground. It had wood stacked up in it ready to be caught on fire. Outside almost every tent were smaller fire pits, some had a familiar wooden tri-pod standing over it, and others were surrounded by stones.

There were people buzzing around keeping busy with their tasks and paying no attention to her. *"Maybe they can't see me,"* Sarah thought to herself.

There were children running and playing with dogs barking at their antics. The women worked together in small groups and laughed with one another. Sarah wished she could hear what they were saying. She almost wished that she could join in.

"Are you ready, Sarah?" a voice inside her head asked. *"Are you really ready to join these people and make them your own?"* Sarah wasn't ready to answer that question. She looked down at the soft dusty earth and at her bare feet peeking out from under her new deerskin dress. It even had fringe on it just like Talking Bird's. Sarah took a deep breath and sighed, then slipped back into her

tipi.

Elizabeth Bourgeret

Chapter Five

As time went on, Sarah was allowed to participate in tasks outside of her tipi. She had gotten used to the stares and the whispers thinking that she would probably have done the same thing if one of them had ended up in her town.

Talking Bird never again mentioned the episode at the water and when Sarah tried to apologize again, she said that it was "forgotten."

The others in the tribe mostly accepted her; there were some who spoke a little more harshly to her as if she were a child or stupid. And still others would spit on the ground when she came close. She was taught to dig up turnips from a hidden patch and was shown to harvest specific herbs that Grieving Mother needed for her poultices and to spice her food.

The tribe stayed in a specific area except when the men went off further to hunt. A security fence of trees surrounded their patch of pasture. The grass under her feet was thick and green and smelled fresh and sweet in the mornings under a fresh coat of dew. If it was quiet you could hear the gurgling of the river that sat just beyond the tree line hidden within the forest. It was rarely quiet. And Sarah was becoming accustomed to the daily noises that made up these people.

Sarah was taught things that applied to

Grieving Mother's duties, as if she was assigned to her. *"It makes sense,"* she thought. *"It does seem as if she has no one else. Talking Bird has her own family, and tends to them. I have yet to meet her son, but she has me gather things that he likes or needs. He is a most generous man,"* she smiled to herself, *"I wonder if he is as handsome as he is generous."* Her thoughts wandered as she somehow separated herself from the other women while scavenging for sticks for the fire. She had found herself alone in the woods and discovered its serenity most welcomed. They didn't have places like this where she was from. The parks of her home were very elegant. The trees were all the same size, the grass was beautifully tended, and small benches and tables were set about in key locations. Sarah immensely enjoyed the wildness of the trees, the colors and smells all around her. With every step the old leaves crunched beneath her feet. The birds and animals fluttered about with purpose. And yet with all this activity, there was a certain stillness. Sarah began to hum a tune as she gathered, unaware of the danger that could befall her peaceful serenity at any moment. She felt safe and sang on.

"You should not be out here all alone," a man's voice said.

Sarah screamed and threw her bundle of sticks in all directions. She turned to face her attacker and saw… him. Was he smirking? "You! What are you doing out here?" she snapped at him.

"Following you. You have not learned to stay near the others where it is safe," he spoke calmly and the sound of his voice made her heart race.

"Humph, safe, No one is safe around you," she spoke under her breath.

"There are many things that could happen to you, out here alone. The trees hide many enemies."

"Yes, as you have just proven." Sarah bent over to start picking up the sticks again to help her hide the fear that was running through her veins.

"I am not your enemy." His voice was soft. It unnerved her.

"What do you care if anything happens to me?" She stood up and faced him, "Do you not have to go kill something, somewhere?" she seethed allowing her anger to say things she would otherwise have kept to herself. She was trying to be hateful. She hated him, didn't she? Sarah bundled her sticks close to her body, sure that he could see her heart racing. He followed.

"Did you need more food or another deer skin?"

This caught Sarah off guard. Was he actually trying to be nice? No. He was most likely trying to buy her forgiveness! "No, thank you. Talking Bird's brother is taking care of me very well, thank you." She looked up and caught his gaze. She stomped off when he smiled at her. He followed her back to the tipi. She dropped her sticks off at the outside pit and was almost inside when his words held her still.

"I am sorry about your son." He paused. She did not turn to look at him, but he knew she heard. "I did not mean to pierce him."

When she slowly turned to face him, her jaw was clenched tight and there were tears in her eyes, but her stance was strong. She took a step towards him and looked deep into his brown eyes. She opened her mouth to speak, but no words came out. Her lips trembled as she struggled to maintain control. When she blinked, the tears rolled down her cheeks but she did not break eye contact with him, or he with her.

She unclenched her fists and reached up to put a hand on both sides of his face. Her hands were gentle but her actions were determined. She pulled his head down to her chest and placed his ear against her heart.

"Do you hear that?" she asked, "That is the sound of my broken heart. It will never be mended again." She let him go and thought she saw true compassion in his eyes. "I have forgiven you… but I will never forget." She turned from him and stepped into her tipi, where she fell to the floor and cried.

Talking Bird, after witnessing the whole episode, called out to her, "Sarah, wait."

The Indian man reached out to grab Talking Bird's arm. "I know what you are thinking. It is not time. Do not say anything. She is grieving."

"But Little Feather, she does not know."

"I know. We will keep it that way for a little longer."

"But brother…"

"She must work through her grief, and nothing you say will change that. She needs to hate me now, to help her heal. Say nothing."

The next day, the men went out on their last hunt. They were gone before Grieving Mother woke Sarah.

"My son is gone. We must prepare for our

Captive Heart

journey," Grieving Mother explained.

"Oh, I wish you would have wakened me. I have not been able to thank him for his care of me."

"You do not need to thank him. He does it willingly for you. He chose you."

"I do not understand... your word... chose."

"Other women like you... gone. But you stay."

This was the first time the other women were spoken of since she was brought here. She wanted to ask more questions, but Talking Bird came in with her youngest son, Donisuma, which means 'Sleeps a lot'.

"Sarah, come with me. I will show you how we prepare for a great feast. You were not able to join us for the last one, but this one is very special. Special for you."

Sarah followed her out into the sunshine while Grieving Mother grumbled a few lines about having to do all the work.

"Is that alright, mother?" Talking Bird tucked her head back in the tipi, "Or would you rather have Sarah's help here?"

"No, take her. Go. But do not forget that we pack soon."

"I will not, but do not forget that we feast first!" she smiled. "We do not pack until tomorrow." Talking Bird linked arms with Sarah and began to walk off. "It is a beautiful day today, do you think?"

"Yes, it is. What is all the activity?"

"Our men are out hunting and..."

"All of the men?" Sarah interrupted.

"Most of them, all of our hunters, anyway."

"Good."

"As I was saying... all of our hunters are hunting and when they return, we will have a huge feast!" Talking Bird grew more excited with every word. "And Sarah, please do not get angry, for I love you like a..." Talking Bird paused but Sarah anticipated her words.

"A sister? I know. I feel the same way." Sarah laughed and was surprised at her good humor. She continued, "You, I can say honestly, are my favorite Indian sister."

"Oh, Sarah." Talking Bird stopped and reached for both of Sarah's hands. "I am so happy to hear you say that, because, the feast... will not only be for thanking the Great Spirit for the hunt and the food, but we will be thanking him for you. It is then that you will be brought in as one of us."

Sarah's feet froze in mid-stride. She felt a pang of sadness and fear, but also excitement. Talking Bird looked at Sarah and smiled while trying to read her expression. Sarah smiled back as best as she could and in turn was trying to decide her own feelings.

Talking Bird hooked Sarah's arm again and they went back to walking. And while Talking Bird explained about the events of the evening, Sarah prayed silently. *"Am I ready, Lord? Can I love them like my own family? Can I be happy here for the rest of my days on earth? Is this where you want me to be?"* A warm feeling came over her and Sarah stopped. She looked up at the sky and said, "Thank you, Lord."

"What did you say?" Talking Bird asked.

"Nothing... so tell me, what does all of this mean, when I become one of you? Does it mean that Hissing Crow has to stop spitting on the ground every time I walk by?"

Talking Bird laughed out loud and Sarah found that it felt good to laugh. "All that and even more!"

All morning they collected vegetables and herbs to be used for seasoning. Talking Bird explained what everything was and what it was to be used for. Sarah followed along and listened to everything that she was saying, but since she had never learned her way around a kitchen, she did not understand why she needed to know about spices and herbs. But she followed along, happy for the diversion.

Then, that afternoon, they started building the smoke house. They gathered young birch branches and bent them over to make a half circle. They tied them to other pieces weaving them into a domed frame. Sarah fumbled with the knots; her dainty fingers becoming blistered again with the unfamiliar work. Over the skeletal structure, they hung a heavy pelt and set it to the side. "This will keep the smoke inside and dry the meat. It will make the meat last a very long time this way," Talking Bird taught her.

As they dug the deep hole that the fire would be built in and the dome would rest over, Talking Bird mentioned, "You know that after the feast is over and you become one of us, you are free to marry."

Sarah stopped digging and looked up at Talking Bird who was grinning at her, "Do... do... I have to?"

"No," Talking Bird laughed, "But do you not want to?"

"I had not really thought of it, I guess."

"You had a husband before, yes?" Talking Bird inquired.

"Yes." Sarah spoke just above a whisper, "His name was Frank. He died of... a... sickness in his chest." Sarah patted her chest to be sure that she was speaking correctly. Sarah grew quiet and Talking Bird waited to see if she would share more. But she did not speak. Instead, she burst into laughter. She dropped her digging stick and pushed her curls out of her face and laughed. She wiped the single tear from her eye with her dirt-covered fingers. Talking Bird watched her laugh and cry at the same time and didn't quite know how to respond.

"I am sorry," she spoke between breaths of laughter. "I was trying to picture Frank out here, living this way." She wiped away another tear. "You think I am bad. The first day you made him walk without shoes, he would have cried like a baby! And, he would never, never...have been able to eat your food. No offence, but he has a ... 'weak constitution'" she spoke in a deep English voice.

By this time, Talking Bird was laughing along with her. "Not a good hunter?" she asked.

"Hunter? Ha!" she laughed. "He would have been afraid of the horse!"

"How did he provide food for you? What did you eat?" Talking Bird was appalled and fascinated all at the same time.

"Oh, we always had food. But where I live, we do not have to hunt. I do not even know how to cook. This... this way of life, it is all very new to me. I do not think I have been out of doors this much in my whole life." Sarah did not see the disbelief in Talking Bird's eyes; she was too lost in her memories. "He was a good man. There are times when I miss him, a lot."

"It must make you sad, not to have a man."

"Sometimes. I was afraid to be alone at first, but I have to remember that God is always with me, no matter where I go or what I do."

"What is 'God'?"

"He is what you call your Great Spirit, I think. They are one and the same." Talking Bird nodded as Sarah continued. "I was on my way to live near my sister, so my son and I would not be alone. The thought of another husband did not really cross my mind." Talking Bird smiled knowing that the thought was now tiptoeing across her thoughts. "Hmmm," Sarah shrugged saying to no one, "I wonder where my furniture is."

Two days had passed and the men had not returned. Grieving Mother worried more with every passing hour.

"She lost two of her sons while they were out on the hunt," Running Deer leaned over to explain to Sarah while they sat in the sewing circle. Sarah nodded and said a quick prayer for the safety of the hunting party.

Running Deer was around the same age as Sarah, perhaps a few years younger. Sarah thought that she was beautiful, but saw that her heart was shallow. Her hair was soft and shiny and straight as a board. Her face had high cheekbones and piercing eyes. She had lost her husband at war and both of her children, one at birth and one at a very young age, Sarah heard.

The more Sarah learned of these women,

and their lives and trials, the guiltier she felt for feeling sorry for herself. The Indian way of life is so hard and so full of dangers that many don't even make it to their thirtieth birthday.

She learned that these people felt that family was very important. There have only been two "divorces". One, the wife went back to her mother to live, because he was physically cruel to her. In this scenario, the woman was not allowed to remarry, but the husband was shunned; they acted as if he did not exist. He was not allowed on hunting trips, or at the council meetings. He was not spoken to or heard. Eventually he left the tribe.

The other, the man took his wife and her belongings into the woods and left her there. It was explained to Sarah that another man could have claimed her but, in this instance, her mother came to get her.

Either one is highly frowned upon. Most men have only one wife, which is the opposite of what Sarah was taught through her church. If a man had more than one wife, it usually meant that she was his wife's sister, and the sister's husband died. The sister would choose to go back to her parents or to her brother-in-law's home and become a second wife. He did not have to take her and she did not have to go.

She was not allowed to marry again from the same tribe, if she chose not to go with her brother-in-law, but could marry into another tribe of the same family group. This kept jealously and gossip to a minimum.

Many of the myths of Sarah's upbringing had been dispelled as she watched this group of people live, work, and love. For instance, Sarah was told that the "heathen savages" took several wives, if any, but mostly just raped and ravaged as they pleased. They had no respect for the land, and they abused the women and children. This was obviously not the way. Although, from an outsider's view, it could be thought that they abuse the women, because the women do most of the "home" work. They prepare the food, keep the home, care for the children and their husbands come first. It seemed pretty biblical to Sarah. But where she came from, the women were pampered. They took care of the home, yes, but that was done by telling the servants what was in order. Two different worlds.

Overall, in this Seapaugh tribe, as they are called, marriage is "till death do us part". Sarah liked that. She was continually surprised that if one cared to look close enough, the two worlds were not so different.

They call themselves "People of the Earth", and they are separated into several different groups. It was this time of the year that all the groups gathered together and hunted and talked and made marriage arrangements. When the final hunt was over, the separate tribes would all go their separate ways, until the next united Seapaugh gathering the following year. Talking Bird explained that not all of the tribes are the same, even though they originally came from the one "seed". As the tribe grew and they divided, some tribes chose to seek out war, while others, like this one, try to be peaceful. Sarah listened and learned about her new people and was thankful that God placed her with this tribe and not one of the others.

She did eventually learn that the other

women of her kind were taken among other tribes and sold. The ones, who were not sold among their own people, were taken further away and sold to white men, to be used as slaves. Running Deer, who apparently had no qualms about telling Sarah anything about anything, told her that one of the women was accidentally beaten to death before they even left the camp.

Running Deer told her the man that had tied them all together was called Wild Dog. The women were his find. "He called your women his pay for helping with the attack," Running Deer confided. Sarah could only listen as the sights and smells of that horrid afternoon came back to her thoughts. She knew exactly whom Running Deer was referring to. He was a cruel man. Running Deer told her that sometimes he came to help them with hunts or would gather his men up for a war party. But he was rarely seen. Their chief did not trust him and did business with him, only when he felt that there was no other way. Sarah would remember him forever. He had scars all over his body and his face was always a frown. There was evil coming from his eyes. He shaved his head on one side and let his long hair hang over the shaved section.

Sarah shuddered at the thought of him. Wild Dog had stood so close to her she could smell his breath. She could smell his sweat and the scent of horse on him. He had grabbed her hair and smelled it while one of the other men tied her to the rope. She could see the lust in his eyes as he ran his hands down her body. He had whispered words that she could not understand and tried to kiss her. Then he had slapped her face and pulled on her hair when she tried to turn away from him. Some of the others did not get off so easily. Wild Dog's lust and desire got the better of him, and some of the other girls suffered great pains. She was helpless. Sarah is still amazed that she lived through the ordeal, and hopes she will never see Wild Dog again. She would never allow that to happen to her. She would rather die first. Her body shook with a newfound conviction. She blinked and came back to the present conversation. Two ladies were discussing who would be eligible for marriage in the summer.

They believed, once a girl stayed in the "red tent" or "woman's tent" she was able to marry. That meant that some were as young as ten years old. Sarah couldn't imagine having to enter a lifelong marriage commitment at such a young age. *"I wasn't even ready at eighteen,"* she thought to herself. But the young ladies in question today smiled shyly and took the older women's teasing in stride.

Some of the boys coming home from the hunt were hoping to marry. For them, they had to make their first kill. Not rabbits or squirrels, but a deer or even better, a buffalo. Most chose to wait to down a buffalo, because there was great honor plus a celebration and storytelling that went along with it.

Young Flower Blossom was hoping that her beau would come home a warrior.

"Maybe this year will be the year someone catches Little Feather," Running Deer was saying. "I know I have certainly been trying to get his attention," she giggled.

"That is no secret!" someone commented. "You have him eating at your tipi often enough."

"That is how you catch a man," she defended.

"You must not be a very good cook, for you have not caught him!"

The whole circle laughed and Running Deer pretended to pout. Even Grieving Mother chuckled and added, "No one cooks like his mother."

Sarah started putting the pieces together. They were talking about Talking Bird's brother! She had never heard him called by a name. It was always Talking Bird saying "my brother this, my brother that."

She paid a little closer attention as an odd twinge of jealousy ran through her. Even though she had never met him, she knew that it was in his tent that she was sleeping and his family that was looking after her. Was it jealousy that she was feeling? Maybe it was how she would feel looking out for her own brother if she had one. Protective. That was it. Running Deer was very pretty, but she seemed more and more like a vixen every moment.

"Why does he not choose a wife, Grieving Mother?" someone asked.

Grieving Mother shrugged. "Maybe his heart is already taken." Everyone turned and looked at Sarah who was oblivious to the implications. She looked around at everyone's faces and felt a blush come to her cheeks.

Running Deer's eyes flashed and she spoke while looking down at her handiwork. "Little Feather would not marry outside of his own kind."

The subject was quickly changed but Sarah heard the deeper meaning. Sarah fought her inner thoughts about how it wasn't her choice to be here and how she would rather be with her own kind too.

She tried to concentrate on her sewing and was thankful when Grieving Mother announced that it was time to prepare for the evening meal.

Elizabeth Bourgeret

Chapter Six

At long last the men finally returned. There was much fanfare and this time, Sarah was able to watch it first hand.

The chief of the tribe, Spotted Eagle, lead the men into the village. He looked very noble on his horse dressed in his formal dress attire. Two others similarly dressed closely followed him. They were his two eldest sons.

Little Feather was following two men after that and when he saw Sarah as part of the audience he smiled and winked at her.

Sarah gasped at his audacity and frowned at him then turned away. But as quickly as he passed, she looked up again wondering which one was Talking Bird's brother. It was difficult to tell, as there were several men looking in her direction. Some of them smiled, some also nodded, and some paid her no attention at all.

The shouting came to a fever pitch, as the bounty was dragged in near the end. The young boy whose horse pulled the travois smiled and shook his bloodied spear over his head while shouting. Sarah followed his gaze and it led directly to Flower Blossom. Sarah smiled and was surprised to feel the envy of young love.

But amidst all the triumph and joy, a heart was grieving. A scream of agony rose above the shouts of joy and pierced Sarah's ear. She turned toward the direction of the heart-wrenching cry and saw a woman that she had not met. She was older and her graying hair was bound in two braids. Two men brought the limp body to her and placed it across her knees. She wrapped her arms around him and pulled him to her chest. She cried and wailed and rocked his body back and forth. Sarah's heart went out to this poor woman and she wanted to comfort her, but didn't know what to do or say. She decided that a shared grief does not need the same language, and started to walk towards her.

She was silently stopped by Grieving Mother's hand and solemn face. Sarah stopped, respecting Grieving Mother's guidance but her eyes never left the scene. The woman pulled a knife from her husbands sheath and ran it across her left arm.

Sarah gasped and tried to push past Grieving Mother to help the woman who had blood pouring down her arm and into her husband's hair.

"She will bleed to death." Sarah hissed in a whisper.

"It is our way," Grieving Mother said simply.

Sarah looked around at the others and saw that everyone was giving her the space that was accustomed. They clearly knew that she was there but again, pretended that they could not see her. Everyone cheered and patted the brave hunters for their abundant kill, but Sarah's heart went out to the woman.

Grieving Mother pulled her away from the painful sight. "There is much work to do," Grieving Mother said gently as she looked up into the sky.

"There is not much time left in the day. Come." Sarah looked back over her shoulder and ached for the woman and the pain she was feeling, but then turned her attention to where Grieving Mother was leading her.

"This is where we will work," Grieving Mother said. Sarah looked to see a whole buffalo lying on the ground almost directly in front of her. Sarah had to swallow hard as one woman she recognized from the sewing circle took out a knife and started slicing down the center of the bull's belly. The contents of the buffalo spilled out all over the ground. Sarah felt the color leave her face. The images in front of her became blurry and seemed to sway back and forth. She was having trouble standing. Sarah turned away from the sight to catch a breath of fresh air and saw that there were other buffalos scattered about the village with circles of women kneeling around them. There was blood everywhere. The women did not even seem to notice that entrails and blood were standing all around their knees. They chatted amongst themselves as if they were digging a hole.

Her eyes went back to the men where she saw Talking Bird in the arms of her husband, Two Spear. They had never met, but she looked extremely in love with that man that was holding her. He stroked her hair and leaned down to kiss her.

Sarah was feeling a little less dizzy, so she watched the couple. Shortly, another man came up to them, clearly teasing them about their open displays of affection. Sarah smiled as Talking Bird blushed, but held her own, teasing right back. Running Deer was not too far behind flirting with everyone. The man was strong and fit. He looked like he could be a handsome man under his face paintings. His hair was pulled back into a single braid and decorated with colored feathers and beads. His smile was charming and he enjoyed the attention Running Deer was giving him. He was shorter than Talking Bird's husband and she wondered if this man could be her brother.

Sarah was enjoying the scene from afar; then HE joined the circle of friends. Sarah's heart stopped. Her face instinctively frowned as she saw him being greeted warmly by all. She couldn't take her eyes off him. She kept waiting for him to show his true colors. The cruel, insensitive man she knew that he was. But he didn't. Instead, he was warm and loving and hugged Talking Bird and Running Deer. Running Deer kept trying to steal his attention but he kept her under control without her even knowing it by putting an arm around her and keeping her at his side. Sarah couldn't help but see how gentle he was with her. He was obviously not interested in her, but did not want to humiliate her at the same time.

Other men joined around them as they talked and laughed. Running Deer flitted from man to man. Some welcomed her attentions and others just ignored her. But HE, this terrible, terrible man, smiled and laughed and talked with everyone. Sarah would not believe that she could be wrong about this man. They must not know what he has done.

Her mother called out to Talking Bird to have her sit at the buffalo next to Sarah. She stole another quick kiss from her husband and rushed off. She ran toward Sarah smiling, "Is this not exciting?"

"It is a little… too much," Sarah answered. "That poor woman…"

"Yes. It was her husband. The buffalo charged him and he could not move out of its way fast enough. Her sons will most likely care for her now or her husband's brother."

"But she's cut! She cut her own arm! She's bleeding."

"Do not worry. She will be tended to and cared for. It is a part of our grieving."

"But…"

"Come on, we have much work to do." Talking Bird tugged on Sarah's arm and forced her to turn back towards the work. But there in front of her were stripped down chunks of flesh and innards being gathered and put into bowls.

Women were scraping the skin from the muscle; others were reaching inside the carcass and pulling out intestines, while others were boiling the meat off of the smaller bones. The sights, sounds and the smells were more than Sarah could take. Her eyelids fluttered and her eyes rolled back into her head. Then she fell to the ground.

When Sarah came to, almost the entire buffalo was pieced out and the area was clear. A small fire was burning off the last bits of blood and fragments where the huge beast was dissected.

She looked around her, completely embarrassed, but no one paid any attention. She woke up in the same place she had fallen. *"Great. I'm invisible again,"* she thought.

"Good. You are awake. Can you help me?"

Talking Bird asked as she struggled with the huge buffalo skin.

Sarah stood up immediately. "I am so sorry. I do not know what came over me. I am not used to…"

"It is okay. I am sure no one noticed." She smiled.

Sarah grabbed one end of the foul smelling pelt and followed Talking Bird to an angular scaffold.

"Drape it, fur side down," Talking Bird instructed. The skin was extremely heavy and Sarah labored under its weight.

"Welcome back!" Flower Blossom teased in passing. Sarah shot a look to Talking Bird who just smiled and shrugged her shoulders.

Running Deer carried a basket of turnips and stopped long enough to comment, "Oh you are awake. Do not worry. We did most of the work."

"She becomes less beautiful with every passing day," Sarah thought. A few more giggles caught her ear as people continued their work.

"No one noticed, huh?" Sarah laughed.

"We are not used to people falling asleep while standing up."

"It is called 'fainting'," Sarah explained. "I do not think I have ever seen so much blood and… and… insides, in my whole life."

"You will get used to that. You will have to prepare the food your husband brings home…"

"I do not have a husband."

"Someday you might." Talking Bird enjoyed poking fun at her new friend.

"Who would want me now?" Sarah laughed. "It was so much easier being confined to the tipi."

Captive Heart

"For you, maybe!" Talking Bird tacked the last bit of fur to the ground to dry. They put a thick black, tar-like substance over the skin to help it dry soft and supple.

Sarah took a lot of ribbing the rest of the night, but she wasn't upset. In fact, it was all in good fun and it actually made her feel more welcome.

As Sarah was drying her hair beside the fire, Talking Bird and Flower Blossom came into her tipi. Grieving Mother was out helping for the evening's preparation, so Sarah was happy for the company. Tonight was a big night for her. She was letting go of all of her yesterdays to begin a new tomorrow with a new culture and a new people. She had accepted her fate and decided to embrace it instead of fight it.

Talking Bird brought her a new dress. This one was very decorated and had patches of different colors sewn to it and long raccoon tails dangling from its edges. It was a very fine piece of work. "That is beautiful!" Sarah exclaimed. "Is that what you are wearing tonight?"

Talking Bird giggled. "No, it is what *you* are wearing."

"Me?" Sarah stood and walked over to the new dress. "Can I try it on?"

"Not yet," Flower Blossom said. "We have to get you ready first."

The two ladies first put a thin layer of white make-up covering Sarah's face then outlined her eyes in black. They put two red stripes on either cheek and a dark black stripe down her nose and her chin. Her lips were colored white except for a small circle in the middle that was red.

They brushed her hair and braided it into two braids that would hang down her back. They decorated her hair with feathers and strings of beads. Sarah would have felt silly if it weren't for the seriousness of Talking Bird and Flower Blossom. They smiled, but there was very little chatting. It seemed that the getting ready was a ceremony in itself.

When they were finished, they sat back and admired their work.

"Well?" Sarah asked reluctantly.

"You look beautiful," Flower Blossom said with a timid smile. "I am so glad that you will be a part of our tribe."

"Thank you, Flower Blossom. That means a lot to me. You have always been very kind to me, and I am grateful." Sarah felt a tightness in her throat and willed her eyes to stay dry so as not to ruin all of their beautiful make-up. Her eyes darted over to the last link of her past life with her own people. Her wooden box of letters.

"Of course you know how I feel," Talking Bird leaned in to hug Sarah, careful not to mess up her hair or make-up. "I will count you among my family."

Sarah blinked back to Talking Bird and smiled at her sincerity.

"Perhaps soon, she might really be your sister. If your brother has…"

"Well, I guess our work is done here," Talking Bird interrupted.

"I cannot be married to someone I do not even know," Sarah teased.

"But I thought..." Flower Blossom looked confused, "Did you not speak..."

"Come, Flower Blossom, we have a lot of things to do. Or do you forget that this is a special night for you as well. You will want to be there to see Grey Horse light the fire tonight."

"Oh yes, I nearly forgot!" Flower Blossom was distracted from the former conversation. "I must go," she blushed. She stood and smiled back at Sarah and Talking Bird, then exited.

Talking Bird explained as best she could the details that would be taking place this evening. She was very excited. "It is a wonderful celebration, but tonight is even more special, because of you. Just have fun, and do what the chief tells you. Now, I must go." Talking Bird leaned over and gently kissed Sarah on both cheeks. "Goodbye, Sarah. For tomorrow, you will have a new name."

Sarah's heart skipped a beat with excitement. She was happy for her decision, but she was also happy for Flower Blossom. It was clear to see that she loved Grey Horse. He was chosen to light the ceremonial fires, and tonight, he becomes a man. He made his first kill on the buffalo hunt so he has earned the right to tell the story in front of everyone, and then claim his bride to be married in the fall, when they return home.

Sarah had been taught her whole life that these people were savages, heathens. She wondered if this would affect her place in heaven. She knew she was saved, but by joining these people, would God see it as her turning her back on Him? After living with these people, she did not see savages. They were good people, loving people. She prayed for strength to let go of the past. She wished that she knew the missing pieces of the puzzle. "Why did they even attack the caravan? Why... why my son?" She wondered if she would ever be able to forget about the murder of her son and move on. She says she forgave the man who took the final shot... but did she really? She could still feel hate that was eating away at her soul. "Lord, help me let go. I give all of my pain and hatred to you. Please take it off my heart. Let me start again." She felt a calming feeling and hoped that it would last. She suddenly needed some fresh air. Sarah decided to go and check on the fires at the smoke house. They needed to be kept going all through the night and the water replenished. So she stepped out of the tipi. It was nearly dark and Sarah could see Grey Horse with his torch lighting each corner of the huge stack of wood in the center of the village. He was smiling and dancing from corner to corner. Sarah saw Flower Blossom looking on beside her mother. She smiled to herself, knowing that she has never felt that kind of love for a man. So strong, so deep. There was no duty about it. It was not arranged; they just obviously loved each other with their very core.

Sarah scooped some water from the water vessel and walked toward the smoke house. Everyone was busy with the feast so no one really noticed her out in her ceremonial clothes and make-up.

She enjoyed the moments of solitude that will soon be replaced with moments in the spotlight. She crouched down and lifted up the flap of the dome. She added a few more sticks to the low burning coals and topped off the water container that sat just above them.

"So, dried meat is a little more your speed?" a voice behind her said.

Sarah did not even have to turn around to recognize it. She silently spoke up to God, *"You're testing me aren't you?"* She turned to try and attempt reconciliation but when she did, he jumped back and gasped.

"What have they done to you?" he teased.

"I thought... it..." she was suddenly embarrassed.

"I am just kidding. You look about as pale as you did earlier today when you fell asleep while standing. And I did not think you could get much whiter!"

Sarah took in a deep breath, "It is called 'fainting'. I am not used to so much blood." she said clearly annoyed. She didn't like his teasing her.

"Do not be mad. I am only playing. You will learn." There was a silent pause and then a grin crossed his face, "You have to admit, it is kind of funny. There you were with Talking Bird one minute, then the next you were on the ground. No one knew what to do," he laughed.

Sarah, against her better judgment smiled and looked away.

"A smile. That looks nice."

Sarah's smile faded instantly and a furrowed brow replaced it. "I have things to do," she said coldly.

"I will not keep you. I will see you tonight."

"Not if I can help it," she said under her breath. He walked away from her and Sarah was angry with herself. "I failed that test. Oh, but he just makes me so mad," she said to no one as she

Elizabeth Bourgeret

walked back to her tipi.

Chapter Seven

The fire was roaring and the entire village was sitting around it on blankets. Sarah was sitting watching everyone with their families. It reminded her of the days of her youth when her mother would dress her and her sister up in their Sunday clothes and all would walk to the park for a fair. There were booths and stages everywhere. Food and games and entertainment. Her heart beat much the same way as those days so long ago. She loved watching all the people in their pretty clothes and the ladies with their pretty hairstyles and bonnets. So many different kinds of people.

Here everyone had black hair and brown skin but they were all unique shapes and sizes, unique in their own ways. Sarah was enjoying every minute.

Talking Bird came over and whispered into her ear, "Come with me, we have to serve." Sarah followed Talking Bird willingly and was just amazed at how many women there were. They were all dressed in different dresses and had decorated their hair with beads and other fineries. They too had make-up on, or what Sarah would call make-up. Their eyes were done up in dark colors and they had markings on their foreheads and cheeks.

Two fires with spits going across them

roasted large pieces of the buffalo meat. One young woman on each spit slowly turned the handle to cook it entirely. The smell made her mouth water. It brought her back to the first night that Grieving Mother brought her a plateful in the tipi. Has it really been that long ago? Just then, she saw Grieving Mother past a group of women. She was smiling and laughing. Sarah had never seen her in such a good mood. *She must be extremely happy that her son came home safely… either that or she really loves a good buffalo roast*, Sarah thought.

Sarah followed Talking Bird and did what she was told. It was a great way for her to meet many of the women that she had never seen before. This was the final night for the tribal gathering. Tomorrow, everyone would be packing up and going back to their own villages. But this was all new to Sarah and she was determined to enjoy every moment of the evening's activities. Everyone was nice to her, but she could feel some unease with others. They were uncomfortable having her around. Sarah had asked Talking Bird about this one time and she merely said, "The white man has done us great harm," and would speak on it no further.

As all of the men were served and seated, the women filled their plates and took their seats. People sat and ate and chatted. There were some women that Sarah had met while they were working with the vegetables that came and sat beside her.

"You are from… a white man's village?"

"Yes. I lived beside the great waters," she answered. This meant she lived close to the ocean. These were people who had never seen the great waters but have heard of them. They loved to ask

Sarah questions of her home.

"How many live in one of your villages?" the other woman asked.

Sarah struggled with the answer. She did not really know how to do numbers past ten. "Many, very many," she stumbled, "maybe about six of these villages," she guessed.

The two women looked very offended. "That is impossible!" one cried out. "How do you have so many?"

"I speak the truth, and that is just my village. There are many more in the other villages that are all around us, in all directions. I was going to a village that is said to be growing quickly. It already has... umm... five of your villages," she shrugged. Sarah was not bragging and she had no idea why the women were getting so upset. "Many people come on big boats from other lands across the great waters."

"You are a liar!" The second woman said.

Another woman who was listening joined in. "It is true. I have heard of this before. Many are crossing our grounds, and want to take our property and our food."

"I do not think they want to do that. I, for instance, was moving to a town that was already growing. I am sure they do not want to take something that does not belong to them."

"I am only telling you what I have heard. I am Sun Prarie. I want to welcome you to our village. It is a good place to live."

The two older women calmed down and asked other questions of her. "Does your skin not burn in the sun?"

"Oh yes, it does. When I first came here, I

was so burned it hurt to move."

"Your hair is very beautiful," Sun Prairie said. "I wish I had such a color."

Talking Bird came and sat down beside Sarah. She greeted the other ladies and leaned over to Sarah, "How are you surviving?"

"I am fine," she smiled. Donisuma, Talking Bird's youngest crawled up into Sarah's lap. She set aside her plate to make room for him. He smiled up at the other women and they smiled back. "It is gonna start," he announced.

"Oh!" Sun Prairie stood up, "I have to get back to my family. "I have enjoyed meeting you. I hope we meet again." She bowed down in formal parting and smiled.

"I am sure we will," Sarah smiled in return. The other two women stood also and nodded down to Sarah.

"I hope that you will be happy as one of us," one said.

"She will never really be one of us, sister," the other added and they walked away.

"Do not let them bother you. They are always angry. They have never had a husband and they are inseparable."

"I am glad that they are not in our group," Sarah admitted. Talking Bird laughed with her.

Several chiefs from the various tribes stood around the fire and faced their groups. Everyone was in attendance and was listening and watching to each as they spoke in their turn. It was finally time for Sarah's group.

Their chief stood up beside the fire and raised his hands. Sarah thought that he made a pretty intimidating figure, standing with the flames roaring up behind him casting shadows across his full Indian garb. His headdress of feathers fell down his back all the way to his feet. He wore dark-skinned pants made from the hide of a deer and a tunic top. It was decorated with quills and fringe and feathers. His staff was held up high over his head waiting for the mass of people to quiet down. He was very tall and had strong squared shoulders and a barrel chest. His hair was still more black than grey, but the grey was making its appearance around his temples. His cuts and scars showed that he had earned his place as chief, but his tenderness with its members showed that he was much respected.

He spoke softly, but it managed to carry across to all of his people.

"We are here to give thanks to the Great Spirit for providing us with plentiful buffalo to hunt and much food to eat. We give thanks to the Great Spirit for the safe return of the men. We know that those lost to us have died with great honor. They will fly into the skies to rest among the stars. They will be missed, but their souls live on in our stories as they become part of our histories."

Sarah was deeply moved by the chief's speech and bowed her head to pray. She did not hear the chief call out her name, but Talking Bird nudged her and told her to walk over to the chief.

Sarah scooped up Talking Bird's son who was already starting to nod off. "Save my seat for me, will you?" she whispered. He nodded vigorously and watched her walk through the crowd.

The people she passed made a low sound and by the time she made her way to the huge fire, the entire village was chanting, but Sarah hardly heard it. It sounded so natural. Sarah stood across from Spotted Eagle, the chief of this village and stared into his eyes. They were intense but not unkind. Her heart pounded in her chest with a twinge of fear and a heavy dose of nerves.

The chief placed his hand on Sarah's shoulder and sang words that she did not understand. Two women came up behind her and draped a white, heavy fur covered pelt over her back and head. They gave her a bowl of bitter tasting liquid to drink. The women spun her around and began to sing while dancing her around the fire. Drums joined in the background. They were low, deep and dominated their steps. Sarah was beginning to feel dizzy and wasn't sure if it was from the drink or the spinning. On top of the women's low rhythmic chanting the chief joined in with a higher pitched song. They stomped and spun her and stomped again. They took her all the way around the fire so all could see. At each side, each of the chiefs from each tribe stopped her and gave her a gift, some placed them in her hands, others decorated her with jewelry, but each one had her drink another swallow of the bitter liquid, and each spun her around, as they continued around the circle of fire.

The medicine man joined in the dance and brought a huge fan. As they continued the dance, the medicine man would fan the smoke under Sarah's cover. Sarah was getting dizzier and more light headed with every turn. *"Please don't let me faint. Please don't let me faint,"* She was saying over and over to herself. *"I couldn't bear it twice in one day!"* She coughed as the smoke blew over her and got caught under her cover. She tried to peek out from underneath but they would just turn her head back down.

The music matched her heartbeat. It was pounding throughout her whole body now, getting faster and faster along with the pace of the music. Just when it reached a fever pitch, and Sarah thought for sure she was going to faint, a bright flash blinded her from the fire and her cloak was taken from her body. Sarah struggled to stay on her feet. With the extra weight off of her back and all of the spinning, she stepped over her feet, back and forth trying to regain some balance. The medicine man was waving a rattling gourd all around her body. The chanting grew softer so the chief could speak. He walked back over to her and placed his hand back on her shoulder. She was thankful for something to ground her.

"You were not born to us but you have become one of us. You came to us against your will, and were as fragile as a newborn fawn. But your strength has made you adapt to your surroundings. You have shown strength and courage, yet you are still learning as a babe learns to walk. You are one of us now. It matters not that you were not born from us because as of today, we see no difference in your skin. Your new reborn name will be Natayah, which has the meaning of Fragile but Strong Woman. Natayah!" he finished with a shout and the village cheered with him.

Sarah smiled and blushed. She scanned the faces closest to the fire and recognized many. They smiled and cheered for her. She looked over the entire circle as she was paraded and announced at every quarter, but did not see him anywhere.

"What do I care whether he is here or not?" she thought to herself. *"Good. I'm glad he's not here. He'd spoil a perfectly good evening."*

The two women dancing with her took Natayah back to her spot as she stumbled through the crowd. The other members of the village stroked her dress as she passed. She sat down and gave Talking Bird a drunken smile. Talking Bird just giggled. Donisuma found his place back in Natayah's lap.

"Natayah." Talking Bird reached around her two sons to embrace her. "I am so happy."

The evening went on announcing the boys who had made their first kills. They were a proud bunch. Each one was recognized, and told their tale of the hunt. There were only three this time, but their stories varied wildly. One was very shy and could barley make the words escape his lips. The other two must have been planning what they would say on the return trip. They were very colorful and expressive. They used their arms and faces to express emotion. Grey Wolf, of course, had a biased audience member in Flower Blossom who listened eagerly to every word.

Natayah was quite caught up in the evening and never passed up the opportunity to refill her cup with a sweet but toxic juice that came around. It made her feel relaxed and giddy all at the same time.

Following the young boys' stories, the more experienced hunters came around the campfire and began to tell stories of hunts in the past. They were told with such passion, one could almost feel as if they were there. The stories became intense and drums and rattles were added for emphasis. A flute carried a tune as the storytellers' word became more blended and became a song. Men wearing buffalo heads with the skins trailing down their backs emerged from the crowds and began dancing around the storytellers. Smoke puffs would rise up out of the fire as if on command and swirl around the dancers to create an eerie effect. The storytellers became the hunters once more and re-enacted a hunt or two from history with the assistance of the buffalo dancers. The story/dance built to a heart pounding crescendo as the buffalo received the final death blow. The drums came to a dramatic halt and the silence lasted for only a moment before the crowd roared and cheered.

The musicians began playing again and the buffalos stood from their death poses and went out into the audience to find a dance partner. One such buffalo came over and held out a hand to Natayah.

"Go," Talking Bird said. "He wants to dance with you."

"No... no... I do not know how."

"You can do it, Auntie Natayah," Donisuma said with his fingers in his mouth. He got up and let Natayah stand. The dancer took her out by the fire and danced around her. He showed her the steps with his feet and she followed. Natayah found that she caught on quickly and enjoyed herself. The dancers joined hands and traveled in a circle around the fire and then back the other way.

When the dance was finished, the "buffalo-man" took Natayah back to her seat. He turned her hands over so that her palms were face up. He put each one to the buffalo's nose as if placing a kiss there. He bowed his big furry head to her and danced back off again.

"That was fun!" Natayah said breathlessly.

Everyone ate and drank into the early hours of the next day. Natayah was eager to get to her bed.

She was stroked and welcomed everywhere she went. Talking Bird ran up to her and grabbed her shoulders. Her smile was wide and sincere. "Welcome, Natayah," she hugged her and stepped back again. "You and Little Feather make a nice couple."

"What? When?"

"While you were dancing!"

"He was the buffalo?"

"Yes!" Talking Bird laughed, more than a little tipsy herself. "I know that you are tired, but I just had to hug you once again. Good night my friend. I will see you in the morning." She leaned in and kissed Natayah on the cheek then turned to leave. "Oh yes, I almost forgot. Before you go to sleep drink a lot of water, so your head will not hurt when you wake up." She turned and disappeared into the crowd.

Natayah watched Talking Bird walk away and scanned the crowd for Grieving Mother. She found the older woman in a circle of her peers laughing and singing. She looked about for Flower Blossom, but could not see her. Running Deer, as usual was in a circle of men, laughing and flirting with them all, not leaving anyone out. Natayah smiled to herself. She was content with her decision. These are her people now.

Passersby would stroke her dress and make some kind of welcoming comment. She would smile cordially, but now she was tired and just wanted to get back to her furs. She hung her head

Captive Heart

down, hoping that if she didn't make eye contact with anyone, they would not come to speak with her. It worked for a few steps until she ran right into him. He stood a full head and shoulders above her. She looked up to smile and apologize at the abrupt meeting but her smile melted from her face as her eyes met his. He smiled at her and stroked her hair. He was feeling brave. He wished that she knew it was he under the buffalo mask. "Welcome," he said, and stroked her hair again, softly, gently, almost intimately. "You are one of us now."

She pushed his hand away and took a step back so as not feel the nearness of him. "No thanks to you," she snapped.

"Can I walk you to your home?" he asked undaunted.

"I can find it myself, thank you."

He took in a deep breath, "Let us start over. Can we?" his voice dropped just above a whisper.

"I want nothing to do with you," she answered coldly.

"We can not all be as perfect as Talking Bird's brother," he said glibly, not expecting the reaction he was soon to get.

That comment pushed Natayah right past her tired and tipsy edge. She exploded back with, "You are nothing like Little Feather! He is good and kind and patient and caring!"

"How do you know that I am not all of those things?" he spoke, not changing his tone.

Natayah gritted her teeth and let the anger run freely through her. She spoke with a growl, "Because you are a cold blooded murderer. And I hate you!" No sooner had the words escaped her

105

lips, did she regret them, but it was too late. Her words hit their mark as clearly as an arrow through a heart.

A shadow fell across his otherwise bright brown eyes. He swallowed hard and clenched his teeth. "I am sorry that I bothered you." He turned and walked away. Natayah could not make herself call him back.

She walked numbly on to her tipi. She turned back hoping he would be there, but he was not. She slipped inside and fell onto her bed with a heavy heart. *"What makes me say things like that? I said that I forgave him, but my words did not have an ounce of forgiveness in them,"* she thought. A tear fell from the corner of her eye, *"What kind of person have I become? Lord, I have asked you to change my heart, but I lack the courage to live it. Please, help me to do Your will. Help me be the new woman that You would have me be,"* she prayed then drifted off to sleep.

She heard the Indians yelling in their high-pitched shouts. She saw them riding on their decorated horses. They were all around her. She was running toward Thomas.

"Thomas!" she yelled. Her sleeping body stiffened and she shook her head trying to fight off the visions that she knew were coming next.

She saw Captain Pike lying dead, riddled with arrows. She looked up and saw Wild Dog jump from his horse and bring a knife into a soldier's back then quickly remove it. He pulled the man's head back and brought his knife across the man's scalp removing it from his head. She turned

Captive Heart

and ran towards Thomas. The dust burned her eyes. Her long skirts tangled around her feet. Her eyes did not leave her son. "Thomas!"

She ran into a soldier with fear in his eyes. His face was caked with blood and dirt. She tried to push past him but he held her tightly.

"Don't shoot! I have a pretty lady. You want her? Don't shoot."

"Let me go!" she screamed, but he would not release her. She saw the sweat beading on his forehead and rolling down his cheeks making rivers of dirt though his face.

"Momma! I'm coming!" It was Thomas... get to Thomas... he was coming out from under the wagon.

"No! Thomas, NO!" she screamed. The soldier released her with one hand, "I'll kill 'er. If I die, she dies too."

She pushed him off; he lost his balance and fell back. No sooner than he cleared her, he was shot with arrows. He shot off his gun. Then one and then another arrow came at him. The soldier tripped and fell back causing the arrows to fly past him. Everything was moving so slowly. Perhaps she could out run the arrows this time.

"Thomas!" she screamed. "Get down!" she thought she was screaming but no sound came from her mouth. She tried to run to her son.

The shouting had died down and as she held her dying son in her arms. The Indians spoke behind her.

"Stay back. Leave her there."

"I cannot. I killed her son."

"She is just a white woman. They do not care about their children."

107

"Look at her. She will die out here."

"Let her man have her."

"She has no man! We have killed them all. And what good has it done us? Did it bring our brothers back?"

"Come. We must go."

"I cannot leave her."

A third voice joined in. "I will take her. And the others. The Otter Tribe will pay good money for them …"

Natayah woke in a panic. Tears wet her face. "It was an accident. He was protecting me?... from my own kind? Is that what you were showing me, Lord?" She sat up in the dark and wiped the tears from her cheeks. "Oh, I was so cruel to him... I don't... I don't even know his name." She stood up and poked her head out of the tipi to see if perhaps the celebration was still going. It was dark and quiet. A few bodies lay around the fire; they slept where they fell. Her head was throbbing. She put her hands on either side of her face to try and squeeze the pounding into submission. "I forgot to drink water." She snuck back out into the darkness to the water chamber and drank her fill. Natayah slipped back in, mentally and emotionally exhausted and lay down in her furs. "Thank you, Lord for opening my eyes. Tomorrow I will make it right." She massaged her temples until she fell back to sleep.

Natayah woke early the next morning, even before Grieving Mother, which she thought, was impossible. She darted out of the tipi and looked around. The people were already out and about, packing things up. She could not see him anywhere.

She saw Talking Bird's tipi fall to the ground, so she ran over.

"What is happening?" she asked.

"It is moving day," Talking Bird responded while pulling the poles out from under the heavy skins.

"Where are we moving to?"

"We are going back home," Talking Bird replied. "Where is my mother?"

"She is still sleeping," Natayah said. "I thought this was home."

"Oh no, this is where we come to do our spring hunting. If we are running short of supplies, we will return in the winter also. Our permanent home is many days away. You will like it there. It is so beautiful. And no more tipi's," she whispered.

"But I like it here."

"Here? It is beautiful, yes, but everything is so… so primitive."

Natayah couldn't argue, but if Talking Bird thought this was primitive, she couldn't wait to see the other place. Running water at least, right?

"I am so surprised that mother is not up yet. She is always so anxious to get home."

"Oh, she is. That explains why our tipi was pretty bare last night. Everything was tied into bundles. Not even any extra wood for the fire!"

"So that is what she did! I am not surprised anymore. She loves to dance and this way she can dance late and sleep in, because she has done everything already!" Talking Bird laughed.

"Have you seen your brother today?" Natayah asked.

"No, but he will be around, helping everyone pack."

"Oh."

"Why do you need him?"

"I just... I was... why have I not met him?"

"I do not know," Talking Bird lied. "Maybe he is shy around you. But I will tell him you asked for him."

Natayah blushed, "No... that is okay. It was... nothing really."

"I am sorry, Sar... I mean, Natayah, I love that name. Chief Spotted Eagle chose wisely. I have to get this done before Two Spear comes to try and help. Never a good idea," she laughed.

"Sorry to keep you. I am sure that I am supposed to be doing something too."

"I *know* you are. Mother is probably looking for you," Talking Bird warned. "But I will see you later today."

Natayah ran back to where her tipi was and it fell right in front of her. And just behind it, he stood holding a pole. He did not look at her but kept his eyes on his work.

"What are you doing here?" Natayah asked. She was happy to see that she could get this mistake corrected first thing in the morning.

"I am almost finished, and then I will be out of your way." His voice was deep but emotionless.

"I did not mean..."

"Natayah!" It was Grieving Mother. "Where have you been? We have much work to do. Go and get the meat from the smoke tent."

Natayah nodded and turned back around, but he was already gone.

Everything stayed at a pretty fast pace and Grieving Mother kept Natayah running all day. The entire camp was packed up in a matter of hours. The horses were draped with baskets and blankets, and poles were tied to either side to create a travois, which was also laden with supplies.

Grieving Mother gave Natayah a pack to wear over her shoulders and down her back. It was heavier than anything she'd ever carried in her life. She tried not to grimace and fell in line behind Grieving Mother riding her horse.

Children ran along, close to their families or their friends' families, or if they were small, they rode on a makeshift wagon. The wagons were made from the tops of the smoke huts, without the cover, and tied them to a travois covered with soft furs. It created a comfortable "cage" for the little ones.

As Natayah walked along, she noticed that her pack was so much smaller than everyone else's. She felt guilty even thinking about how miserable she was and how much her back and legs already hurt.

The sun was hot and she could feel it burning her scalp. At their first break, the women began making food for the men and children. Natayah took the opportunity to reach into the pack and find her old skirt. She tore a thick strip and tied it across her head and under her hair, creating a scarf. She tucked the rest of the fabric back in her pack and her hand brushed against something hard. She peeped into the basket. And there wrapped in a soft piece of leather, was her box. She had forgotten all about it. She had been so busy with her new life... suddenly she felt so lonely. She looked around her. She was one in a sea of people, and yet she felt all alone.

She thought about reaching in and grabbing a letter for comfort, until she saw Two Spear walking toward her tugging a horse. Natayah smiled up at him and shielded her eyes from the sun.

"Little Feather asked me to bring you this horse. He said that he could not stand you looking so pathetic walking with your pack. So he sent you this. Why he could not bring it to you himself, I do not know," Two Spear sighed heavily obviously not in the gift-giving mood.

"Oh, that is so thoughtful!" She stood, and came around Two Spear to stroke the horse. "He is beautiful."

"He is a she," he corrected.

"Oh," she blushed. "I have never ridden a horse... or... is this a pack horse... or..."

Two Spear sighed impatiently. "Whichever you want. I must go. Here," he said handing her the rope and turning to leave."

"Thank you. And please tell Little Feather thank you for the gift also," she called after him, but he did not respond. She smiled at the horse, which nuzzled Natayah under her neck. "I don't think he likes me very much," she whispered to the horse in English. "What should I call you, girl?" She cooed at her while scratching her ears. "How about Clara? That will do nicely. That way I won't be all alone. Do you speak English?" She laughed.

The break did not last long and soon all were up and ready to go. Natayah did not attempt to climb on the back of her new friend, but she did

Captive Heart

tie the pack on her, thankful for the relief.

The village of people walked for miles and miles, even as the sun was setting on their first day.

When they finally stopped for the night, Natayah was leaning on her horse for support. She had the rope wrapped loosely around her hand, but the horse seemed to know its purpose and stayed close by her. She was so thankful for finally being able to stop and rest.

Grieving Mother and Natayah sat together eating dried meat. Grieving Mother counted the pieces to make sure they would have plenty for the remainder of the trip. Grieving Mother didn't talk very much but a smile crossed her face when Natayah told her about the gift of the horse.

"My son must have taken to you," she said.

"But why can I not meet him? I want to thank him for all that he has done."

"The time will come... when he is ready."

Elizabeth Bourgeret

Chapter Eight

Natayah's body hurt so badly that she could hardly get up the next morning. The night was hot and they slept out on the hard ground. Natayah was able to enjoy the vast sky of stars for only moments before sleep over took her. Her legs ached, her back ached, her feet were not very happy with her either.

Natayah tried to ignore the hustle and bustle that went on around her. When Clara came over and nudged her with her nose, Natayah knew she had to get up.

She stood and stretched and tied her pack to Clara. "I am so thankful for you," she whispered to her horse. "I will be ecstatic when I figure out how to ride you!"

Grieving Mother climbed on her horse and rode up to Natayah and handed her a strip of dried buffalo meat. She had a big grin on her face as she rode on. "Where's the eggs and bacon?" Sarah laughed at her own personal joke. But when others began to walk past her looking at her oddly, she rolled her eyes, "What have I gotten myself into?" She watched Grieving Mother ride away holding her breakfast in her hand. Clara's nose pushed Natayah in the back and urged her to follow the others. "Traitor," she said over her shoulder. Clara nudged her again, and Natayah obeyed. She forced her feet to walk while she gnawed on the dried breakfast.

As they walked, Natayah took pleasure in the rising of the sun, the colors spilling out across the sky was a thing of beauty. It was so beautiful that it inspired a song. Natayah and Clara walked side by side while Natayah sang softly to her.

The group walked on for hours. "Apparently we are not stopping for lunch today, Clara," Natayah said to her walking companion. Natayah leaned against her for support.

A rider trotted up alongside Natayah and she looked up to see who it was. She perked up and smiled and was ready to apologize to him, but then he spoke first.

"You know you can ride that horse, right?"

Natayah sighed, too tired to be embarrassed. "I do not know how to ride," she admitted.

"Whatever suits you," he snapped and sped up to leave her, then thought better of it. "I was just worried about your feet that is all," he spoke looking straight ahead.

Natayah was surprised by this unexpected kindness, and then he added, "How do you not know how to ride a horse?"

"We had… 'carriages' at home," she could see that he did not understand the English word "carriage" so she explained. "They are pulled… by horses, but we ride on a seat, with cushions and a cover over our head. It has… "wheels"…" she waved her hands in a circle.

"I have seen these 'carriages'. It was where we found you."

Natayah tried hard not to take offense and to keep the vivid images from entering her mind, so she pushed ahead, "Yes, those are similar, but ours were much more comfortable," she smiled.

"We will have to teach you."

Natayah was touched. She decided to try and make amends. "I was hoping that we could... start over again. I was very rude when you suggested it. So... I..." she took a deep breath. "Hello, my name is Natayah."

"I know. I was at your party last night."

"You were? I did not see you."

"Were you looking for me?" he grinned at her enjoying the blush that rose up on her otherwise pale white cheeks.

"No, I just... I was..."

"I saw you." He smiled down at her and kicked at his horse to pull away from her. Natayah blushed, and then realized that she still did not find out his name. She was too embarrassed to ask Talking Bird, not to mention everyone practically had her married off to Little Feather. So if she were to ask about this other man, who is quite handsome, what would people think? She would not want Talking Bird to think her ungrateful for everything her brother has done for her. Natayah smiled to herself and felt her stomach do a "flip-flop". "Oh this is silly," she said to Clara. "I am a grown woman for goodness sake." But still she smiled.

Thankfully, the caravan came to a stop with barely enough light to find the blankets. There was not a lot of conversation once the beds were made.

Natayah was lying on her blanket with her horse standing close by. "I have got to learn to ride a horse," she drifted off to a deep sleep.

The next morning came too soon. Again Natayah's muscles screamed at every movement. As she lay there trying to decide if she should even stand up she was wondering if it might not be better to be left behind.

But she pressed on. Today, Talking Bird came back to walk with Natayah. "I can teach you to ride, if you want," she offered.

"I would love to know how to ride. My feet are so angry with me," Natayah made light of the situation. As they walked a silence came over the caravan. Natayah could feel a heaviness in the air. She instinctively knew not to speak but looked over at Talking Bird for explanation.

Talking Bird tipped her head in the direction of the North. Natayah followed her line of vision and saw.

There, slowly coming into view over the hill were tall poles with feathers and animal skulls hanging from them. There were maybe a hundred such poles forming a circle. In the center of the circle were what looked like stacked beds made from wood and hide. They crept up closer. The silence was haunting and even the horses made no noise. Natayah looked to her right at the structures and saw that there were bodies on each of the platforms. They were bundled and laid peacefully decorated with feathers, beads and flowers. Natayah looked to Talking Bird for understanding. Her eyes were filled with tears and she stared straight ahead. It seemed that no one would look the direction of the platforms, but it was a very solemn procession.

Natayah waited patiently until everyone from the caravan passed the sacred area. The chatter started up again and Natayah turned to Talking Bird.

Without prompting, Talking Bird offered,

"That was a mass burial of our people. They were all killed on the way to our spring hunting grounds. My brother was one of them."

"What happened? Why did they all die?" Natayah asked.

"Your people," Talking Bird shook her head and restarted the story. "The white men attacked us and began shooting our people. They rode on horses and had fire sticks that killed many of our people in a matter of minutes." She looked down at her shoes to contain her sadness then continued. "We did nothing to anger them. We must have just been in their way on that day. They killed us for no reason. Our men retaliated... you were a product of that retaliation." Talking Bird took in a deep breath, "I must go to my mother." Talking Bird climbed onto her horse with ease and rode up to where Grieving Mother rode with her head down, as did the others.

Natayah felt awful. She railed against the Indians because of her people being attacked for no reason, that they were innocent bystanders... suddenly Natayah recalled one of her sister's letters... *"The Indians would not be a threat because the Army had "cleaned out" the area for travelers."* Cleaned out... is this cleaned out? Natayah felt sick to her stomach. Her people were responsible for this. For all of it. If she was to be angry with anyone for the position she found herself in, it should be at her own people.

Natayah wanted to apologize for all of the wrongs her people have done to them, but what could she say? She walked on in silence watching the sun climb higher into the sky, thinking on the war between the two peoples and wondered when and how it could come to an end. In her world, she had never known such a war raged. In her world, she discovered she was sheltered from many things.

Natayah had learned her lesson from yesterday and did not eat all of her dried buffalo meat at one time. She rationed it out for herself for the day, just in case the chief decided not to stop for lunch. But it was much to her great pleasure that he did decide to stop early today. They could have easily made it into their village before nightfall, but Chief Spotted Eagle did not feel that the time was right. His "dreams" told him it was not safe. Natayah thought his idea was brilliant. While the chief sent men out to investigate, Natayah and Clara walked over to the edge of a river and put their feet in. The water felt cool and soothing on her hot sore feet. She slipped off her moccasins, already regretting getting them wet. "These are going to take hours to dry," she said to no one tossing her shoes on the beach.

Natayah took a moment to take in her surroundings. The valley was beautiful. The river had a rock and shell beach that was a little difficult for her tender feet to handle, but she tried to stand still and let the water rush over her feet and splash against her legs. Down the river to her left, the terrain rose up high, steeply forming a bluff. Natayah looked down the river and saw that the bluff dotted the landscape as far as she could see. "This is beautiful, Clara," she said. "I could stay here forever." To her right the trees swallowed up any view she might have. They were thick and close together making Natayah feel very alone.

Talking Bird, Flower Blossom, Speckled Doe and Running Deer all came to join Natayah at the water's edge.

"We are going up stream to bathe. Would you like to join us?" Talking Bird asked.

"Oh. I would love to," Natayah said sighing. "We are home then?"

"Not yet," Flower Blossom answered. "We are about a half day's walk down and across the river. But the men, for some reason, have left the group, so we will probably be here for the night."

"I do not care why we are here. I am just happy we can stop for a while!" Natayah laughed. "I will join you, but let me go back and tell Grieving Mother where I will be so she does not worry."

"I already did!" Talking Bird laughed, "Come on."

The girls walked up the river and around the bend for a little privacy. Natayah was getting used to the group bathing, but was still the most shy. They hobbled down the rock beach until they found a spot they liked.

"Are you sure they can not see us here?" Natayah asked.

"Relax! The men are gone anyway!" Speckled Doe teased her.

"The cute ones anyway!" Running Deer laughed. They stripped off their dresses and threw them on the shore. Clara, the faithful horse she has become, followed them upstream and stood in the water waiting her next orders.

They all got in and splashed and giggled. Flower Blossom was telling them that she almost had her wedding outfit finished. Talking Bird teased Natayah about the horse that Little Feather had given her. Running Deer bragged that White Cloud had killed two rabbits for her to make new fur lined moccasins for winter. They chatted amongst themselves and paid no attention to Clara snorting and nodding her head up and down. It wasn't until she kicked up her front feet and whinnied that Natayah asked her in English, "What's wrong, girl?"

"She's talking to that horse in white man's tongue," Running Deer scoffed, "does she not know that it is an Indian horse?"

Natayah heard her but chose not to comment, as Clara was getting more and more agitated. Natayah stood up and started walking toward her.

"It is probably a snake." Talking Bird called out. It was no snake, for as soon as Natayah started walking toward Clara she reared back. At the same time from the trees hanging over the river, two Indian men dropped into the water. Their faces were painted with red, black and white. Most of their head was shaven smooth except for a long ponytail or braid that was decorated with horsehair and sticks.

Three more came from the woods on horseback. The women screamed as the men came toward them.

One of the men on horseback rode by and grabbed Natayah by the hair and rode to the opposite side of the river. They were shouting and barking. One of them clubbed Talking Bird in the head with a stick and scooped her up onto his horse. She was knocked unconscious and the blood from her wound trickled down the horse's leg.

The three men on the ground grabbed Flower Blossom and Speckled Doe who were clinging to each other and screaming.

Running Deer tried to escape by running down the river but the third horseman grabbed her by her hair and pulled her across his horse.

The screams and cries from the women drifted down the river and when Natayah's horse showed up without her, in front of Grieving Mother, she knew something was wrong.

She ran to Night Owl, one of the teenagers left behind, and begged him to go and find the men. She knew the women were in danger. He immediately jumped on his horse and rode off.

The women were taken to a clearing. Talking Bird was still unconscious when he threw her from his horse to the ground. Natayah was dragged most of the way because her feet could not give her balance. Her naked body was scraped and bleeding from her waist to her feet.

All the women reunited in a huddle close together around Talking Bird's body.

The men shouted at them in a language they did not understand. When the women were unable to respond to the commands, the impatient men came over and grabbed the first woman, which happened to be Flower Blossom. She screamed and cried and clung to Speckled Doe and Natayah's hands.

"No, No please!" she screamed. The man with a red handprint on his face hit Speckled Doe's arm with a switch over and over, to have her let go. When Speckled Doe could no longer hold on she shrunk back from the switch that had spread to her chest and back.

Natayah clung to her hands and wrapped her arm around Flower Blossom's neck even though the switch came down heavy across her bare back.

They pried Flower Blossom away and struck Natayah hard across the face, which sent her falling backwards onto Talking Bird's still body.

They dragged Flower Blossom's naked and dirt covered body over to a protruding boulder and threw her down across it. Her face hit the boulder and blackened her eye. The man tied her hands together over her head.

Natayah stood back up, her face bloody and her eye was already starting to swell, but she grabbed a handful of rocks and began throwing them at her captors. Few of them hit their mark and the ones that did made no impact whatsoever. She could see the lust in their eyes and knew what was coming next and had to do whatever she could to prevent it. The three men standing around Flower Blossom's body were talking and stroking her smooth bare skin. They seemed to be playing some sort of elimination game as to who was to have the first turn. They did not pay any attention to Natayah's rock throwing. The man with the handprint on his face won and got down on his knees behind Flower Blossom. He untied the string on the side of his pants.

The two men that were guarding Natayah and the others were watching and cheering. Speckled Doe and Running Deer were cowering over Talking Bird's body crying. Natayah didn't think, she was acting on impulse. She ran over to the other three men and threw herself at the one who was untying his leggings down on his knees. She scratched and bit for all she was worth. The two even stepped back and laughed and pointed. The other two men joined in the laughter as their friend was being mauled by a she-cat. After a particularly deep bite the man with the red face yelled at his men to help him control her. But she only fought harder. One would throw her off, but she would be right back in the fray biting whatever she could sink her teeth into.

The man with the handprint was able to escape while his partner was trying to pry her teeth from his thigh. He stepped over to Flower Blossom and picked up her small body. He called out to Natayah and taunted her in a language she did not know. But she understood its meaning. He held up Flower Blossom in front of him and danced her around. Flower Blossom's tears rolled down her sweet, young face. There was blood trickling down the corners of her mouth and her eye and cheek were swollen. Natayah let go of the man in front of her and gave the other man her full attention. He was talking to her. She could hear the other men laughing amongst themselves. It was as if he was daring Natayah to come closer. "You want her? Come and get her," he seemed to be saying. The red-faced man had his arms under Flower Blossom's and made her bounce and dance in front of Natayah, taunting her.

Natayah's chest heaved gasping for air, but she lunged forward and was caught by two of the bystanders. "Let me go!" she screamed and kicked into the air. "You animals! Leave us alone! Let her go!"

The man to her right had eagle feathers decorating his hair and his face was painted like a skull. He picked up a handful of Natayah's hair and spoke to the others. She tried to pull her head away and when that didn't work, she reached over and bit the hand that held her.

The man that held Flower Blossom yelled out a single command and the others grew silent. He dropped Flower Blossom to the ground and came over to stand in front of Natayah. He spoke to her close to her face in a venomous tone. He nodded to his men and two came over and held Natayah by her arms. He reached for her red curls and brought a handful to his lips. He dragged the handful of hair across his face and whispered through it. He came back close to her. Natayah could feel his breath on her cheek. He whispered something into her ear and the other men snickered.

The Indian kicked Natayah's legs apart and grabbed her breast. He looked her in the eye while his hand made its way down her body and rested between her legs and he made a remark. He paused waiting for a response from Natayah. Natayah's body shook with anger and she sneered. But then, she spit.

This made him crazy with anger. With a closed fist, he struck Natayah in the face causing her to fall back on the ground. She curled into the fetal position and held her knees close to her chest. One of the men who was holding her began kicking her tightly wrapped body.

The hand-printed man shouted again and the others stopped. He told them to pick her up and turn her toward him.

Natayah's face was bloody and bruised. It hurt to breathe. Tears came from her eyes but she made no sound. They held her face so she could not turn away. She watched in horror as he picked up

Flower Blossom's body in a very slow and deliberate manner.

Flower Blossom was shaking her head "no" as tears were coming from her eyes. He put a knife in her bound hands, and wrapped his hands around hers.

Natayah tried to stand barely uttering the words, "No, please... not her. She is just a baby...." but her lips were too swollen that nothing could be understood.

He raised Flower Blossom's hands high over her head and with a single plunging motion; the knife was forced into her stomach. Flower Blossom folded in half and coughed up blood. The man let her fall to the ground and pulled the knife from the gaping wound. He cleaned the stone blade off on her arm as the blood spilled onto the ground.

Natayah cried, "No... I am so sorry. I'm sorry." She mixed her Indian and English words. Flower Blossom laid on the grass covered earth and quivered as her life spilled from her stomach. She held on to her middle trying to contain the blood, but with the other hand, she reached out for Natayah.

Natayah reached out for her as well and when the men released her she tried to crawl toward her. Their fingertips met and locked. Natayah heard Flower Blossom say, "Tell Grey Horse... I love him..." Natayah nodded and clutched her hand.

The hateful red-faced man grabbed Natayah by the hair and straddled her back. He put the bloodied knife to Natayah's forehead ready to take her beautiful red haired scalp.

Suddenly his body fell heavy onto Natayah.

She felt a piercing in the back of her neck. She heard him gurgle and felt warm liquid roll down her shoulder. His lifeless body lay heavy on Natayah's bruised and beaten one. She could scarcely breathe.

Natayah was fighting for consciousness. She heard a battle going on around her. The women were screaming again and crying. It only lasted for a brief moment and soon the clearing was silent. Natayah opened her eyes wondering her fate and saw Flower Blossom lying dead in front of her. Their hands still clasped.

She heard a familiar language, but it seemed so far away. She heard a cry of anguish and saw Grey Horse roll Flower Blossom's dead body over. Their clasped hands slipped apart. He fell to the ground beside her and brought her close to him. He cried into her hair and yelled out into the air as he pressed her body close to his. Natayah tried to speak, thinking they might not even know that she was there, but she could make no sound. Her vision was slipping away, perhaps into death.

The body that lay dead on her was crushing the breath from her and she decided to go peacefully. She has hurt enough for one lifetime. "I am ready," she prayed silently. She saw Thomas running towards her surrounded by light. She tried to reach out to him but could not make her limbs move.

"Momma…" he called out to her.

As soon as she saw her hand and white sleeve reach out to him, she was being pulled back. The light spun around her and she saw the scene beneath her. She saw a man hovering over her. He pushed the dead man that was crushing her to the side.

Captive Heart

Air returned to her lungs and she was in her body again. She saw the green grass stained with blood, she felt her body being flipped over and she felt strong arms around her.

She let out a cry of pain and the arms held her closer. A deep voice spoke to her and she felt a gentle hand brushing the hair from her face.

She fought to open her eyes again. It was him. She tried to speak, but he silenced her with gentle kisses. She brought her hand to her face and felt the swelling. Then the flush of pain ran through her. She cried out and then screamed. Her cries were haunting and gut wrenching, but he held her still. When her cries were exhausted, she fainted away.

"You are safe now. I have you…"

Elizabeth Bourgeret

Chapter Nine

It was two days before Natayah opened her eyes again for any length of time. She went through fever and talking out of her head in both English and the language of the people. The medicine man came to her and rattled his instruments over her and chanted. He blew red powder over her body and smoked his pipe. He told Grieving Mother that his medicines probably would not work on her because of her skin color.

So Grieving Mother took it upon herself to heal her. She wrapped Natayah tightly to heal her broken ribs and tended to her other wounds. She forced her to drink by inserting a straw into the corner of her mouth and giving her broth. Grieving Mother stayed with her night and day, and Talking Bird came frequently to check on her as well. For a while, Grieving Mother had two patients, but the medicine man took credit for healing Talking Bird's bump on the head.

Natayah finally opened her eyes and saw a high thatched roof over her head. The room was dark, save for a window that was propped open on the wall across from her. The room she was in was long and narrow with support beams in the center. A fire pit was dug out close to her bed, which was on a raised wooden platform. There were two other pallets laid out on the platform that she could see. She looked over her head and saw Grieving Mother sitting with her head down. She had fallen asleep on her vigil. Natayah tried to smile, but it hurt her. She raised her arm to touch her face and saw the raised welts on her forearms. She let out a quiet sob as she remembered the reason for her pain. Her hand reached her face and felt her swollen lips, cheeks and eyes. There was a cut at the back of her neck from where the arrow pierced her when her attacker fell to his death from the fateful arrow that was sent through his throat.

She pulled her covers back and saw that she was bound by tight hides wrapped from under her arms to her hips. The scratches and gashes were swollen and red and covered in green poultice. She dropped her head back down and whimpered in pain as she put the cover back over her mid-drift. It hurt everywhere. She cried again.

Her cries alerted Grieving Mother to her consciousness. "I grow weary of taking care of you child," Grieving Mother smiled over her.

Natayah tried to speak, but could not force a sound.

"Shhh, do not talk."

Natayah shook her head "no" and tried again. "Flower... Blossom?" She barely made a sound but Grieving Mother knew her question. She dropped her head low and shook it from side to side. "She is among the stars."

Natayah's tears ran from the corner of her eyes. It hurt to cry, but she was so filled with grief. She pointed to herself. "My... fault..." Her sobs caused her so much pain that she wrapped her arms around her chest.

Grieving Mother soothed her forehead with a gentle hand and soft words. "Do not be sad. She is hurting no more. You are a good friend."

Natayah still cried and said "no" with her head.

"You saved the lives of the others," Grieving Mother went on. "Chief Spotted Eagle is thinking he should change your name to Wildcat, according to the stories of Running Deer. She claims that you fought hard to try and save Flower Blossom." Grieving Mother reached out for Natayah's hand and held it close to her. "That shows great courage. Especially since she is not your kind. I have misjudged you."

The tears poured from Natayah's eyes. She felt she did not deserve such words of kindness. She was so consumed with guilt.

"Running Deer has been here every day to see you. And," she said with a bit of a twinkle in her eye, "so has Little Feather. He sat by your side for hours."

Natayah didn't know what to think. She was so grateful for everything Little Feather has done, but why won't he let her see him? And why wasn't he in the rescue party? But as much as her curiosity would let her think on Little Feather, the majority of her thoughts only went back to the one who saved her. She longed to ask after him, but would surely insult Little Feather's mother, the one who has brought her back to life... twice. Grieving Mother gave her a drink that made her feel sleepy, and she fell into it willingly.

In her drug induced dreams she saw herself in the arms of this man. The man with no name. He was carrying her to safety. She felt calm, safe.

Elizabeth Bourgeret

Until another man came up to them and tried to take Natayah from his arms. He was wearing a buffalo mask. It must be Little Feather. She clung to the man's neck, "No, I want to stay here."

"After all I have done for you..." it was Grieving Mother.

"I thought we were friends!" Talking Bird yelled at her from behind Little Feather.

"You owe me. I have taken care of you," Little Feather was saying to her. Suddenly the man with the red handprint on his face came from the woods with his knife and pushed past Little Feather. "No! I love him!" Natayah heard herself shouting. But the evil man pulled her from his arms and plunged his knife into the smooth breast of her love. He kept stabbing and pushing until they had come to the edge of a cliff. The man fell to the ground. Natayah cried out. Little Feather dragged Natayah over to the edge as well. "You want him? You can have him!" He threw her on top of her love, which lay in a bloody heap. The Indian with the handprint laughed and kicked them both over the edge.

Natayah woke with a start. Her heart was pounding and there was a hand holding her still. She fought against it until her eyes saw that it was Running Deer.

"Lie back, rest." Running Deer said with a barely audible voice and without looking at Natayah's eyes. She wiped her forehead with a cool cloth and said again, "You need your rest." Running Deer's voice was hoarse from screaming and her throat was tender, but her other injuries were minor. She pressed on. "Natayah," she swallowed hard, "I am grateful to you."

Natayah shook her head "no" and reached

Captive Heart

out to touch Running Deer's arm. Running Deer took her hand but kept her eyes cast down. "I am filled with shame for myself. I did nothing and you… you… who were not born to us, risked your life and your beauty to save one of us. I was so afraid that they…" she stumbled on her words, "that they would take… my… pureness. I could do nothing." Running Deer wrapped her other arm protectively around her own waist.

"It is alright," Natayah whispered.

"No," Running Deer said again with tears rolling down her cheeks. She briefly looked at Natayah's swollen, bruised face, "It is my shame and I must deal with my pride." She nodded her head and stood from her kneeling position and left the room.

Natayah watched her leave the room and looked up to the ceiling. She shook her head from side to side not wanting the images to return. "God, I need to rest, please, take these evil dreams from me. I am so grieved for Flower Blossom. I was so frightened. What are your plans for me? Couldn't you tell me? Why am I kept alive? Flower Blossom had so much to live for. I have had my family… and lost them."

Natayah nodded off to sleep again and when she woke, Grieving Mother sat beside her. "You have visitors." She touched her forehead and tucked the covers close to her body. Then mumbled under her breath, "How is anyone supposed to get well, with people coming and going all day…" Natayah heard her barking orders outside then adding, "…and do not stay too long. She needs her rest!" Then, he came in.

Her stomach did a "flip-flop" and suddenly

she was concerned about how she looked. She watched him stride towards her with his strong muscular legs and solid lean body. He was a beautiful man on the outside and she was learning that he was beautiful on the inside too.

He came up to the platform and sat beside her pallet.

"You are looking better today," he said.

Natayah shook her head "no" and she was blushing underneath all of the bruising.

"Thank…you…" she swallowed and tried to make sound come out, "for saving me."

He placed a finger on her lips to silence her. "Grieving Mother says that you are not to try and talk yet," he grinned, "They are calling you a wildcat. Said you are not afraid of anything."

She shook her head "no" again. "I… was… afraid… So afraid," she strained.

"Stop trying to talk. Otherwise Grieving Mother will make me leave. Unless… unless, you want me to go."

Natayah gave her best attempt at a smile and shook her head no.

"You will not try and talk?"

"No."

"Good. I like being the only one who gets to talk. What should we talk about?"

Natayah thought he had the most beautiful eyes she had ever seen. Had they always been so piercing? It is amazing what you can see when you strip the hate away.

"The rumor is that you will soon be betrothed to Little Feather. Is that true?"

Natayah shrugged her shoulders.

"Has he been here to see you?"

She nodded. "Sleeping…" she whispered.

"You are sleeping in his bed, did you know?"

Natayah looked surprised and embarrassed. She started to lift up, but he touched her shoulder, "No! Do not get up!" He shielded his eyes. "I do not know you well enough, yet!"

Even though it hurt her ribs, she laughed. She grabbed her stomach and laughed again. "It hurts."

"Well, stop laughing." Which only made her laugh again. "Let us get back to the subject at hand. Why do you think that Little Feather only comes around when you are sleeping? Maybe he is hiding something?"

Natayah furrowed her brow and shrugged.

"He does all these things for you and showers you with gifts, and still you have not met him?" Natayah could not see the smile he was trying to conceal.

"No."

"Strange, do you not think so?"

She nodded her head yes.

"Are you madly in love with him?"

Natayah stared into his eyes for a moment before she reluctantly shrugged her shoulders.

He stared a moment too long before they were both embarrassed. "I almost forgot. I have a surprise for you myself. We can not let Little Feather have all of the fun." He stood and walked towards the door. "Here is the real one you should thank for your rescue." He opened the door and whistled and Clara trotted in obediently and went immediately over to Natayah's bedside. She stopped at the edge of the platform and reached her nose down to Natayah.

Natayah untucked her arms from the blankets and rubbed them against Clara's nose. "Hey, girl," Natayah whispered. Clara, so happy with the attention nuzzled her nose into Natayah's ribs. "Oh, ow… ow…oww. Yes, I've missed you, too."

Little Feather tugged back on her rope but Clara fought against it and it appeared she was trying to kiss Natayah's open hand.

"She sounded the alarm when you were taken. She came running back without you and Grieving Mother knew that was a bad sign." He walked back over beside her and took the hand that was petting Clara's nose. "You are safe here. If you need anything…"

"I owe you… an apology…" she whispered, "I am sorry…"

"It is forgotten," he interrupted. He held her hand as he stroked it with his thumb.

Clara shook her head and threw his hand out of the way so Natayah could get back to petting her nose. They laughed.

"C'mon animal, we need to let her rest. Grieving Mother's orders." He took her hand again and gave it a gentle squeeze, then took Clara by the rope and headed straight out the door.

Natayah's heart fluttered inside her tightly wrapped chest. It hurt to smile, it hurt to laugh, but she found herself doing both. What was this feeling? Was it true love? Or could it be forgiveness? Either one, Natayah drifted off to sleep a little happier that day.

Natayah was determined not to spend another day in bed. All of the other women were mostly healed and about their business, but here she was still being pampered like a newborn.

Talking Bird came in to see Natayah while she was struggling to get up. Talking Bird now and forever had a scar beside her right eye and lost a couple of back teeth, but otherwise she was back to good health. Natayah was so thankful, because if the club had struck her just a few inches over, Talking Bird would have lost her sight.

Natayah's outer scratches were healing rather quickly thanks to Grieving Mother's care, but her internal wounds still made her body ache the same as the first day. The bruises showed clearly and colorfully on her pale white skin and her face was still swollen. She, too, would most likely have some scarring on her face and legs.

"What are you doing?" Talking Bird gasped, "Grieving Mother is going to be so upset with you!"

"Why do you think I waited until she had gone?"

Talking Bird had to laugh at her stubbornness. No more was she the pale, helpless white woman with an endless supply of tears. Now she had become a strong, courageous, Indian woman.

Talking Bird helped her to slip a dress over her head. She winced as it ran across her torn skin. This being her first attempt at putting clothes on since the attack, she drew short breaths with every movement. She was still wrapped around her chest to limit her movement, which was almost a blessing as it gave her a little extra support on her back. She looked down at her bandaged wounds and saw the blood seep through a couple. Grieving Mother is not going to like that, she thought to herself as she pulled her dress down below her waist.

"I do not mean to sound stupid, but is this our home?" she asked as she adjusted herself on the edge of the raised pallet.

"Yes," Talking Bird smiled. "This is our village."

"I seemed to have missed out on the last bit of the journey."

"So did I. When you are well, I will take you outside and show you everything."

"Whose home am I in?"

Talking Bird sent her a look that meant to say, "Isn't it obvious?" but she merely answered, "This is Little Feather's weetu."

"I was afraid of that. Is this his bed?"

"Of course it is. Do not worry. He insisted. He is staying with my husband and me. Would you like to know a secret?" Talking Bird did not wait for Natayah to answer. "For many nights after you were first brought here, he slept just outside your tipi. If the wall had not been there, he would have been beside you."

"That is so sweet," Natayah found herself saying.

"This building is very large for one man and his mother, do you not agree?"

Natayah looked over at Talking Bird, "You are not very subtle, are you?" Talking Bird could only giggle in response.

Natayah was just about to her feet with the help and support of Talking Bird when Grieving Mother came through the door.

"Daughter!" she shouted.
Both Natayah and Talking Bird replied, "What?" as innocently as they could.

"You are not well yet. You should be resting."

"I tried to tell her, but she would not listen," Talking Bird admonished but couldn't stop smiling.

"Please, Grieving Mother, I am in a new place and I have not been able to see any of it," she begged.

"If you are so ready to get out and about, I will tell Chief Spotted Eagle that you are ready to meet with him. He is waiting to see you."

"I do not want to see him! Look at my face! I look terrible!" Natayah grew worried.

"Then back to bed you go."

"Why does the chief want to see me?"

"He probably wants to plan a name change ceremony and wants to know if you are going out to battle any of our enemies... Wildcat..." Talking Bird teased.

Natayah shook her head, "I am not so brave. I could not save her." Her eyes glazed over as she stared off into the distance. "She was just a little girl... ready to make memories of her own... I had her killed."

"Do not do this to yourself." Grieving Mother came to her and sat beside her. "It could have been much worse. It is not an easy life for a woman."

"Yes. It could have been much worse," Natayah sighed and wiped away a tear. Grieving Mother patted her leg roughly and Natayah grimaced.

"Oh, I forgot to show you," Talking Bird interjected, trying to change the subject, "I brought you my cane. Two Spear made it for me, because it was difficult to walk at first." She ran over to the door and grabbed the cane that leaned against the wall.

"Thank you. I think that I will need it. I feel dizzy just sitting up."

"Too much, too soon!" Grieving Mother stood up and lifted her legs back onto her bed. "You lay back down."

"But, I was half way there!"

"Rest!" Grieving Mother wrapped the blankets around her again.

"But what about Chief Spotted Eagle?"

"Tomorrow!"

Tomorrow actually came two days later. Natayah was glad that she waited. She could sit up without feeling dizzy and she could open her eyes completely without feeling the swelling on her cheeks. She had no idea what she looked like and was in no hurry to find out.

Talking Bird came in the late afternoon. Natayah was already sitting up with her dress on and Grieving Mother was putting her shoes on for her.

"Are you ready?" Talking Bird asked.

"Oh, yes! I could use some fresh air." Her first few steps were so excruciating that she almost crawled back into bed.

"Is it too much?" Grieving Mother asked.

"We are almost to the door. Let me at least walk outside." Natayah took small steps and relied heavily on Grieving Mother, Talking Bird and her cane. When Talking Bird opened the door and Natayah stepped out, her breath was taken away by the beauty that surrounded her.

The trees were so tall and green and offered

just the right amount of shade while still letting the blue sky and rays of sunshine peek through. There were dozens upon dozens of wooden huts made of thin sticks tied together. Half way down each "building" a dark brown paste sealed the gaps between the sticks. Each weetu had windows cut from it or built around to form one; and they each had thatched roofs. Some were very long and others were more square. Others followed no real pattern at all. Talking Bird explained that the different sizes had to do with the family size and the number of animals the family owned. Some have added on, but tried to keep the rectangular shape. The weetus were scattered everywhere yet in an orderly manner. People were out and about doing their daily chores or sitting in groups. She heard the voices of small children and followed the sound with her eyes. She could see little bodies running around at the end of a path through a patch of woods. There was a clearing in the center of the village that was covered with beautiful green grass. It had a pit dug in the center for village gatherings.

  Natayah took a couple steps forward and looked down at her feet. She saw the dirt paths that went from place to place that have been worn into the ground from much use.

  Natayah could hear water and looked around for where it might be coming from.

  "I think this is the most perfectly situated weetu in the whole village," Talking Bird said proudly. "This was my home when I was a small girl. The river is just over there, but from here, you can see the tips of the beautiful red bluff."

  Natayah looked in the direction that she pointed and followed the trees up to their very height. She could see it. The tips of the bluff.

"The elders would send the children and women to the top of the bluff if they thought there might be danger. I would go up there and play with my brothers when I was little, too. It is beautiful from the top. You can see clearly down here to the village, so I could see when my mother was looking for me," Talking Bird laughed.

"So that is how you got home so fast!" Grieving Mother smiled.

"Do you want to see it? The river flows at the base of it."

"I can hear it. Yes, I would love to see the river and the bluff."

"I do not think Chief Spotted Eagle will mind if we take a detour!" Talking Bird wrapped her arm around Natayah's back as they prepared to walk. Natayah's body was screaming out in pain but she was determined.

They walked along the dirt path to what looked like the edge of the village, but the ground actually sloped down toward the riverbank.

When Natayah saw the rocky beach, her heart began to speed up and she pulled back, too afraid to go forward remembering the rocky beach leading up to their kidnapping. Talking Bird swung around in front of her, "It is okay, Natayah. You are safe here. We are home. Come closer. You will see... it is different. It is much further downstream. You are safe."

Natayah nodded her head, but could not settle her heart.

"Can you make it?" Grieving Mother asked again. "We can wait for another day."

"No. I can make it," Natayah said, trying to

believe it.

As they started down the slope, a young woman came up and walked in front of Natayah. She did not look too much older than Natayah, herself. Natayah saw immediately the mark of a grieving woman. Her left arm was healing from the gash cut into it with a knife. The wound had been heat-seared, but it still looked fresh.

The woman grabbed Natayah's free hand and turned her palm up. She bent over to kiss the delicate white palm.

"I am Quannah, the mother of Flower Blossom. I thank you for trying to save her." She kissed Natayah's palm again and disappeared into the heart of the village.

The three women's eyes grew moist, but no one said a word.

Natayah's steps grew weaker as they made it to the waters edge. They helped Natayah sit down on the rocky beach. Tears ran down her cheeks. She had had about all she could take for one day.

The river was beautiful. The water was clear and the sound was music to her ears. She forced out the images that were formerly linked to those sounds. Straight above her loomed the mighty red bluff. It was awe inspiring. This is where God could be found, Natayah thought to herself. She let her body relax and gave herself to Him knowing that he was keeping her alive for a reason. She looked up and gazed at the bluff again and let the sounds of the river soothe her soul.

The huge bluff had streaks of red and orange bleeding through it. Talking Bird told her that it was the blood of her ancestors reminding them of the trials they had to face to become the people they are today. Natayah did not say anything but she did not believe the same thing. She believed that it was God using his colorful pallet and showing off His wonders.

Natayah stretched her neck back and shielded her eyes to see the top. "It is amazing," she said breathlessly. She closed her eyes to hear the river sing to her and feel the warm summer breeze blow through her hair. The sun felt so soothing on her skin. She opened her eyes again. "This is the most beautiful place I have ever seen." This time her tears were not from pain but from the mercy of God's love, even in her darkest hour, showing her that He always has been and always will be here.

The three women sat in silence on the rocky beach and stared out at the water. Natayah's fingers ran across the rocks lazily and finally she scooped up a handful.

"I have never seen such colorful rocks." she picked out ones that were striped with cream and reds and others that looked like crystals shining in the sun. Others that might look plain and dirty on one side, but when you turn them over, there is a tiny cavern of crystals.

"I had forgotten how wonderful a place this is, having grown up here, but seeing it through your eyes makes me thankful again that we live here," Talking Bird said.

Grieving Mother nodded her head in agreement and happily joined in searching for additions for the growing pile of exceptional rocks Natayah was collecting on her dress.

Natayah began humming a tune she recalled from her days of being a member of the Baptist congregation. Two women came down to the river to fill their woven baskets with water and looked over at the rock collecting threesome. What an odd sight seeing two Indian women sitting on either side of the red-haired white woman when there was so much work to be done.

There was always work to be done. And it will be there later.

After several hours had passed, they knew it was time to get back.

"Do you think the chief would mind if I waited until tomorrow for that visit?" Natayah asked. "I am awfully tired."

"It will be fine. Let us get you back to bed. You have had a busy day."

"What about my rocks?" Natayah sounded like one of the children.

"There are hundreds more where those came from. We can come back another day." Grieving Mother said gently pushing Natayah back up the beach.

"Thank you for spending the day with me." Natayah said as they got her back inside the weetu. They got her tucked into bed and they didn't hear another peep from her until morning.

Elizabeth Bourgeret

Chapter Ten

Natayah woke early the next morning with Grieving Mother sitting by her bed. She greeted her with a smile.

"Are you hungry for some solid food today?" Grieving Mother asked.

"I think I am. My throat still hurts when I swallow, but my empty stomach hurts even more!" Natayah answered.

Grieving Mother and Natayah ate breakfast and chatted. Natayah enjoyed this new friendship with the older woman.

"Do you think you are ready to see the chief today?"

"Yes. I want to know why he calls for me."

"I would like to know myself. Maybe I am just a nosy old woman," Grieving Mother laughed.

After breakfast, they cleaned up and slowly made their way to the chief's weetu.

Natayah moved along slowly with the use of the cane. Her body ached with every step.

"You are walking better today," Grieving Mother noticed as she held Natayah's left arm for support.

"Am I? It really does not feel like it."

"It will get better. It takes time."

"It is not like I have some where else to be. No "schedules". No "clocks"…" Natayah laughed to herself.

"What do these words mean? skejul and clok?"

Natayah explained a bit of her busy life as they walked. She was the wife of a merchant. Did she miss those days? She thought back on her friends and her social engagements and obligations. She would have never gotten kidnapped and almost killed on the streets of her home town, would she?

"My deerskin clothes are much more comfortable... not as many layers," Natayah added.

"I like the feel of your old clothes."

"They are lighter on hot summer days," Natayah continued by explaining briefly that her clothes were made from a plant called cotton. Grieving Mother was amazed that something so soft could come from anything but an animal.

"I would like to see this cotton plant," she said.

"Well, honestly, I have never seen one myself," Natayah explained. "I purchase the cloth already colored and prepared at a place called a 'General Merchandise Store'"

Grieving Mother stopped for a moment. "No wonder you were so fragile. You did not have to provide for yourself."

"You are right. We have had very different lives," Natayah admitted.

They continued walking. Suddenly Grieving Mother slapped Natayah on the back, "You will make a good Indian woman. I will not give up on you."

Natayah winced and tried to recover from the rare display of affection.

When they reached the chief's weetu, Grieving Mother told Natayah to wait outside to make sure he was ready for her.

A few moments later a group of men and smoke came pouring out of the weetu before Grieving Mother came back out to get her. "He said you can come in now," Grieving Mother announced as she waved Natayah to the entrance.

Natayah walked into the dimly lit room. A layer of smoke swirled around near the ceiling fading in and out through the beams of sunshine coming through the open windows.

Chief Spotted Eagle sat at the far end of the weetu on a platform. His legs were crossed and he quietly puffed on his pipe. Natayah looked around his weetu. It was much larger than the one that Natayah stayed in. It had many fire pits running down the center. There were several beds along the walls and many tools and weapons hanging from the ceiling. There were neat stacks of furs and piles of dishes tucked under the beds. The beds lowest to the ground were made from a platform but other beds hung above the lower beds in some places. *"How many people live here?"* Natayah wondered.

Chief Spotted Eagle waved her to come closer. She approached with respect and did not sit until he pointed to a bear skin rug with the head still attached laying on the floor in front of him to the left side of the low burning fire. Sitting was a struggle. She tried not to make a sound but it was obvious that she was in pain. Grieving Mother came over to assist her down to her knees. Natayah was learning that emotions, especially those of pain or anger, from a woman were meant to be kept to

151

oneself.

She sat quietly waiting for him to speak. Even in her own culture it was customary to wait for the man to speak first... when she could hold her tongue that long.

After a few more puffs on his pipe, he told Grieving Mother to leave and wait outside. "I will take care of her," he assured Grieving Mother who looked like a wounded puppy being sent out.

"How are you feeling?" he finally asked her.

What kind of answer was he looking for? She wondered. If I tell him the truth, it would be, *"It's killing me to stand up and sit down, to breathe in and out and even to eat. I live in fear of going near the water again...."*

"I am fine," she answered.

"There is something I must tell you," he paused. She waited. "Your wagon train was attacked because of what your people did to my people."

"Yes. I know."

He nodded, thankful that he had to say no more on that subject. "You were not killed..." he thought about his choice of words, "You were not killed because my cousin Wild Dog takes pleasure in... trading or selling your kind to other tribes or back to the white men." He puffed his pipe. "Little Feather, he is a good man. A brave man. He has killed many enemies and much game in his years. But he is... soft... here," pointing to his chest, "for you."

Natayah dropped her head and blushed. Chief Spotted Eagle smiled, "He purchased you from Wild Dog." Natayah's head shot up, she gulped air in and was going to object, but he silenced her with a raised hand.

"He does not wish to own you. But he knew what was in store for you if he did not. I hope you never hear of the outcome of the other women. I have forbidden it to be spoken of in this village." Natayah furrowed her brow and was sad for the other women. "You are very kind," she acknowledged. She tucked her head down and allowed the chief to continue. "Since you have no father, I have decided to act in that role, if that would suit you."

"I would be most honored," she answered humbly.

"Daughter, then." He smiled down at her and she smiled and nodded back to him.

"Daughter, Little Feather has come to me to ask for permission for tomah-wee-ha... to court you... to win your heart. What do you say to this?"

"Does this tomo.... tumo...tomah-wee-ha mean that you have promised me to marry him?" she asked.

"No. It is to give permission for him to make you interested. Marriage is the purpose for this courting ritual."

"Oh," she said unenthusiastically.

"Does this displease you, daughter?"

"No, I suppose not. He has been very good to me, but I really do not know him. I have not met him formally."

Chief Spotted Eagle furrowed his deeply lined brow, "Have I not seen you two talking?"

"Have we? Maybe we have and I just did not know it." Her brain was frantically trying to retrace a time when she was talking with a group and one of them might have been him.

Elizabeth Bourgeret

"But I may tell him, you will welcome his advances?"

"Yes, I suppose so. But what happens if we do not get along?"

"You do not have to marry."

"Was there anyone else that asked you about this tomo-wee-ha thing… for me?"

The chief raised his graying eyebrows in surprise, "Is there someone else making advances to you?"

"I guess not," she sighed.

"Then it is settled," he announced in his authoritative voice as if there were a whole room full of people. She sat still waiting to be excused, but he only stared at her. "Daughter, there is something else," he began. He spoke softly and cautiously. "Do you find yourself happy with us?"

Natayah was caught off guard and didn't know how to answer.

"Would you think of running away?" he added.

"No," she answered honestly. "When I became a member of this tribe, I knew I had to give up my old life. It has been difficult, but I have made the commitment. And I could never repay all that has been done for me by running away."

"I am happy to hear this. He sat silent for a moment and puffed on his pipe. He nodded once and continued, "I have a request of you."

"How can I help you," she asked.

"A man came to us this morning… he is… one of your kind."

Natayah gasped and her heart raced, not wanting to believe it was true.

"He seems to come in peace." the chief

continued, "We have been hidden in these woods and protected by the bluffs for many, many seasons. I do not recall many of the white man finding us." He puffed again, remembering. "We are having trouble communicating. He wants something from us and I do not know what it is. Would you be able to help us without betrayal?"

"Oh, I would never betray you. I would be happy to help," she said resolved. "But I thought it would not be safe for a white man to see me here. For the safety of all your people…"

"I have had no bad dreams or bad feelings about this. I feel it will be fine."

"Then yes, I would be happy to help."

"Do you remember your old language?" he asked.

"Yes, I talk with my horse in that language all the time. It will be nice hearing it spoken back to me. I like the way it sounds."

"Very well, then. I will send for him." He tapped his staff against the wooden platform and one of Chief Spotted Eagle's sons stepped inside. He nodded and the son left the room once again.

"What is it you wish to know from this man?"

"What does he want? Why is he here? Are there more of his kind? Try to find out if he would mean us harm."

Natayah nodded her head in understanding, "I will find out what you need to know." She stood slowly and painfully from her kneeling position.

The door opened and four men walked in. Three Indian men and one white man. He was dressed in deerskin trousers and had on a dark red printed top. His hair was a sandy brown and hung in uneven layers to his shoulders. His beard was thick and unruly.

He smiled as he came forward and held out his hand to Natayah. His blue eyes sparkled as he spoke, "I was told that there was a beautiful red-head hidden in these parts."

It was her language, but he spoke with a slight Southern drawl. Natayah reached out her hand and smiled in return. As he got closer to her she could see a change in the look on his face. It was a look of concern. He spoke in low tones. "Have they done this to you? Are you alright?"

He held her hand firmly and came close to her, but she could not speak. She could only stare at him while inside her head she was screaming at herself, "Say something! Don't just stand here! Tell him these people did not hurt you!"

Chief Spotted Eagle interrupted her berating thoughts and spoke to her, "Ask him to sit and talk with us."

Natayah released his hand and took a step back. She directed him to a place on the floor and stuttered out the words, "please...sit."

He sat where he was told but his eyes never left her. He looked her over mentally assessing the wounds she had sustained.

Natayah felt uncomfortable under his scrutiny and could not look him in the eye, "What... is your... name... please?" she finally asked.

He smiled at her again, "Forgive me for staring. It looks like you have had a rough time? Is there anything I can do for you?"

"What is he saying?" Chief Spotted Eagle asked.

Natayah turned to him and said; "He is

asking me about my health." She turned back to face their guest and said, "My name... is Natayah."

He stood up and stared into her deep blue eyes. "Have they threatened you not to tell me what has happened to you? I can protect you."

She shook her head "no" growing impatient with herself and with him for all the extra questions throwing off her train of thought. "What is your name?" she stumbled through her words, as if it was a foreign language.

"I'm so sorry. You must think my manners are terrible." He held out his hand to shake hers again, and helped her sit on the bear blanket. "My name is Josiah Cooper." He spoke loudly and used big motions with his hands.

Natayah had to turn away so as not to laugh. He continued, "I hail from down Arkansas way, but I am working out of St. Louis. Headed back that way, actually."

Natayah's eyes lit up at the sound of the city. "You are... going... to St. Louis?" she asked.

"Yep, I do some huntin' for a store owner there."

"What is he saying?" Chief Spotted Eagle demanded.

Natayah's head was spinning, *"St. Louis? Was she really so close?"* She told the chief that he was just passing through.

"What does he want here?" the chief asked through Natayah.

"Oh, just a place to stay and possible, do some huntin' while I am here."

"What does he hunt?"

"I hunt deer, beaver, coon, mostly."

"What does he offer in return for our

hospitality?"

"If I can stay for a couple weeks, I would be willing to share the meat with you so long as I have enough to eat and I get to keep the skins."

"It is done. Eat with us tonight, and my wife will set up a tipi for you."

Natayah smiled a genuine smile, "You can stay. He has invited you to be his guest for dinner. They are going to give you your own place to sleep, just outside of the village."

"Can I spend more time with you?" Josiah asked.

"Yes," Natayah smiled, "I would like to hear my language, more. I am a little rusty."

Josiah stared at her a moment too long and Natayah turned away.

"I almost forgot!" Josiah jumped up which startled all the men. Josiah raised his hands in peace, "I... uh... forgot. I have gifts..." Natayah laughed as she translated. "Can I go and get them?"

The chief nodded.

"I'll be right back." Josiah exited the weetu.

"Daughter, does this bother you?" the chief asked her.

"No, not at all," Natayah smiled sincerely.

"He seems to be no threat."

"I do not like him. He seems false," Black Elk interjected. As the chief's oldest son, he was very suspicious of everyone.

"He is very nice. He seems like a good man," Natayah said worried that Black Elk may sway his father to go back on his decision.

"We will watch him, and Natayah, you will tell us if he is deceiving us."

"Yes, I will," she answered solemnly.

Josiah came back in with a large parcel in his hands. Upon closer inspection it was made of canvas with a sturdy handle. There were words printed on the side, but all that Natayah could see was the word STORE, the top of the bag was covered. He dropped the bag to the floor and knelt down on one knee beside it. He leaned his one arm on his knee and carefully opened the bag. He peeked inside and looked up at the chief then back down into his bag. Josiah knew what he was doing as he felt everyone in the room lean in a little closer.

Using all of the flair of a performer, he pulled out a small, shiny copper pan. "Here, this is fer your wife." He handed the pot to the chief.

The chief accepted the gift by its long handle and stared at wondering what to do with it. He tapped on it, enjoying the metallic sound it made and then asked, "What could this be?"

"This gift was a humble gesture for your wife, if it would please you. It is used for cooking." She stepped up to the platform and took the pot from his hand and flipped it over and held it by its handle. "The contents go here and it rests on the fire. It will not burn up and it cooks quickly."

"I will give it to my wife," the chief announced, "I accept your gift."

"There's more!" Josiah went on. He pulled out two steel bladed knives with bone handles and gave them handle side to the chief.

"And this is for you and your family," he said to Natayah and handed her a smaller but similar knife. "I am sure you can find many uses for this."

"I can, yes," she smiled and looked to her chief to see if she was allowed to accept it. He nodded so she thanked him. "You are very generous."

"Are you married, Natayah?" he asked.

She blushed, "No, my husband died a couple of years ago."

"I am sorry to hear that, ma'am."

"Thank you," she said barely above a whisper.

"I am surprised they didn't force you into a marriage already. How long have you been with them?"

"I am not sure, really. Four, maybe six months."

He nodded his head. "I have one more thing for you. I am truly grateful for all of your help dealin' with these savages…" Natayah's skin prickled for the second time with him. For sometime now she has considered these people her own. Her equals, not savages. But her heart was quickly melted when he pulled out a beautiful ivory brush, comb and mirror set and handed them to Natayah.

She stared at them and stroked the delicate design on the back of the mirror. The bristles of the brush were so soft. Her thoughts went back to the top of her dresser in her room that she shared with her sister, Katherine. "Josiah, it is beautiful. I had a set very similar to this when I was a child. They are so beautiful. I don't know if I should accept them.

"Please do," Josiah said closing Natayah's hands around them. "It seems that I gave them to just the right person."

Captive Heart

Chapter Eleven

Natayah was floating on a cloud. She was so happy. She slowly made it back to the weetu with the aide of her cane.

It was agreed that Josiah could stay with the tribe for a season and in addition to the meat he promised that he would give one of every four hides that he took from the territory. Chief Spotted Eagle was very pleased with this arrangement.

Natayah was thrilled as well. Someone of her own kind to speak with on a daily basis. She hoped that he was up to date on the latest information so she might get some kind of idea about how Katherine is living.

As she thought about it, there was nothing so important that she really missed in her old life. The people of course, her family, but she was discovering a strength within her that she never knew she had. She missed going to church, but here, she found God everywhere she looked. She missed running water but... no, she missed running water! She missed her books, her Bible especially, her photographs, and piano... Could she live without them forever? "I believe so," she smiled to herself. But then there was Katherine. Surely she could not possibly know that her sister was still alive. Perhaps she could send word back with Josiah when he left. That would not be a betrayal, right? Katherine, must think her dead. And she could have been... if...

Before her thoughts could turn sad, Talking Bird emerged from her weetu just as Natayah was passing. *"God's hand at work,"* she thought as God provided her with a distraction.

Talking Bird smiled at her and walked along in step with her. "Natayah, how much better you look today!"

Natayah smiled her swollen, lopsided smile. "Thank you. I am feeling better."

Talking Bird stood there and grinned at Natayah. Natayah looked down at herself and lifted her shoulders, "What?"

"I am... so happy that..." she took in a deep breath and spoke very quickly like an excited child, "that you have accepted my brother's tomeh-wee-ha!" She giggled to herself and jumped around in a little circle. "I am so happy. Soon, you will be my real sister!"

"News travels fast," Natayah lifted her eyebrows pretending that Talking Bird's little dance was strange behavior, but inside, she was smiling too.

"I am sorry. Two Spears was there when the strange white man came in and knew that Chief Spotted Eagle would not have allowed you to speak with him if you had not accepted."

Natayah looked at her questioningly, so Talking Bird explained further, "It shows that you are willing to make a life here, among us. If you had not accepted my brother's attentions, he would have worried that you still had ties to the white man's world."

"But I do still have ties," Natayah was distressed, and tired, "I will always have ties. I cannot forget who I am or where I came from. I have family out there somewhere."

"I am sorry. I did not mean to upset you. I always seem to say the wrong thing. Of course you must never forget your history. It is as important to you as it is to us, I am sure. I meant that you are willing to start a new life, a family, with us. Blending our two worlds." Natayah did not respond so Talking Bird grabbed her free hand, "Please do not be angry with me. I am so happy that the Great Spirit has brought you to be among us. I sometimes talk so much I do not think about what I am saying."

Natayah listened. She too thought God had brought her to be with these people. And she did commit to a new life here, for better or worse. She shook her head humbly and squeezed Talking Bird's hand, "I am not angry with you. I must have had too much excitement for one day. Too much on my mind... it is forgotten."

Talking Bird jumped up and down clapping her hands. She hugged Natayah gently, "Now, tell me about the stranger. Is he handsome? Is he nice? Will he be staying? Why is he here?"

"Hold on! One question at a time!" They walked and talked and giggled like two teenagers all the way to Natayah's weetu.

The lifeless body of the rabbit lay still on the ground. Natayah knelt over it with her new knife in her hand knowing what she had to do, but not being able to do it.

"It is just a rabbit," she said softly. "God

gave it to us for our nourishment.... Just do it!" She rolled the willing participant onto its back and lifted up its chin. The legs automatically flopped open to the sides making a clear cutting area for her. She took in a deep breath and swallowed hard. She held her knife tightly with her fist. Poised, her knife hovered over the neck for a minute, and then another. "It's dead... it will not feel anything." she told herself.

"Does that help? Talking to it?" a voice said from behind her.

Startled, Natayah screamed and flung the knife. It landed directly between his feet.

"Hey! Watch where you throw that thing!"

She looked up and smiled, happy to see the familiar face, but still nameless, Little Feather.

"I am sorry, I did not see you," she smiled realizing that she was blushing madly for the heat in her face.

He reached down between his legs and pulled the blade from the dirt. "This is a nice knife. What is this material that it is made from?"

"It is called 'steel'. It is a metal. It will not break as easy as bone or stone and it is very sharp."

"Where did you get such a thing?"

"A man gave it to me," she teased. A twinge of jealousy ran through him and he was unable to hide it, much to the pleasure of Natayah.

"What man?"

"A white man came to the village a couple days ago. Where have you been?"

"I was hunting. I have heard of no such man."

"You sure do disappear a lot. No wonder you do not know what is going on."

He crept closer to her, "Were you missing me?" he spoke in a gruff whisper.

Her body shivered as she could feel his breath on the back of her ear. "Not particularly, but you would have known about the handsome stranger."

"Handsome, too? Are you not promised to your beloved Little Feather?"

"Oh, so you heard about that, but not the white man?" she enjoyed the teasing and she enjoyed the comfortable feeling that she now felt around him.

"Well, I... thought... I mean... You have accepted the tomeh-wee-ha, have you not?"

Her smile faded, "Yes, I have. Does that bother you?"

"No," he answered quickly.

Almost disappointed with his answer, she proceeded cautiously; "We can still be friends, right?"

His smile grew wide and he knelt down beside her. "Yes. We can." He grabbed her hand. "I am glad to hear you say that." His thumb stroked the back of her hand gently. He caught himself staring into her eyes and he placed the knife roughly into her hand. He cleared his throat and asked, "So, you are to marry?" He stood up and turned away from her lest his feelings would have been at her feet.

"I do not know," she paused, "I am quite sure that he would not want me for a wife. He does not even know me. And I do not know him. I am constantly in the midst of trouble or getting hurt. I can barely cook, I have this fancy knife but I cannot bring myself to skin this one little rabbit that *he* brought to me." She stood up and threw the knife down into the ground. "And... I have been told that I have a slight temper."

"I would believe no such thing," he joked with her.

She laughed, "So you see? It is a hopeless case. I would not want to marry me, would you?" She was caught off guard by the serious look in his eyes. She froze in place as he came near her. Her heart jumped in her chest as he reached his hand out to touch her cheek. She held his gaze and leaned into his hand.

"Nuh-tay- uh!" the shout came from the other side of the village and repeated again.

The sound of her name made her jump back away from him as if she had been caught doing something wrong. She laughed nervously and brought her hand up to her neck. He looked down to the ground and back up to her from the corner of his eye.

"The white man?"

"Yes. His name is Josiah and he will be with us for a while."

"You know his name? Do you spend all day with this man? Is that safe? Do we really know anything about him?"

Natayah interrupted him, "Amazing is it not? I found out his name in only one day, and I still do not know yours!" She raised her eyebrows and put her hands on her hips in a moment of triumph.

"Why do you need to know my name? Can you not be my friend without one?"

She dropped her hands to her sides. "I hope I can always be your friend," she said sincerely not looking at his handsome face, "but it would be nice to be able to refer to you as something other than, 'that guy'! I cannot even tell my best friend about you. She would ask who you were... I have no name to give her."

"What would you tell your best friend about me?" He came closer, loving that fact that it made her uncomfortable. "Would you tell her that I was handsome, strong, and brave?" He was almost close enough to hold her but she put her hand up to stop him. "No," she said abruptly, "I would tell her there is this crazy man that keeps stalking me, that will not tell me his name."

"What if I do not have a good name? What if my name embarrasses me?"

"You? Embarrassed? I do not think so."

"No, really, what if my name meant Deer Droppings or Rabbit Insides? You would get sick every time you heard it. There we would be and someone would say my name, and you would fall asleep standing up, again!" he laughed as he teased her.

She couldn't contain her laughter. "It is called 'fainting' and I have not done that in a long while, thank you." They were laughing when Josiah came up to them.

"A rose by any other name, would still smell as sweet," she said to him and held his gaze for a moment and just before he looked as if he was about to lean in to kiss her she then turned her attentions to Josiah. "I just quoted Shakespeare in an Indian language!"

Josiah and Little Feather looked at her confused.

"Never mind," she told Josiah. "Did you need me for something?" The two men were silently sizing each other up. "I'm sorry," she said in English, "let me introduce you. Josiah, this is Tonica," she giggled when she saw the look on Little Feather's face.

"Did you just tell him my name is Deer Droppings?"

"Yes, I did. But it is alright; he does not know what it means. But see how important names are?" she laughed.

He looked wounded, "I will let you get back to your rabbit."

Natayah looked over her shoulder at him, "I will see you later, right?" she smiled at him softly and sincerely.

"Yes," his frown softened. She watched him walk away until Josiah interrupted her thoughts.

"Yes, I need you," he spouted, "These goons are followin' me around and I can't understand a word they're sayin'."

"Be thankful. When I first got here, I wasn't allowed outside the tipi for weeks!"

"What?" he shouted.

"Never mind. What shall we talk about?" She asked giving him her full attention.

"Why don't you tell me how this happened to you? You look awful hurt."

"This is nothing!" She looked down at herself and put a hand to her face, "You should have seen me a week ago." She tried to laugh it off but a flash of fear ran past her eyes.

"Did these people do that to you?" When she didn't answer, Josiah put his hands on her shoulders and asked her again.

"I... I don't want to talk about it," she

looked down at the ground to avoid his burning stares and the tears welling up in her eyes.

"I can get you outta here," he whispered.

She looked up at him and said nothing at first, but furrowed her brow. But finally she asked, "Have you been down to the river?" She knew that her every move was being watched and did not want to give anyone cause for alarm.

"So tell me Josiah," she hooked her arm through his and began walking toward the river, leaving the dead rabbit where it lay. "How are things in the big city?"

"I'll get to all that, but first, tell me your name… your real name."

She stopped for a moment and thought. She looked up at him almost wishing he could give her a clue.

"What is my name?" she asked. "Sarah," she said. "My name is Sarah," she smiled.

"Sarah," he repeated. "It is sure nice to meet you."

Elizabeth Bourgeret

Chapter Twelve

The days went by and the summer was in full swing. Josiah had not attempted to learn the language of the Indians but had become completely dependent on Natayah. He spent most of his time with her and neglected his duties and the very reasons for stopping here at this village, or so they all thought.

Natayah grew more and more fond of the man she jokingly called Deer Droppings and was unsure about the promise she made to Chief Spotted Eagle about the tomeh-wee-ha with Little Feather. He would find excuses to come and talk to Natayah and would tease her like they were still two little children in school. One afternoon while she was talking with Josiah, he would throw acorns and twigs at her just for the sake of distraction. Natayah, too, caught herself looking for this annoying man whenever she was out, hoping to catch a glimpse of him.

The person she thought of as Little Feather, as far as she was concerned, remained in hiding but was ever faithful with gifts and wooing her from afar.

This morning when she woke, she found a special treat, a bowl of summer strawberries, outside her door. Natayah was deeply touched but longed for someone to share them with. It created much confusion in Natayah's heart. She had all the players for a wonderful romance, but she was anxious for the end of the story. On one side she had the illusive but attentive Little Feather that has made her an offer of marriage, but has never even held her hand, then on the other side, her beloved Deer Droppings who was there, one afternoon for example, sitting behind her, gently combing her long, waist length hair with the ivory comb, but never giving a clue of commitment. And then there was Josiah. His bright sky-blue eyes would sparkle every time he smiled. He was charming and she enjoyed hearing his stories, but there was something missing. A sincerity, perhaps. He was all smiles and laughter on the surface, but she was unsure if there was anything beneath that layer.

The women, when they would get together for their sewing circles would ask her about the white visitor. Then the women questioned what they could find to talk about for all those hours they spend together. Which would lead to questions about Natayah's past life.

"Did you live in a weetu?" Running Deer asked one afternoon.

"Something like it, but ours is called a 'house' and it was like three weetu on top of each other."

"How can that be?"

"She is just teasing, Running Deer, they cannot put one on top of another."

"Actually they can," Natayah defended herself. "I do not know how they are structured, because it is all hidden when the house is finished. The walls are smooth. You cannot see the wood that built them. Our walls had pretty designs on them, usually flowers. And we had steps to get from level to level," she made examples of stepping up with her hands. "Where we cooked, was in a room that was dug into the ground. It was like digging a hole, putting the weetu into the hole and making the roof flat, then adding another. That is the best way I can describe it."

"You had an entire weetu, just for cooking?"

Natayah blushed. It sounded so extravagant in their eyes. "We would store our food there, and prepare everything there then it was brought up to the next level, where we would eat it around a 'table'." They listened intently as Natayah described a table and chairs to them. It never dawned on them to sit on anything other than the ground. They thought that Natayah was strange when she put a flat piece of wood on top of two stumps to create a bench, but now they understood why.

"Do you sleep the way we do?"

"They do not do anything the way we do!" Running Deer laughed.

"We slept on a 'bed' that sat up off the ground about this high," she showed them. "It was a frame made of wood, but it had a 'mattress' on it, which made ALL the difference! A mattress is like a giant pillow for your whole body."

"Tell them about the water!" Grieving Mother coaxed. She had grown fond of Natayah and her stories.

"In my home, we did not have to go to a river to get water. The water came to us in big… reeds. They were like… this big around…" she demonstrated the size of one of the pipes of what she imagined the size to be, "and we would pump a handle and water would come out." she shrugged her shoulders. "It was that easy."

"You see?" Grieving Mother laughed, "Now you can see why I am having such a hard time making her into a good wife?" All the women laughed, including Natayah.

"Do you miss it, Natayah?" a little girl named White Dove asked.

"Sometimes," she answered honestly.

"You will not leave us will you?" White Dove looked at her with her big brown eyes.

"No," she paused, "How could I leave a place as beautiful as this and a face as pretty as yours?" she cupped White Dove's chin and kissed her nose.

One afternoon, Natayah and Josiah walked through the village. Talking Bird watched as Natayah was trying to explain something to him in English. Natayah looked up and waved to Talking Bird as they walked past.

"Are you going to hide behind that tree all day, brother?" Talking Bird asked Little Feather.

"He is with her all the time!"

"So, when are you going to tell her? It is not fair that she thinks two men are courting her when it is really the same man."

"I do not know anymore. She is always with that white man… what if she…"

"She loves *you*, brother," Talking Bird interrupted, "both of YOU."

The clouds rolled in across the valley and the sky was thrust into darkness. The whole village sensed that there was a storm in the air and all seemed to be on edge.

Josiah and Natayah walked along and gathered some raspberries still clinging to their bushes. Natayah carried a basket under her arm as she regarded the clouds with respect and caution. "It looks like a bad storm is coming."

Josiah did not comment but nodded. He had thoughts of his own. "Sarah," he began, "I have really enjoyed my time with you. More than I thought I would."

"And, I, you," she replied.

"And... you are... looking well."

"Thank you. I feel so much better. It's good to be back to my old self again. I hate being a burden to anyone."

"You could..." he cleared his throat. " You could travel soon, if... if you wanted, then, right?"

"Yes, I suppose. But we won't travel again until winter, and I can't say that I'm looking forward to ..."

"I meant, with me," Josiah interrupted.

Natayah stopped picking and looked up at Josiah who was now nervously twisting another leaf around his fingers.

"Josiah, please. I thought we had been through all this."

"Sarah, you are not makin' this very easy on me. I was supposed to ride in here, a blaze a glory and rescue you from your miserable existence and save you from a life of savages. I would go home a hero. You aren't supposed to be so happy here."

Natayah looked at him confused and said nothing.

"I haven't been completely honest with

you," he paused. Natayah instinctively took a couple steps away from him.

"I was sent here to find you." He waited for the meaning to sink in. "Yes, I am a trapper, and yes, I work for a merchandiser in St. Louis. A man we both know. His name is James Tobias."

Natayah gasped at the sound of her brother-in-law's name. She couldn't speak. All she could do was shake her head back and forth in disbelief. She brought her hands to her lips and then to her forehead. Her eyes burned with tears.

"I... I... don't believe you," she stuttered. "You would have told me... you wouldn't..."

"I've been lookin' for you everywhere. You have no idea how close you are to your original destination, do you?" Josiah spoke emphatically as the thunder sounded over their heads. "I have found a couple of the other women, but I have been looking for you and your son."

"My son?"

"Your bodies were not found at the massacre so your sister gave me the brush set to give you... and this." He pulled a book from his knapsack and handed it to her.

"My sister?" Tears no longer quivered in her eyes, but rolled down her cheeks as the first drops of rain began to fall. She leaned against a tree to keep from falling to the ground.

"Your sister was sure that since your bodies weren't found that y'all were still alive. She hired me to find you. Since I am a trapper, I am familiar with much of the countryside and am able to slip into Indian camps without much threat. But I found this village on accident. I don't think anyone knows about your little hidin' place here, tucked between the bluffs. I guess that it was lucky that I didn't know the language; otherwise, I might never have found you. Here. Your sister said that if I was sure it was you, to give you the brush set and she said that you would be missing this, more than anything." He held out the book again and reached out for her hand. He placed the book in her hand and wrapped her fingers around its crisp new leather binding.

She turned the book to look at its cover. The Bible. A sob escaped her lips and she clutched the book close to her chest. As she did, a slip of paper fell from its pages. She slid down the tree that she was using for support to pick up the delicate, folded paper.

"Sarah, your son, is he not with you?"

She didn't hear the question but unfolded the paper and recognized the signature at the bottom and she could not control her anguish. She heard Josiah's voice, but could not understand the words that he was saying. Her eyes drifted back up to the top of the page. She blinked the tears from her blurred vision to read:

My dearest sister,

If this note finds you alive, then my prayers have been answered. I hope and pray that you are safe and unharmed. This Bible is for your comfort, and strength. If you and Thomas can escape with Josiah, he knows how to find us. We will find you safe transportation to our home.

If you find that it is too dangerous at this time, Josiah will tell us of your whereabouts and we will find a way to bring you home.

Elizabeth Bourgeret

Until that time, my dear sister, know that you are in my prayers every night and every day.

I miss you so. My love for you and Thomas,
Katherine

Natayah tipped her head back against the tree and cried out to the rain. Her emotions were torn and drained. Why didn't they find her son's body? Could he still be alive? Did Wild Dog sell him to someone else? "Where is my son?" she called out to no one in her grief.

Josiah became uncomfortable with her making so much noise. He did not want any unwanted attention to be drawn to him especially since he was trying to steal one of their captives.
He crept slowly over to her slumped body, "C'mon, now. Let's get you home. No need for all this cryin'. We can leave after this rainstorm passes." He reached out to her but she pulled away.

"Please, just go away!" she yelled at him.

"Be reasonable, Sarah, you'll catch your death o' cold if you stay out here."

"Go away!" she shouted. "Leave me alone!" She covered her face with her hands to shut out the world. Josiah startled, slipped away from her, looking back over his shoulder, not knowing what to do. When he reached the edge of the village, he tucked his head down and shoved his hands into his pockets as he walked back to his tipi. The rain poured off his hair in big drops but he made no eye contact with anyone.

The storm came on in fierce bursts. The thunder clapped and the rain poured down in heavy bullets. "God?" she called out, "Where are you? I need you! What am I supposed to do? Where am I supposed to be?" The thunder rolled and the lightning lit up the sky. The rain pelted her skin; still she did not rise. The tears came as quickly as the rain on her face. She fell over onto her side clutching the book and the note from her sister. This was a deep gut-wrenching cry, her breath caught as she tried to keep up with the waves of emotion tightening every muscle in her body.

When Josiah came back from the woods without Natayah, Little Feather ran to find her. Fearing the worst, he found her body curled into a ball with the book pressed tightly against her chest.

"Natayah!" he ran to her. "Are you alright?" He crouched down beside her. She did not answer. He moved her hair away from her face and she blinked as the rain hit her. "Natayah, are you hurt? Did he hurt you?"

She opened her eyes and looked up at him.

He lifted her to a sitting position and kept his arm around her. "Why are you out here in the rain?" he shouted over the storm. "What has happened? Can you not see that this storm is fierce?" He held her close to his warm body and moved the hair that was pasted to her face off to the side. Her eyes were filled with pain, but as he gently stroked her cheek, he saw the emotion change to anger and hate.

"Where is my son?" she asked him through clenched teeth as she pushed him away.

"Natayah, why do you ask me this?" Little Feather tried to pull her back to his body.

She crawled away from him and stood up. Her body was shaking and her teeth were chattering from the cold. "Where is my son?" she shouted again.

"You know where he is. Why do you…"

Forgetting herself, she spoke in English, "My sister, sent a note with Josiah. They said they didn't find his body. Where is my son?"

"I do not understand what you are trying to tell me. Please, use our language."

"Why could they not find his body? What did they do to my son?"

"Nothing, they did nothing." He spoke gently as he tried to reach out to her.

"Then where is he? Is he still alive? Did he escape? Was he sold? Did your people take his scalp? Is it not enough to kill a small child without torturing him as well?" She was screaming uncontrollably now and Little Feather took every blow that she handed out.

"Woman!" he finally shouted back at her, "Your temper is like the fire in your hair! When will you come to trust me?" He sighed heavily and softened his voice. "Your son is dead. By my hand. I cannot take that back. Your people did not find him, because… because, I went back and I buried him, the Indian way. I saw your pain. I felt your pain. And if it was my son, I would want him to have a safe passage to the other world to wait for you there."

The rain seemed to slow and the thunder quieted. She stared into his eyes that looked black. She stopped struggling and allowed him to draw her close.

"You buried my son?"

"I gave him safe passage. I built him a platform and wrapped him. I said the prayers for our ancestors to come and find him and take him to the stars. I gave special instruction that he was to

Captive Heart

be treated with care since he did not know our ways." He looked down at her, "I told them that his mother was very special, and would be looking for him someday." He paused. "It was my hope that you would become one of us..." He held her close not wanting his eyes to betray his emotions.

"You... did that... for me?" she asked blinking back the rain and struggling to keep her shivering body still. "I do not know how to thank you. Thank you, for doing that."

"Will you, someday, ever be able to forgive me? Will this tragedy that brought us together always be between us?" He took her hands in his and looked deeply into her eyes.

"I know that it was an accident and I have forgiven you long ago. It is... hard." she hiccupped, the lump in her throat still dangerously close to more tears. "I still have the pain of losing him everyday. And the nightmares still haunt my dreams..." she spoke with jagged breaths. She knew what he wanted to hear. Their word for "forgiven" is "forgotten". She knew that she would never be able to forget but she uttered the words that would give them both peace.

"It is forgotten..." she said softly.

She could see the relief pass over his eyes. He put his finger under her chin and lifted her face. "Thank you. How long I have waited to hear that." They stared into each other's eyes as the rain turned to a mist. "Should I steal a kiss from your husband-to-be?" he asked.

She closed her eyes and breathlessly whispered, "Yes."

183

Elizabeth Bourgeret

Chapter Thirteen

The next morning, Natayah's emotions were at war within her. Grieving Mother watched her as they ate raspberries.

"You are awfully quiet this morning." Grieving Mother mentioned.

Natayah shrugged her shoulders.

"Did something happen with your new friend?"

Natayah looked up and wondered if she should tell her about all that happened yesterday. About Josiah's plans to take her back to her own people, about the note from her sister, about her kissing another man when she is promised to this woman's son, about this terrible ache in her head and heart.

"Josiah… he wants to take me back to my people," she confessed.

"And do you want to go?" Grieving Mother asked.

"My heart… is confused. I do not…"

The door flew open and Talking Bird ran in holding a flower in her hand. "It is time!" she shouted. She ran over and tackled Natayah, sending her raspberries in every direction. She hovered over Natayah's face and told her matter-of-factly, "It is time!" Natayah was laughing along with Talking Bird and tried to wriggle out from under her.

"Time for what?" Grieving Mother asked calmly, the only one with any raspberries left.

Talking Bird held out the now bent flower, "He sent you this! He is ready to meet with you… finally!"

Natayah sat up and sent Talking Bird tumbling off to the side but not before Natayah snatched the flower from her hand. "Really?"

"Who is ready?" Grieving Mother asked bewildered.

"Your son!" Talking Bird hissed.

"But I thought…"

"Mother!" she stopped her in mid sentence and took the flower back from Natayah. "You are to take this flower and wait in the strawberry glen. He will meet you there with a matching flower."

"That is so romantic!" Grieving Mother smiled. "He must get that from me." The three women laughed.

"Come on," Talking Bird stole a berry from her mother's bowl. "We have to get you ready!"

The early morning sun filtered its way through the trees to shine down on the dew-covered grass. Yesterday's storm has given way to blue skies and a warm breeze. Natayah stood at the edge of the strawberry fields and watched the sun glisten on the changing leaves. Her heart was filled with turmoil. What am I even doing here? She thought to herself. I kissed another man. Her stomach fluttered at the thought of that kiss and a smile crept to the edges of her mouth unwillingly. *What am I doing here?* She stood twisting the flower in her fingers. Talking Bird had braided Natayah's hair in a loose braid and tucked in flowers through the finished style. All was quiet and she took advantage of the moment to send a prayer up to God.

"Lord, please help me to know what to do. Is this man that I am to meet here, meant to be my husband? Or have I fallen in love with the wrong man? Or, am I supposed to leave and go back to my people with Josiah? I want to do Your will, Lord. Please, can You make Your will obvious to me?"

Her thoughts were interrupted by a loud whisper behind her. She turned to look over her shoulder meekly. She gasped when she saw him peeking out from a bush behind her.

"What are you doing here?" she hissed. "You are not supposed to be here, right now!"

Little Feather came out from hiding and smiled at her. "I thought I would sneak out to see you before you became a married woman." He smirked and wrapped his arms around her. She gasped and tried to wriggle free of his hold.

"What are you doing? You must go! He might be here any moment!" She escaped from his hold and took a step away to try and calm her pounding heart.

He came up close behind her and whispered in her ear. He folded her into his arms, "Do you really want me to go?"

"Please, you must." She pushed against his hands that were locked in front of her. He spun her around to face him and put his finger to her chin. She resisted and he lifted her chin to force her to look into his eyes.

"Are you sorry you kissed me?"

She could feel the tears burning the back of her eyes, threatening to spill over. She turned away and did not answer.

"What does he have, that I do not?"

"Nothing... I do not know... I just..." she stumbled for words, "The chief said that no one else was interested... so I thought... that you..." a single tear made its way down her cheek.

"Wait, wait. Calm down," he wiped her tear away. "This is no way to meet your future husband."

"Please... just go." She knew her heart was breaking. She knew the answer to her questions. This was the man that she loved, but she had promised herself to someone else.

"Here," he smiled down at her, "Would it help if I had one of these?" he stepped back and pulled a smashed daisy from the waistband of his buckskin trousers.

Her face showed her shock. Her mouth dropped open as she looked down at his smashed flower and then to her own wrung and twisted flower. "It was you? All along?"

"Would you be my wife, Natayah?"

"It has been you this whole time?"

"What kind of an answer is that?" He gently wiped the tears away with his thumb, "Are you sorry?"

She smiled at him, "I was hoping... wishing that it could be you. I did not think..." she threw her arms around his neck and her feet came off the ground. She kissed him on the mouth, while he tried to catch his breath.

"Whoa, Whoa, we cannot have this, I am

proposing and you have not answered," he smirked at her. She smiled up at him and stretched up to her toes to kiss him again. "Is that your answer?"

"Yes. The answer is yes!" She couldn't contain her smile.

The smile faded from his face and he looked deeply into her eyes. "I have never loved another. I will love you all the rest of my days and into the next life." He tipped her head back and kissed her passionately. "When can we be married?"

"Whenever you say!" she laughed and covered his face with kisses. She knew this was the right choice. Everything in her soul, told her that this was where she belonged, with this man who has made her heart beat, perhaps for the first time.

Little Feather went to Chief Spotted Eagle and asked for permission to marry before the next summer. The majority of the weddings happen in the early part of summer when they return from the hunting trip, but summer was almost over.

"You have waited a long time to marry," the chief said to him. "I would not ask you to wait longer. But have you asked yourself, if she is truly the one, or are you attracted to her because she is so different from us?"

"I have to admit that she is the most beautiful woman that I have ever seen. But she also has great beauty from the inside. She will be a good partner for me, Chief Spotted Eagle, if you will allow us to be married."

"I see no objection. Can you wait until two days from now?"

"I will do my best. It will be difficult," Little Feather smiled broadly.

They were indeed married in two days. The women complained because there was not much time to prepare for the festivities. Natayah could find nothing to complain about. She was so happy and went about her duties with the biggest smile.

Quannah, the mother of Flower Blossom insisted that Natayah wear her daughter's bridal dress. The beautiful soft, bleached white dress was elegantly designed with fringe and quills. Natayah, herself, embroidered the flowers that decorated the shoulders and the back. It was her gift for Flower Blossom. And now she was wearing it for her own wedding. A shadow of sorrow passed through Natayah as she ran her fingers along the fine stitching, but it did not last long. She promised to love Little Feather as deeply and passionately as Flower Blossom would have loved her beloved Grey Wolf.

The ceremony took place as the sun was setting, offering a brilliant lighting display. The fire was built, but kept low so all could see.

Natayah wore her hair in one long braid decorated with shells and flowers. She looked beautiful in her white dress, and she carried the Seapaugh tribe marriage band draped over her flat outstretched hands.

Natayah had never really seen Little Feather in his full garb, but he looked so handsome in his full length feathered headdress, and porcupine quill chest covering. He wore a matching neckband, and his hair was worn loose.

The marriage band was a strip of white leather that was meticulously beaded with an elegant pattern. The long fringe at both ends were tied off with more beads. This band was the same that Grieving Mother used when she united with her husband many years ago.

The couple stood before the chief. Little Feather and Natayah faced each other. Chief Spotted Eagle took the marriage band from Natayah and placed Little Feather's left hand on top of Natayah's right and said, "His hand is not to go on top of hers, so as not to dominate her." He flipped the flat hands over so Natayah's rested on Little Feather's. "Her hand is not placed on top of his as she does not rule above him." Chief Spotted Eagle took their hands and placed them palm to palm, side by side. "They will work together, live together and love together as man and wife. Side by side. Equal partners in this marriage for life." He wrapped the marriage band around their joined hands symbolically binding them together. Little Feather wove his fingers between hers and smiled at her. She clasped his hand and returned the smile as well.

Chief Spotted Eagle continued the ceremony. "This is a special day," he said to those gathered around him. The small crowd of people quieted. "This day stands for so much more than a man and a woman joining together. *This* union can also stand for two worlds joining together. We welcomed this woman into our world and she has accepted our ways. And now she is one of us. But today, she becomes part of our future. Uniting the whites and the Indians to live peacefully together starts with one man and one woman. This man... and this woman.

"The man in this union is to be the protector and the provider. He must be sure that he will love and care for this woman no matter what comes their way. There will be good days and there will be bad days. Never treat her badly, and your union will strengthen.

"This woman is to be the care giver and the supporter. She must be able to use all that her husband provides to care for him and your children. She must love and obey her husband and give him children. There will be good days and there will be bad days. Never be harsh and hateful and your union will grow.

"May the Great Spirit bless you in this union. May he grant you many sons and may you never grow weary of being together."

He touched them on the forehead with a feathered scepter and shouted. The crowd shouted back and the music began. They were married.

The couple stayed and feasted and sang with the others until Little Feather took his bride and put her atop her horse, Clara. He climbed on his own horse and leaned over to kiss Natayah. The crowd shouted and cheered.

"My son, I am so happy. She is a good woman," Grieving Mother kissed her son's hand and stepped back.

Little Feather grabbed the ropes that guide Clara then nudged his own horse forward. They rode into the sunset toward their wedding night tipi hidden away from the rest of the tribe.

Natayah leaned over to her new husband as they were leaving the village, "Do I still get to call you Deer Droppings?"

Everyone watched them off and waved and cheered and seemed genuinely happy for them except for the white visitor who lurked in the shadows. He looked on with disdain. He drank himself to sleep that night vowing to make it right.

Elizabeth Bourgeret

Chapter Fourteen

The couple rode back into the village a week past their wedding night. Family and friends greeted them, then the work day continued as normal.

Talking Bird hugged Natayah as she slid off her horse, "Oh sister! I am so happy to see you! How was your time away? No, do not tell me, you will just have to say it again at the sewing circle. So quickly, get changed! We must go!"

"Do I have to go? I am not ready for the honeymoon to be over yet," Natayah whined as she wrapped herself into Little Feather's arms.

"Go, wife. And do not tell the embarrassing parts. I will be here when you get back," he kissed her ear.

"Oh, no. If I must sew, you must go out and hunt something. You heard the chief, you must provide for your wife. Go and kill us a fine deer." She spun out of his arms and smiled at him.

He looked for sympathy from Talking Bird, "Already so demanding!" He drew Natayah close. He leaned his face close to hers and traced a small circle with his nose along her cheek and made his way to her ear. He touched her earlobe ever so gently with his lips and then he whispered in her ear, "Are you going to clean it when I return?"

Natayah pulled away and wrinkled her face. Little Feather added, "The chief said…"

"We can discuss the details later." She reached up on her toes to kiss his cheek and whisper in his ear, "I love you."

"Will you come on!" Talking Bird tugged on her impatiently.

"But you said I could change first."

"I know now, that if I let you do that, we will never get out of here!" she laughed and pulled Natayah away. Husband and wife held on until their fingers slipped away from each other's. Natayah finally turned and walked arm in arm with Talking Bird and they gigged with their faces close together whispering secrets. The sewing circle was to be held at Quannah's weetu where the women would gather and laugh and gossip and maybe even get a little sewing done.

Josiah stepped out from behind a weetu directly in front of them. He had been drinking and his odor made that quite evident that bathing was a thing of the past.

Natayah reached out to hold his hands in hers. "Josiah. It's good to see you. I have missed you."

He looked at her with disgust, but his words were kind. "You look so beautiful."

"Thank you," she blushed and glanced nervously at Talking Bird who looked on with concern.

"You... you could have had... had any man....you wanted," he hiccupped and stammered. "Now, you consider yourself married...to this...savage?"

"Josiah, why don't I take you back to your tipi so you can rest?" She looked over at Talking Bird and explained that she would be along momentarily. Talking Bird nodded, but was not eager to leave her side. "Natayah, he is not thinking right. I worry for you."

"He is just a little drunk. I will take him back to his tipi so he can sleep it off. It is okay. I will be along." Natayah encouraged Josiah to take steps toward his tipi. She held on to his arm to keep him from falling.

"God don't recognize this marriage, you know," he slurred. "He is a savage. A heathen savage... unequally yoked, and all that stuff."

"Josiah, please don't say things you might regret later."

He stopped and pulled his arm from hers. "I am here to rescue you! You are supposed to be grateful that I'm here!"

"I am grateful that you are here. Your friendship means so much to me..."

"Friendship? Friendship? What's your sister goin ta say?" He looked at her eye to eye. "She thinks you're out here... being abused and raped... and beaten, and who knows what else! Wait till she finds out that you're married to one of 'em. By your own free will!"

"Josiah, it's a good thing that these kind and gentle people don't understand your slander or you might not be so attached to your scalp." Natayah tried to speak calmly but was shaking with anger.

"You see? You see? And this kind of barbaric punishment is okay with you!"

"No, you misunderstand me. I know them and I respect their ways. I don't like or approve of everything they do, nor do I like or approve of everything my own race does."

"These are not your people."

"Yes, Josiah ... they are."

Without thinking, Josiah reached out and slapped Natayah across her face. She gasped and held her hand to her cheek to stop the stinging. The tears burned at her eyes but she tried desperately to keep them from falling.

"Sarah... I'm... I didn't mean..."

"I think that it's time for you to leave." Natayah turned from him and started walking away. Her body trembled and her face burned.

He shouted after her, "How's your sister going to feel knowing that you chose to stay with these heathen savages instead of coming home to her? And now you are bedding one of them! What does that make you? How can you stay with the people that killed your only son?" Natayah stopped but did not turn around. The tears fell from her eyes to the ground. She took in a deep breath and wiped her tears away. She held her head up, and began walking away from his ranting.

By the time Natayah made her way to Quannah's weetu, she had managed to compose herself. She hoped that the handprint didn't look as bright red as if felt.

As she walked into the weetu, the women shouted. She was startled, but immediately recognized a celebration was at hand. The women gathered around her and hugged her and all were talking at once.

They presented her with gifts for her new married life and teased her mercilessly about "poor Little Feather starving, because his new wife can not cook"! They laughed and talked and ate and asked her questions about her honeymoon.

"We walked and talked and held hands..."

Natayah said dreamily.

"And other things married couples do!" someone interrupted. The whole place roared with laughter. Natayah blushed.

"Look! You can see her blush. Your white skin betrays you, sister." Talking Bird teased.

Natayah enjoyed her female companionship, but Josiah's words still burned fresh in her mind.

That night was the first night in months that Little Feather got to sleep in his own bed, in his own weetu and now he lay next to his new wife. He slept soundly with his arms wrapped around his bride, but she still lay awake. Josiah's words haunted her. *"Katherine would want me to be happy, no matter where I am,"* she thought, *"God loves all His people..."* Sleep eventually came to her, but morning came much too quickly.

She was awakened with kisses on her forehead and gentle fingers moving her hair from her face.

"Good morning wife. You are supposed to be making me breakfast," Little Feather whispered.

Natayah opened her eyes and smiled. She stretched her arms over her head then wrapped them around his neck. "Not yet," she muttered and pulled him back down with her. She opened her eyes and saw him staring back at her. He stroked her cheek and said, "I would stay here with you all day if I could. I love you, Natayah."

"Then stay."

"I cannot. The chief has called me to him. I must go. He says that it is urgent."

Her eyes opened fully. "Is anything

wrong?"

"I do not know. But I must go and find out."

Natayah sighed and released her grip around his neck. She looked up at him coyly, "Should I wait here… or should I get dressed."

He laughed, "Woman, you will be my undoing!" He kissed her again and got up. "I do not know when I will return."

"Okay, I will get up. I am sure Grieving Mother has things for me to do. When does she come back to this weetu? It is strange to wake up and she is not here."

"She will probably give us a moon's cycle to be alone, then she will return. I must go."

"Wait!" she called out urgently. He stopped and looked back at her, "no goodbye kiss?"

He came back over to her and crawled up alongside her. "Oh, woman, how you move me," he whispered and kissed her passionately. He pulled back and she kissed him again. He propped himself up on his elbow to stare into her eyes before standing…again, "Are all of you white women so…spoiled?" he asked.

She smiled and stretched again, "Yes, and are you not lucky to have the only one in the whole village!"

Little Feather covered her head with the fur blanket and made his escape. "I will see you later today," he called back to her on his way out.

She slid the blanket off her head pulling her hair down across her face and lay still for a few moments watching her hair fly up every time she breathed out. "I could not possibly be so happy and be out of God's will," she said out loud.

Natayah left the weetu on her way to see Grieving Mother when Josiah came up to her.

"Sarah," he spoke low, "Please, just give me one minute. I have to speak with you."

Natayah stopped, but did not say a word.

"I wanted to apologize for yesterday. I was... out of line." He paused allowing her to speak, but still she remained quiet. "I'll be leaving in about a week. Please take that time to at least think about coming with me. Let me take you back where you belong." He saw that she lowered her eyes and was listening to him, so he continued. "Don't you remember? Indoor plumbing? Servants? Shoes? Why would you want to give up all of the modern conveniences that our race has aspired to? These people are beneath you! They can't even read or write." He saw her stiffen, "Alright, alright, they are very nice and yes, they have been very hospitable, but Sarah, do you really want to live this way for the rest of your life?"

Natayah looked up at his face and knew in her heart that he really believed all the things that he was saying, but suddenly those modern inventions didn't mean as much. She began walking away and he called after her, "Just think about it, Sarah."

Little Feather found her later near the river's edge with his mother and sister washing out clothes against the rocks. He called her to the side and spoke quietly. "Natayah, something bad has happened. Let me say first that our tribe had nothing to do with it."

Elizabeth Bourgeret

"What happened?"

"Another wagon train has been attacked," he said solemnly, "Spotted Eagle thinks that it was Wild Dog and…"

"We have to go!" Natayah shouted, "There might be survivors! We have to go and help!"

"I am going right now." Little Feather looked past Natayah and saw Two Spear coming to speak with his wife, Talking Bird, about the same thing.

"I want to go with you."

"No." He put a hand on her shoulder, "You cannot go. I know you mean well and want to help, but I do not think you should see this."

"How am I just supposed to wait here and do nothing?"

"You will have to. Trust that I am doing what is best for you."

"Little Feather, please, I want to help."

"No." He leaned down to kiss her forehead and he and Two Spear disappeared back into the woods.

Natayah tried to concentrate on her work, but not more than an hour passed when a commotion was heard in the village.

Grieving Mother advised her daughters to stay hidden in the trees in case they would have to escape to the bluff. So they watched as the tail end of a group of Indians on horseback rode into the center of the village.

They saw Wild Dog approach Chief Spotted Eagle and spoke with him. Since they recognized the other Indians, the women moved in closer, but kept the children back.

"Please stay hidden, Natayah. Wild Dog is

not fond of the white skinned people. And he probably forgot that you are here. I believe it is best to keep it that way. We will go in closer and see what is happening." Grieving Mother and Talking Bird moved in closer while Natayah stayed hidden. She did move to a position so that she could hear more clearly and see a little better.

"But cousin, do not send me away so quickly," Wild Dog was saying, "I bring gifts for you."

"I am sure we have no need for your gifts," Chief Spotted Eagle responded.

"Would you insult your cousin in such a way?" Spotted Eagle did not answer. "If you, yourself will not accept these gifts, I am sure someone in your tribe might wish to purchase them for a small price." Wild Dog waved to one of the others in his group and five men each brought before the chief, and the gathering crowd, a white prisoner each, bound from the back and burlap sacks covering their heads.

Natayah gasped as the sacks were taken off their heads revealing two young teenage boys and three women.

"Look what I have brought you. How can you refuse? Use them for whatever you want." He walked along the row of prisoners and stopped at the young woman at the end. Her long brown hair was tangled and fell into her face. He pulled her hair back and breathed in the smell. Natayah could see deep cuts on her face. One of the other woman's clothes were torn and ripped from her shoulder. Wild Dog grabbed a handful of her hair and forced her head against his chest. He reached down and putting his hand under her skirts, "I have to tell you, that I sampled this one myself. You cannot say no to this." Tears ran down the woman's face and she looked like she was about to vomit. He turned her around so he was behind her and placed his hands on her chest. Wild Dog spoke through her hair over her shoulder, "There is still some left for you, cousin."

Natayah's eyes filled with tears and she was ready to step forward when she heard the chief speak. "Wild Dog. I have told you. We do not take white slaves. We do not accept your 'gift'. We are trying to be at peace with the white tribes…"

Wild Dog interrupted. Fury crossed his face. "You would make peace with those animals? They steal our lands, they kill our people, they bring sickness to our children and you want to be friends with them?"

"We believe that there is hope that the two tribes could share…"

"Share? Why should we have to share? This is our land!" He fumed and paced in front of his captives. Then barely above a growling whisper, "If you do not want these gifts that I bring to you, so be it!" He threw his right hand in the air and yelled out. He grabbed the woman again and took his knife and ran it across her throat. The men that held them killed the other four the same way.

"NOOO!" Natayah came running out of hiding. She ran through the crowd making her way to Wild Dog. She screamed and raised her hand and brought it across his cheek leaving four bloody streaks in its wake.

Little Feather rode up and jumped off his horse in time for her to be saved from the same fate as the other white captives.

"You are pure evil!" she screamed and tried to pull away from Little Feather, "How could you be so cruel?"

Wild Dog wiped the blood from his cheek and laughed out loud. He stepped over the lifeless body of the woman he just killed and spoke to Little Feather.

"You still have this one, I see. I thought you would have used her up months ago."

"Take your prizes and leave this village." Chief Spotted Eagle spoke firmly.

Wild Dog ignored the order and walked over to Natayah. He picked up her hair, "Oh yes, I remember you." He breathed his hot breath on her face. "I got a nice price for you."

Within seconds, Little Feather pushed Natayah to the side and had the point of his knife digging into Wild Dogs neck.

Natayah dropped to her knees over the bleeding boys, still coughing and struggling for their last moments of life.

"You will leave here and never touch my wife again," Little Feather spoke through gritted teeth.

"Your wife? You have married this white animal?" He pulled away and threw his head back with laughter. "I should have charged more!" He strutted among the crowd. "And this is okay with you? You are comfortable with your enemy living among you, AS one of you?" He turned back to Little Feather and spit on Natayah's kneeling body, "I hate them. I will kill them if I get the chance." He squared off with Little Feather, "Keep that in mind if we meet again. This is your only warning."

He shouted to his warriors and they mounted their horses and left. The five dead bodies lay on the ground in pools of their own blood.

Natayah worked along side the men in digging graves for the five. Her breaths were ragged and she could barely see for the tears in her eyes, but she worked on and was able to give instructions as to the white man's ways of burial.

"Let me do this," Little Feather said, "You need to rest." She shook her head and shoveled dirt over the bodies. She prayed for each one and placed a cross made from sticks at the head of their graves.

"I did not even know their names," she cried.

"How do they find their way to the Spirit World when you have weighed their souls down with this heavy dirt?" Little Feather asked as they were finishing up.

Natayah took Little Feather's hand and stared at the graves. "Their souls were gone before they were even put into the ground."

The whole village was quiet. Solemn. Everyone did their part to clean up the mess but kept a respectable distance from Natayah. Several woman came to her and offered condolences as if these people were closely related. Natayah did feel a sort of kinship with them, although she had never seen them before… or will again…

"Are you alright?" Talking Bird came to Natayah. She looked up at her and felt such love for Talking Bird and for her true sister that her emotions could not be contained. The tears came freely and she embraced the emotions of being caught between these two worlds. Would she have felt different about this woman who was holding her and consoling her if she had read about this incident in the newspaper? Yes. She was ashamed to think that she would. It might have been something that would have been brought up over tea… but then never mentioned again. Hate knows no color, she thought.

Suddenly, she gasped, "Josiah!" she said out loud. "Have you seen him?"

"No," she replied, "He doesn't speak to anyone but you."

"I have to find him. What if Wild Dog found him? He could be…" Natayah rushed toward his tipi that lay just outside of the village perimeter. An easy target.

Natayah flung open the flap and tried to see inside. A scream told her that she had found him. As her eyes adjusted, she could see that he lay curled in a ball on his bed pallet.

"Josiah! Are you hurt?" Natayah asked him in English.

"Sarah! Is that you?" he whimpered.

"Yes, of course it's me. Are you alright?"

"I saw everything…" his voice quivering with every syllable, "I thought they were going to kill you and then me next."

"But they didn't. You are safe." She tried to console him but he crawled over to her.

"For how long?" he snapped. "What if they're waiting in the woods for me? How will I ever sleep again?"

His eyes were red and swollen, and sweat beaded on his forehead. "You will be fine. You are strong." Natayah attempted to comfort him even as she pulled herself from his frantic grasp.

"No! No I'm not! I tried to be... I wanted to be a trapper; you know, get out and see the world... so when I met your family and they offered me this job, I took it."

"So this is your first experience with Indians?"

"Yes!" he shouted, "When I came up from Arkansas, it was smooth sailing. No Indians, no blood, just beautiful wide open spaces." He grabbed Natayah's shoulders again as she knelt at his door and looked urgently into her eyes. "You can't stay here. You need to be with your own people. It is too dangerous for you here. We obviously were not meant to mix."

Natayah looked into his eyes. They betrayed his deeper fears. "I will think on it."

He held her shoulders for a few moments more and then dropped his arms. "Good. We can get out of here."

"I will think about it Josiah," she repeated and stood and left his tipi.

Chapter Fifteen

Her mind was reeling as she walked back to her weetu. She stopped and watched everyone's activity. Could she ever really belong here?

She saw one woman returning from the river carrying water for her family. "It was just the turn of a handle..." she muttered. Another woman was scraping the hide of a deer and still another woman was hanging up strips of meat for drying. "I used to purchase my material and food." The men were chatting around a blazing fire as the sun began to set. "A flick of a switch brought light to a room." She turned back to look at her weetu... "And we had more than one room... and furniture... and dishes..." Winter was coming. How would she survive the cold? Her head began to hurt. The memories of her two worlds spun about her thoughts. She saw her sister laughing in the sunshine, "Come with me sister!" Her son was running toward her. Her maidservant was asking her a question. Her legs began to quiver and her mouth went dry. She reached her hands out in front of her, "Father?" He stood in front of her and was scolding her, "Sarah, you don't belong here." What was he saying? The flashes came quicker until they were just a blur rushing past her. She heard Little Feather's voice but it seemed so far away. She saw Wild Dog jumping out at her with his blade over his head already dripping with blood. "Little Feather!

Save me! I am not supposed to be here." Then suddenly, her heart sped up and she could no longer stand, her world spun around her until she fell to the ground.

She woke up in her bed with her husband looking down at her as he propped himself up with one arm. "We are going to have to work on this stomach weakness of yours," he smiled and kissed her nose.

Tears welled up in Natayah's eyes. She reached out her hand and placed in on Little Feather's cheek, "I love you." she said.

"Why do you say that with tears?"

"I do not know... it is just..." a tear rolled from the corner of her eye, "you deserve so much better."

He wiped away her tear and spoke lovingly, "I have waited a long time for you." He smiled, "I prayed many times to the Great Spirit for you."

"You prayed for a white woman who cannot cook?"

"That is what I get for not being more specific!"

"Do you think..." she paused searching for the right words, "that... I belong here?"

"My love. You belong with me. As long as we are together, that is where we belong."

"But Wild Dog..." she couldn't finish her thought. She saw the anger flush Little Feather's face.

"I should have killed him!" he smoldered. "He will not be back."

"But..." she began while another tear made its way down her cheek.

"You think no more of it, my wife. He is

gone. And I will be here with you. We will be together, forever."

The next day Natayah could barely think straight. Her husband left the weetu before she woke, which means that she didn't make him breakfast like the other wives would have. "Who knows what he is eating," she said out loud, and then thought about it, "Whatever it is, it's probably better than what I could do."

Natayah walked out to the field. The prairie grasses were so tall that she saw the sons long before she saw their mother. Talking Bird was sitting in the middle of the field with Running Deer weaving baskets. This is one task that Natayah enjoyed and was slowly but surely getting better at.

"There you are. We were wondering what had happened to you," Talking Bird greeted. "You look tired."

"Our she-cat was probably out all night protecting our village from intruders," Running Deer teased.

Natayah smiled briefly and sat with a heavy sigh. She pulled three pieces of the long prairie grass and began braiding. "Did you feed my husband today?" she asked.

"You do not know where your husband is?" Running Deer questioned. "Anytime you do not want him, I will be happy to take him off your hands."

Natayah looked at Running Deer, but almost like she didn't see her. "Yes. You would make a good wife for Little Feather."

Both women reacted with a look of shock,

"But he chose you, Natayah."

Natayah blinked and looked at Talking Bird. "Your husband was at our weetu this morning. He said you did not sleep well last night. Mother made us all breakfast."

Natayah looked down at her hands and could feel tears threatening. She stopped braiding and looked at her now callused hands. No longer the hands of a lady. Her nails were short and ragged and there was dirt around the edges and underneath. She reached back and brought her hair over her shoulders. It was filthy. She hadn't worn it down like this since she was a child. She stretched out her arms in front of her. Her once lily-white skin was now freckled and tan.

Running Deer and Talking Bird looked on with concern. "What is wrong with you today?" Talking Bird asked.

"Are you still upset from yesterday?" Running Deer offered.

"I do not know." She looked up at them with tears on the brink of spilling over. Grieving Mother walked over to join them and looked at Natayah but said nothing and sat down to begin her weaving. Talking Bird and Running Deer looked at Grieving Mother wondering why she didn't say anything about Natayah's strange, moody behavior. "What is wrong with people today? Am I missing something?" Running Deer whispered to Talking Bird who just shrugged in response.

"Maybe I am still upset from yesterday... well, of course I am. It is not everyday that you see five people murdered for no reason..." she mumbled on. "Maybe I am just tired, or maybe it is almost my time for the red tent... I just feel...

unclean," she sobbed.

"We can weave later if you want. Let's go to the river," Talking Bird suggested. Talking Bird nudged Running Deer who quickly added, "Sure. My baskets can wait for another day."

"Are you sure you do not mind?" Natayah asked again.

Talking Bird stood and took Natayah's hand, "You go on down and we will clean up here. We will be there shortly." She squeezed Natayah's hand and gave her a wink. "Go on, it will only take us a minute."

"Thank you…so much," Natayah cried and began walking toward the river.

"What has gotten into her?" Running Deer asked.

Talking Bird shrugged as as they began to walk away they heard Grieving Mother giggle.

Natayah was sitting outside her weetu combing her hair when Josiah came up to her. He held four dead otters by their back legs and stood in front of her. "My obligations are now fulfilled," he said, "I will be leaving tomorrow."

She looked up at him, "I'll go with you."

"You will?"

"Could you wait until after dark?" she asked looking down to the ground.

"Sure. Why don't you meet me… east…" he pointed, "at the edge of the trees before the fields." She nodded. "You're doing the right thing," he added, and then walked away.

She made it through the day in a daze. That night, she made love to her husband. He was so

213

gentle and loving. Did he see the tears? Did he know that this was their last time?

The next morning he was gone before the sun came out. She knew he was going hunting with Two Spears. Natayah ignored the dizziness she felt and made herself get up. "What should I take?" she wondered. She had none of her English clothes left. She had torn those to pieces and made other things out of them. How would she be received if she shows up in a big city dressed like an Indian squaw? Would her sister treat her differently when she finds out that she was married to an Indian "savage"? Willingly?

"Caught between two worlds, belonging to neither." Her eyes welled up with tears. She looked to the corner of the platform. A stack of blankets took up the space, but underneath, she knew, her precious box of letters lay hidden. She had purposefully taken them out of her daily view so she wouldn't constantly be reminded of her past life. "Josiah ruined that plan." she slipped her dress on over her head and crawled over to the corner. She pulled out her box and leaned against the wall. She put the box on her lap and opened the lid.

The familiar scent of the musty papers filled her senses. She pulled a letter from the box, unfolded it and began to read:

Oh Sister~

How I wish you were here. No, that is wrong. How I wish I was with you. I simply abhor this place! I am sorry that I have moved here, I just don't belong.

Those words hit a nerve within Natayah. She didn't remember this letter. She only remembered Katherine being happy with her new life in the big city. She continued reading:

There is so much work to be done. The city is new, the streets are still dirt and the sidewalks are still wood! Oh! I just hate it, remembering what we left. I feel so out of place! This pregnancy has made me so emotional and tired.

I know. I can hear papa now quoting scripture: 'But let patience have her perfect work, that ye may be perfect and entire, wanting nothing.' I keep those words running through my mind whenever I am running short of patience! Forgive my complaining, but I am so lonely for your company and understanding countenance. There are times I wish I could just come back with you and mama.

But then, I remember how much in love I am with James and I can't think of life without him. He is worth staying here and changing for. The Bible reminds me to cleave to my husband and 'What God has joined together, let no man put asunder.' These verses give me comfort. I know without my Bible to give me peace, I let myself get so confused!

Natayah's eyes drifted over to her Bible lying untouched beside her pallet. A sadness washed over her as she realized that she was attempting to make these life-altering decisions on her own strength. Her own sister sent her that Bible to help her get through whatever life sent her; not knowing that the most horrific of situations could turn into one of deep love and friendship.

Natayah looked back down to her box full of

letters when the door opened and Talking Bird poked her head around, "Do you mind if I come in?"

Natayah looked up and smiled. Talking Bird leaned against the door and smiled at Natayah still sitting in the corner.

She walked over and sat beside Natayah and stroked the letter box. "My brother has loved you from the very beginning," Talking Bird started, "He knew that when you woke up from your shock and grief that you would need comfort of some kind from your people. He left one day and did not return for several more. When he returned, he carried this box for you." She ran her fingers over the box's unique carvings and let them rest on Natayah's hand. "He said this box must have been very special to you because it was not packed away, like your other items. It seemed to him that you must have carried it with you always." Natayah nodded her head as tears silently fell down her cheeks. "He did not speak again of what else he did while he was away, but I knew when he returned with this box, there was a deepened bond that could not be broken with him for you. It was like he was waiting for you." Natayah knew in her mind those days she was referring to must have been when Little Feather went to bury her son.

"These are 'letters'." Natayah spoke softly, "...They are from my sister."

Talking Bird shook her head in question. "I do not know this word 'letters'."

"In my culture, we have a way of communicating with out speaking, but... by 'writing' similar to your pictures, but more... detailed." Natayah tried to explain, "My sister and her husband moved away to live with… another tribe… but we were still able to communicate by sending these." She held up the letters for Talking Bird to see. "On these 'pages' she is telling me stories of her life and her children, and I would send my news back to her. I saved them. And yes, they are so precious to me."

Talking Bird was fascinated. "You can talk with these symbols?"

Natayah smiled. "Yes, we can rearrange these symbols in different ways to say anything."

"Anything?"

"Everything!" Natayah emphasized and laughed.

"Can you teach me these symbols?" Talking Bird asked. Natayah thought about her impending journey in the middle of the night, "I… I do not know..." Natayah stuttered.

"I understand. It is just for your people?"

"Oh no!" Natayah held her hand, "It is for all people. I just do not know if I am a good teacher." She looked away ashamed of her lies.

"It is okay. I do not need it. Who would I talk to?" Talking Bird stood up, "Come. We are supposed to be weaving baskets."

Natayah put her letter back in the box and stood up to leave with Talking Bird.

"I am so glad that you are my sister now and that we are close so we do not have to make symbols to talk." Talking Bird smiled meekly and hugged Natayah. A wave of guilt ran through Natayah but she tried to swallow it away.

Grieving Mother joined the weaving party and brought lunch to everyone.

"Oh, thank you, mother." Talking Bird said,

"But I do not think I can eat anything. I have not been feeling well, these last few days."

Grieving Mother smiled, "I know. But both of my daughters need to eat."

"Thank you for feeding my husband," Natayah spoke softly with tears welling up in her eyes. She wiped the tears away. "I am sorry. I do not know what is wrong with me."

Talking Bird teared up, "It is okay. You will learn to cook someday and you are turning into a fine wife." Talking Bird laughed as a tear slipped down her cheek. She wiped it away with her free hand, "Whatever is wrong with you must be contagious!"

Grieving Mother laughed and laughed. She shook her head and held onto her stomach. The others turned to look at her wondering what the outburst was about. "Both of you! How wonderful!" She turned and walked back out of the field, laughing the whole way. Stopping only once, she turned back and tried to say with a straight face, "You need to eat!"

They all looked at each other, but Running Deer put words to their thoughts, "What is wrong with her?"

Little Feather came home to find Natayah sitting outside their weetu with her Bible in her hands. She was leaning against a woven support that he had made for her so she would be more comfortable while relaxing. He snuck up behind her and nuzzled into her neck. She giggled and threw her head back. He took the opportunity to kiss her cheek. He tipped her chin toward him and kissed her lips. "I have missed you all day," he whispered in a husky voice that barely cloaked his passion.

She smiled and leaned over to lay her head on his shoulder. He slipped in behind her and wrapped his arms around her waist and pulled her back against his chest. "We are a perfect fit."

"Are we?" she asked fighting tears again.

"Yes. I would love to prove it to you… right now." He kissed her neck again. He nuzzled into her neck and it threw her into a fit of giggles. He laughed, loving the reaction and kept it up until she slid down and away from him. She wiped the tears from the corners of her eyes from laughing so hard. "What? I was just showing you my affection!" he laughed. He reached his hands out for her to help him up. She grabbed hold of him and he pulled her back down to him instead. She squealed and protected her neck. "I wish I could take you inside but we have to go to White Owl's weetu for tonight. He lost the games. His wife has to cook!" he laughed.

"It sounds more like he won, to me," Natayah said discouraged.

"It will be a nice night, with friends."

She sat up and turned toward him. "Could we just stay here instead? I wanted to spend some time alone with you."

"I thought you might be tired of just spending time with me. Besides, I want to show off my new wife to everyone."

"Please, Little Feather."

"Oh, this is serious. You called me by my name… my *real* name!" he teased her. "We can stay here if you would like."

"I would. Thank you." He turned her back around and squeezed her close to him again. She stiffened, guarding, "I am not going to bother your neck… for right now." She relaxed against him and opened her Bible once again. "Why do you stare into that black box?" he asked.

"Box?" He nodded pointing to her book. "Oh," she said understanding, "This is a 'book', and each one of these 'pages' has a lot of information on it. So I 'read' it to learn more."

"What does it teach you?"

"This particular book is called the Bible. It is filled with what God… what you call the Great Spirit, wants us to know. How to live, how to treat others, what happens to us when we die…"

"The Great Spirit tells you this? In this 'boook'?

She smiled back at him. "Yes, many, many seasons ago, He sent His son to walk among the men and He told these men many things that He wanted put in this special book. Then man made this book so everyone can know what God wants for us."

"I have heard that the Great Spirit has come to visit us in human form. I thought it was just stories that were handed down from generation to generation."

"That is something like what this is, only it was printed so no one would forget and it could be shared with everyone, not just the next generation of children. So your people can know, and my people can know, and people who we have not even met can know."

"Why does our medicine man not have this? He speaks to the Great Spirit."

"It is not just for him, it is for everyone."

"How do you know what it says?" he asked

holding the book flipping through the hundreds of onionskin pages.

"You only have to know how to read," she giggled.

He stood up quickly and looked insulted. "Why do you laugh? Is it just for women? I do not want any part of woman's work."

Natayah reached out for his hand and brought him back to sit in front of her. He followed her lead but still frowned. She wrapped her arms around his waist and held the book in her hands. She leaned over his shoulder to see the Bible, "No. I said it was for everyone. Listen. Here it is telling us that He promises to provide for us. This chapter is called Matthew." She translated as best she could as she read from the book of Matthew: *"Do not worry about things, such as food, drink or clothes. You have been given a body and life, and they are more important than what to eat and wear. Look at the birds. They do not worry about what to eat. They do not plant and gather and store up food, for your Great Father feeds them. And you are far more important to Him than they are. Will all your worries add a single moment to your life?"*

"This is what you were reading when I came?"

"Yes."

"Do you think I cannot provide for you?"

"No, that is not what he is saying. He is telling us that when you go out to look for food, He will be sure you find some. He thinks of you as one of his children and a father would not let his child go hungry."

"I understand. Can you read some more?" Natayah flipped through the pages to find another of her favorite verses.

She read a few more of her favorite passages and translated as she went. He was patient and listened. He loved the sound of her voice and he loved the words she read.

"I want to know more," he said, "I like to know what your God has to say."

"He is your God too," she said, "He is just called by a different name."

"But you call Him God," he looked back at her and she nodded. "Then I will call Him God, too." He leaned in to kiss her. "Will you tell me more tomorrow?" he rolled over to his hands and knees.

"Why tomorrow?" she asked.

"Because I have other things on my mind," he murmured and kissed along her cheek and down her neck.

"But..." she tried to resist, "but... I made food!" she giggled.

"You did?" he stopped and looked at her.

"Yes, I can cook; I just have trouble getting the meat out of the deer!"

He laughed and held her close. "I love you, wife."

"I love you, too, husband," she held him tight and swallowed the sobs that threatened to pour out of her. *"Oh, Lord, am I doing the right thing by leaving this man?"* she prayed silently as she held on to him, *"I love him so much."*

"Come on!" he pulled away from her and jumped to his feet. He pulled Natayah up to her feet then lifted her effortlessly up and over his shoulder. "Show me this food you are bragging about!"

The night was still and Natayah stared into the burning embers left in the fire pit. Little Feather's arm lay over Natayah's stomach as it always did, protecting her even as he slept.

She lifted his arm up gently so she could slip out and he stirred. He opened his eye and looked for any sign of danger.

"It is alright, husband," Natayah whispered as he lay his head back down. She stroked his hair and kissed his forehead and then his cheek.

He pried his eye open again. "Hurry back," he whispered. She kissed him again and rose off the pallet. She slipped her dress and moccasins on, grabbed a small sack hidden at the foot of her bed and went out the door.

Elizabeth Bourgeret

Chapter Sixteen

The village was quiet with the exception of a few of the dogs barking at her. She shushed them as she went past. The moon was almost full so it gave her a little light as she made her way through the woods. There was a chill in the fall night air and she regretted not bringing a cloak.

She spotted Josiah near the edge of the woods. He was pacing back and forth looking at the moon. He saw her walk towards him with her satchel and smiled at her. "I thought you might have changed your mind! Let's go. We can put some distance from this place with the moon being so close to full. We'll have plenty of light." He shook his hair from his face as he moved to gather his belongings.

"Josiah," she spoke softly.

He stopped picking up his stuff and looked at her. He started shaking his head from side to side in disbelief. "No…no…no…no. Don't say it," he said dropping his things back to the ground.

"Josiah. I can't go," she said looking directly into his eyes. "Here, this is for you." she held out the satchel to him. "It's some dried meat and corn cakes, and…"

"Sarah," Josiah interrupted. "We've been through this. You don't belong here."

"But I do," she said calmly. "This is exactly where God wants me to be. He showed me that over and over today."

"What if God sent me to find you?" he shouted.

"I believe that He did. You *were* meant to find me and teach me that without a doubt, I am where I belong," she stated. "Just because they are different from us doesn't mean…"

"Different? They're barely one step above animals! And I'm being generous!"

"I'm sorry, Josiah. Please tell my sister that I love her and that I am well." She tipped her head to him and turned to leave.

He stomped the ground with his foot and reached down to grab his rope. "I didn't want to have to do this," he muttered.

He walked up behind her and put his hand over her mouth. She tried to scream but his hand stifled the noise. She struggled free of his grip and started back into the woods.

She screamed out, "Help me! Little Feather!" He grabbed her ankle causing her to fall forward. She put her hands out in front of her to control her fall, but he pulled her foot back. She landed on her chest and her face.

"I'm sorry it has to be this way, Sarah," Josiah strained to say against her struggling. "I'm only doing what is best for you!"

"You don't know what's best for me!" she screamed and tried to slap him wherever she could make contact. He ducked and dodged her flailing arms and tried to keep hold of her. She managed to flip completely over onto her back and used all of her leg muscles to kick back away from him.

He reeled back holding his stomach. "You are talking crazy, Sarah. When you wake up with your own people, you'll remember this as just a bad dream."

"No! You'll have to kill me first."

"I don't want to have to do that, Sarah, but I will."

Sarah was suddenly terrified. She saw by the look in his eyes that he was serious. "You wouldn't kill me just to get your way would you?"

"No, I would kill you for the reward money."

"How could you?" Sarah scooted away from him as he lassoed his rope.

"I'll just blame it on the Injuns. Everyone knows they are blood thirsty animals, except you!"

She turned over to get back on her feet, but he was on top of her again tying her hands together with his rope.

"No!" she yelled. She flung her hands in all directions to keep him from being able to grab them. She screamed and kicked, striking where she could.

"Look at you!" he stepped back to catch his breath. "You are no lady. You are turning into one of them."

"I'd rather be one of them than to be compared with you!" she yelled and threw a rock at him. It hit its mark on his head. A small trickle of blood slid down his forehead. She took the time that he was holding his head to get to her feet. She turned to run again, but in no time, he was upon her. He tossed the rope around her waist. She tripped and folded in half. Josiah used this opportunity to grab both of her hands and pull them up behind her.

Natayah cried out in pain and he pulled up harder. She screamed out again. "Are you going to cooperate?" he yelled.

"Josiah, please…"

"Do you know how much you are worth? There is no way I am going back without you. So you can make this easy or hard! But you are going back with me!"

He bound her hands with the rope. She wept and pleaded. "Josiah, please… don't do this," she cried. "This was how I was brought to this village and sold, my hands bound in ropes, my freedom and choices taken away from me. What makes you any less of a savage?"

He threw her to the ground, while he gathered his belongings, "Sarah, I meant to come here as a hero… your savior…"

"Instead, you have become my captor," her voice seethed with anger.

He breathlessly stooped to pick up his pack and supplies. He took a few steps and stopped. He looked all around him. He appeared to be lost. The look of fear came across his face. "Where's my horse?"

Natayah looked around and her heart skipped a beat, knowing, yet not knowing, what was to come next. She stayed silent.

Josiah turned toward Natayah clearly terrified. His fear amplified his rage. He pulled out his knife from its sheath and walked toward her.

"I'm not going to let you go," he growled between clenched teeth. He grabbed Natayah's rope-tied hands and lifted her roughly to her feet.

Then without warning or sound, an arrow came from the darkness of the forest and pierced Josiah's leg. He fell just at Natayah's feet.

His face shifted from anger and power to

fear. "Don't let them kill me, Sarah!" he panicked.

Within seconds, Little Feather came running out of the woods and was straddling Josiah with his knife at his neck.

"Oh, God! Don't let him kill me!"

"Why should he spare your life? You had no qualms about taking mine," Natayah hissed.

"I...I wouldn't really kill anyone... we're friends, right?" Little Feather tightened his grip, and pressed the knife into his skin near the breaking point. "Please, Sarah!"

"Husband," Natayah spoke calmly, "Do not kill him."

Little Feather broke his glare at Josiah and looked up at his wife, "Are you alright?"

"I am." Little Feather tightened his hold and barely pierced the skin as the white man yelled out. Natayah spoke again softly, "Please, husband. There has been enough killing."

He looked up at her and saw the goodness and forgiveness in her face and relaxed his grip on his throat. He took a handful of the hair that he held and pushed Josiah's face into the ground. He caught the look from his wife. "He slipped," he shrugged.

Little Feather cut the ropes that bound Natayah. She threw her arms around his neck and he embraced her but never took his eyes off of Josiah who was trying to stand.

Little Feather pushed Natayah to the side and walked over to Josiah. He bent over and grabbed the arrow and pulled it back out of his leg. Josiah screamed again and fell back to the ground.

Little Feather reached down and picked up Josiah by his shirt and stood him up on his feet. He spoke to him in his native tongue and pointed. Natayah translated, "My husband tells you that the only reason you have been saved is because of his love for me. You need to go and never come back."

"But my leg!" Josiah cried out, "I'll bleed to death!"

Natayah translated as Little Feather spoke, "Your horse is tied to a tree in that direction."

"Sarah, you can't send me out like this!" Josiah pleaded.

"You have your life," Natayah spoke plainly. "Go to your world and leave me to mine."

Little Feather gathered Josiah's things and handed them to him. He picked up Natayah's bag and looked at her questioningly. She took the bag from him and saw the hurt cross over his eyes.

Natayah walked over to Josiah and offered him the bag again, "God go with you, Josiah."

Josiah took the bag and looked to the ground. He situated his things over his shoulder and looked up at Natayah. "We'll meet again."

"No, Josiah. Take this gift of your life that my husband has offered you, and live a good life. For he won't offer it again."

Josiah looked at her with hate before he turned and limped away.

Natayah watched him walk a few paces before she went to stand beside her husband. She drew close to him and put her arms around his waist. "Will he be alright?" she asked.

"Yes. It is only a small wound." He showed her the arrow. "The head is very small. I use these for rabbits." Natayah giggled. This was just a game for her husband.

They watched Josiah for as long as the light

would allow, then turned back towards the woods to go home. Natayah rubbed her shoulders, and stretched out her back. "What took you so long?"

"I had to get my pants on!" he smiled at her.

"You could have stepped in a little sooner."

"You looked like you were doing just fine, my little Wildcat." He squeezed her shoulder and kissed her temple.

They walked home in silence. When they walked inside, Little Feather tossed his bow and arrow to the side and picked up a couple of logs to put on the fire. He said nothing and did not look at her as he sat to take his shoes off.

Natayah walked over to him and knelt down in front of him. "Husband?"

He let out a heavy sigh, and rested his elbows on his knees. "Were you going to leave with him?"

Natayah swallowed hard. "There was a time… that I thought… you would be better off without me."

Little Feather dropped his head and sighed. He looked up at Natayah and she saw the sheen on his eyes. He put his hands on her cheeks, and tipped her face up to his, "Do not *ever* think that. I would be lost without you."

"I am sorry," she raised up to be face to face with him. "I will never think about leaving you ever again." She leaned in and kissed him.

He wrapped his arms around her waist tightly and pulled her over him into their bed. "I love you… so much," he whispered into her neck.

"I love you too," she whispered back, but in her mind she thanked God for His care of her and for sending her this man that she loved with all of her heart.

Natayah woke the next morning with a new purpose and a full heart. She got up despite the dizziness in her head and the soreness in her muscles.

As she and Little Feather sat together and ate their breakfast, Natayah read to him from the book of Genesis, translating as best she could. Explaining the English words that she had no translation for.

"So it is only one God who created the earth and sky and everything in it?" Little Feather asked in earnest.

"Yes. He has helpers; those were the angels that I mentioned. But, yes, there is only one God. He is the beginning and the end."

"I do not think that the chief will believe this. Our history tells us differently."

"That is why there is this book. Your ancestors were not exposed to all of God's words. Your people only know some of these stories."

"Yes. We have a story that tells us that the Great Spirit will return to take us to the great gathering in the sky."

Natayah smiled. "Yes, that story is in here too."

"It is?"

"It is." She fought the tears that were burning her eyes. This is where she belonged. To be here, right at this moment, to spread God's word. "As we read on, you will find that he wants everyone, everywhere to know His stories."

"How is that supposed to happen?" Little

Feather asked.

"One person at a time, my love." She leaned over and kissed his nose. At that moment, a loud rapping was heard at the door.

"Enter," Little Feather announced.

Talking Bird ran into the room straight for Natayah. "Oh, sister! I have the most wonderful news!"

"What? What is it?" Natayah laughed getting caught up in her excitement. "Here, sit down and have something to eat."

"Oh no, nothing for me. I cannot keep food in my stomach!" she smiled.

"And is that the good news?" Little Feather teased.

"No!" she scowled at her brother, "If I am correct, which Mother believes that I am, I am with child!"

Natayah reached out to grab her hands, "Really?" she embraced Talking Bird's neck, "Oh, I am so happy! I love babies!" They held each other and laughed as tears ran down their cheeks. Little Feather added his congratulations but rolled his eyes at their carrying on.

"Are you wanting a daughter this time?" Natayah asked.

Talking Bird blushed. "It is my duty to ask the Great Spirit for a son, for my husband, but I secretly hope for a daughter."

"Oh, I am so happy for you!" Natayah repeated. "Is there anything we can do for you?"

"Not right now, but I do want you to be with me... when the time comes. Would you?"

"I can think of no where else I would rather be," she replied glancing down to her husband, who

233

was still laying on the floor trying to eat his breakfast, but caught the meaning of her look.

"Tell her about your exciting evening," Little Feather prompted.

"I am sorry, sister, could you tell me at sewing circle? I must go and tell Running Deer."

"Yes, it can wait. You should go and spread the good news."

"Running Deer might not be as happy for you as we are," Little Feather told her. "I think she will be jealous."

Talking Bird shrugged. "Let her. I do not care! Besides, it is not as if Natayah was having the baby. THEN she would be jealous!" Natayah and Little Feather looked at each other and Little Feather bounced his eyebrows as if to say, "Not a bad idea!"

"I have to go!" Talking Bird hugged Natayah again and kissed Little Feather then skipped out of the weetu.

Natayah sat back down by her husband still smiling, "It will be nice to have a new baby."

Little Feather crawled to Natayah and picked up her foot, kissing each toe sending a wave of squeals through the weetu. Natayah laughed as Little Feather made his way up to her knee covering the area with his tiny kisses, "Stop!" she laughed.

"Come on, wife, let's make a baby!"

"But... breakfast!" she sputtered through gales of laughter.

"It can wait."

Chapter Seventeen

All the women were laughing as Natayah retold the events of the night before, putting a comical spin to it.

"And he stole his horse and hid it across the field!" Natayah laughed out the punch line.

"That sounds like Little Feather. He loves to play jokes!" Running Deer said.

"Were you not scared?" spoke up shy Little Pebble, who had just become old enough for the sewing circle.

In a more serious tone, Natayah answered, "Yes, at the time I was scared. But looking back, now that I know the outcome, there were some pretty funny parts!" she smiled.

"Besides, Natayah is getting the reputation that she can take care of herself!" Talking Bird teased.

Natayah saw Grieving Mother shake her head as she sat across from her.

"So he was just watching you from the woods?" someone asked.

"My husband would have killed him so fast…"

"Oh, he wanted to, believe me." Natayah added, "But I asked him not to."

"Why would you do that?" Speckled Doe asked, "He should have killed him and been done with it."

"Because that is not the kind of life that God

wants for us," she said calmly.

"But they do it to us!" Salt Woman shouted out.

"Yes, they do. But that does not make it right. And when you have killed them, does it bring your lost loved ones back?"

A silence fell over the group and Grieving Mother could stand it no more. "What about the baby?" she shouted out into the silence jarring everyone's attention.

Natayah and Talking Bird looked at each other wondering what she was talking about.

"Mother, we have already told everyone about my baby."

"I know daughter. Is the baby alright?"

"It should be." Talking Bird answered, a little confused.

"Not your baby, daughter, your baby!" she said pointing to Natayah.

They looked at Grieving Mother wondering what she was talking about. Grieving Mother sighed heavily and asked Natayah, "Have you had any bleeding?"

"No... not yet." Natayah blushed having to answer such an intimate question, "But I think it is soon... I have lost track of time."

"Good," Grieving Mother nodded and went back to her sewing. "Then the baby is fine."

Natayah looked at her confused and then a gasp was heard in the room. Then another. And finally the realization came to Natayah and Talking Bird.

"A baby? Me?" She struggled to put her thoughts into words, "Am I going to have a baby?"

Grieving Mother nodded and smiled, but

never looked up from her stitches.

Squeals and giggles filled the weetu and everyone jumped up to hug Natayah and Talking Bird and offer another round of congratulations.

Talking Bird squeezed Natayah's neck, "Oh sister! Both of us!! Having babies together!!"

Tears poured down Natayah's face. "A baby," she could barely speak. "Does Little Feather know?" she directed her question at Grieving Mother.

"He will when you tell him," Grieving Mother smiled.

"I am sorry, friends, I must go... I have to... oh, Little Feather! I have to..."

"Just go!" they all shouted at her.

She stood and dropped her sewing where she sat and ran from the weetu.

"Grieving Mother, you must be so proud. Two grandchildren this year!" Quannah said.

"Yes, but what will this one be when it is born?" Running Deer asked with acid dripping from every syllable, "Is it going to be white, or Indian?"

Talking Bird stood. "It will be both. A union between our two people. Perhaps a peace can come between our two worlds, starting with this child."

Little Feather was as proud as a peacock and showered his wife with gifts and praise. Her dizziness plagued her for a few more weeks, but she didn't care. A baby.

Natayah began saying her prayers out loud in the Seapaugh language. Her horse, Clara, was the only one who heard her English words now since Josiah had been gone.

Natayah would still read from the Bible every morning and soon others joined the couple to hear the words from the book written by the Great Spirit. As word spread through the village that Natayah was reading "letters from God" more and more gathered to hear. To Natayah, this was just more proof that she was where she was meant to be.

It was late one morning after reading that Natayah walked down to the bluff. The leaves had left the trees and there was frost on the grass and even though there was quite a bit of chill in the air, the sun warmed her back. She took this quiet time to reflect on the many blessings that God showered on her. She smiled to herself, *"Who would have thought, that a year ago, when I was contemplating a trip out west, I would have ended up here. A white woman, married to and completely in love with an Indian man with high ranking in his tribe, pregnant, and bringing the word of God to an 'uncivilized nation.* "Uncivilized," she thought, *"how ignorant we all are. The Indian people are quite content with the way things are. I wonder what, if anything, they would want from our culture. Cookware... that would be nice..."* Clara nudged Natayah's shoulder. She unconsciously rubbed the horse's muzzle and continued with her musings, *"Perhaps some fabric, maybe not lace or silks, they would have no place out here, but some nice breathable cottons. Yes. That would be nice. And wouldn't the girls love my jewelry!"* She nuzzled her face into Clara's warm neck and giggled to herself. *"Running Deer especially, she would not be so smug to me if she knew the 'riches' that I had left behind. Not that I was rich by most standards, but to these people..."* She gasped, *"What about books?"* She drifted off to another direction, *"I truly miss my books, but I don't think they would appreciate Shakespeare or Chaucer. They have such wonderful stories of their own... and they are hundreds of years old, some of them."* She bent down around her protruding belly to feel the temperature of the water. *"And my, how I have changed."* She rubbed her hands over her tiny pregnant belly. *"Katherine would never believe that I eat toasted grasshoppers. I find that kind of hard to believe myself. Now I can skin a rabbit, prepare the meat and the skin within a day's time. That is, of course, between trips to the woods to throw up."* She laughed out loud. "I am getting better though." Clara whinnied at her as if responding, and laughing along with her.

Natayah squatted down to put her hands back in the water. "I don't want to have to bathe in that water!" she said aloud to Clara. "It is too cold." Then another thought passed through her mind, just short of panic. "What am I going to do throughout the winter? I can't go all winter without a bath! I can't be expected to get in this river with ice covering it! I would surely freeze! I must speak to my husband on this matter." She thought quietly to herself and then with a look of determination, she decided. *"I can at least bring a small amount of civilization, can't I?"* With a new sense of purpose, she went in search of her husband with Clara following close behind.

Natayah found him sitting with Chief Spotted Eagle and Two Spear and a few other men. Natayah called out to him so as not to walk in on something that perhaps she was not meant to hear. They were getting used to her forward behavior, but it still stunned them every time she did it. In their culture, if the women wanted a moment with her mate, she would come some distance outside the circle, kneel down and bow her head waiting for acknowledgement. Natayah could not and would not conform to that.

"There's my wild cat now," Little Feather said to his friends, who responded with laughter. They mostly thought she was beautiful, but a little too much trouble for their liking. For example, when she walked up to the circle, he opened his arms to her and they embraced. Then he bent down to nuzzle her pregnant belly, right there in front of everyone. If it was anyone else, he would have been called 'soft'. He still gets teased, but he takes it all because he has never been so happy. He might have lost a little bit of weight, and it might take a bit longer for him to get an edible meal… with meat in it, but it was worth it in his mind. She was worth it, the mother of his unborn child.

"Husband," she said as she walked right up to the circle, "In the winter, when it is cold, colder than this…what do you do to keep clean?"

The entire circle burst into laughter, including Little Feather, but Natayah stayed put and waited calmly for an answer.

"I do not think I understand your question," Little Feather answered trying to contain his laughter.

"This is what you interrupted our meeting for?" Two Spear asked.

"Is that what this is? I can never tell from a distance if you are discussing world peace or just telling stories," she smiled sweetly. They all laughed in spite of themselves. "Now, really husband, this is important."

"Same as the summer. The river," he answered. The horror clearly shown on her face. "In the river? Even when it is cold… and snow is on the ground? You bathe in the river!"

"Sometimes we have to break through the ice first," Two Spear added.

"It is a much quicker bath…" Little Feather teased.

"What did you do in your world?" asked the chief.

"We would never bathe out of doors in any season!" she answered almost offended. The men just looked at each other deciding that the white people must be a filthy race.

"Was there anything else?" Little Feather asked.

"Not right now, thank you, but you have given me direction." She kissed him on the cheek and turned to leave when the chief said, "Daughter Natayah, could you…" he re-thought his words, "Maybe you might be willing to give *us* some direction."

"You are asking a woman?" Black Hawk asked.

"Yes, my son," the chief answered. "A white woman."

"I will do my best," Natayah offered. She sat down with her husband in the circle of men realizing the honor that was being bestowed upon her.

"You were very helpful when the white man, Jozah came to us. Even though you were deceived by his character, you were not to blame."

"Thank you, father," she nodded.

"Do you miss your people?" he asked.

"I would be lying if I said that I did not," she answered solemnly. "But I have never been happier than I have been here, with my husband and my new baby."

The chief nodded, satisfied with her answer. "I am glad that you are an honest woman."

Natayah smiled and nodded.

"Grey Wolf has been out riding today and has seen many men of your kind on horses. He believes they were less than a day's ride away from our village. My question to you, daughter, is this, what would they be doing here? Should we be concerned?"

Natayah was taken aback by the question. She had never really concerned herself with why and where men traveled about. Just now, she was wishing that she had paid more attention.

"I do not know for sure. The reasons could be many, father. My first thought was that it might be the 'mail'. Mail is one of our ways of communicating. How we send messages to one another," she explained.

"Letters," Little Feather provided the Seapaugh word.

"Letters," Natayah repeated. "If that is who they were, they could care less if we were here, as long as they had no reason to fear us. They just have a job to do. They usually travel in a large 'stagecoach'. Um..." she thought for a moment, "A sort of wagon that can carry supplies or people on short trips."

The men all nodded and mumbled amongst

themselves wanting, hoping that this was the answer. The chief slapped his leg and pounded his staff into the ground, "I give them permission to pass through our land," he stated matter-of-factly.

Natayah laughed to herself knowing that white men obviously didn't care if the chief of the "uncivilized savages" gave them permission or not.

"It could just be other settlers. Like me. Moving from one place to another to start a home. Since there were no women and children or large wagons, it was probably the scouts."

This brought much grumbling and talking amongst one another.

"My white sister, Katherine, told me in a letter that many people are moving out west in large numbers," Natayah continued.

"They are moving here? Is this West?" the chief asked?

"Close to here, I imagine." She saw the look of panic in his old eyes. "Can you blame them? This must be the most beautiful country in all the world." She smiled and placed her hand on his. He smiled and patted her hand.

"It might be other trappers, like Josiah. It could be the army…"

"Here is what is heavy on my heart," the chief spoke bringing things back to business, "We cannot survive the winter without the meat of the buffalo and the skins they provide us. And you know the great loss of life we suffered on our last hunting trip." He stopped and sighed momentarily lost in his thoughts. The others stayed silent, respectful. "I believe," he began again, "that just the men should make this trip. We will leave the women and children behind. We will be able to move quickly. We will hunt and clean then return home. We will have our celebrations here."

"Do you think," Little Feather asked, "that we should leave some men here, for their safety?"

"From what I hear," Spotted Eagle chuckled, "your woman can look out for herself!" Everyone laughed and Natayah blushed. "But we can leave Black Elk and Red Rock here to guard the village and the other men's wives. We should be back within two moon cycles."

The men nodded in agreement and it was done. But in the back of Natayah's mind, she wondered if her husband would be back in time to witness the birth of his first born…or… be back at all.

Natayah excused herself from the men and was anxious to get started on her new project. The bathtub. "There's nothing like a project to keep your mind from anxious worry," she told herself as she walked towards her home.

Natayah was putting the final coats of tree sap mixed with ash to make her human sized basket completely waterproof. It was in the shape of an oval and a light color of tan with the exception of a thick stripe of a dark green color.

"I got bored with tan," she explained when Little Feather asked. He teased her regularly about her basket.

"How are you going to be able to lift it when it gets full?" "What are you planning on carrying in that?" "I know! It is a place to store our heavy blankets in the summer." "Does it hold wood?"

Captive Heart

Natayah would just smile and keep weaving while he asked questions and made silly guesses. "If that is for the baby, that is going to be one big baby!"

The basket took all of two months to finish and it was only two weeks before Little Feather and the others would be leaving on the buffalo hunt.

Tonight, when Little Feather would come home for his supper, she would have a surprise for him.

She made his dinner... with meat, and began to boil water. She was so pleased that the basket held water and didn't leak all over her smooth, level dirt floor.

When Little Feather came home, he was so used to seeing the basket around that he didn't even see the steam coming from the hot water setting in it. He was distracted by the smell of food.

She could barely contain her smile all through dinner. Finally, he asked, "What are you smiling about?"

"Hurry and finish your dinner and I will tell you." Little Feather stuffed the last bite of the deer steak into his mouth. "I am funished," he barely uttered around the full mouth of food and stuffed cheeks.

"Good!" she jumped up, as best as a seven month pregnant woman could. "Now, get undressed!"

He grabbed her in his arms, "I like your surprises!"

"No, no, no." She pulled away giggling as he tried to kiss her neck right where she is ticklish. "Go on, take your clothes off," she laughed.

He did as he was told and wrapped a narrow deerskin around his waist as she poured one last container of hot water into the basket.

"Is that what you use that for? To store water? That is a great idea!" Little Feather said.

"No, it is better. Come over here."

"Finally!" he threw off the deerskin and came toward her. He spun her around to kiss him, which she did, gladly.

"Here. Climb in," she instructed. He looked at her like she had just lost her mind.

"You want me to ruin the water supply?"

"This is a 'bathtub'." She used the English word. "This or something somewhat like it is what we used to get clean when it is cold outside. No ice, no snow... no rivers in the middle of winter." She smiled so proudly. He didn't get in and was wondering what exactly had happened to the intelligent woman he had married.

"Just try it. It feels so nice and relaxing. I am letting you go first...trust me. You will love it."

Little Feather took a deep breath and reached one foot over the high wall into the basket of water. He gasped at the temperature and hopped around on one foot. Natayah laughed at the look on his face.

"Are you trying to cook me?" Little Feather shouted balancing his leg on the edge of the basket.

"Try again, nice and slow."

He did and his tightened jaw relaxed as he got used to the water. He lifted his other foot in and went through the same process again.

"Feels nice, does it not?"

"Yes, I guess so. Now what?" he asked while standing in the basket of water reaching his knees.

"Now you sit down."

Slowly, he did. His knees were pressed against his chest and the water flowed up around his shoulders. Natayah knelt down beside him and scooped the warm water up and over his neck and hair.

"Is this not better than that icy cold river?" she asked.

"Yes. This what your people do?"

"Yes." She smiled as she rubbed his back with warm water. "We had a helper and she would pour water over our head to get the soap out. Just lean back and relax." She coaxed him to let go of his legs and lean back against the woven basket. He could feel the basket give against his weight and he straightened up again.

Natayah grabbed a smaller basket and poured water down the back of his long black hair. He wiped the water from his face and pushed his hair back. He leaned back again and rested his arms along the edge of the basket. "I have decided that I like this," he said. He leaned his head back and suddenly the entire basket, with him included and the gallons of water filling it, tipped over backwards. Natayah gasped as the entire bathtub flipped up and tossed her naked husband out onto the now muddy floor. Little Feather ended up face down and spread eagle surrounded in a river of water.

She didn't know whether to laugh or cry, but laughter won out when her husband made his way to his feet, completely covered in mud.

He stood in front of her as the water flowed around his feet and stared at her as she laughed uncontrollably. "I am more dirty now than when I started!" He used his index fingers to remove the mud from his eyes. "Was that supposed to happen?"

"No!" was all she could blurt out through her laughter and now tears.

"You think this is funny?" he said walking toward her with a menacing look on his face.

"No... husband, no!" she squealed, "Now, do not..."

Little Feather reached out and grabbed her hands and pulled her into his mud covered body body. They wrestled and laughed until they both ended up in the mud puddle again. He grabbed a handful of dirt and smashed it into her hair. He painted stripes of mud on her face.

"This is your war paint," he laughed.

"I am going on the war path, all right, look what you have done to my dress!" she couldn't stop laughing even though she was doing her best to scold him.

"I can fix that!" he said as he stripped her dress off over her head and rolled her back over into the mud.

They wrestled in the mud until there was no sign of who was white and who was Indian. They finally fell into each other's arms and lay in the puddle of mud. She rested on his arm and he lay on his back. "I guess we should go and wash this off," he said as they settled down.

"What am I going to do about this floor?" she wondered, patting her hand in the thick mud that was once smooth and flat... and dry.

"You will think of something. Another project for you while I am gone." He leaned over and gave her a muddy kiss. Little Feather helped lift her out of the mud.

They each got another set of clothes and made their way to the cold river, hand in muddy hand.

For the next two weeks Little Feather and Natayah were practically inseparable. It was hard for them to believe that they would have to spend the next two or three months apart. They stayed in bed later, and walked everywhere together. At night he would lay his head and hands on her belly to feel the baby kick his face.

Together, they leveled the floor and he even built shelves for her.

One morning, she snuck out before he woke to pick some of the last few berries, before the end of the season. They had frost on them, but their color and flavor was still preserved. When she came back, she found Little Feather sitting inside the dry bathtub.

"What are you doing?" she asked laughing, remembering the last time he was in it.

"I like your idea. I think it could work. It just needs support, here and here," he said as he rocked from side to side almost flipping it again.

Natayah walked over to him and leaned down to kiss him. "I love you," she whispered.

"I love you, too," he answered as he wrapped his arms around her and pulled her into the woven bathtub.

"No! No! It cannot hold both of us!" she protested, but it was too late. He pulled her in and they both toppled to the side.

"Hmmm, I have decided that it cannot hold

both of us," he laughed.

That afternoon they went out and cut down some saplings. Little Feather cut them into thin planks and set them in the river.

Later, they bent the planks along the outside of the bathtub making it look more like a sleigh. He tied the planks together to hold them in place. He also built a rectangular box for the entire woven bathtub contraption to fit in. They painted it with more sap and ash.

"There," Little Feather announced. "That should work." They stood there together and stared at their creation feeling most pleased. She beamed with pride at her husband's ingenuity.

"Should we try it?" Natayah asked.

"YOU go first!" Little Feather answered.

And so she did. It took several hours to have enough hot water to fill it so they spent the in-between times getting Little Feather packed and ready to go, for the next day was his departure.

The mood was heavy over the entire village and hardly anyone spent anytime outside their weetu. Natayah and Little Feather were no different. They cooked their meals inside, packed his things inside, and took their baths.

Natayah went first. Little Feather gently and tenderly washed his wife's hair and then went on to wash each part of her body, stopping to give extra care to her belly that poked out of the water. Natayah returned the favor for her husband. They ended up turning in to bed early and did not separate from each other until the early light.

Little Feather was wrapped around Natayah

with one arm supporting her head and the other arm on her pregnant belly.

"It is time," he said barely above a whisper. He knew that she was awake even if he couldn't see her face.

"I know." She rolled over to face him. "Please be careful. Our son will need his father."

"Son? Do you not secretly wish for a daughter, like my sister?"

"No, I want a son for you. But you need to teach him to grow up to be just like you." She paused, "Please, be extra careful."

"If I am too careful, I will not be able to bring home food for us to get us through the winter," he reasoned, but he saw the sheen of tears in her eyes and decided that reasoning was not what she needed to hear at this time. "I will be extra careful," he promised and kissed her forehead.

She lifted her head so he could get up. He leaned down and kissed her belly. "My son." he talked to it and watched the skin roll as the baby moved around. "I will be home soon. Then I will teach you to hunt."

"Maybe we could wait a few months before we put a weapon in his hand," she giggled as she stroked his hair.

He looked up into his wife's eyes, "Will you come to see me off?"

"Yes, of course." He stood and reached his hand down to help her up.

The hunting party left with great fanfare… and Natayah felt so alone.

Elizabeth Bourgeret

Chapter Eighteen

The winter seemed to come on quickly. The men had been gone for only four weeks. The women helped Natayah and Talking Bird with the things that they would need to get through the winter and for their new babies.

Natayah's weetu was the hub of activity once word of the bathtub got around. It was time consuming to fill up and empty, but how nice it was once you were in it!

Grieving Mother moved back in with Natayah and they were both happy with the situation. They were sitting quietly by their small fire working on clothes for the baby when Talking Bird's oldest son came running through the door.

"Grandmother! My mother needs you! I think the baby is coming!" he shouted.

Grieving Mother nodded, "I thought it might be today. Go and take your brother out to Quannah's and wait there until we send for you."

"Yes. Grandmother. But hurry!" he ran back out the door.

"Oh, how exciting!" Natayah squealed. "What do I need to do?"

"I will go right now. If you could heat some water and bring it to her that would be very helpful."

"We can use this water, it is almost hot."

"That will be fine. I will see you over

there."

Natayah waited until the small bubbles formed along the side of the gourd that held the water. "That should be warm enough. We don't want to burn the little thing." She wrapped a blanket around the water and darted out the door.

A crowd was gathered around Talking Bird's door bundled in blankets and huddled together for word of the good news. Natayah pushed her way through and went inside.

"Oh Natayah, just in time. Tell everyone that it is a boy."

"A boy? Already? I missed everything?"

"Bring us the water."

Natayah walked over to Talking Bird who was lying on her back with the baby nestled to her breast. His beautiful black shiny hair was plastered to his head with blood and baby slime. Tears welled in her eyes. "Oh, Talking Bird, he is beautiful."

"He was in a hurry to get here!" she answered as Grieving Mother wiped Talking Bird's face with the warm water and cleaned off the baby.

Natayah struggled to turn away from staring at the beautiful newborn but everyone outside would be anxious for the news. She went back over to the door and announced, "It is her third son!" A roar of cheers came from the outside and congratulations were passed along.

Natayah went to help clean up the baby mess as mother and son gazed at each other.

"I am sorry that you did not get your daughter," Natayah offered.

"It is alright. My husband will be very proud. Three sons. Yes, he will be proud of this one. He is big and strong. He will be a good warrior."

Grieving Mother stayed with Talking Bird for two weeks before she came back to Natayah's weetu.

"He is a fine baby," she bragged. "You will have a good sized baby yourself. It may be difficult for you."

"Oh, I am ready. I want to hold him in my arms. I ache to count his fingers and toes, feel his soft skin. I hope his hair is like his father's." Natayah smiled as she daydreamed. "I hope that Little Feather returns in time to see the birth of his son."

"It is not common for the husband to be with the woman during childbirth."

"It is like that in my culture, too. The husband waits outside until everything is over and the room is returned the way it was. No sign of childbirth other than the baby."

"Yes, our men like to have little to do with it as well. But you say that my son wants to be here?"

"That is what we talked about."

Grieving Mother rolled her eyes. "My son is growing soft."

"I like him soft. He will be a good father."

"I think he will."

Every night Natayah would pray for the safe return of the men. All of the men rode on horseback which would mean they could cover more ground and travel faster. They carried with them, "snow shoes" which looked like tennis rackets and were made from willow branches. They attached them to their shoes to keep them from sinking too far into the snow. The men would do the bare minimum to prepare the buffalo for travel. Therefore, much of the innards and brain would be left behind or eaten along the way.

Natayah prayed for a prosperous hunt, and a safe one. She knew they needed food to help them through the winter, but selfishly, she just wanted her husband at home, with her.

Her baby grew bigger every day, so she added to her prayers that Little Feather would return in time to see him come into the world.

There were two boys on this trip that were expected to return as men. Their mothers were more emotional than she was, and she thought that was impossible. In two years, Talking Bird's oldest would be striving for that honor. Natayah was amazed that with a blink of time, her son would also be on that same journey.

Natayah was restless. She knew that the baby would be coming soon. She couldn't sleep. She got up and stepped out into the cold night air with the buffalo robe wrapped around her, barely covering her belly. The moon was full and a light snow was falling. The snowflakes were big and melted when they hit the ground. *"My favorite kind of snow,"* Natayah thought to herself.

The village was quiet as everyone was asleep. Natayah followed the gurgling and bubbling sound to lead her to the river. The moon sparkled over the shallow water as it bounced off the rocks. Ice was beginning to form around the edges and the snow was starting to stick.

The snow covered the ground lightly and made the world seem to glow. The furrows from their crops were stripped with snow; the rocks around her seemed to soak in the snow as it fell. She tipped her head back to watch the snowflakes fall right to her face. She smiled remembering her sister and herself walking to church.

"Catch them, Sarah," Katherine called out as she darted back and forth.

"I just like to watch them. It looks like the stars are falling," she answered quietly.

"Then just stick your tongue out, like this." Katherine pressed her tongue flat against her chin and tipped her head back. Her long blond braid swung behind her as she chased the flakes.

Sarah smiled and stuck her tongue out, and soon the girls were giggling and running into each other trying to catch the tiny frozen treats.

Natayah closed her eyes letting the memory surround her. She thought only for a moment where Josiah was. Did he speak with her sister? Would she know that she was safe and in love? "Katherine," she spoke out loud, "I am waiting for my son. My first in this second marriage. I wish you were here. I wish you could meet him." She closed her eyes and stuck her tongue out flat.

The first pain hit her while she stood there letting the cool drops melt on her warm tongue.

She grabbed her stomach and felt the tightness. "Not yet, little one, your daddy is not here yet." she spoke in English.

The contractions continued to come but they were far apart. She stayed out by the river for as long as she could breathe through the contractions, but when they cut off her breath, she started back to her weetu.

When she got to the weetu, Grieving Mother was already awake and bustling around the room. *"How does she always know?"* Natayah thought.

Grieving Mother looked up from her activity and smiled, "It is time?"

Natayah nodded and went over to her pallet to lie down.

"What are you doing?" Grieving Mother asked her, "Why are you in your bed?"

"Am I not supposed to be?" Natayah answered. "When Thomas was born, as soon as my water broke, the... the... 'doctor' put me in bed and would not let me out for two weeks!"

Grieving Mother shook her head, "No, no, no, no, you need to be up... walking. Go over and tell Talking Bird that the time has come."

Natayah's face said everything, and Grieving Mother had to swallow her snickers. "Are you sure?"

"Go, go, go." Grieving Mother waved her out the door. Another contraction hit before Natayah walked out the door. She held onto the door frame and breathed deeply through the pain. Grieving Mother stopped and watched. "Plenty of time," she said, "I may have you fetch some water!"

Natayah did have to fetch some water and pick up some sticks, even though she knew there was enough in the weetu. Talking Bird made thick porridge with powdered dry meat mixed in and had her eat the entire bowl.

"You will need your strength," Talking Bird told her.

"I know! Especially if you keep having me do all of these chores!"

The contractions grew stronger and Grieving Mother whispered to Talking Bird, "It is time." Grieving Mother pointed Natayah to her bed, which she made it to slowly between crippling contractions.

She lay down on her pallet on her back and drew her legs up to her chest.

Grieving Mother and Talking Bird looked at each other wondering what she was doing. "Did she not already have a baby once before?" Talking Bird leaned over to ask Grieving Mother.

"It must have been too long ago. Perhaps she has forgotten," Grieving Mother replied.

"You must roll over, daughter," Grieving Mother told Natayah as she moved to position at Natayah's feet. Natayah just stared at her. "Over," she said again and showed her hand motions. "On your hands and knees."

Natayah was in too much pain to argue, so she slowly rolled to her side. Another contraction. It caught her breath and she screamed out from the pain.

Talking Bird put a cool cloth on her forehead, "Try not to cry out. You must use that power to help you push."

Natayah nodded and made her way to her hands and knees. She found immediately that it took the pressure off her lower back and she was able to breathe easier.

"If you want to, you can put your arms around my neck to push, or you can stay like that," Talking Bird offered, positioned at her head.

"I like this," Natayah said breathlessly, "I do not want to move."

Grieving Mother looked over her shoulder to

see the first rays of sun shining in through the cracks around the closed window. "Your baby likes to start early," Grieving Mother commented.

"Unlike his mother!" Talking Bird teased.

Natayah's response was cut off by the next contraction. She began to scream but remembered the advice and used it toward pushing.

Natayah pushed and pushed, but the baby continued to slide back up the canal.

"I am getting tired," Natayah said. She dropped down to her elbows and sat back on her feet to catch her breath. Her belly lay on the ground between her knees. The baby was still.

"This is a stubborn one," Grieving Mother said.

"He is waiting for his father," Natayah replied. And then as if on cue, Little Feather came bursting through the door.

"Am I too late?" he asked running over to Natayah. Natayah started crying, "You are home. You are safe... I am so happy to see..." another contraction. Her arms were around Little Feather's neck and he supported her through the pain.

"What are you doing in here, son?" Grieving Mother scolded.

"This is my child. I did not want to miss it!"

"This is for women!" Grieving Mother tried to argue, but Natayah shouted out and Grieving Mother went back to her job. "The head! I see it!" Grieving Mother shouted. "With this next one, do not push so hard, nice and easy."

Natayah nodded her head into Little Feather's neck. He supported her with all his heart and his strength. His hands were on her lower back and her arms were around his neck. The contraction came and Natayah breathed through it controlling the push.

He put a cool cloth on her neck and spoke words of encouragement in her ear as the head was delivered.

"Is it a boy?" Little Feather asked.

His mother looked at him and explained, "Just the head is out and it is not talking yet. You will have to wait." She shook her head and leaned down to tend to her newest grandchild mumbling about men butting in where they don't belong.

One more contraction, one more push, and there it was. "It is a boy!" Grieving Mother shouted out through tears.

"A son," Little Feather repeated. "You gave me a son." He kissed her cheeks, nose, forehead and hair. "A son!" Little Feather helped her lay down on her back and propped her head and shoulders up with a pillow. Grieving Mother placed her new son in her arms.

Tears ran off Natayah's face and landed on her slimy little son who was now feeding at her breast.

"He is so beautiful," Natayah said through her tears. Little Feather looked over her shoulder and gently touched his coal black hair and counted the fingers on his tiny little hand, as they wrapped around his daddy's finger. His skin was a shade lighter than his father's and the only thing that gave away a different heritage was his deep blue eyes. Just like his mother's.

"Oh, woman. He is so beautiful. You have made me so proud." Little Feather kissed her temple and then her cheek. He leaned over and kissed the little fingers that clung to his. The baby's blue eyes connected with his fathers and then looked over to his mother.

"You are alright for a moment?" Little Feather asked her. Natayah nodded and Little Feather said, "Good, I will be right back." He stood up and ran outside. The women watched him go out in only his breeches, but then they heard, "I HAVE A SON!!"

When the naming ceremony came along, there were four babies to be announced. Two girls and two boys.

Talking Bird's son went first. His name was to be: Ta-wan-ah-hay-su which means; Son Number Three of a Warrior. His name may change as he grows older and begins to develop different qualities or traits, but for the next few years this was his title. Two Spear strutted around with his son over his head and Talking Bird looked on with pride.

Natayah had spoken to the chief about the naming of her son. She requested that part of it be from the Bible, and that the chief could choose the other part. The chief nodded in agreement and said he would give great thought to it. "It is lucky that I consider you my daughter. You happen to be a favorite of mine."

Natayah went against protocol, again, and leaned over to kiss his wrinkled cheek.

"Thank you, father," she whispered.

Natayah and Little Feather waited anxiously for the announcement of their son's name.

The chief stood beside the couple and brushed the baby's face with his feathered staff.

The little babe wrinkled his nose and sneezed. Little Feather looked out to the crowd and announced, "My son sneezed!" The crowd laughed. "New father," Natayah looked past him and explained to everyone. They laughed again.

The chief came and stood in front of this new family. "You have been blessed. The name for this strong young warrior, the first of the house of Little Feather is; Jacob Na-nah-hae. Jacob Blue Eyes."

Elizabeth Bourgeret

Chapter Nineteen

Sometimes, for revenge to be as sweet and painful as it is intended, some time has to pass. Time enough that people have forgotten about past hurts and humiliations. Time enough to make the poison of bitterness consume a soul. It was to be that time…
Two worlds collide and find a common link. A plan was made, a price was paid and revenge was set in motion.

The village was all a buzz about the army encampment that had settled less than fifty miles from the village.

The chief called for a meeting and invited Natayah along. Jacob was now three years old so Natayah and Little Feather walked him over to play with his cousins.

As they walked on to the meeting, Natayah spoke, "Did you hear that your son is teaching his cousins to speak English? I do not know whether to be embarrassed or proud!"

"He knows more than I do, and I have known you longer," Little Feather replied.

"You never wanted to learn," she teased.

"What would I need with English? Besides you seemed happy enough talking to your horse."

Natayah elbowed him and laughed. "I guess you will teach this boy to speak English too?" Little Feather asked.

"Oh, no. This one is a girl," Natayah said running her hands over the tiny bump at her stomach. "There are too many men in my house!"

"What do they want here?" the chief stood and paced the length of his platform.

"We should take no chances," Black Elk stood to speak. "We should attack now before they have the chance to attack us!"

"They have shown no signs of aggression," Little Feather said. "They might just be resting their horses."

"Or they might be here for good!" Black Elk shouted.

"But if we attack first," Little Feather continued, "and they did not even know we were living here that will mean more will come in retaliation."

"Let them come!" Two Spear shouted.

"We are ready for them!" Grey Wolf joined in.

"No. You are not," Natayah spoke softly. The room grew quiet and all eyes turned toward the woman. She gathered her confidence and raised her head to meet the men head on. "You may feel like you are great in number, but believe me, we are very small. The village that I came from is the size of five or six of this village. And there are so many more than just my village." She lowered her head hating to have to say these things to this proud group of men. "When my village divided and I left to join another, there were only a few wagon train trails, now, I have seen many. You know, more men and their families will continue to come."

"What do you suggest, daughter?"

"Why do you not try and talk with them? Ask them why they are here," Natayah spoke meekly and humbly. "If they are here to do us harm, you will know and can respond. I would be most honored to be your voice with the white man, father."

Little Feather looked over at his wife and smiled. He was proud, but he was also concerned for her safety. "I understand that you want to befriend them, but I do not want any harm to come to you and our child."

"They will not harm me. It is against their beliefs to harm a woman. I am certain that no harm will come to me. And if I go with the Chief of a great tribe, they will know that I am there for business."

"I like your plan, Natayah," the chief said, "but let us wait for another moon cycle to see if they do not move on their own first."

Natayah lay nestled in her husband's arms as he slept, wrapped around her. Her thoughts were of the men in uniform. She lay awake as she remembered unwillingly, the last time she saw the likes of them. It was many years ago now. A left-over painful memory.

"Husband," Natayah whispered barely nudging Little Feather. His head shot up and he looked over his home and looked over to his son's pallet. "Are you well, wife? What is wrong?"

Natayah giggled, "All is well, husband."

"Why did you wake me?"

"Would you..." she rolled over to face him. His arm lifted enough for her to move then he placed it back over her body. "Would you... take me to see the grave of my son?"

Little Feather raised up to his elbow, and looked down to her face. "Why do you want to do that? He is not there. Have you not told me time and time again that when we die, our soul leaves our body and joins God in His heaven?"

"I did. Yes. And that is so, but I just miss him. When I look at Jacob, I think of what great brothers and friends they could have been. And now, with this one coming, my thoughts..."

"I understand."

"I never got to say goodbye," she added.

"It is a few days ride, but we can go tomorrow if you like."

"I would, thank you." She smiled meekly at him. "I will make arrangements with your mother to stay with Jacob."

"As you wish, wife. Can I sleep now?" he dropped his head down on his bent elbow.

Natayah smiled, "I guess you can... if you want."

He popped open one eye, and a smile spread across his face.

The next morning Natayah packed a sack of food for their journey.

"Are you sure you should go with all the white men everywhere?" Grieving Mother asked, with Jacob standing in front of her.

"We will move quickly, and stay to the

woods."

Grieving Mother nodded and kissed them each.

"Jacob, you are the man of the house while I am away. You take care of your grandmother."

A wide grin crossed his face. "I will father. She will be safe with me."

Little Feather nodded and pat his shoulder. Natayah, however, was much more affectionate. She scooped him up in her arms and smothered his face with embarrassing kisses. "Mother!"

"Just because you will be the man of the house does not mean you will ever be too big to be kissed by your mother!" Natayah snuggled her nose into his neck and tickled him with tiny kisses. He squealed out and she attacked his ribs and soon he was wriggling out of her arms in peals of laughter. They were both laughing as he crawled between his grandmother's legs and peeked around them.

Natayah bent down and held her hand out. Jacob came back to his mother and allowed himself to be wrapped in her arms. "I love you, little man."

"I love you too, mama."

Little Feather cleared his throat and Natayah stepped away from her second born son, with first-born status, to visit the grave of Thomas, the brother, he would never know.

Their ride was quiet and thoughtful.

When they reached the sight of the massacre, an eerie silence blew across the open prairie. There was no sign that this had once been covered with blood and bodies and destroyed wagons. A vision of a new tomorrow, a different future, that these people had risked their lives for, ended here.

A lump grew in her throat and Little Feather stayed back as Natayah rode on to survey the land. Deep ruts tracked across the land to show that their train had not been the last. It showed that the efforts made by the Seapaugh Indians and their kind to stop the white invasion had failed. Natayah's emotions were torn. She looked back at the man that she chose for her husband. He sat on his beautiful cream-colored horse with his head down, deep in thought.

Natayah sent up a prayer as she took in the land as far as the eye could see. She turned back to her husband and gently asked, "Where is the grave?"

Saying nothing he clicked at his horse and turned him away from the pasture. Natayah followed. They rode until they came to a wooded area. Little Feather dismounted and came back to assist his wife. Then, he pointed into the woods.

Natayah followed his direction and saw the raised grave nestled into the trees. A person would have to be looking for it to see it. She walked slowly, reverently towards it. Tears stung her eyes and it was difficult to swallow.

The poles of the raised shrine were decorated with feathers and a bull's skull. She looked up and saw that a small, child sized bow and quiver of arrows hung close to edge. A tear slipped from her eye as she went through the motion of attempting to reach it. She pulled her arm back down to her body. She saw that he placed his toys at the foot of his "bed". He was too high for her to reach, so she leaned her head against one of the poles. "My baby," she whispered. "Thomas, I miss you so. I have forgiven the men that made these actions come to pass. I hope that you have too. I know that you are with the angels in Heaven and feel no pain or worry. I am sure that you are happy. If I thought otherwise, I surely would not be able to go on. This man that has taken care of your needs is now my husband. He is a good man, and loves me very much. It is obvious to see in the care he has given you, that he loved you as well," she drew in a ragged breath and wiped the tears from her face. "I will not be back here again. I know that you are no longer of this earth. We will meet again, when our Lord deems it is time. I wait patiently for that day, my son. I love you and will never forget you." She sniffed in again, and ran her fingers down along the pole. She turned to leave and looked back again, knowing it would be for the last time, "Goodbye, Thomas."

On the night before they were going to meet the white men, Chief Spotted Eagle gathered everyone together for a feast. The nights were warm and the crops had been planted. They deserved a celebration.

There was dancing and music and food. Jacob and his cousins danced around the fire just like the adults. Natayah and Little Feather looked on as their son grew into a man, almost right in front of them. The people dressed in their finest clothes and talked and mingled, sang and danced, while rejoicing together for a good harvest and a peaceful meeting with the white man. Even as the festivities went on, no one wished this more than Little Feather. There was no fear in his wife's eyes. She was strong and courageous. He was overcome by the music and got up to take his wife's hand and danced with her around the circle of fire. Jacob joined in between them and they celebrated together as a family.

As the night wore on, the chief addressed his people.

"Tomorrow, we go and visit the white army. We will take them gifts to show that we come in peace and offer good will. My daughter, Natayah, will come with me and be my voice. We are hoping for a peaceful union with our two tribes." He looked to his sons who stood beside him, "My youngest son, Runs With The Wind, will stand by as our lookout. If there is any cause for alarm, he will alert our warriors. And…" he paused, "if anything should happen to me, Black Elk, my oldest son, will lead you into battle." The men in the crowd roared with support and raised their fists in the air. The chief continued, "I hope it does not come to that."

"Mother," Jacob asked as the chief continued his speech.

"Yes, son," Natayah whispered still trying to listen.

"I think I should go with you."

Natayah smiled down at him and ran her hand over his smooth black hair, and he looked up at her from her lap, "Why is that?"

"Because, I am the eldest son of my father and I speak English, too."

"That will make you very valuable to your

chief one day, son, but not yet."

"Why not?"

"Because if anything happened to me, you will need to look after your father."

"Mother, I do not want anything to happen to you."

"I do not either. But you need to stay here, just in case."

"Yes. Mother."

"And we hope to create a working union between our two peoples." the chief concluded.

The next morning, Natayah braided her hair in one long braid down her back. She wore a dress that covered her belly so as not to bring attention to it.

Little Feather came up behind her and kissed her neck. He reached his arms around her stomach. "Are you sure about this?" he asked.

"I am nervous," she answered truthfully. "What if my English is not right anymore? What if I have forgotten?"

"You could not have forgotten. That horse will not listen to anyone else but you!"

"I am serious."

"You do not have to do this."

She turned to face her husband, "I love you... so much," she began slowly. "If... something... were to happen to me..." she took in a deep breath, "husband, please. Do not seek revenge. Jacob needs you and if you attack the white men, you will surely die."

He saw her lip begin to tremble and he

lowered his head to touch hers. "I cannot make you that promise. I would not be able to sleep… eat…breathe until I paid for your…" he shook his head. "I cannot make you that promise."

She cupped his face in her hands, "Then, I shall just have to return." She smiled as she looked up at him. She ran her fingers over his ear and stroked his hair drinking in the sight of him.

"Yes," he leaned down to kiss her. "Yes, come back. My life is not complete without you." He wrapped his arms around her and held her tight.

"I promise. I will return," she whispered. He squeezed her and breathed in the scent of her hair. She pulled back and looked up at him. "I promise," she said again. He nodded and leaned in to kiss her deeply.

A horn blew outside and Natayah and Little Feather stepped outside their weetu. Jacob jumped onto his dad and Little Feather effortlessly lifted the boy up to his shoulders.

The woman began a chant while men joined the chorus in low humming. Someone was keeping time with a drum. Natayah could not see; her eyes shimmered with tears. She lifted her chin and settled things with herself. No tears. No tears.

Chief Spotted Eagle, Runs With the Wind, and Two Spear mounted their horses. Natayah reached up to kiss her son perched on top of his father then she hugged her husband again, before he helped her onto her horse.

"If there is any sign of trouble, run," he whispered to her. "Two Spear will ride along half way and wait to hear from Runs With the Wind. Be safe and take care of our son," he smiled and rubbed her belly.

"Daughter," she smiled, blew a kiss to Jacob and nodded to the others. She nudged the horse and they rode off. Natayah turned one last time to see her husband and son…but not again, for fear they would see the tears in her eyes.

Elizabeth Bourgeret

Chapter Twenty

As they rode on the chief explained some of the things he wanted to say. Natayah nodded and offered suggestions about proper etiquette.

Runs With the Wind stayed far ahead of them and Two Spear stayed behind. So Natayah and the chief rode much of the way with just each other for company.

"I see that you are in love with Little Feather and that he made the right choice with you."

"Thank you. I do love him."

"You make a pretty good Indian," he chuckled, the creases growing deep around his eyes.

"It took long enough!" she laughed.

"But you did not give up. I thought you were going to die of grief before we ever left the hunting grounds many years ago."

"I am sure that I will never completely heal from those wounds, but God has blessed me and that helps lesson the pain."

"Did your God give you direction in this?"

"I prayed and prayed, father, but I did not get a response. So I travel on faith."

"Yes. I believe that is all that we can do sometimes."

In the distance, they could see Runs With the Wind talking with three other Indians.

"Who is he talking to?" Natayah asked.

"I do not know. I cannot see." Chief

Spotted Eagle answered. They rode further and Natayah gasped, "Is that Wild Dog?"

"It looks like it could be. I wonder what he is doing out here."

Natayah rolled her eyes and took in a deep breath, "I cannot stand him father."

"I know. Let us see what he wants."

Natayah pouted and slumped her shoulders. She let her horse fall a couple of paces behind the chief.

"You are the one always promoting peace, if I remember correctly, daughter," he called back to her over his shoulder.

Natayah laughed in spite of herself and the chief smiled back at her. His eyes shone and he looked pleased to be in Natayah's company. That look was recorded into her memory for all the rest of her life.

Natayah straightened up to face the unexpected guests.

"Greetings to you cousin," Wild Dog hissed.

Natayah stayed silent and kept her horse behind the chief.

"Wild Dog," the chief spoke with authority. "We do not have time to visit now. We have important business to attend to."

"Yes, I know all about your plans to visit with the white troops. And I am afraid it would interfere with my dealings with them." He smiled and looked past the chief to Natayah. In English he spoke, "Hello, Sarah."

Natayah's eyes grew wide and her heart skipped a beat. Wild Dog withdrew a knife from his waistband and lunged at the chief. Chief Spotted Eagle thwarted the attack with the side of his spear by knocking Wild Dog's arm away.

"Go, Natayah ride!" the chief shouted. Natayah kicked her horse to run but the chief's horse was in the way, so Clara reared up on her hind legs. Natayah held on tightly until Clara found her balance. She kicked her once again and Clara took off running with one of the men close behind her. He jumped from his horse to hers and took hold of her reins. She fought against his grip of her and slid down off the horse. Natayah ran back toward the chief, but found him slumped over his horse with blood dripping down the horse's leg.

Wild Dog rode alongside her and picked her up by the back of her dress. He threw her over his horse and rode back to his other two men.

"I knew we would meet again, Sarah." Wild Dog spoke in English. He threw her down to the ground and slid off his horse in front of her. She fell next to the dead body of Runs With the Wind. His throat had been cut open and blood rapidly draining from the gash. The screams she felt inside would not leave her throat. She stared in horror as the body flinched and pulsed.

"As much as I would love to just kill you, I am afraid that our mutual friend wants you alive. But, luckily for me, he wants you battered and abused. He doesn't have the stomach for it… so, this might hurt a little," he struck her with the back of his hand across her face.

Natayah cried out and brought her hand to her mouth. He kicked her in her back. She wrapped her arms around her belly, her head scraped against the ground.

"Please…" she barely muttered through her bruised face, "… my baby…" Her plea fell on deaf ears, but thankfully the next blow knocked her unconscious.

They gathered her limp body and tied her onto her horse. Wild Dog hopped on his horse and the three rode away with Clara and her unconscious passenger, Natayah, following behind.

Not long after, Two Spear came upon the scene of the two dead men. He jumped off his horse and checked for signs of life. He swore at the clouds and fell to his knees. He saw the blood on the ground. He crawled over to it and knew that it must have been Natayah's. The blood trail led away from the gruesome scene. Was she alive? Was she a trophy?

He was torn. Should he follow the fresh trail of blood or return to the village to sound the alarm. He followed the trail for a time and saw that it led away from the white village. "Who has done this?" he wondered. To his left the white man's village, to his right, the trail continues. "Little Feather will want to know," he decided, and he turned toward his village to tell his best friend and brother-in-law.

Natayah heard voices as she regained consciousness.

"… the amount we agreed upon." a voice said.

"A war will be started against the white man as soon as they discover the chief and his son lying dead on the trail. They will no doubt blame the whites and will attack before the end of the day," Wild Dog was saying in English.

"I don't care about a war. I care about my

reward and Little Feather dying."

"It will be done. He will come after his white wife, so I would make your exchange soon," Wild Dog instructed.

Natayah's horse was pulled into motion again and she slipped back to unconsciousness.

It took no time at all to gather the warriors to go after the chief's murderer.

"I knew those white men could not be trusted!" Grey Wolf called out.

"It was not the white men," Two Spears said. "It was not their kind of horse prints. I believe it was one of our own."

"And Natayah was not with them?" Little Feather asked.

Two Spear shook his head. "I cannot be sure she was still alive. Four horses left the area, all had riders."

"How do we know that she did not betray us?" Tree Owl yelled.

Little Feather jumped from his horse and pulled Tree Owl from his. Little Feather put his hands around his throat and had no intentions of letting go.

"Little Feather! Stop. We are wasting valuable time. If you want to find your wife alive, we must go." Two Spear held his arms until he stopped his struggle and let go of Tree Owl. "Calm yourself, brother. This will do her no good."

Little Feather nodded and walked away from Tree Owl.

Two Spear looked down on Tree Owl as he gasped for air. "You are a fool. Natayah would not betray her people." He kicked a spray of dust at Tree Owl before returning to his horse.

Little Feather looked over at his son who was playing quietly with his cousins, unaware of the panic of the village men. Jacob looked up and caught his father's gaze. Little Feather did his best to smile, which Jacob returned. Little Feather winked and got onto his horse. Jacob did his best to wink back, but ended up scrunching up most of his face in the effort. The proud father smiled even as the lump in his throat threatened to choke him. He nodded after him and turned and followed the other men out of the village.

Two horses galloped at full speed into the army barricade.

"Help! Help! Please somebody help me!"

A dozen or so men ran out to meet the man on the horse. A woman was draped across his lap. "Help her first. Please hurry. She's been badly hurt. Probably for some time."

Two men pulled her limp unconscious body from his lap. Another man took the reins of the Indian marked horse that was tied to his saddle.

"What happened to her?" one man asked.

"She was a captive of the Indian tribe that has a village about sixty miles from here. I saved her and now," he sputtered breathlessly, "I think they are after me."

"Her wounds are quite severe. I'll have our doctor take a look at her Mister…"

"Cooper, Josiah Cooper."

The group of warriors came upon Wild Dog and his two other men.

They stopped and smiled at their "cousin" group.

"Black Elk," Wild Dog said, "What brings you out here?"

"Do you not know?" Black Elk growled at him.

"No, why should I?"

Black Elk nodded and was just about to ask them for their assistance when Wild Dog added, "How is your father?" It was the slightest smirk that sent Little Feather from his horse.

"Where is she?" he yelled. "Where is my wife?" Little Feather grabbed his leg and pulled Wild Dog to the ground.

"Honestly, Little Feather, I do not know where she is."

Little Feather pulled his knife from its sheath. "You are a liar!" he placed it at Wild Dog's throat and spoke through gritted teeth, "Where. Is. She."

"Alright. I will tell you what I know. But I had nothing to do with it." Wild Dog stood up and stared at Little Feather. "The last that I saw her, she was still alive. A white man was taking her into the white man's camp."

Little Feather lowered his knife and was ready to walk away when Wild Dog added, "Here is an extra piece of advice," he sneered, "You should probably go back and hide your families, because the white man is coming to kill them."

The men looked at each other wondering if they should believe him or not.

"What have you done?" Black Elk pointed

his question at Wild Dog while sliding off of his mount.

"Nothing you did not deserve." He spit on the ground at Black Elk's feet. The spit still hung from his mouth and there were scratches covered with dirt on his chest. "I gave you a warning of what is to come. Take it and leave me."

"You have turned against your own people," Black Elk accused.

"This coming from you? You, who let a white woman into your village and bed your warrior? You allow her to ride alongside your chief?" Wild Dog walked over to Little Feather and finished his statement, "It is you who turned against your people. I made it right."

"What did you do to her?" Little Feather grew impatient.

"Like I said, your wife was alive when the white man took her from me, but I cannot say the same about the baby. There was a lot of blo…"

Little Feather pulled his knife from Wild Dog's throat as quickly as he had thrust it in. Wild Dog grabbed his throat trying desperately to keep the blood from pouring from between his fingers. His eyes rolled back in his head and he fell to the ground. Dead.

Black Elk nodded to his other two warriors that held Wild Dog's accomplices and they were killed.

"Do you think he was telling the truth about the white man attacking?" someone asked.

"I do not know. He was probably lying to regain our trust," Black Elk said. He looked to Little Feather, "Are you still going after your wife?"

"Of course I am!" Little Feather shouted.

"But the white man has her," Red Rock reminded him.

"She is my wife. I must go."

"I am sorry, about your wife," Black Elk said. "I cannot risk all of our lives for this one woman. You have avenged my father's death, and I am grateful. But the duty of the village has become mine. I must think about the village now." The two men clasped forearms and nodded to each other. "I must attend to my father's funeral."

"I understand," Little Feather said. The two men turned and mounted their horses. Two Spear gave him details as to where he could find his father's and brother's bodies. Black Elk thanked him and headed away from Little Feather.

Two Spear pulled his horse alongside Little Feather's. "I will go with you," Two Spear said. "We will find her."

"Good luck and safe return," Black Elk called after them.

They waited until they could no longer see Black Elk. Two Spear leaned toward Little Feather, "My wife would kill me if I came home without you and Natayah."

"I am glad you are here, my friend and brother." The rest was left unsaid.

"My baby! My baby… is my baby alright?" Natayah asked in her moments of consciousness.

"She is speaking some kind of gibberish," a voice said.

"Her face is swollen, give her some morphine for the pain," another voice said.

"Help me." she said in English, "I have to

get back home."

"That poor girl. What a trial she must have gone through," the voice said. "There now, you rest. We'll have you home in no time."

Natayah drifted back to sleep.

"Doctor, can she travel?"

"I'm sorry son; she needs at least a few days rest." The doctor wiped the sweat from her forehead and washed his hands in the bloody basin of water.

"I'm only takin' her to St. Louis. Her sister is there waiting for her. And those Injuns, they'll be after me soon, if they ain't already."

"Mr. Cooper, I'm sure they won't try to attack the United States Army."

"Yes, sir, they would. They killed five white folk right in front of me. I'm telling you, they have no souls."

The doctor rubbed his chin in thought. "Perhaps it would be in her best interest to get her safely back home as soon as possible. I'll talk with the captain to see if we can expedite things."

"The tracks lead right into their camp." Little Feather said as he crouched low to the ground.

"What is your plan?" Two Spear asked.

"I do not know. There are too many men for us to charge in. Natayah strongly believes that the white people will not harm her. So I do not want to do anything to risk that. You said there was blood?" Two Spear nodded. "She is probably hurt. I am going to have to trust that the white men will help her. We will wait until she is rested. The white man will use his white medicine on her. We will have to sneak in at night in a day or two and bring her back."

"Look at all of those tents. How will we know where she is?"

Little Feather smiled up at Two Spear, "That horse of hers. It will be where she is."

"I do not see it from here."

"Watch carefully... Here she comes," Little Feather said and put his fingers in his mouth and let out a shrill whistle.

Suddenly, Clara reared up on her hind legs and whinnied.

"I see her!" Two Spear called out.

Clara broke free from the ropes that had loosely bound her. She was tied to a post near the rear of the encampment. She took off running with about twelve soldiers running after her. She ran towards the center of the camp and knocked down a clothes line but refused to be captured. The men would not give up the chase either. One man had a rope and was tying a lasso in one end. Clara stopped as the men circled around her. She looked confused. Little Feather whistled again and all the soldiers' plus one horse looked up to the hills. Clara galloped back to the rear entrance and made her way out of the camp and ran towards the two Indian men waiting for her just over the top of the hill.

A group of men in uniform shot their guns blindly in the direction the horse was running.

"What are they shooting at?" Two Spear asked.

"They had better not kill that horse," Little Feather shook his head. "My wife will be furious!"

"There is no way their guns can reach us," Two Spear laughed. He stood up from his crouching position and waved. Half of the men turned in the other direction and began shooting. Two Spear could barely contain himself, "What are they doing?"

"Two Spear, look over there, to the left. Is that Josiah?"

Two Spear crouched back down. "The white man that stayed with us?"

"Yes! That is him! I should have killed him when I had the chance."

The horse bounded up the hill and stopped short of running over Little Feather. They took the horse deeper into the woods.

Little Feather spoke in English, "Good girl… good girl…" he patted her on the neck.

"What did you say to her?" Two Spear asked.

"I have no idea, but Natayah says that to her all the time," Little Feather tied Clara to his horse while the army continued to shoot into the air. They snuck away, back to their village to work out a plan.

"Hold your fire!" Captain Dunbar called out to his men, "Hold your fire!"

Josiah walked over to the captain, clearly pale and afraid. "You see? They're coming. They want their captive back and they will steal your horses and kill us all! They're just toyin' with us now. They'll be back. I promise ya."

"I was told that the indigenous people that lived in this area were peaceful for the most part.

Captive Heart

Apparently, I have been misinformed."

"Please, Captain Dunbar, you gotta get me outta here."

"Mr. Cooper, I am not in the habit of uprooting my men…"

"Captain?" It was the doctor. "I'm afraid I have some troubling news. The girl… she is…"

"Well, spit it out, man!"

"The girl is… expecting."

"You mean a baby?"

Josiah held his breath not knowing what their response would be, and the doctor nodded.

"The heathens!" the captain growled through his breath. "That poor woman has been through enough." He turned to Josiah and tugged on the brim of his hat, "Mr. Cooper, your request will be granted. In light of this new information, she should be transported to St. Louis. I will send two of my men to escort you." The captain started shouting orders and men began running in every direction.

"Mr. Cooper. You say you know the exact coordinates to that village?"

"Yes, sir," Josiah said as the unseen glare of retribution flashed across his face.

"Those savages will be dealt with accordingly," Captain Dunbar said almost to himself.

Elizabeth Bourgeret

Chapter Twenty- One

The soft smell of roses filled her senses. Soft cushions surrounded her. She was unable to open her eyes. Someone was humming nearby.

"Grieving Mother, are you there?"

"Sarah... Sarah honey, are you alright?"

She lay there quiet and still, listening for clues. Her thoughts were spinning and the pain was intense. *"I am losing my mind,"* she thought. She wanted to open her eyes. "Grieving Mother, tell me you are here. Am I dead? I am hearing the voice of my sister. Am I going crazy?"

"Sarah, oh Sarah, please come back to me. Can you hear me?" Katherine put a cool cloth on her face and neck. "It's me, sister... your Katherine."

Is this a dream? She could feel her heart race. Tears burned her eyes. *"Why is God doing this to me?"* she thought. Her mind raced through the possibilities. Is she back at home in the bedroom she shared with her sister in the days of her youth? Did any of it happen? She tried to take in a deep breath and she smelled again the familiar scent of roses. Her sister's favorite.

"Katherine?" she spoke in a whisper.

"Yes! Yes! It's me!" Katherine smiled and sat down on the bed alongside her sister. She wiped a tear from her cheek and re-soaked the washcloth with cool water and wrung it out.

Elizabeth Bourgeret

"Where is mother? Why can't I see her? Why is she not here?"

Katherine furrowed her brow and thought, she doesn't know where we are. Should I tell her? "Sarah, you had an... accident. Your eyes are bandaged and your hands and legs..."

"I don't remember..."

"It's alright, sister, you're safe. The doctor says you should rest."

"Am I at home or in a hospital?"

"You're at... my home." Katherine said gently.

Sarah furrowed her brow as the thoughts went racing through her mind. Her home. Her home?

"Where am I? Where is mother? Mother!" She sat up in bed and tried to pull the bandages from her eyes.

"Sarah, no, don't do that! Nurse! Help me quickly!"

Sarah struggled to be allowed to see against the pain she felt. Was it real? Did everything happen? Did anything happen? She kicked against the arms trying to hold her down. She shouted out in her Indian language, "Little Feather, take me home! Where are you! I need you!" A moist cloth covered her face and a bitter smell overtook her senses, then, she felt herself drifting off to sleep. "No, Katherine, don't do this." She stopped fighting and before she drifted off, she heard her sister crying.

"What have they done to you, Sarah?"

Several days went by and the doctors kept Sarah mostly sedated with laudanum.

She barely ate and was too tired to sit up. Every day, she could feel someone come in and roll her from one side and then to the other. Some days she would be pulled up higher on the bed and be expected to sit. The drug made her dizzy. All she wanted to do was sleep. She could no longer feel the pain of her wounds; she could feel nothing.

Katherine held Sarah up while the nurse stacked the pillows behind her.

"Sarah, I have good news for you. The doctor will be here soon and he says that it's time for the bandages to come off. Isn't that wonderful?"

No response.

"Perhaps that will help to improve your appetite. Food always tastes better when you can see it." Katherine did her best to keep talking; maybe more for her own benefit than for Sarah's. "Soon you'll be up and walking again." she searched for conversation. "The doctor says that you can stop taking the laudanum now, but if you feel you need more, I can…"

"Katherine," Sarah spoke in a meek hoarse voice, "I wanted to thank you for all of your letters."

Katherine didn't know what to say. She looked down at the sheet she was folding and toyed with its corners. A silent tear slid down her cheek.

"They helped me through some difficult times," Sarah paused before adding, "Thomas is dead."

Katherine went over to Sarah's bed and picked up her bandaged hand, "Yes. We know."

Sarah nodded and said nothing.

The doctor came to take off the bandages. He instructed that the shades be pulled and for Sarah to keep her eyes closed.

He used the scissors to cut the first layer and slowly unwrapped the second layer. He removed the pads from her eyelids and said, "Alright, now Sarah, whenever you are ready, you may open your eyes."

The first thing she saw was the pattern of little yellow rose buds scattered across a pure white background. She saw her own hands next. The scrapes were healing but were still tender. She lifted her head and saw a grey haired man with spectacles smiling at her. To her left...

Uncontrollable tears poured from her eyes as she looked upon her sister's face for the first time in years. Katherine's face was also wet with tears as they gazed at each other. No words could describe this moment for the two sisters.

"Your hair," Sarah finally said, "has it always been so blonde?" The two laughed.

"Me? Your hair used to be so much darker. Look at all the blonde in your red curls."

Sarah laughed as she cried, but couldn't take her eyes away. "I... never thought I would see you again," she said through tears.

"You are such a beautiful sight to me too, sister. I have prayed every day for this moment."

The two sisters embraced and cried. The doctor showed himself out, "I think my work here is done..."

As Katherine pulled back to grab a handkerchief for herself and her sister, all they could do was stare at each other. Katherine's hair was piled on top of her head in a nice, neat bun. The dress she wore was a silver-grey fabric and was cut to show her body shape. "I made a dress with that shape out of leather. It was beautiful. They all thought I looked silly. I thought it was pretty," Sarah mumbled sleepily.

Katherine took the washcloth and wiped her sister's face.

"Sister," Katherine began, "It is so good to see you. We have so much to catch up on. You'll have to meet my brood and James is so looking forward to seeing you." She caught herself talking again to keep from touching on sensitive issues that filled the room like a heavy weight.

"Katherine," Sarah began.

"You're so… tan" Katherine kept on. "Whatever are we going to do with all of those freckles," she laughed nervously. She picked up Sarah's hand and turned it over in her own. Katherine traced her fingers over the callused and cracked skin on Sarah's working hands. Another wave of tears. "I'm sorry, Sarah. I told myself that I would be strong."

"Katherine…"

"Sister, you don't have to talk about it until you are ready…"

"Katherine. I'm not supposed to be here."

"I know. It's a miracle. The doctor said that you will be back to your old self in no time. There will be some scarring…"

"How did I get here?" Sarah interrupted.

Katherine's face lit up. "Oh Sarah, that's the

wonderful part. I am happy to tell you that Josiah Cooper is your hero! He saved you. We wanted to thank him with a reception when you were feeling better, but he would have none of it. What a humble servant. He really wanted no fanfare at all. We are so indebted to him. The meager reward we offered could not begin to show our gratitude." Katherine brought Sarah's hands up to her lips and kissed them gently.

Sarah felt nauseous. She felt used and betrayed. Sarah shook her head from side to side and cried. It was a deep aching cry that came from her soul. She withdrew her hands from Katherine and covered her face, as the tears would not stop.

Katherine was powerless to console her so she excused herself from the room and cried for her sister's pain outside her door.

Katherine's husband, James came to her side when he saw her sitting on a small parlor chair in the hall.

He heard Sarah's wailing on the other side of the door. "What happened?" he asked his wife quietly bending down to kneel beside her.

"Oh, James, she is so distraught. I can't bear to know the agonies she has suffered. I told myself that I would listen, but I don't think I'll be able to... listen to her, James. How she suffers. I don't know that I can stomach to hear the events of the past several years."

James took his wife's hands in his own, "This will take time, my love. It will be an adjustment, for all of us. We just have to do the best that we can."

Katherine nodded, but was not comforted.

"Does she know?" James continued with

hesitation.

"About the baby?" Katherine answered, "I don't know. It would have been more merciful if it had died." Katherine shook with another burst of tears. "How could this have happened, James?" She hiccupped through her tears, "My poor, poor sister."

Sarah cried herself to sleep that night. The next morning when Katherine brought breakfast into Sarah's room, she found her sitting at the window looking down at the street.

Sarah looked at all the people, their clothes, the tall buildings; even taller than she remembered. There was glass on the windows and cushions on her chair. The walls of her room were smooth and covered with a pretty flowered design. Sarah laughed to herself... shoes.

"Good morning, sister," Katherine forced a smile and brought the breakfast tray over to the table beside where Sarah was sitting.

"I had forgotten," Sarah began as she fingered the silver fork. "All the... luxuries."

"It's good to see you up," Katherine smiled. "I thought you might like something a little heavier than broth this morning. Do you think you are up to it?"

Katherine pulled the lid from the plate to reveal eggs, bacon, new potatoes, and biscuits with honey. Sarah smiled and thought, luxuries.

"It looks delicious. I couldn't possibly refuse such a splendid looking meal."

Katherine sat in the chair opposite Sarah at

the same small round table. She nervously played with the lace trim that was sewn along the edges of the tablecloth.

Sarah ate the food as though she hadn't eaten in days. She stopped for a moment and looked at the utensil in her right hand. "A fork," she said amused.

"You look so much better today. It's amazing what a little sunshine can do to your complexion," Katherine smiled gently. "I thought that you might like a bath today... if you were feeling up to it."

"A bath?" Sarah asked, "In a real bathtub?"

"Yes. A real bathtub," Katherine snickered. "I'll have Matilda draw one up for you. And I'll have some new clothes put in the washroom for you, too." Katherine's eyes drifted down to Sarah's midsection. She blinked in embarrassment for staring, "Sarah, I hate to bring up... unpleasantness...um, so early in the day, but," she drew in a deep breath, "are you aware that you... are... with child?" Katherine breathed out and looked down at her hands uncomfortably.

"Sister, don't be silly. Of course I know. How could I not? Look at the size of me!" she laughed nervously.

"Yes, of course. I'm sorry. I could look into... places that...take... those kinds of children... and you would never even have to see it." There. She said it.

Sarah was shocked. She couldn't speak. She could only stare at her sister that could not bear to bring her eyes up to look her in the face.

"How... how could you say such a thing?" Sarah managed to say.

Katherine was obviously shocked by Sarah's question. "My dear sister," she began, "your ordeal... the savages..." she paused. "How will I explain that you are with child and your husband is long dead?"

Sarah fought the urge to lash out in anger at her sister's opinions, but thought better of it and decided to deal with her ignorance in another way. "My sweet, protective sister." Sarah reached across the table to take Katherine's hand. "You are mistaken and have been much deceived. This child that I carry was conceived in love... with my husband."

Katherine let out a deep sigh of relief. "Then you are married? Josiah told us you were a captive with the Indians this whole time."

"I was living among the Seapaugh Indian tribe, yes." Sarah let the implications set in and watched the expression change on her sister's face. It was one of disgust and then it turned to pity. "Would you like to hear about it?" she finally asked simply.

"There is plenty of time for that. You're home now. I just need to check on your bath for you, just at this moment." Katherine stuttered nervously and left Sarah alone with her breakfast and her memories of the true love and her son living somewhere else in this world without her.

Elizabeth Bourgeret

Chapter Twenty-Two

CAPTIVE LOVE
Read the true story of a beautiful woman of culture kidnapped and forced to live among a tribe of savage Indians. Beaten and abused every day for years. Forced into hard manual labor!
Read of the daring rescue by the trapper who managed to escape their evil clutches and return the beautiful maid to her loving family.
Ladies! You may wish to set this story aside for it contains the nightmarish horrors that few live to tell about. These images are liable to haunt your imagination for some time to come and are not meant for the weaker sex.

The door to Sarah's room flung open and Katherine breathlessly rushed in. She was dressed in her nightgown and robe which came untied in her rush.

"Oh, Sarah, I'm sorry, I was trying to get to you... you weren't meant to see that." She walked over to Sarah's bed and gently pulled the newspaper from her hands and folded *The Missouri Republican* so she could read no further. But the damage had been done. The tears that rolled down Sarah's face spoke volumes and Katherine felt that she had been punched in the stomach.

"I'm sorry, Sarah." Sarah cast her sister an angry look. Katherine continued, "I'm sorry about all that has happened to you. About the newspaper, about…believing in someone who had such a black heart." Sarah furrowed her brow and shook her head not understanding her meaning. Katherine set the paper on the table and came to sit along side Sarah on her bed, "I didn't know." Katherine paused trying to gather her thoughts. "I was so distraught when I heard of your attack. I was sure we had lost you. But when we received the wire that they had not found your body, I had hope. My husband hired a young, handsome trapper to bring back furs. He was cheaper than getting them sent over from Europe. He was familiar with the territory and said that he knew some Indian tribes that might take captives. We wished… rather than believed it to be true." Katherine's hands stayed busy twisting her handkerchief around and through her fingers. Her eyes looked up nervously and then back down to her hands. "When Mr. Cooper had become captured himself…"

"What?" Sarah interjected. She caught herself and took in a deep breath, "I'm sorry… please, continue."

"He… he told us that he had escaped but had nearly bled to death. He said that he tried to take you with him but the Indians attacked him and took you back."

Sarah rolled her eyes and gritted her teeth and Katherine went on. "Sarah, when he returned to us and told us that you were still alive, I wept with hope. I knew your character was strong and could carry you through anything… anything." Katherine looked up and smiled and ran her fingers along Sarah's face wiping away her tears. "You did receive the things that I sent?"

Sarah smiled and nodded. "I did. And they were of great comfort to me."

"Good. I had no idea what the situation was where you were. I could only hope that he could get them to you. He told us that he was barely able to see you without your guards or your being let out of your small filthy prison. He said he went through great peril to get those items to you." Katherine's voice caught in her throat. "He said you had been badly beaten..." Katherine broke down into heart wrenching sobs, "I begged James to double the reward money if he could find a way to bring you back. Please understand, sister... we thought..."

"I do understand," Sarah tried to console her sister. "For I would have done the same thing were it you." Sarah wiped the tears off Katherine's cheeks with the hanky she pried from her sister's closed hands. "But you have to understand, it was not that way. Yes, at first I was terrified, grieved for the loss of my son. I wanted to die, at that moment, but slowly, I began to heal... inside and out. Your letters and God's grace saved me."

"My letters? I thought all of your belongings were at the..." Katherine swallowed not being able to say the words.

"They were. But there was this one man. It's kind of funny now that I look back on it..."

Sarah told Katherine everything. They laughed and cried and held each other all day.

"A son? Another son?" Katherine smiled, "Jacob. What a wonderful name."

"And sister, they don't give birth lying on their backs!"

"No!" Katherine tried to be offended by the subject matter but then looked about the room and

Elizabeth Bourgeret

back at her sister, "Do tell!"

And they talked.

"The doctor told us that you had several fractured ribs that didn't heal properly and other injuries."

"I'm not surprised. That could have been the time we were attacked by a different tribe of Indians when we were at the river."

And they talked.

Sarah was laughing, "And the water spilled out all over my smooth floor with my husband rolling out after!"

And they talked even more.

"And I didn't even know they were the same person until he handed me the matching flower there in the glen."

"That is so romantic!"

"It is now, but it was frustrating to live through!" Sarah smiled reminiscing. "He truly is a good man."

"I am sure he is. I never even thought they were capable of such feelings, such…"

"Emotions?" Sarah finished for her. Katherine nodded her head, embarrassed.

They talked late into the evening hours until Matilda came in to clear their evening meal dishes.

"Ma'am? The kids is wonderin' ifin' yous gonna do they prayers wit 'em"

"Yes, Tildy, I'll be there. Thank you."

"Yes'm"

Katherine turned back to Sarah and sighed, "You know, it never crossed my mind that you might actually find happiness. I am sorry for your pain, sister. Oh, that Mr. Cooper! I'll have the sheriff arrest him first thing in the morning!"

"Katherine, don't bother, I am sure he is long gone by now. He can do me no more harm."

Katherine walked over to the chair that Sarah sat in, still in her dressing gown and reached her arms out. Sarah grabbed her outstretched hands.

"I am so happy to see you, sister."

"As am I," Katherine responded. "What would you say about meeting the children tomorrow?"

"I would love to!" Sarah smiled and squeezed her hands. "For soon I will have to return to my husband. I want to spend as much time with them as I can."

The statement caught Katherine off guard. "Yes, well…we can discuss that another time. Get some rest, sister. Perhaps we can run over to James' store and get you some material for a new dress. Do you still like to sew? Or should we just get a store bought one?"

"A dress already made? How would they know my size? That must cost a fortune!"

"A subject for tomorrow! Good night, dear Sarah." She kissed both of her hands. Before she left the room she turned back and said, "I am so happy to have you here. I do love you so." And she slipped from the room.

The next morning Matilda came in to help Sarah dress. Sarah found that she fell easily back into her old routine of having servants.

"I'm glad that you stayed to help me, Matilda. I might have been all day trying to remember how all of these layers go on!" Sarah smiled with her arms above her head as Matilda wrapped the corset over her shift. "Ach! Why do we wear these things? Don't crush the baby, now."

"No ma'am, I ain't gone crush da baby, but da missus say to make you look like you ain't spectin."

Sarah looked over her shoulder, "Humph, good luck with that." Matilda shrugged her shoulders and added, "Er'body knows Ms. Katherine. They knows she always do was right. She don't want no bad talk 'bout her only sister. She love you, Miss Sarah. She would cry and cry fo you all da nights."

Matilda hooked up the back of Sarah's dress, while Sarah struggled for air. "Really, these are so uncomfortable!" Sarah tried pulling at her waist to no avail. "I can't breathe!"

"You get used to it again, Miss Sarah," Matilda giggled. She instructed Sarah to sit in her chair while Matilda slipped shoes on her feet.

"You sho gots a lot a callus on yo feet. Miss Katherine ain't gone believe this."

"I am sure that it is not necessary to tell my sister how callused my feet are."

Matilda got up from the floor and looked Sarah over and smiled and nodded her head in approval. "Missus say she got a big breakfast waitin' fo you downstairs but want ta know if you wanted yo tea in yo room afore coming down."

"Real tea? With cream and sugar?"

Matilda nodded. "Yes'm"

"Oh, I have missed sugar! I didn't realize what a sweet tooth I had until I didn't have it any longer." She laughed and mused, "It's funny what you miss."

Matilda gathered up Sarah's dirty nightgown and linens, "You sho' is brave Missy Sarah, I read all about you in da paper dis morning."

Sarah dropped her head, "It's not what you think. I'm sure it was more story than fact."

Matilda shook her head as she walked toward the door, "Still… you sho is brave… sho is."

Sarah looked at herself in the full-length mirror. Her hair was piled neatly on top of her head with long curls dropping down on either side. Her face and hands were clean. Her fingers traced the scar that lined her eyebrow and the one that gave her a permanent part in her hairline. She is older since she last saw her reflection. The brilliantly green dress was quite a contrast to the tans she was used to. She was amused that the latest fashions added an extra petticoat. She managed to draw a shallow breath under her layers and layers of tight, uncomfortable clothing. She did look like a lady, though. The only thing that betrayed her was her darker freckled face and of course, the calluses on her hands and feet. Apparently long sleeves were all the rage even in the heat, but it would hide her scars and scrapes that decorated both arms.

She followed her figure down and placed her hands where the bump was barely showing. Matilda hid it well, she thought, and with this shawl, you can't tell at all.

She breathed a heavy, painful sigh. As happy as she was to see her sister and meet her nieces and nephews, she longed for her son and her husband. Do they know where I am? Do they think that I am dead? Do they even know that I am missing?

She sighed again, "Well, I had better get

downstairs before they send up a search party." She tried to walk to the door, but the shoes were squeezing her feet. She walked back over to her mirror and looked down at the hem of her dress. It went past her shoes and brushed against the floor, she noticed. So, with a swift kick, the shoes came flying off her feet, hitting the wall by her chair. "Perhaps they won't notice." She shrugged her shoulders and lifted her dress and enjoyed the feel of the soft carpet under her feet.

Breakfast was almost overwhelming. As Sarah walked into the dining room, all eyes turned to her. She scanned the faces of her nephews and nieces. How beautiful they all were. James stood from the far end of the table and smiled at her. His dark brown hair framed his handsome face. He had grown a mustache since the last time she had seen him. He wore a black vest over his white shirt with a black bow tie. He walked around the children sitting in their places and extended both of his hands. "Dear sister, you always could light up a room with your entrance."

"Oh, James," Sarah held his hands, "I knew my sister made the right choice of husbands," she flirted back, "Oh, it is good to see you again."

He pulled her into an embrace. "You, standing here, is the answer to so many prayers." he whispered.

Sarah looked across the table to her sister who was sitting directly next to her husband's chair. She was smiling and Sarah saw the silent tear that slipped down her cheek.

"Let me introduce you to my family... your family," James said, placing Sarah at the seat of honor at the end of the table. "This is James, our eldest," he pointed to the young man at Sarah's left. He resembled his namesake, the spitting image of his father. Young James nodded politely and Sarah smiled back. "Next, we have Joseph."

"I'm nine!" Joseph spurted out. Sarah nodded, thinking her Thomas would have been nine this same year...

"This little lady is our Sarah Jane."

"We really had no choice," Katherine chimed in stroking her daughter's hair, "she looked so much like you... if I hadn't been there myself, I would have thought she was yours."

Sarah Jane looked down shyly, but stole a glance, her blue eyes sparkling.

"Over by her mother is Grace, our youngest daughter. Next to Grace is Adam. Adam just turned four." James pulled out the chair for Sarah to sit. "He insisted on sitting by his Aunt Sarah."

Adam giggled and looked at his mother and covered his face with his hands.

As Sarah sat, she said, "It is so nice to meet all of you." Sarah pat James' hand that was resting on her shoulder. He went back to his chair and nodded to Otis to serve breakfast.

"I am looking forward to getting to know everyone better."

The children chatted away amongst themselves throughout breakfast and Sarah enjoyed every moment.

The children were excused from the table and the adults remained. "Breakfast was wonderful. I do love pork," Sarah admitted as she poured herself more tea into her cup. "And this tea is wonderful. I must remember to take some with me when I return home."

James and Katherine glanced at each other with concern but it went unnoticed by Sarah.

"Sister, would you like to visit James' shop this afternoon? Is that alright, dear?"

James nodded and Sarah was excited to get out of the house.

"Darling, you might take her down to Lafayette Park while you are out. I am sure it will be quite warm today." James suggested.

"I could see a river from my window," Sarah said. "Do you mind if we go and see it?"

"Of course, I'll have Otis ready the carriage. You don't think it will be too much for you on your first day out?"

"No. I am looking forward to seeing a bit of civilization."

Katherine, feeling encouraged by her sisters comment, ordered the clean up of dishes and the carriage to be readied.

Sarah adjusted her new bonnet as she was jostled around in the carriage. She suddenly missed her horse. *I could never ride on my horse in this outfit,* she thought. She wondered where and how her horse was. Her mind drifted back as they passed building after building to her horse riding lessons with Little Feather.

"You know you can do a lot more with that horse than talk to it."

"I do not know how to ride and *she* does not tease me."

It was before she knew that Little Feather

was Little Feather and that she would fall madly in love with him.

"Who would tease you?" She flashed him a disbelieving look. "How have your people survived for so long? Our young children learn to ride a horse soon after they learn to walk," he laughed.

"Is this you not teasing me?" she asked.

"No. Not teasing. Wondering. You are so fragile. And all of your women seem to be."

"I was raised to be that way! In my world, ladies are treated like… like LADIES!" She was shouting. Very *un*-lady like. "We do not *have* to ride horses! We do not *have* to collect firewood, or dig up roots or do anything dirty! We are taught to… to…. 'read' and 'sew' and play 'piano' and to be good wives…"

He ignored the words he did not recognize and asked, "How can you be a good wife if you do not have to do all of those things?"

"It is different!" she huffed and started to walk away feeling the tears begin to sting. Clara obediently followed behind her.

He called after her, "Do you want to ride or not?"

"NO!" she yelled back over her shoulder.

"What about Little Feather? He is not from your world. Do you not want to make him a good Indian wife?"

She stopped and the horse stopped.

"Come back. I will not tease."

She looked back at him and sighed. She turned the horse and returned to him.

"The first thing we have to do is get you on your horse. Stand here in front of me and put your foot in my hands." He held the horse steady and placed the rope reins on the horses back. She stood in front of him and lifted her right foot. He cupped his hands but did not bend down for her foot to reach. She was getting ready to make a smart comment but then saw the intensity in his eyes as he stared at her. "You are too beautiful to be doing all the work of Indian women. I can see why men would cater to you. I am sorry your life has turned this direction."

A look of pain passed through her eyes, but she heard the compliment as it was meant to be heard. "Thank you," she whispered.

He held her stare only a moment longer before he lowered his hands; it was enough for her to feel a new tingle run through her body.

"Sister, are you alright?" Katherine asked again.

"Oh, yes, I'm sorry. You were saying?"

"Nothing important... where were you?"

"Thinking... remembering," Sarah said with a slight smile.

"It will pass," Katherine tried to comfort.

The sisters had a picnic lunch under a gazebo a few blocks from the river. The park was bustling with people walking, riding bikes, pushing baby strollers and Sarah enjoyed taking it all in.

Katherine explained that they had to keep some distance from the river because it was more for business than socialization. Sarah watched the huge steamboats and paddleboats move smoothly up and down the river.

"It all seems so long ago," Sarah commented.

"What?"

"That I was a part of this world. It seems so

distant. There are times that I struggle to even see Frank's face in my memory."

"It has been a long time, sister. And you have been through so much," Katherine spoke gently and placed her hand on her sister's knee.

"Yes, I have. More than I would have cared to! But now, this world seems so different to me."

"It is! So much has changed! This is going to be a city of the future, sister. We are growing by leaps and bounds. St. Louis is already a leader in furs and shoe manufacturing, our streets are expanding and you saw how tall our buildings…"

"What did we used to do all day?" Sarah interrupted. "I am feeling lazy. By now I would have gathered wood, sewn or repaired my husband's leggings, woven baskets, tended the garden, prepared breakfast and lunch and would probably be skinning the deer that my husband killed for dinner."

Katherine waved her handkerchief in front of her face to keep from fainting, "Sister, please!"

"I'm sorry, I had forgotten," she gazed off into the distance, "They used to tease me for being like you…so fragile…" she turned back and looked at her sister and took her hand, "Your hands, are so soft… It's in my name, you know…"

"What is?"

"The word fragile. When they named me, I couldn't do anything, they compared me with a baby. But I was a fighter… strong… learned the language and their ways. I was called "Natayah." It means fragile but strong." Her Indian name rolled off her lips like a warm sip of coffee.

"This must be difficult for you," Katherine dabbed a tear from her eye.

"It is. Please do not misunderstand, I am so happy to see you again and finally meet your wonderful family. I will have memories of this forever. But I miss my people also."

"But sister, we are your people," Katherine furrowed her brow with concern.

"You will always be my sister, my blood, but I am one of them now. I have changed."

"Now, now, it won't take long before you are your old self again."

"I don't want to be that person again. There was a time when that was all that I wanted... but now that I have it back, I see that I don't need it... don't want it. I want this child to grow up knowing her traditions and history and way of life. I want her to know her father and brother..."

"Please, sister, give it some time. You'll fall back into your life and your child will be able to have all the privileges that our culture has to offer. Why should you sleep on the floor when you have a bed? Why should you gather sticks when your home is safe and well lit? Why would you deprive your child of these things?" Katherine inquired.

"I'm not so sure they are better. I do miss many of the luxuries, but isn't there a place where the two worlds can combine? Do I have to choose?"

"It is an easy decision. This," Katherine pointed around her, "progress, expansion... future. This is better."

Sarah looked around her, past the neatly groomed grass and trees to the river's edge where black smoke billowed into the air and tall buildings blocked out the sky. "I'm not so sure it's better," was all Sarah could say.

Captive Heart

Elizabeth Bourgeret

Chapter Twenty-Three

Katherine had Otis drop them off at the corner and instructed him to meet them at the store. "It's a lovely day for a walk. Thank you, Otis."

The sisters walked down the main street with their matching parasols while Katherine filled Sarah in with the details and gossip of each business along the way. She nodded and shook hands with several people as they crossed each other's path. Sarah responded cordially to everyone that she was introduced to.

"It's funny," she said quietly to Katherine, "It does all come back." Her words and smile came easily. Sarah found that she enjoyed the polite, meaningless conversations.

"Oh no. Bother, she's seen us." Katherine said through the side of her mouth.

"Who?" Sarah inquired.

"Mrs. Barklege. She is such a busybody."

Sarah noted the heavyset women walking with purpose straight for them. She looked as if someone was after her, her face pained, and her hanky dangling from her hand wiping her brow and neck every few steps.

"Oh, Mrs. Tobias. It is scandalous, I tell you. I certainly hope your husband does not intend to sell his wares to the likes of them!" Mrs. Barklege blurted out.

"Of what are you speaking?" Katherine

asked politely, trying desperately to veil her dislike.

"Why, of the Clairmont's, of course!"

"Pastor Clairmont?"

"Calling himself a man of the cloth," she huffed. Sarah and Katherine looked at each other perplexed.

"I am afraid, that I don't know of what you are referring to," Katherine said.

"Why, the wagon train crew that is coming through. They have brought with them a real injun. He is supposed to be navigating with the wagon master."

Katherine paused before speaking, still not quite understanding the problem, "With the attacks on the wagon trains out west, I should think it would be rather helpful to have one... of... their kind along for safety." Katherine shifted nervously and glanced over to her sister, hoping that she would remain quiet. She did but was listening intently.

"But my dear Mrs. Tobias that is not the scandal... Pastor Clairmont has allowed that heathen into his home!" She looked at her audience and did not get the reaction she was looking for so added with emphasis, "He is allowing that savage beast to sleep in his *home*. You know how they are. That one savage could kill them all before daylight. It's all they know. Rape and pillage. They can't help themselves." Mrs. Barklege threw up her hands and wiped her brow and the folds under her neck again.

"Heaven forbid, he gets one of them pregnant," Sarah spoke up. Both women gasped. Katherine for the shock of Sarah being so blunt, and Mrs. Barklege swooned for the mere imaginings of an Indian and white woman "coupling." She stood there with her mouth agape and stared at Sarah, not noticing that Sarah had placed a protective hand across her blossoming abdomen.

"Mrs. Barklege," Katherine began, "I'm... I..."

"No matter. I must go and see to this myself. Reverend Forrester would have never allowed such an event, God rest his soul. These pastors from the east, I tell you, I just don't know what to think." She nodded her head to each of the ladies and bustled off, handkerchief waving in the wind.

Sarah and Katherine walked on but could hear Mrs. Barklege's high pitched voice, "Mrs. Simmons, have you heard!" about a half a block behind them. Sarah clenched her jaw and kept her eyes down.

"Thank you," Katherine whispered, linking her arm with her sister. "Thank you for not saying anything."

"I can see what it would have cost you. How can people be so shallow?" Sarah thought for a moment. "Did you know that the Indians think the same things of us? They think the white race is cruel and lazy. My husband had to deal with much ridicule for loving a white woman. I appeared lazy and stupid because I didn't know their ways. They often asked me how I survived in my world for so long without knowing the necessities of living. It's funny now, but then, it was quite painful."

"How can they think us lazy? Look at all we have accomplished!" Katherine defended.

"They don't see your tall buildings and bricked streets. They see that you have taken something that did not belong to you and killed whomever stood in your way. That is why they attacked my wagon train in the first place, because the army slaughtered many of their families to make way for the coming white people. I just happened to be in the wrong place at the wrong time."

Katherine stopped and looked at Sarah taking her hand, "Sarah, I am trying to understand. Please be patient with me," Katherine pleaded with her sister.

"I pray for you, sister. I pray that God opens your eyes and helps you see past the color of skin. I am sure you will think differently when you see the beautiful children that I can make!" she giggled.

"Really, sister. I don't remember you being so brazen!" Katherine laughed in spite of herself as they continued walking.

"It's all that savage living!" she teased back.

The two sisters chatted and laughed and window-shopped as they walked the blocks of St. Louis. Sarah was deeply amazed at all the new gadgets she saw in the windows of passing stores. Things that were created to make life easier. *What will they think of next?* Sarah wondered to herself. She wondered too, if she would ever be able to walk down a street such as this holding the hands of her children with her husband walking beside her. She laughed.

"What?" Katherine asked.

"I was just trying to imagine my husband in one of those suits with the fancy bowler hat," she laughed again.

They came to the end of the block when Katherine said, "Here we are. What do you think?" Sarah streched her head back to take in the height.

Captive Heart

It was a brown brick building with its opening at the corner with two large double doors beckoning entrance. A large vertical sign was attached to the edge announcing the proprietor. Tobias General Merchandise. The name Tobias was also engraved in stone high above the door under a second story window. The large windows displayed women's dresses and the newest bonnets on one side, and tools and supplies decorated another. Katherine spoke with authority, "It is the largest in the city. And half of it belongs to you, sister."

Sarah looked at her puzzled.

Katherine explained. "Frank sent money to James to help him expand our small store. The pioneers and the wagon trains made us rich. They bought everything, as fast as we could stock it! By the time we were going to start sending money back to you, we received your letter about Frank passing. Then, you were coming here, so we waited. But the money is here for you, in the bank. James has been quite faithful. You have enough money that you could set up a home, with servants, and running water. They say that in the future we are to have gas-burning lamps in all the homes! Can you imagine?"

Sarah shook her head trying to take it all in. Katherine came and linked her arm with her sisters, "Wouldn't father have been proud?"

Sarah nodded her head and smiled, "Indeed he would. It is a fine looking store. Can we go in?"

"I thought you'd never ask!" Katherine hugged her sister's arm and opened one of the large double doors.

Once inside, Katherine took their parasols and tucked them behind the wooden counter that spanned the length of the room. She removed her gloves and assumed her business voice. "Good afternoon, Timothy. How are you today?"

"I'm good, Mrs. T. Mr. Tobias is in the back. You want I should fetch him?"

"No, thank you. Did the candy and sugar and flour come in…" Timothy was a young clerk of maybe eighteen and followed Katherine around as she inquired about the morning's activities.

Sarah barely moved inches from the door. Her eyes could not stay focused on one thing for long, as there was so much to see. People came in and went out around her, but she paid no attention to them. She tried to keep her mouth from gaping but caught herself several times and shut it promptly.

Crackers, flour, sugar, cornmeal, oatmeal, and coffee were displayed in large barrels in the center of the main entryway. Boxes of foodstuffs lined the shelves. Bright colored candy covered the main counter with homemade baked goods under glass enticing passersby.

Tools, pots and pans, kettles, toys! Dolls with pretty little dresses and curls, wooden trucks and guns, animals stuffed with soft material. Shoes and boots lined one wall of shelves. Sarah looked over everything and then she saw a set of stairs. Her eyes followed the stairs up to a second level. She tipped her head back and held her bonnet in place.

Animal heads were displayed along the second floor railing. "I wonder if any of those are Josiah's handiwork," she said under her breath. She caught a glimpse of stacks of fabric bolts on the second level through the railing. She made her way to the stairs trying to see the other contents of the upper lever and never saw Cylus Greer until she ran into him... quite literally.

"Oh! I do apologize! I am... I did not see..." she brushed her hand across her hot blushing cheeks and tucked her head down hoping that he could not see the color in her face.

"It was my pleasure," he said in a deep, smooth voice. It had just a hint of a southern drawl.

"I was just... looking... I...I'm sorry."

He smiled down at her as he helped right her stance by holding her elbow. He could not take his eyes off of her.

"Oh, Mr. Greer!" Katherine called out as she walked over to the base of the stairs, "I see you've met my sister."

"Yes, rather abruptly, I'm afraid," he said, as his eyes never left Sarah who was still so embarrassed that she scarcely brought her chin up.

"Well then, let me introduce you formally," Katherine interjected. "This is my sister, Mrs. Sarah Dobson. Sarah, this is one of our merchants, Mr. Cylus Greer.

Sarah put her hand out and curtsied, "Well, actually..." Sarah began.

"Actually, her husband passed away..." Katherine interrupted. He bent to kiss her fingertips but Sarah barely noticed. It was the sound of her own name that sent her back into her own thoughts. Sarah Dobson. How long has it been since she was addressed by that name? Was it appropriate? What would she be called now? Mrs. Little Feather? Do Indians even have last names? Is our marriage even recognized here? It was a subject Katherine preferred not to discuss, let alone acknowledge.

She would rather pretend that Sarah was not married and not pregnant with an Indian child. *You can only hide that for so long*, she thought. Her quiet reverie was interrupted with Mr. Greer speaking to her. "I should have recognized the familiar beauty in the two sisters," he charmed. "Are you enjoying your visit, Mrs. Dobson?"

"Oh, oh yes, I am. Very much," Sarah stuttered. The silence stretched to an uncomfortable level.

"Mr. Greer," Katherine recovered, "those lace gloves that you brought in are just lovely. Wherever did you find them?"

"Those came straight from Paris, France, ma'am. I will see that you get a pair."

"Oh, thank you, you are too, too generous," Katherine giggled.

"I love to see beautiful women dressed in beautiful things," He nodded his head toward Sarah.

"Mr. Greer, would you do us the honor of having dinner with us tomorrow evening?" Katherine asked.

He smiled genuinely. "I am honored," he bowed, "but I am afraid I can only accept if I am guaranteed more time to visit with the lovely Mrs. Dobson."

"Why, Mr. Greer, I am not sure that I should not be offended," Katherine teased.

"Madam, I apologize, no offence was intended, but I am absolutely mesmerized by your sister's charms," he purred through his drawl.

"Then please, say you'll be our guest. Tomorrow, at eight?" Katherine spoke before Sarah had a chance to protest. "We will look forward to seeing you then, won't we, Sarah?" Katherine

Captive Heart

nudged her sister.

"Oh, yes, of course," Sarah smiled shyly and looked back down at her toes peeking out from underneath her dress. She quickly adjusted her hem to cover them.

"Until tomorrow then," he caught Sarah's distracted gaze and held it all the way down to her fingers where he placed another kiss.

"Thank you, yes, tomorrow," Sarah smiled politely.

During dinner that night a package arrived.

"Excuse me, sir, this come for Miss Sarah, sir." Otis politely poked his head in.

"Bring it in, Otis," James instructed.

He took the box over and handed it to Sarah. "Thank you, Otis," Sarah smiled up at him. He nodded and left the dining room. "Do you mind?" Sarah's eyes questioned the others sitting around the table.

"Please, continue," James spoke for everyone.

"What's in the box Aunt Sarah?" Sarah Jane asked.

"Open it!" young James shouted.

"Can I open it?" Adam asked.

"Children," Katherine admonished, "Let Aunt Sarah open her own package."

"I wonder what it is!" Sarah nervously said as she untied the cord. She lifted the lid from the box and the most beautiful pink colored silk shoes complete with heel and a top strap. "Shoes," Sarah announced to all anxiously awaiting. She tipped the box so everyone could see.

"Shoes? That's an odd gift. Is there a note?"

325

Sarah lifted the shoes from the box and revealed a flower tucked into the toe of one of the shoes that was tied with a dainty ribbon to a card that read: *I hope you don't mind my furnishing the missing piece of an otherwise impeccable ensemble. Your servant, Cylus Greer*

"Oh, I am so embarrassed!" Sarah blushed.

"That's what you get, walking around without shoes! Really, Sarah, it is so, uncivilized," Katherine teased. "I think it's charming that he bought you shoes. He has excellent taste, too." Sarah could not hide the blush in her cheeks.

"Do you not like wearing shoes, Aunt Sarah?" Joseph asked.

"Not particularly," she whispered as she leaned toward him, "They hurt my feet."

"Mine too," Joseph admitted.

"Why don't we go to the drawing room?" James suggested.

"Oh yes, the children have something special prepared for you, sister."

Happy to have the attention taken off her, they moved away from the dinner table allowing Matilda and Otis to clean behind them.

The children played the piano and sang songs, and recited poems and scripture for the amusement of their parents and Aunt Sarah. Sarah's heart was so full; she thought that it might burst.

Adam bellowed out four verses of "America the Beautiful." The words stirred Sarah's heart, and her thoughts went back to the most beautiful country she had ever seen. And it had been only a few steps from the door of her weetu. This big city held no allure for her. The applause drew her back to her nephew bowing with his hand across his stomach and the other behind his back. *What a handsome young man,* she thought.

Next came Sarah Jane. She smiled timidly and curtsied. Her pale peach ruffles swayed from side to side as she nervously rocked back and forth and narrated her piece from the 23rd verse of Psalms.

"The Lord is my shepherd; I shall not want.

He maketh me to lie down in green pastures; He leadeth me beside still waters

He restoreth my soul; He leadeth me in the path of righteousness for his name's sake…."

Sarah glanced over to her sister and saw that she was mouthing the words right along with her daughter. Sarah remembered many a time these very words comforted her when she had nothing else to grab hold of.

"Yea, though I walk through the valley of the shadow of death, I shall fear no evil; for Thou art with me…"

Little Grace toddled over and crawled up onto Sarah's lap and watched her siblings perform with her thumb in her mouth. Sarah wrapped her arms around her niece and breathed in her rose scented baby smell… and longed for her son's sweaty, musty, dirt-caked hair smell.

Sarah Jane was finishing up and Katherine couldn't have been more proud of her oldest girl. "… and I shall dwell in the house of the Lord forever."

As the eldest boy stood to do his rendition of Lieutenant Colonel William Barret Travis' "Victory or Death Speech" he grew very solemn. As the speech intensified, so did the speaker, "I shall never surrender nor retreat! Then, I call on you in the name of Liberty, of patriotism and of everything dear to the American character, to come to our aid with all dispatch..."

James sat proudly and puffed lightly on his pipe. He nodded in approval whenever his son would glance his way.

"... and *die* like a soldier who never forgets what is due to his own honor and that of his country. Victory or Death!" He raised his right fist up and pointed his nose into the air for his dramatic finish. The room poured out their praise in applause and young James relaxed from his position and fell to the floor at Sarah's feet.

"That was wonderful, James." Sarah leaned over Grace to be able to see his face. He shrugged his one shoulder, and lightly responded, "I messed up, some."

"Oh, I didn't even notice. You are quite a fine orator."

"Was I good too?" Adam asked.

"Yes, of course, dear. I loved hearing you sing."

A long silence ribboned through the room and it was comfortable. Sarah stroked Grace's soft blonde curls, and James reached out to hold Katherine's hand.

"Aunt Sarah," young James asked, "Did you really live with the Injuns?"

"Yes, honey, I did."

"Do the Injuns play the piano and sing, too?" Sarah Jane wondered.

"Well, they do sing, a lot, and they love to dance, but they don't have pianos. They play other instruments like drums, and flute-like instruments and they have lots of noise makers that they shake."

"Can you sing us a song?" Adam asked.

Sarah thought about it as the children begged her to sing, "Alright, here is the song we sing to put our babies to sleep." Sarah's voice was soft and gentle as she sang out the high floating notes in words they couldn't understand, but held them riveted. She rocked from side to side with Grace on her lap and sang while a silent tear slipped from the corner of her eye.

When she finished, Young James whispered, "Hey look, it worked! Grace is asleep."

Sarah smiled and kissed the youngest Tobias child's head.

"Is it a sad song, Aunt Sarah? You're crying," Sarah Jane observed.

"What did the song say?" Adam asked.

"It was about a boy." Sarah began.

"Like me?" Adam interrupted.

"Yes, just like you." Sarah continued. "He was talking to the moon and asking that it watch over him while he sleeps, and to help him dream about where to find all the best animals to hunt. So when he would wake up he would know just where to look."

"Does it work?" Joseph asked.

"I suppose it did. They never came back from hunting trips empty handed."

"When they went out on the warpath, did they paint their face with blood?" young James asked bravely drawing out the word "blood" for the effect of his brothers and sisters.

"James!" his mother admonished.

"Sorry, momma," James put his head down.

"It's alright," Sarah said. "My people are a

peace loving people. They do not like to have to fight. They will, only when they are forced to, for the protection of their own, usually."

"Shucks." James sounded disappointed. "I heard that the Pawnee tribes kill just for the fun of it."

Sarah shuddered for just a brief moment remembering the time she was introduced to their type of fun when they took her from the river. "Yes, they are very cruel. But my people are not like that at all."

"Who are they?"

"They call themselves The People of the Earth. You would know them by the name, the Seapaugh Indians."

"Do they eat raw meat?"

Sarah could see her sister bearing the conversation as best she could from the corner of her eye, but Sarah secretly enjoyed having the children's attention. "Some of the men do, when they are out on the hunt. They sometimes eat the tongue as soon as the animal is dead, for luck."

The room of children "eeew-ed."

"…but most of the time we cook the meat, just like you do," Sarah laughed giving them exactly what they wanted- something gross.

"Alright, I think that is enough questions for your Aunt Sarah for one night," their father spoke up after his wife nudged him.

"Yes children, it's time for bed," their mother chimed in.

"Aunt Sarah," Adam came over to kiss her goodnight, "They are pretty much like us, huh?"

Sarah tussled his hair, "Yes, they are very much like us," she smiled and hugged her nephew

Captive Heart

with her free arm. He kissed her cheek and shouted, "Goodnight!" as he ran up the stairs.

Katherine came over and lifted the sleeping Grace from her lap and smiled down at her sister. "Thanks for being so patient with them," she said.

"I love them so much, Katherine. It is a pleasure spending time with them. I have a lot of catching up to do."

"Aunt Sarah?" It was Sarah Jane. She came up and stroked Sarah's hair and coiled a lose curl around her tiny fingers.

"Yes, sweetie?"

"Did you miss us while you were gone?"

"Oh honey, of course I did. I honestly didn't know some of you were even born yet, but there has always been a place for you in my heart, and I prayed for your family everyday. And now that I've met you, I love you so dearly." Sarah pulled her in for an embrace.

"You won't ever leave us, will you?" Sarah Jane pulled back just enough to be able to look into her face.

Sarah looked at her mirror image and ran a finger along her face and cupped her chin. "I will have to leave, someday. I need to get back to my son... your cousin. But anywhere I go, you will always be with me... here." she put a finger to her temple, "...and here." she moved her finger to her heart. "I will love you no matter where I am."

Little Sarah Jane smiled and squeezed her aunt's neck again. Sarah looked up to see her sister's face covered with tears.

The children were all tucked into bed and the house was quiet. Matilda came to help Sarah

331

dress for bed, but Sarah sent her along to her husband, Otis. "Why don't you call it a night, Matilda? If you could just unhook me, I am quite sure I can handle the rest myself."

Matilda was obviously grateful and nodded with a smile as she slipped out of her bedroom door.

She was alone. As she turned down the key to turn out the lights, the darkness engulfed her. She pulled the covers up over her shoulders and let the sadness come in. Her heart, despite the house full of people, felt so empty. She was so lonely. She longed for the other pieces that completed her heart. She ached to feel her husband's arm around her while she slept. Her eyes burned with the tears that ran across her nose and into her pillow. My Jacob, do you miss me? How she wished she could have both worlds. Her tears led her into a sleep of memories.

Chapter Twenty- Four

"Joseph! Go put some shoes on!" Katherine reprimanded as he came running through the drawing room.

"I'm an Indian brave, mamma!" he shouted followed by whooping noises and leaps.

"I'm sorry," Katherine apologized to their guest.

"It's quite alright. I was young once myself," Mr. Greer smiled sipping his tea. "That was truly an excellent dinner, Mrs. Tobias. When one travels as much as I, a home cooked meal is always a treat."

"You flatter me, Mr. Greer. We are so happy to have you."

Mr. Greer," James spoke up, "I'm sure you are bored with this tea as I am, perhaps I could interest you in a glass of brandy?"

"I am sure I could be persuaded." he laughed, "Not that I didn't thoroughly enjoy your tea, Mrs. Tobias."

"You are all politeness, Mr. Greer, but perhaps, husband, Mr. Greer might want some time alone with my sister."

A rattling of china and the spilling of some tea brought all eyes to Sarah who was trying to swallow her tea so as not to choke on it. "I'm sure Mr. Greer did not come all this way to see me," she blushed, eyes nervously darting about.

"On the contrary, Mrs. Dobson."

Sarah looked everywhere but up.

"But it is getting quite late. I'm afraid that I must take my leave, perhaps a rain check on that brandy, James?" Cylus stood and held out his hand to shake.

"Anytime," James nodded and shook his hand firmly.

Cylus turned to Sarah. "Miss Sarah, or may I call you that?" he paused.

"I don't think we know each other well enough for such informalities, as yet, Mr. Greer," Sarah responded shyly.

"Of course, Mrs. Dobson... may I... stop by tomorrow for a walk?"

"She'd love to!" Katherine spoke out of turn.

Sarah shot her sister a look, but smiled before Mr. Greer could catch it. "How could I refuse?" she answered looking directly at her sister.

He took his hat from Matilda and walked over to Sarah and kissed her fingertips. "Goodnight then, until tomorrow."

She curtsied slightly, "Goodnight."

A week went by with Mr. Greer's continuing attempts to court Sarah. She was polite and cordial and was entertained by their conversations and was surprised that she could feel comfortable around him, but would not be wooed.

One evening, Cylus Greer came to escort Sarah and her sister and her brother-in-law to the theatre. Despite her original objections, Sarah found herself quite excited about the outing.

Cylus had ordered a fancy carriage to carry the party to the theatre on the other side of town. Sarah was growing increasingly uncomfortable in the tight corsets, and the heavy shawls. Her unborn baby would push against the restraints showing its displeasure.

"Here, take my jacket." Mr. Greer draped it across her shoulders. "How can you possibly be cold on such a lovely evening?" he teased as Sarah pulled her shawl tighter around her body deciding not to comment. Katherine usually stepped in with her excuses and tonight was no exception, "She has been feeling a little under the weather. She really is a rather frail little creature." Katherine tried to giggle through her blatant lie.

"You look the picture of health, my dove, but perhaps you just need someone to take care of you," Cylus spoke through a raspy whisper.

"Oh, look! Is that the theatre?" Sarah distracted the party, and Cylus laughed enjoying the "thrill of the chase."

A man opened the massive door and the two couples entered the beautiful foyer of the theatre. Sarah looked up at the beautiful ornate decorations on the ceiling and the walls. The delicate sculptures adorned every alcove.

"Perhaps you ladies would like to freshen up?" James suggested as he directed them to the powder room.

Katherine looked beyond her husband to a group of men with their cigars puffing madly and then back to James. "James, dear, do not get so caught up with your talk that you leave us unattended," Katherine warned but with a smile.

"My lady, I am at your beck and call," he

Elizabeth Bourgeret

laughed.

Katherine rolled her eyes and linked arms with her sister and disappeared into the powder room.

"Those silly men and their talk. How they are attracted to politics." Katherine mused as she tucked hairpins strategically into place. Sarah adjusted her corset and attempted to gather a few deep breaths.

"Oh! This thing is so uncomfortable!" Sarah complained. A pair of women left the powder room and nodded at Sarah sympathizing with her condition. Sarah rubbed her belly to try and sooth its tenant.

Katherine slipped her gloves back on, and started on her way back up the stairs toward the lobby. "Don't worry sister, it won't be much longer. I believe that after tonight, you will have him in the palm of your hand." She looked back over her shoulder and reveled in the look Sarah shot at her. Oh, how Katherine loved to play matchmaker.

Sarah knew that the time finally came that she needed to bring up the tender subject with her sister. The evening at the theatre made it inevitable. She waited until the next day when the house was quiet and the two sisters were alone, engaged in their sewing.

"Sister," Sarah began gently, "I hate to even broach this subject with you, knowing how it makes you feel, but I am afraid that I can put it off no longer." Sarah paused waiting for some type of response from Katherine, but she purposefully kept her eyes on her sewing.

"Sister… I must go back." she spoke barely above a whisper.

Katherine said nothing but her back straightened as she took in a deep, silent breath, her needle never missing a stroke.

"Please do not be angry with me. I have enjoyed every moment with you and your family. As much as I have longed to see you again..." she paused, "There was a time when... all that I wanted was to escape from my lot in life and return to you and your 'civilization.' Sometimes the fear of having to stay trapped in that world would eat at my soul. The pain of missing you or the thought of never seeing your face would cause my heart to beat so hard that I could barely breathe. But now, I feel those same feelings for *that* world and for my husband... and son. God has made a place for me there. A family. A family of my own. He has allowed me to start over again."

Katherine stopped sewing and her hands dropped to her lap. She said nothing, but Sarah could see the tears falling on her sewing hoop.

"I know that you and James went through great expense to find me and... rescue me." Sarah continued, "But I have been thinking about it. I can no longer stay with you. I must get back home."

"But Mr. Greer... I do believe, that he means to marry you," she said casually.

"Katherine, Mr. Greer is a pleasant sort of fellow, and I do not mind his company, but if your purpose is for us to marry, then that cannot be. For I am already married."

Katherine looked up; her face was red with tears. "But... Sarah...they are... Indians," she said the word with disdain. "They are heathens. You would be giving up your life, a good life, which you could have here with us to a life of sin."

Sarah snickered to herself, "No, they're not heathens. I have seen to that. Many of them have been saved. They know that Jesus Christ is their Lord and Savior."

Katherine furrowed her brow, not understanding. Sarah explained how she read the Bible to them in their own language and that so many responded that they had to find new lodging to hold everyone that was interested. She told her that many of them had chosen to be saved. "I am no preacher, but I hope that God heard their prayers." Sarah smiled.

"My sister, a missionary?" Katherine tried to bring up the sides of her mouth into a smile.

"No. Not at all. I just try to live the way God wants us to and His light shines through me. I did not ask for this role. It just… happened," Sarah laughed, more to herself.

"I am really not surprised. Only you could turn, most likely the worst experience of your life, completely around to bring glory to God. Sister, how I admire your courage."

"It wasn't easy. I don't mean to lesson the amount of fear and heartache and physical pain I had to travel through, but only God can bring light to the valley of the shadow of death. He brought me through… for a purpose." Sarah paused for a moment. She decided to press on, "So, you see, my husband and I *are* equally yoked. My place is with my husband."

Katherine shook her head from side to side as the tears rolled down her cheeks.

"Katherine, I don't mean to hurt you…"

"No. It's not that," Katherine stopped her. "I know you love me as much as I love you… I just

Captive Heart

don't know how to tell you…"

Sarah stood from her chair letting her sewing fall to the floor. She walked over to her sister sensing the seriousness of her last comment and knelt down on the floor in front of her chair. She held Katherine's hands in her own as Katherine's tears turned to sobs.

"What is it sister? You can tell me anything," Sarah said softly as a shiver ran down her spine. Sarah's eyes were gentle and willing but Katherine could see a twinge of fear hidden just behind her calm exterior.

Katherine pulled her hand from the embrace of her sisters. She could see the near panic in Sarah's eyes as she gently stroked her hair. Katherine shook her head and looked down, "I was hoping that you would be happy here, with us," she hiccupped through her tears, "… hoping that we would be enough, that you'd forget your… other… family."

"Sister, is that what this is about? I could never forget them… just because they have different color skin and live differently…" Sarah saw Katherine shake her head from side to side, but Sarah continued, "How would you feel if James and your children were taken from you, and you had the chance to…"

"They aren't there," Katherine said, plainly forcing herself to look into her sister's eyes.

Sarah shook her head, wiping a tear from her sister's chin. "I don't understand, honey, what do you mean?"

"Sarah. They are all dead."

339

Elizabeth Bourgeret

Chapter Twenty- Five

Sarah lay in her bed grief stricken. Her mind struggled to make sense of the news she was given. She stared at the ceiling, motionless. Her mind drifted back to the fateful day when she last saw her husband.

"Do not seek revenge," she said quietly and ran her fingers down his perfect cheek.

"I cannot promise that."

Sarah rolled over to her side and wrapped her arms around her pillow. The pillow soaked up the neverending supply of tears and muffled her cries.

Katherine snuck into Sarah's room in the early hours of the morning when she heard Sarah speak quiet words in her Indian language.

"Sarah, are you alright? Darling, it's been two days. Won't you please speak to me? Won't you please eat something?" Sarah did not respond but her eyes stayed open as she stared into space. "Sister, I'm sorry... I... I didn't want to tell you. I had hoped that you would be happy here and ..." She moved to Sarah's bed and sat down on the mattress behind her. "Honestly sister, I would rather have taken that information to my grave than to hurt you so."

Without moving Sarah spoke, "How did it happen?"

"Sarah, now I'm sure you don't want to..."

"How did it happen?"

Katherine looked up to the heavens and sent a quick prayer of thanks, then took in a deep breath before she began. "From what I understand, I was told that once you were safely within the army compound, Mr. Cooper warned them that he was under attack. He told the Captain that he believed the Indians would come in the night to reclaim their hostage."

Sarah rolled onto her back, "But I'm not a hos…"

"Yes, honey, I know that… now." But then, they thought they were rescuing you. Or Mr. Cooper made them believe it to be so. They were protecting you. Mr. Cooper told us that while they made arrangements to get you safely to us that a group of Indians charged the compound, so they returned fire." Katherine choked back the tears as she tried to continue. "They said that they waited for a couple days knowing that the Indians would try again, and then they sent out a group and found the village and…" she couldn't finish. "Sarah." She stroked her sister's head and pushed the curls from Sarah's face, "Sarah, I am so sorry."

"Why would they do that?" Sarah's cries were uncontrollable again.

"I'm sorry, I wish…"

Sarah rolled back over to her side and buried her head into her pillow. "My son! He was just a baby!" she cried out.

Katherine kissed her sister's head and whispered, "I'll get you some cool cloths…" and she tip- toed from the room.

Sarah did not hear her leave and cried on. "My husband, oh my husband. Why couldn't I

Captive Heart

have died too?" she bawled. "God! What are you trying to tell me? Why do I have to go through so much pain? Oh God, I ache so much... my heart is broken. Please God, take this pain away."

She looked up and saw a letter opener setting on her desk. She remembered the Indians custom. She tore the sleeve of her nightdress and sat up to drop her legs over the side of the bed. She went to pick up the letter opener as it gleamed in the sun. She quickly ran the edge across her skin, disappointed that it left no mark. She looked back to her desk for a sharper instrument and found a pair of scissors. She separated the blades and held them tight. "This is for the loss of my husband," she said as she raked the edge of the blade across her upper arm. She cried out in pain as the blood poured from the jagged, gaping wound. The blood was warm as it covered her arm and hand.

"Ow, that hurt! That was so stupid! That is a stupid custom!" she fumed as she squeezed her arm with her right hand. "I hate blood. I don't feel so well..." The room was beginning to spin and Sarah felt the weight of her eyelids press down. "Katherine," she was barely able to whisper. She clutched the wound, and fell back against her bed. Sarah slid down the edge of the bed dragging the sheets down with her. Her vision clouded, she was sure her life was passing away from her. "Maybe this was meant to be. When I wake, I will be with my husband." She watched the blood pour down her arm and soak the sheets beneath her. She was ready to give in to the endless sleep when Katherine returned with her towels.

"Sarah! What have you done?" Katherine ran over to the edge of Sarah's bed and wrapped the clean towel she brought around Sarah's arm. "Matilda!" she shouted, "Matilda! James! Fetch the doctor!" She ran to the doorway and James met her there. Katherine had blood on her dress and a streak of blood across her forehead where she wiped her hair back from her face. "Katherine! Are you alright? Are you bleeding?"

"I'm alright, James, its Sarah! Please fetch the doctor!" Katherine ran back to her sister and squeezed her arm. "Don't leave me Sarah. Don't die this way!"

"I... don't... want to ... die," Sarah murmured.

"Okay, honey, hang in there... the doctor's coming."

"I don't understand..." Sarah mumbled in a daze, "They do it all the time in the village."

"What?" Katherine said alarmed. "Hold on, sister, hold on."

"I hate blood," Sarah slurred and lost consciousness.

When Sarah woke again, she saw shards of light streaming through the cracks of the heavy drapes. Katherine was asleep by her side in a chair and the nurse slept in another chair at the foot of her bed.

Her room was filled with bouquets of various flowers and gifts. She could smell the fresh cut flowers and took in a deep breath. A smile managed to cross her lips. *I imagine James is tired of me stealing his bedmate,* she thought. Her sister lay still as the sun shone on her blond hair. Strands had fallen loose from their former bun. Katherine wore the same dress; it had Sarah's blood staining the front. *What have I done?*

She tried to use her arms to help her sit up but was surprised by the pain in her left arm. She looked over and saw the bandages wrapped around her upper arm with a slit of blood staining through. *That didn't help me feel any better. If anything it postponed my return,* she thought. "Why was I so stupid?"

"Mrs. Dobson? Are you alright? Shall I give you something for the pain?" It was the nurse. She made her way to Sarah's bedside and ran a damp cloth across Sarah's forehead.

"No, thank you. I'll be alright. Could you help me sit up, though?" The nurse tucked her arms under Sarah's back to help her sit.

"Sarah! Are you alright?" Katherine asked waking up.

"Yes, sister. I am fine… really."

"What were you… why would you…"

"It is an old Indian custom with the women," she began her explanation a little embarrassed by her former actions. "When they lose a loved one, a son or… husband," she swallowed hard, "they cut themselves in mourning. I must have cut too deep or something. None of them ever pass out… believe me, they can have their custom."

"Why that is absolutely barbaric!" Katherine said with shock, "What on earth made you think…"

"I'm sorry I frightened you."

"Frightened! If I hadn't come back just when I did, you might have bled to death."

"I know…" Sarah furrowed her brow, "maybe that was in the back of my mind. Sleep seemed to feel so much better than the empty aching in my heart. But then I thought of my baby." She moved her hands over her protruding belly. "I must not give up for her sake."

"Oh honey, God must surely have plans for you. He has saved you over and over again. And all of the suffering that you have endured must be turned to good. It's His promise." Katherine assured her sister.

Sarah moped around the house for another week. Bouquets of flowers arrived daily.

"Sister, here's another lovely arrangement from Mr. Greer. He has been in town now for a week." Katherine brought the huge vase of flowers into Sarah's room. "You had better consent to see him soon; you are running out of space!"

Sarah looked up from her place in the Bible that she was reading and snickered, "He certainly is persistent."

"He is," Katherine laughed, "That has to count for something, doesn't it?"

"I suppose so. But I just don't…"

"Now, Sarah, you can't go the rest of your life living in the past." Katherine arranged the flowers as she spoke. She plucked the withered ones out of the vase and joined the more vibrant ones with the newcomers.

"Katherine, I know that, and I don't feel that I am. But I have a baby coming… a fact that no matter how many shawls you have me wear, eventually, it can't be hidden. And…" Katherine heard the tone in her sister's voice change and went over to sit across from her at the small window table. "I just don't feel..." Sarah continued, "that my husband is dead."

Katherine placed her hands over her sister's, "I know, but we've talked about this. It's time to let go."

"I can't, Katherine, I can't." Sarah stood and crossed the room. "I may not have been the best Indian wife, but oh, how I loved... love him." Her fingers ran across the soft petals of flowers. "He still feels very much alive. And this is his child that I carry." She looked down at her figure. "How can I raise her alone? She needs her family to teach her and hand down to her the history and customs that have been in her family for hundreds of years. I don't know enough. And you know, as well as I, that she will not be accepted as a citizen, barely even a human. She needs to be with her own people, or we will have to go away." Sarah paused and touched the scar under the sleeve of her left arm. "He can't be dead." She looked over at her sister whose head was down and she was concentrating on the wedding band of her finger. Sarah didn't even have one. "I ache for my husband, sister."

"Sarah," Katherine drew in a deep breath, "I know this may be a bit uncomfortable for you, but... I'm just trying to think of your future," she paused, "I heard that across the river, there is a reservation of Indian families and they would take the baby and raise it as one of their own."

Sarah's shocked expression said more than the words that finally formed from her open mouth could have conveyed. "Katherine, really! How could you even suggest such a thing? Would you love any of your children any less than another? Would you be able to give away any one of your children?"

"Of course not, but that is entirely different."

"No! No its not! There is nothing wrong with my child! Just because my child will have skin that is a little darker than my own, does not mean that I could love her less. I don't care what she looks like. I love her! God sent her to me, to love and care for and raise her up in His name," Sarah spoke with new determination. "She will know her Indian heritage, and I will be the one to teach her!" Sarah's lip quivered as she struggled to contain her anger. She stood and walked to the other side of the room.

"I don't mean to upset you, sister. But I believe that Mr. Greer might propose. Do you want to throw that away?"

Sarah sighed and sat at the edge of her bed. "Katherine, I'm not like you. I know that you love James, with all your heart. But if anything happened to him, could you just marry someone else, no love, no…"

"Yes, Sarah, I could. I have my future and my children's future to think of. Women just don't go off by themselves. We have to have a man to take care of us! What else would we do?"

"Katherine, I don't love him… I barely know him!"

Katherine changed her tone and stood beside her sister on the bed. "That will come in time. Mr. Greer is a good man. He is a good match for you."

"I will not give up my baby. If Mr. Greer is unable to accept me for who I am and the things that have happened in my life, then we are better off without him."

"Sarah, you are a stubborn one."

I am Natayah, she thought.

It took a couple more days before Sarah was ready to face Mr. Greer. He happily accepted her dinner invitation to the Tobias home.

The conversation remained casual over dinner, but Cylus Greer barely took his eyes off of Sarah.

"Matilda, that was the finest lobster I have ever had the pleasure of eating!" Cylus exclaimed, winking at Matilda.

"You can thank Mr. Tobias fo dat Mr. Greer; he done got it all da way from Nantucket. But I be takin da credit fo the good cookin'," she nudged Cylus and burst into laughter as she exited toward the kitchen.

"Mr. Greer, are you going to marry my Aunt Sarah?"

"Joseph! I don't think that is any of our business," his mother smiled nervously.

"I thought we had to watch over her," he said defending his question.

"You are absolutely right, young man and I applaud you for that," Mr. Greer praised Joseph but then turned his attentions to Sarah, "Perhaps that is a question your aunt and I should discuss."

Sarah blushed and looked down at her plate looking for something to busy her hands.

"Are you going to be the daddy?" Adam asked innocently. Katherine and James looked at each other anxiously, and their eyes darted over to Sarah who kept her eyes timidly down to her empty plate.

Mr. Greer shifted nervously in his seat and cleared his throat; "I hope so, someday." He nervously glanced over at Sarah.

"What about the new baby?"

"Adam, please! This conversation is inappropriate for the dinner table!" his mother admonished. James stirred his tea rapidly. The tension in the room was obvious to all the adults, save the innocent Mr. Greer.

"What?" he asked unpretentiously, "What did I say? I was talking about the baby in her belly..."

"Adam!"

"Mr. Greer, would you like some more coffee?" James interrupted.

Cylus Greer sat silently letting the implied information sink in. "I don't think I'll have that coffee, James. I think, perhaps that I should go."

Sarah stood and dropped her napkin on her plate. She squared her shoulders and allowed her shawl to fall to her chair as she addressed their guest, "Mr. Greer, would you like to join me in the parlor?" She could feel his eyes drift down to her midsection and linger there. He stood and looked away from her. "Please," she asked again.

"Thank you again, for the lovely meal and company," he stuttered.

"You are always welcome, Cylus." James replied offering his hand feeling that he was betraying his friend. Cylus Greer took his hand and clasped it firmly.

"I thank you. Mrs. Tobias... children," he

nodded and followed Sarah from the dining room while Katherine fanned her face as she slumped toward the table. *Children,* she thought.

Matilda met them just outside the dining room, "Y'all be wantin' some tea in the parlor room, Miss Sarah?" she asked.

"No, thank you," she answered as she walked past her into the parlor. Sarah crossed the room and turned back to Cylus and indicated the sofa. Matilda closed the parlor doors behind them. He sat and then she sat. The silence in the room was deafening.

"I can see plainly now," Cylus said low. "I feel so foolish."

"Please don't," Sarah apologized. "Deception was not intended… well…" Sarah took a deep breath and sighed it back out. "I was expecting when I had arrived here. My husband has recently … died." She unconsciously smoothed the pleats of her navy blue dress as she continued, "My sister knew that my child was going to be born fatherless, so she attempted to save my reputation in a new town by covering up…"

He raised his hand, "I understand." He rubbed his forehead with his fingers.

"I'm afraid you have been caught in the middle, Mr. Greer. Honestly, I had no intentions for this… us…"

"I'm afraid that this forces my hand."

"I am truly sorry. You are a good man and I never intended…"

Cylus was quiet when he stood. He walked over to the liquor cabinet and poured himself a small square glass of bourbon.

"Sarah," he spoke still facing the cabinet, "I

travel a lot." He turned to face her. "I have met many women. I have honestly been outrunning marriage 'opportunities' for some time. I did not see myself as one to settle down. None have captured me… until now." He turned and walked towards her. "Sarah, you are the handsomest woman I have come across."

Sarah blushed and looked down at her hands, "Mr. Greer."

"Please, let me finish, while I have the courage," he asked of her. He gathered her hands in his and while stroking the back of her hands with his thumb, he looked down at her and she nodded. "Your child will need a father. I don't have any fancy words ready for you so I will speak plainly. Sarah, would you consider me… for… your husband?"

"Mr. Greer… I…" Sarah was speechless.

Cylus laughed as he crossed the room to grab her hands and bring them to his lips. He kissed the backs, turned them over and kissed her palms and then her wrists. "I honestly don't know what kind of husband I would make, but the thought of you with someone else…" He caught himself and cleared his throat. "Don't answer now. I have to go away on business again in the morning. I wish that I could postpone it, but I should be back in two weeks. You can think on it and let me know when I return." A smile spread across his face as the idea slowly sank in.

"I am very flattered," Sarah started, "but I think there are some things that you should know. I mean we hardly know each other…"

"We have the rest of our lives."

"Yes, but my baby… my baby is…"

"Going to have nothing but the best. Let's talk about it when I return." He leaned down and kissed her fingertips on each hand. "Please tell me that you'll think about it," he looked deeply into her eyes.

Sarah remembered the words of her sister. "I will think about it, but I don't want you to think...." Cylus gently put his thumb on Sarah's lips silencing her, and he cupped her chin with his fingers. He gently stoked her bottom lip. She thought he was going to kiss her. She waited for that familiar tingle in her stomach, the one that precedes new love and a first kiss. But there was nothing. She raised her eyes to look into his and saw passion and restraint there.

"I will see you in two weeks and I'll bring gifts for you... and our... little one." He leaned in and impulsively kissed her forehead.

Sarah pulled back startled, and then blushed, embarrassed. Something didn't feel right, but she smiled her best and he did not notice her discontent. He took her hand and held onto it as he walked her to the front door. He turned and kissed her cheek. "I won't be gone long." He kissed her hands again and closed the door behind him.

Sarah turned and leaned against the closed door, wondering what the emotions were that swirled around her head. It wasn't long before Katherine descended the stairs in her nightgown and robe. Sarah kicked her shoes off and fell against the wall with a heavy sigh.

"What happened?" Katherine whispered, "Was he terribly angry?"

"He asked me to marry him," Sarah said surprised even as the words left her mouth.

Elizabeth Bourgeret

Chapter Twenty- Six

Smoke filled the room. Her eyes began to burn. She sat up in bed and gasped. Her lungs rejected the smoky air and she coughed convulsively.

Sarah slipped out of her bed and hovered close to the floor. She felt her way toward the door of her bedroom. The heat was intense, the air dark and grey. She felt for the handle and pulled the door wide open.

Outside the door she was kneeling at the edge of her village. The flames were climbing up the weetus on both sides of her. In the distance she could see Grieving Mother standing there as others of her tribe were running and screaming from the horse-mounted devils.

Sarah stood and shouted through hoarse voice, "Mother, run! You must run!" she called out, but Grieving Mother just stood there with a smile on her face, her arms extended waiting for her embrace. It felt as if she floated toward Grieving Mother feeling the heat of the fire all around her. She wrapped herself in Grieving Mother's arms.

"Oh, child, I have missed you," Grieving Mother whispered in the Seapaugh language that sounded so welcome to Sarah's ears. Grieving Mother stepped back to arms length to look her over. "This one will come early. She will be smaller than Jacob Blue Eyes."

Sarah's eyes filled with tears as the building

began to crumble around her. "Mother, please, we are in danger. Where is my husband?"

"Natayah. He is a good man. He loves you. He will be alright. He waits for you."

"We must go find him. I need to see him. Come, we have to get you out of here!"

Sarah didn't know if her tears were from the burning smoke or her breaking heart. She dare not take her eyes off of Grieving Mother for fear of what she would see beyond her. Bullets flew past her and lodged into the faceless bodies running past her.

Sarah tried to move Grieving Mother forward but she was slow to move. "Natayah, I have loved you… always." Grieving Mother stepped away from her grasp and smiled at her. "I must go." She turned and walked away from Sarah. She looked back over her shoulder, "It is a girl, you know." She smiled again and walked into a burning weetu, moments before it collapsed and was engulfed in flames.

"No! Mother, NO!" Sarah cried out. She took a few steps toward the burning rubble and a wall of flames roared up in front of her and sent her falling backwards. She covered her face, protecting it from the heat. She tried to crawl toward the remnants of the weetu that Grieving Mother disappeared into.

She reached her hands out in front of her and touched wooden spindles. She blinked the tears from her eyes and found herself on the balcony outside her bedroom clinging to the banister in front of her. It was still dark and the house was quiet. She looked beyond the banister and saw the flower arrangement in the foyer on the lower level and the front door to the left.

"A dream?" she asked herself wiping the tears from her cheeks. "It was so real." She looked down at her stomach and ran her hands across her belly. The little one kicked back against her hand in response, which brought a smile to Sarah's tear streaked face. "I wish your father was here," she whispered. She rolled off her knees and turned to lean back against the banister. "My little girl... sweet baby girl," she sang softly to her unborn child. Her ramblings turned into a lullaby that she sang to Jacob while she waited for him to be born. There she sat singing in another language, afraid to close her eyes again. But feeling a strange new hope.

Sarah was much happier not having to wear the constrictive corsets. Even though being pregnant was nothing to flaunt, she kept herself modestly dressed, but it was more comfortable than trying to make the pregnancy disappear. She loved being pregnant. The baby was getting more active every day.

The table was empty after breakfast; so the two sisters enjoyed the quiet while sipping their coffee.

"Sister, what if my husband still lives?"

"Sarah, honey, why do you trouble yourself like this? Especially since Mr. Greer is going to be here any day now. Are you getting cold feet?"

"Katherine, my feet have never been warm on this matter."

Katherine laughed. "You are silly. Don't borrow trouble."

"Don't tease, I am completely serious. What if he still lives and I am on track to marry another man?"

"Sarah, it's not like you to worry this way. What has troubled you?"

"Dreams," Sarah admitted. "I've been having dreams."

"Oh. There now, you can't put any stock in what happens in your subconscious. Perhaps your dreams are just the things you want to see."

"Maybe," Sarah considered but then thought to herself, these are images I do not want to see.

Katherine could see that Sarah was truly distracted by her dreams so she offered, "Sister, you have been through so much. Your trials have been many. Maybe God has sent you Mr. Greer to ease your heart. Maybe it's finally time for your life to become easier. Would that be so wrong?"

Sarah considered her sisters words for a moment as she silently sipped her coffee. "I would welcome a life without pain and strife," she mused. "I am tired of hurting. But even through all of my trials, I could see that God was with me, even in the darkness. There were times that it was more difficult to see Him, but once I stilled my fretful heart, He was there. Embracing me."

"There, you see? He is here and He has sent Mr. Greer."

"But it doesn't feel right."

"Sister," Katherine reached across the table and placed her hand over Sarah's. "Let go and let God show you."

Sarah nodded in agreement. *Lord, I trust you. Please show me Your will. You are my light in the darkness.*

The light was just peeking through the curtains when Sarah rolled over to see Kinsi, the young kitchen maid putting coals into Sarah's fireplace.

"Thank you, Kinsi," Sarah said in a raspy morning voice.

"I sorry to wake you Miss." she answered in her young, high-pitched voice.

"Not at all, it was just too cold to get up, but I think you've fixed that," she smiled.

"Yes, Miss. Thank you Miss." She curtsied. "Miss?" she continued, "What rooms of the house you think you be settin in today?"

"Whatever Miss Katherine decides is fine with me."

"Yes Miss." She curtsied and took her empty coal pail from the room.

Sarah stuck her arms out from under the blanket to stretch and pulled them back under the heavy layers of blankets. "I lied," she said out loud. It was not warm enough yet. She smiled and nestled back down deep into her blankets. "What I wouldn't give for a nice bear skin," she giggled to herself.

A tapping was heard at her door followed by her sister's voice, "May I come in?"

Sarah poked just her face from her fortress of blankets. "Of course you may."

Katherine scampered in across the room and crawled into bed next to Sarah. She was wearing her nightgown and robe and her hair was still in a long braid that hung down her back.

"Just like when we were children," Sarah

giggled.

"Yes, but now there's a baby between us." Katherine poked her head under the covers. "How could I have ever thought you would be able to hide that?"

"Oh stop!" Sarah laughed and protectively wrapped her arms around her belly, "Don't you listen to her my sweet baby. You grow as much as you want."

"How are you going to get your figure back for your new husband?"

"Running after the baby, of course!"

"Don't be silly, sister. Your husband will have a nursemaid for you. Probably two or three! I am jealous."

"I won't need them. I love taking care of my own, nursing them, holding them… Mr. Greer will just have to deal with that."

Katherine looked at her sister as they lay face to face with the covers over their heads, "Sarah. I am glad that you will be accepting Mr. Greer."

"I have been thinking about what you said. If this is God's will, I need to embrace it."

"No more dreams?"

"Actually, no, not for some time. Not since we spoke."

Katherine smiled and stroked her sister's soft face. Her smile said more than words could say. Suddenly, her expression changed to one of intrigue. "Oh, I almost forgot. A letter came for you this morning." Katherine dug into the pocket of her robe, "I wonder whom it could be from!" She teased and pulled her head out from under the covers and held the envelope just out of Sarah's reach. Sarah tried to grab it from her, but Katherine pulled it higher. She did this a few more times until Sarah threw the covers off and threw her pregnant body on top of her sister who groaned under the weight.

"Give it to me!" Sarah laughed, still reaching.

"Get off me, both of you!" Katherine laughed but still fought for her position.

"I'll get off when you give it to me."

"I'll give it to you when you get off!"

Katherine pretended to gasp for air and allowed the note to fall just into Sarah's reach. Sarah grabbed it and rolled off her sister who was clutching the air as if she was drowning. "You are such a trouble maker," Sarah teased as she tried to right herself and her belly on half of the bed.

Sarah opened the envelope and pulled out the note. "Dear Madam," Sarah read aloud, "Madam?"

"Just read it." Katherine encouraged; pulling her braid out from under her.

"Dear Madam," she began again, "My regiment is stationed near St. Louis for the day until we are to return to our post where you were recovered. I am most eager to see you restored to full health and in the comfort of family. If you have no objections, I will come by your family's home at 3:00 p.m.

"If there are any objections, please send word with my man to our encampment.

"Yours cordially, Captain William Dunbar." "Who is Captain Dunbar?" Sarah finished the letter and asked. "Is this yet another suitor you have snagged for me, sister?"

"Oh no, dear, Captain Dunbar is old enough to be our grandfather," Katherine giggled.

"Then who is he and why does he want to see me?"

Katherine slipped from the bed and adjusted her robe in front of the fireplace. "Sarah, he is the one..." she chose her words carefully, "who assisted Josiah Cooper in bringing you here, to me."

"Oh," Sarah said standing from her bed, "how thoughtful of him," sarcasm dripping from every word.

Katherine was thankful that the questions and attitude ended there.

"I suppose that I do owe him my life. Wild Dog would have left me to die. In fact, he would have killed me if..." she shook the memory from her mind. The pieces of the puzzle were still coming together in small segments. "He said that he wasn't allowed to kill me. I guess he and Josiah..." she put her hands over her face not wanting to succumb to the pain.

Katherine reacted immediately. "Don't let go, Sarah, you've come too far. If it would hurt you too much, I can cancel..."

"No, he did save my life. I can at least thank him."

"I thought as much. I'll make sure Matilda has a lovely tea prepared."

"Thank you, Katherine, for all that you do." *Thank you, God for my sister and her family and her never ending support.*

Promptly at 3:00, the knock was heard. Sarah and Katherine stood up in front of their chairs waiting for their guest to enter the room. Otis slid open the door, a distinguished older man in his army dress uniform stood holding his hat under his arm. His pure white mustache curled up at the ends. His hair, mostly white, yet tinged with the yellowing of smoke, hit just above his shoulders. Otis announced his entrance.

A smile dominated Captain Dunbar's face as he bowed low. He walked over to Katherine and bowed again, taking her hand and kissing her fingers. "Thank you for allowing me to trespass."

"It is our pleasure. So nice to see you again, Captain Dunbar," Katherine smiled.

He turned to Sarah, "A picture of health and more beautiful than I remember. I am happy to see you." He bent and kissed her fingers.

"It is an honor, Captain. Please, won't you sit down?" Sarah directed him to the long couch that sat between the two chairs that the sisters occupied. He sat and placed his hat beside him on the couch.

Katherine prepared the tea and plate as they made small talk on the weather. The topic turned to the poltics of slavery.

"The northerners think they have a right to tell everyone how to live and how to conduct business. Mark my words, one of these days, all hell's going to break loose. Oh pardon me, ladies," Captain Dunbar apologized for his language.

"Do you really think it will come to a war?" Katherine asked.

"Yes, ma'am, I do. It has to. And now that this business with Mexico is overwith, I am most certain the attentions of our government will be forced to address this situation. I am not opposed to war by any means. I've seen my fair share of bloodshed… And being a man of the South, I'll have to choose sides. I have a lot of good men under me that I know will become formidable opponents, and I would hate to see it come to that."

Katherine and Sarah glanced at each other wondering if the entire visit was going to be talk of war, but the Captains next statement would change the events of how they expected the day to go.

"I swear, some days I wish we could take care of those slaves and slave lovers like we can those Injun savages."

"I'm sorry?" Katherine asked.

"Well, the slaves are much too valuable. The Injuns on the other hand, are just worthless, bloodthirsty…"

"Captain, please…" Katherine interrupted seeing Sarah's face pale.

"Of course, my apologies. I get a little carried away and forget that I am in the company of two beautiful ladies. I am usually in the company of the men. I do apologize." Captain Dunbar nodded to Katherine who smiled back, and he reached over impulsively and patted Sarah's knee and confided, "Do forgive my speakin' freely, but you won't have to worry about those redskins ever botherin' you again."

"More tea, Captain Dunbar?" Katherine spoke quickly attempting to intervene.

The Captain nodded and handed his cup back to Katherine as he continued speaking to Sarah who was visibly shaking, but he took no notice. "Yes ma'am, as soon as you were brought to us by

Captive Heart

that poor, fool-hardy Mr. Cooper," the Captain shook his head in disbelief, "thinkin he could handle those devil-men all by himself. But he survived and managed to rescue you as well. That takes some charisma, I tell you! And did you know those filthy savages somehow stole the horse he brought you in on."

"Clara," Sarah barely muttered under her breath.

The captain continued, his eyes lighting up with reliving of the story. "I don't know how they did it, but it was obviously one of their own horses. Anyway, that horse tore off through our camp and right up the hill where there were two Injuns just-a-waitin' for it. I figure those were the scouts. Mr. Cooper told us they were chasin' after him to try and get you back. They hate to lose one of their captives, you know."

Sarah fidgeted in her seat but was unable to speak. Wanting, but not wanting to hear the rest of the story.

The Captain, however, needed no encouragement to continue. "Mr. Cooper tipped us off that they were planning an attack on our base for some time. He knew he only had a short window to rescue you, so he took his chance. Now with you in our base, we knew they would be comin' for sure. And we were ready. We had to get you out of there, right quick." He became more animated with the re-telling. Katherine never took her eyes off her teacup and Sarah stared cold into the Captain's eyes.

"Ol' Cooper, he gave us the exact location of where they were holding you captive. So we got you safely here, to St. Louis, with your lovely family," he briefly nodded to Katherine, "and then we took care of business." Captain Dunbar took a sip of his tea, his tirade apparently coming to a merciful end.

Sarah took in a deep breath, but only Katherine could see the pain in her face and deep in her eyes. "Please, Captain, pray continue."

"Sarah, I don't think that is such a good idea," Katherine said trying to smile.

"No, please, I want to know. Just how did you... take care of business, Captain?" Sarah's words were polite, but her voice was shaking.

"Well, I don't mean to brag... but it *is* quite a story," he mentioned to Katherine obvious in his support of Sarah.

"Captain, my sister is looking tired, perhaps we could persuade you another day," Katherine tried again gently standing.

The Captain stood looking a little confused, but Sarah kept her seat. "My sister worries too much... I am fine. Do I not deserve to know? What with being a captive all those years?"

The Captain set his cup and saucer down on the end table and took Sarah's hand. "Madam, I would be so pleased and honored to tell you the tale that will allow you to sleep peacefully at night." He sat back down in the corner of the couch and settled into his best story-telling position. Not being able to hear the anguish in Sarah's voice, his eyes lit up and he held his hands out in front of him ready to begin. Katherine knew that this would not end well.

"We kept our eye on those two redskins and when they left, we knew that they were going back to get more of their filthy savage friends. So we waited. When we heard that you were safely delivered to St. Louis, we made our move. Now the Army believes in sneak attacks and all, but we decided to give them a fair chance, so we waited until daybreak. We are not barbarians, you know. The light was just coming up over the horizon; we made our move." He leaned back against the couch and slapped his knee. "Whoo! It was like shootin' fish in a barrel! They didn't know what hit 'em." He stood up and leveled his imaginary gun on its target and pulled the invisible trigger, complete with sound effects. He lined up the next "victim", took aim and shot again and again. "Like fish in a barrel!" he said once more. "They were runnin' all over, screamin' tryin' to cover themselves. They sounded like barkin' dogs." He placed his hand by his mouth as if conveying a secret, "I'm not really a dog man, myself." He stood back up and looked off into the distance, "Yep, I was sure proud of my men that day."

Tears filled Katherine's eyes but Sarah's face remained hard, unruffled. "Were there any survivors?" she managed to ask, her jaw was quivering but her voice showing no emotions.

"Ma'am, you are speakin' to a Captain of the United States Army. When we set out to do a job, it gets done," he nodded to her and he fell back down to the couch. "You can sleep well, little lady," he winked at her trying to be tender. Then he laughed to himself and rubbed his hands together remembering the glory of the day, "But you know, just to be on the safe side, we torched it."

"What?" This broke Sarah's countenance. She began to shake and grab her stomach. Fragments of her dreams flooded her mind as Captain Dunbar's words faded in and out of hearing. She saw the flames; she felt the heat. The horses that rode past, she looked up and saw the uniforms, now. She shook her head, the dreams…

"Our post is only about seventy miles away from where this village was," the Captain was saying, "I'm sorry to be vulgar, ladies, but rotting bodies don't exactly smell like a bouquet of flowers, if you know what I mean. So we had to set the place on fire. Not that burning flesh smells much better," he laughed to himself until he heard Katherine gasp as she covered her nose with her handkerchief.

"What of the children?" Katherine managed to ask, "Was there no mercy for them, Captain?"

"Ma'am, to speak frankly, the little ones just grow up to be animals. Just like their parents. Sometimes it's just better to kill off the young. It's the humane thing to do. Stamp them out before they learn to kill…"

Sarah stood up and screamed out. She grabbed hold of her stomach and bent over. Her teacup and saucer rolled to the floor.

"Sarah!" Katherine stood and ran over to her sister. "Matilda!" Katherine called out.

Sarah managed to stand erect. Her face was red and tear stained. She leaned over to hold onto the chair for support.

Katherine stepped over and took hold of the Captain's arm. "Captain," she said, always the hostess, "I believe that events have cut our visit short. I'm sure you understand," Katherine smiled as she began to lead the Captain towards the door. Captain Dunbar, taken aback by the delicate … female… situation, only nodded and leaned over to pick up his hat.

"I don't think it would be safe to have you here when I give birth to my future killer," Sarah sneered at the man.

He walked over to her kneading his hat in his hands and spoke sincerely, "I am sorry we could not have saved you before this tragedy."

Sarah cried out again in agony, "I wish I would have died with my family!" Sarah shouted.

The captain stepped back, obviously shocked by her words.

Katherine stepped between them before the Captain had the opportunity to respond. "Captain, she is obviously not thinking clearly. Do you mind if Matilda shows you to the door?"

"Did she mean…" Captain Dunbar struggled against Katherine to look back at Sarah who had fallen to her knees and rocked against the pain.

"I believe she is referring to the attack on the wagon train…before…" Katherine let her words trail off so the captain could make his own conclusions. He nodded in understanding and kissed Katherine's hand. He glanced back over his shoulder at Sarah, and dropped his eyes to his hat, "Be sure to tell her…"

"I will…" Katherine guessing at the end of his sentence, "Thank you for your visit"

He smiled down at her. "I do want to leave you with these last words of caution," he took a deep breath and patted her hands. "You need to dispose of that abomination as soon as possible. When it is old enough, they instinctively need to kill. And they could kill you and your family in your sleep. How well will you be able to sleep with a savage under your roof?"

Sarah cried out again and Matilda shut the

parlor doors with the Captain on the outside of them. She escorted him to the door and handed him his coat and gloves.

The moment the front door was shut and their guest had departed; Matilda came back into the parlor and helped Katherine take Sarah to her room. "Matilda, fetch the doctor, and start boiling the water."

"But Missus Katherine, it ain't time. That baby ain't done yet." Matilda panicked.

"Try and tell the baby that!" Sarah interjected. She crawled to her bed and got onto her hands and knees. "Please, be okay, little one," she murmured out loud. The voice of Grieving Mother came to her mind, "This one will come early." Sarah shook her head; it can't be possible. It was a dream. Or was it a message?

Katherine rubbed Sarah's back and was oddly interested in her calm. *How much, o Lord, can she take?* Katherine prayed silently while holding her sister's hand. *Lord, be with her and this baby. Please let her days of heartache come to an end with Mr. Greer.*

Chapter Twenty- Seven

Hours passed and the whole house was put on hold. The children were uncommonly quiet and respectful. It was not too long of a wait until the sound of a baby's cry broke the silence.

Sarah crawled back into her freshly made bed and stacked the pillows high behind her head. Sarah breathed through the pain as she situated herself on her bed waiting to be reunited with her daughter.

Katherine held and rocked the baby waiting for Sarah to be settled. She stroked the soft black hair and ran her finger over her cheek. The baby turned her head toward Katherine's finger looking for food. "Oh, no, sweetie, I can't help you, there. Let me give you back to your mother." She walked over to Sarah and leaned her daughter into her arms. "She is so beautiful." Katherine wiped away her own tears.

Sarah pulled her daughter close to her breast. The baby nursed and Sarah ran her fingers gently down the baby's arm and across to her tiny fingers. Her skin was a light tan; her hair was jet black and her eyes, a piercing blue... just like her brothers.

"Grieving Mother said she would come early," Sarah spoke softly, her eyes never leaving the baby. "She also showed me the massacre... in my dreams. I knew it before Captain Dunbar ever said anything. He merely confirmed it." She looked up at Katherine. "He is alive, sister."

"Sarah, let's not ruin this beautiful moment."

"I have to go back."

"Can we talk about this another time?" Katherine stuttered.

"You always say that. I love you; you are my sister... but..."

"Sarah, they are dead. You have to come to terms with that!" Katherine walked across the room and stood beside the window looking out over the city's street. She took a deep breath. "I know this must be extremely difficult for you, but you have to move forward," she spoke more calmly and gently. "You are back where you belong now. You have your family... a beautiful baby girl. You have a man that wants to make you his wife. Sarah, let's think reasonably. Let God bless you. You have been through so much. Let Him bless you."

Sarah looked back down at her precious child in her arms. Their skin colors were dramatically different. Sarah's was so pale, and the babe's was so tan. "You look like your father," she whispered to her daughter. To Katherine she said, "She told me to come and find him."

Katherine looked confused and annoyed. "Do you hear yourself? It was just a dream, a coincidence."

"All of those things? There has to be more!" Sarah wiped the tears from her chin before they fell onto her nursing baby. "I have to see it... for myself."

"I don't think..."

"Katherine. Look at my child," Sarah spoke

sternly. Katherine's eyes veered down to the precious bundle pressed against her only sister. "How do you think she will fair in this world? You heard Captain Dunbar. She is different. She… and I need to be with her people." Sarah paused not wanting to hurt her sister's feelings. She wanted to believe that she was on the path to receive God's blessings and she would eventually get over the pain of her past… her losses. Her throat tightened as the images of her husband and son came before her. She looked down at the new life that was given to her and relished in the fact that this, right here, was one of God's many blessings. She could not settle into a new life until her doubts were salved. This was the direction she was being sent from the words God whispered to her heart.

"Please, sister. Please, just take me out there and if they are all gone, I will come home and marry Mr. Greer… happily, without reservation."

"Sarah, it's at least a day's journey."

"We can leave early and we can stop at the Army encampment on the way back. I am sure they would love having guests from St. Louis. Especially if we come bearing gifts… Mr. Greer said that his visit would be postponed, we would have plenty of time."

"I make no promises," Katherine started and walked over to Sarah's bed gently sitting on the edge and pulling the cover back slightly to see the now sleeping baby. "I will discuss it with James. We couldn't possibly go until spring… "

"But… Mr. Greer…"

"Not until spring… if at all."

Sarah nodded accepting her sister's offer. "Thank you, Katherine." Sarah's eyes glistened with tears as the sisters joined hands.

It was late in February after a heavy storm had passed through St. Louis that Cylus Greer was able to make it back. His return was announced with packages arriving just days before he made his appearance on the doorstep of the James Tobias household.

He was obviously pleased at Sarah's slimmer figure and it showed in his thinly veiled passionate looks. "You are truly beautiful," he whispered, as he kissed her hands and boldly reached to kiss her cheek. "I didn't think…"

"She was early," Sarah smiled, surprised at how well she was accepting his attentions.

"She? Is she as beautiful as her mother?" he asked tentatively.

"More so, I believe," Sarah blushed. "Would you like to meet her?"

He cleared his throat, and loosened his collar nervously, "Of course."

Sarah took him over to where little Emma Grace lay sleeping in the lacy bassinet, one of the many gifts from Cylus Greer.

She pulled back the covers from her face, but was watching Cylus' expression. She saw that his brow furrowed and his eyes darted everywhere. "She is… quite lovely," he managed to say.

"Thank you. You wouldn't be able to tell she was born early. Her appetite has helped her catch up quickly."

Sarah saw the concern in his face. Emma's tan skin and coal black hair betrayed her heritage.

Sarah scooped up the infant and cradled her in her arms and sat in the chair hoping Cylus would sit as well. He chose to pace, searching for conversation.

Cylus finally sat and leaned toward Sarah. "Sarah... I..." he swallowed hard. Sarah could read both panic and pain in his eyes so she decided to help the conversation along.

"How are your travels this time of year? Are the roads clear and what not?" Sarah asked nonchalantly.

Happy for the distraction, Cylus answered, "Not so much really. The snow is melting, yes, but it looks like we will be getting more bad weather here before the week is out."

"So does this mean you will be staying in St. Louis for a while?"

"No," Cylus answered quickly. He glanced down at the baby trying to be discreet, but Sarah saw. "On the contrary, I will be leaving again, immediately. We have... been having... trouble at some of the... boatyards. But I don't wish to bore you with business."

"You are very kind. I don't have much of a head for business." Sarah stood and placed her sleeping baby back in her cradle. "Thank you for all of the lovely gifts."

"Oh, yes, you're welcome, of course." He stared into her eyes for a moment mentally making his final decision. "Sarah," he stood and walked close to her. He reached his hand out and placed it gently on her cheek. She smiled demurely and broke his gaze. "I'm sorry."

"No need to apologize, Mr. Greer. Duty calls you away."

"Yes. Thank you."

"Well," Sarah stepped away and tucked the blankets in around Emma, "I don't think it fair that we keep you all to ourselves when your stay is going to be of such a short duration. You must have a lot of business to tend to." Sarah was pleasant with her words. She didn't want this marriage any more than he did, anymore, but he was too much of a gentleman to go back on his word. Sarah was giving him an easy escape, and he was silently grateful.

"I... I do. Thank you." He looked at Sarah's face hoping that she could not see the guilt that he was hiding in his heart. He felt like a coward. What a prize she would make standing beside him. But this child... He knew he could never love this half-breed and he also knew the mother would never let it go.

Sarah called for Matilda to bring Mr. Greer his hat and coat. He stood in the hallway putting on his gloves, "I'm sorry I couldn't stay longer." He looked up at her again, memorizing her features, "You look absolutely beautiful. Motherhood becomes you."

"Thank you," she smiled sincerely.

"I'll write... when I can," he lied. "But I know that I'll be..."

"It's alright, Mr. Greer. I understand." Sarah held her hand out to him and he kissed it a few moments longer than appropriate.

He looked up into her eyes and his voice cracked, "Goodbye, Sarah."

"Goodbye," she answered back. She knew that he meant it. It would be the last time she saw Mr. Cylus Greer.

Captive Heart

Chapter Twenty- Eight

Sarah had accumulated quite a bit of belongings since she had arrived late last summer. "I couldn't possibly take all of these things back with me. They would make fun of me!" she said to herself. "Or would they?" She held up one of her dresses and looked at herself in her long mirror. "Yes. They would," she laughed. "Uncomfortable things!" She walked over and flopped down beside Emma Grace who was sprawled out on a blanket on the floor. "Although, some of these undergarments could certainly come in handy… wouldn't they?" Sarah leaned over and asked her baby who just smiled up at her.

Sarah looked thoughtfully around her bedroom. "All of these modern conveniences, that I thought I couldn't live without. We will be leaving them all behind," she spoke to Emma Grace who responded by stretching out her arms and gurgling. "Will you miss any of them, do you think?" she asked the babe. "No? Me either." She leaned over and kissed playfully on the baby's belly. "You'll have your daddy, won't you? Won't you?" she nuzzled into Emma's belly again to be awarded with giggles and Emma grabbing her hair. "Daddy will take care of us won't he?" Sarah talked and cooed with her growing child. "But there are some things…" Sarah stood after she kissed Emma's forehead and walked to her desk and pulled out a slip of paper. She sat at her desk and began a list.

"Sweets for the children... a good knife set! Oh, one better, a dinnerware set. Who would have thought that simple utensils like a fork, knife and spoon could make such a difference," she laughed at herself and continued her list. "I don't suppose I could take a bathtub..." she looked around her room and thought for a moment. "Seeds! I can introduce them to all kinds of new foods. Gardening these new items can't be that hard, they already know about corn and beans. But oh, wouldn't potatoes be a lovely addition. If I had to eat one more turnip..." she scribbled her list of seeds. "Cloth for Grieving Mother... and some for me. I will make some comfortable... cool summer clothes. And I will bring everyone a sewing needle and some thread. Something new for the sewing circle."

Sarah could smell breakfast wafting up to her room, so she scooped up Emma Grace and went downstairs. Kinsi was there to take the baby so Sarah could eat in peace, "I would like her back after breakfast please, Kinsi"

"Yes'm."

"You coddle her too much," Katherine said as she poured Sarah some coffee.

"It is the Indian way that a mother is rarely without her child until they are around three years old."

"You are not with the Indians, as yet," Katherine argued trying not to lose her patience.

"But I will be. Besides, I like their way better. I enjoy having Emma with me. I can't even remember any other way."

Katherine shrugged her shoulders wondering

Captive Heart

why she ever agreed to letting Sarah go back. If the scene was anything like Captain Dunbar described, it could damage Sarah forever. But, then again, it might just be what she needs to let go of the past and come back to St. Louis to start a new life. Katherine did her best to humor her sister and prayed that this whole ordeal would be over soon.

Later in the afternoon, Sarah sought out Kinsi. "Would you mind caring for Emma for a bit?"

"No missus, I s'pposed to be carin' fo her even mo. I don't mind. Dis way I don't have to carry coal."

Sarah laughed and kissed the baby and handed her over to Kinsi. Then, Sarah went where few members of the household ever venture to. Downstairs to the kitchen.

She could hear Otis and Matilda laughing and singing. As she walked into the plain grey kitchen she saw Otis in a long white apron, whistling as he dried the dishes Matilda was handing him. Matilda accompanied him with a tune as she poured another bucket of hot water into the sink. Her long grey skirt was "swooshing" along with the music.

Sarah, not wanting to interrupt, leaned against the doorway, listening and smiling.

Matilda saw her first and nudged Otis to stop. They both put down their items and turned to face Sarah.

"Yes, Miss, is they somethin' I can do for ya?"

"Matilda, I am sorry to interrupt, but I was wondering... what is your... most valuable asset in the kitchen?"

"Miss?"

"I mean, what is your favorite thing that you use in your kitchen that you just couldn't live without?"

"Oh," she smiled, "you mean 'sides my ol cook stove there?" Sarah nodded and looked around her domain. "It's likely my stew pot... or my griddle. No, I don't think I could survive without this here clever... but I has to say, I sho do love this indoor pump Mr. James had put in. 'Specially on cold winter mornins' like these. It sho is nice. It sho is."

Sarah nodded because she remembered how it had been to walk down to the river to get buckets of water for everything. Then an idea came to her.

"Matilda, I may only be here for a few more weeks, do you think I could cook with you?"

"Miss Sarah, where you goin', you gots no one to cook fo you?"

Sarah laughed. "No, besides, I like to do it myself... but I'm a little rusty and well, just not very good. And I could use some hints on short cuts," she smiled.

"Oh, Missy Sarah, I knows all da shortcut they is to know," she laughed a full and hearty laugh, "What would the Missus say?"

"Don't worry about her. Would you mind?"

"No, miss, I enjoy bein' here in my kitchen. I could sure use some company."

"What do you call me, some ol' dried bread?" Otis spoke up pretending to be insulted.

"Now you hush.... Fo supper today, the missus call fo chicken. How 'bout we start there."

"That would be fine." Sarah smiled broadly and pushed up her sleeves. "Okay. Where do I start?"

"Firs, I'd be puttin on dis apron so's you don't soil yo pretty things," Matilda laughed.

The two ladies cooked and chatted all day. Sarah added items like salt and sugar to her list and she learned shortcuts and other secrets that she'd be able to take back with her.

"Sarah, the ladies of the church are having a quilting, would you like to go along?" Katherine asked one morning after breakfast.

"I would love to, but I promised Ma…"

"I'm quite sure she can survive for one day without your help," Katherine interjected trying to keep the edge from her voice. "Really sister, when I suggested you not spend so much time with your baby, I certainly did not expect you to take on the domestic duties."

"Don't be silly. When I go back home I'll have to cook much more. I am quite out of practice and actually rather spoiled."

Katherine's face took on the look of watching a pitiful street urchin with sympathy. "Sarah, I don't mean to be unsupportive, but you don't have to go back to…"

"Don't say that!" Sarah snapped but then took in a breath and spoke more calmly. "I can't give up hope."

"Sister…"

"Katherine. He is my husband and my son is out there too. Tell me you wouldn't do the same. Love is love no matter how he was raised, or how differently I was raised," Sarah sighed and fought back tears. "In my heart, there is no difference."

"Alright, I will not make another discouraging remark, but I can't promise that I won't worry."

"That's fair," Sarah smiled as she tried to swallow the lump in her throat.

Katherine moved over to the couch to sit beside Sarah and wrapped her arms around her sister. "I love you so much. I am having trouble letting you go again," Katherine's throat tightened.

Sarah leaned her head over on top of Katherine's and returned the embrace. "I have so enjoyed being here with you and your family."

"Come to the quilting with me. We could certainly use your expertise… and our time together is running out."

"Yes, I will come with you. Let me run and tell Matilda and feed Emma."

From that time on, the two sisters were practically inseparable. They went out and had chocolate soda, lunch alongside the river, took in the theatre and shopped. Katherine was thankful for the chill in the air and the snow on the ground because it meant that Sarah had to keep her shoes on. Sarah still helped Matilda in the kitchen for one meal a day and played perfect hostess for Katherine and James' friends for the rest of her visit.

But then, the day finally came. The sun warmed the ground, the flowers poked their buds from dirt, and the daylight grew longer.

Sarah had been packed for weeks.

It was more difficult to say her good-byes than Sarah expected. She gave Kinsi the mirror and comb set that Cylus Greer had given her for Christmas.

"I gon miss your baby," she said with a tear

slipping down her cheek.

"Thank you for taking such good care of her. She is going to miss you too."

"When Matilda opened her gift, her eyes flooded with tears, "Oh Missy Sarah, dis be too pretty to wear."

"Try it on," Sarah said, pulling out the hand made apron embellished with beads and embroidery.

"It fit, but I can't be wearin' it in this dirty ol' kitchen. It be nice nuf fo church wearin'"

"So be it then," Sarah shrugged. "I have enjoyed our time together immensely. Thank you for sharing your kitchen with me." They embraced warmly then Matilda pulled away and ran back to her kitchen.

"Don't leave, jis yet," she called out.

Katherine and Sarah gave Otis his gift together since they had made it together.

He opened it and stared at it without saying a word.

"It's... it's a jacket," Sarah explained. "It's for when you take the carriage out, or go to church, or run errands for Mr. James."

"I ain't never had nothin' so nice," he said with a shaky voice.

"Well, now you do." Katherine chimed in, "and don't you dare hurt our feelings by not wearing it, because you think it's too nice," she smiled at him and patted his arm.

"Oh no, missus, I wear it everyday. It a fine jacket. Thank you Miss Sarah, thank you, Missus Katherine." He nodded his head several times as he backed away.

"Alright ladies, we have to go if we are

really going to do this," James called out.

"Do you think Otis should come with us?" Katherine asked.

"Katherine, I am perfectly capable of driving horses. We do have to stop by the store and pick up Johnson. We'll be fine," James said, "But we do have to go. We only have so much daylight."

Sarah had said goodbye to all of the children last night since they would still be in bed when they left in the morning. She left gifts for each one of them at the foot of their beds so they would have something to remember her by.

She took the sleeping Emma Grace from Kinsi and tucked her blankets around her. There was a chill in the air so, Sarah tucked her into her coat for extra warmth, and held her with one arm.

Katherine came up and claimed the unused arm and linked her own through it. She laid her head on Sarah's shoulder as they took one last look at the house that Sarah would probably never see again.

"It will be lonely here without you."

"I will miss my best friend," Sarah whispered.

"You can always come back," Katherine said looking at her sister's tear streaked face. "For a visit." Sarah nodded, not knowing what the future holds. "Come on," Katherine warned breaking away, wiping her own tears and tying on her hat, "before James starts complaining about the hours he is losing at the store," she laughed faintly.

Sarah nodded again. She was ready.

"Wait! Wait Miss Sarah!" Sarah looked back over her shoulder and saw Matilda running toward her. "Here, Miss Sarah, dis for you."

Sarah pulled back the opening of the heavy burlap sack and saw smaller individually wrapped cloth sachets. "It's some spices for you. Helps those turnips go down lil better. An dis one, it be real good for tenderizin' venison. And this here, this some lentils for soup. Fatten up that boy o' yours." Matilda dropped her voice to a whisper, "I even put some taters in there so you don have ta wait til they grow."

Sarah was crying and Matilda's eyes shone with tears. "Thank you, Matilda, for everything." Sarah pressed her forehead against Matilda's since her hands were full.

James stepped out of the carriage and helped Sarah and Katherine into their seats.

Matilda and Otis stood on the stoop and waved goodbye until they could no longer see the carriage.

The carriage turned right to pick up the supplies and Johnson from the store.

Most of the town was still quiet when they left the store. The roads were pretty smooth until they reached the cities end.

Johnson, one of the Tobias' workers from the store, drove the wagon alongside James' carriage. The two sisters slept part of the way but chatted most of the time trying to involve James as much as possible.

Emma turned out to be the perfect traveling baby. She slept, she ate and she rode along not causing a fuss. "Her father will be so proud. It will make it easier for our spring hunting trip. Jacob on the other hand, was not so very patient when we had to travel," Sarah told them about the worn path that James would find that would lead them to the village that they took every spring to hunt buffalo.

James said that he sent word along to Captain Dunbar of their visit. *"In return for his most welcomed visit and its unfortunate and abrupt end,"* it said. James also brought along 50 pounds of coffee for the men. He didn't mention if there would be one or two ladies in his party.

They decided to take Sarah directly to the village and spend the night at the army encampment on their return, that way, if Sarah is present on the way there, but not on the way back, it would not need explanation.

Chapter Twenty- Nine

Sarah's heart began to speed up when the landscapes began to look familiar. She showed Katherine and James the worn path that veered off into the distance. "And just up here, there should be a lining of trees..." and as if on command, they came into view. Sarah could scarcely stay in her seat.

The closer they got; the smell grew stronger. A wet musty, rotting smell.

Sarah shifted Emma on her lap. A feeling of dread practically suffocated her. They pulled in between the break in the trees. The carriage could barely make it through.

"Stop, James. Please, stop here." Sarah handed Emma Grace over to her sister and jumped from the carriage and took off running.

"Sarah!" Katherine called after her, but James wrapped his arms around her.

"Let her go," James comforted.

Sarah followed the horse path toward her village. The trees were scarred with burnt limbs and ravaged trunks. The ground was wet with the remains of autumn's leaves that had been buried by the snow. The moist, rotting air accosted her nostrils. She raised her hand to cover her face.

When she finally came to the clearing, she was out of breath and nauseous from inhaling the death of winter. She stopped dead in her tracks when she saw what was left of her home.

Her hand slowly slipped away from her face and fell to her side. Her heart pounded against the confines of her chest. Her eyes scanned the village. James and Katherine had gently maneuvered the carriage along the horse path, but Sarah did not hear. They sat quietly in the carriage and let Sarah grieve.

The weetus were burned to the ground. Only a few frames remained. There was an eerie silence devoid of the normal forest noises and people and families working and playing.

Sarah had to support herself on a nearby tree. There was nothing. Nothing left.

She walked down what was once the center path of the village. She saw human bones scattered by animals, clothes and pottery lying about. All the signs of the life that once thrived here. She walked over to her home… what was left of it. A cradle half charred still stood in the corner. She lifted some of the burned sticks… "The bathtub?" she laughed through her tears.

She picked up a stick and dug through the wet leaves and clay made from the wet ash. She went to where the platform was that held their bed… nothing. She found a pile of mildewed blankets piled up where the head of their bed once was. Her stick moved them so they would fall over. She hit something hard. She dug a little deeper and found… a box. Her letter box. Undamaged. Save for some water spots. She opened it and the letters were just as they had always been.

She could no longer keep her grief silent. The tears poured from her eyes and she struggled to catch her breath between sobs. She shook her head not wanting to believe what her eyes were telling

Captive Heart

her. Her heart fought against the truth that surrounded her. She called out in her Indian language. "NO! You cannot be dead!" She sobbed as her voice echoed across the barren valley. "Little Feather! Where are you? Jacob!" She fell to her knees and cried. "I came back. I came back. You cannot be dead." She whimpered.

Katherine tried to get out of the carriage to comfort her sister, but James held her still.

Sarah pulled herself up with her stick and held her box under her arm. She was so deep in grief that she did not see the carriage. She walked by memory past the other homes of her friends and her adopted family seeing, but not seeing. She walked in a daze to the river's edge and looked up to the mighty bluff standing before her.

She fell to her knees, "God! Please, this is all my fault! I am so sorry!" She was sobbing again. She shouted out, with what was left of her voice, "Little Feather! I am sorry! I love you! Please do not be dead!" She fell forward catching herself with her hands against the rocks. She let her fingers dig into the rock beach and let the tears fall.

A pair of hands touched her shoulders and she let them embrace her. They lifted her up and guided her back toward the carriage.

"Come on, Sarah, let's go back."

Sarah hiccupped and could barely breathe, "Katherine, he can't be dead. Grieving Mother told me to find him. I have to look for him, but I don't know where. All this life... lost. Katherine, they killed them." Sarah was crying and babbling, but allowed her sister to guide her footsteps. "Little Feather, I came back," she murmured.

They reached the carriage and Katherine

climbed in and took the sleeping baby from the much-relieved James.

Sarah stepped up into the carriage and wiped her tears, "I will never love again."

She took a deep breath trying to convince herself that she was ready for her future alone. Raising Emma alone. She leaned over to take Emma from Katherine and noticed the frightened look on her sister's face. Sarah followed the gaze back out across the destroyed village. There he stood.

A man with dark black hair down past his shoulders. His hair hung loose and got caught up in the breeze blowing it away from his face. He stood staring at the carriage, not speaking a word. He wore no shirt, but light colored leggings. He held a long spear in his right hand that he was using as a staff. The only thing that made him look real was the breeze moving his hair as it blew.

Sarah gasped and stared back. She looked over at her sister and brother-in-law, making sure they saw what she did. Their sheer look of terror confirmed it. She looked back toward the figure as fresh tears fell from her eyes. She slid down from the carriage, her heart pounding in her chest.

"Sarah, no," Katherine whispered without moving.

She cautiously took a couple steps forward. Am I seeing this, she questioned herself.

"Natayah..." the wind carried his deep emotion-laden voice to her and wrapped itself around her heart.

No longer could she control her feet or her tears. She made her way to him and stopped a couple steps away still doubting her blurred vision.

"How long I have waited for you," he spoke gently. There were tears in his eyes. He held out his hand to her and she took the remaining steps toward him. He reached out and grabbed a handful of her hair near the scalp. He pulled her close to him and kissed her with the passion of a lifetime of love and the broken heart of separation. She threw her arms around him and laid her head against his chest.

"Is it really you? Am I really here? With you?" she cried, "I have missed you so much."

He pulled her back so he could see her face again. He wiped the tears from her face. "You take a long time keeping your promises, wife," he smiled down at her. "Are you staying?" he looked at her clothes and nodded to the carriage.

She bobbed her head up and down. "Forever." She embraced him again. She ran her hand along his cheek. "Will you come with me; I want you to meet someone."

"Your sister?"

"Yes, but there is someone even more important," he allowed her to pull him reluctantly toward the carriage.

James and Katherine had a look of fear on their face that they were both trying to hide. It made Little Feather laugh inside. Katherine had tears in her eyes when she handed Sarah her baby.

She took her and uncovered her face and handed her to Little Feather. "This is your daughter." Little Feather took her and cradled her close to his chest. He nuzzled her with his nose and breathed her in deeply. James was a little jealous at his ease around such a young child.

"What do you call her?" he asked.

"Emma Grace."

"My wife," he reached up and cupped Sarah's face, "our daughter is beautiful." Sarah placed her hand over his on her cheek and kissed his palm. Sarah smiled in a teasing grin and she kissed Emma's forehead and then kissed her husband. "I knew you would say that, she looks just like you!" she laughed and he leaned in to kiss her again. "Mmm, I have missed that, too." she swallowed hard, "So much."

Sarah broke her gaze with Little Feather and laughed, a little embarrassed, "I would like you to meet my sister and her husband." In English she turned to her sister and said, "Katherine and James, This is my husband, Little Feather."

To everyone's surprise, Little Feather stepped forward and said, in English, "Hello. It is nice to meet you."

"Little Feather! Where did you..." Sarah smiled and looked past her husband at something that caught her eye. She turned and stepped past her husband and baby. She saw a little face peeking out from behind a tree. Sarah's breathing increased as her heart beat faster, "Jacob?" she said in disbelief. "My Jacob?" She said again calling out to him.

"Momma!" he came darting out from behind the tree toward her.

Sarah looked up at Little Feather and he rolled his eyes and she took off toward her son. He jumped into her arms and wrapped his legs around her.

"Jacob. Jacob... oh, my baby. Oh... you are so big and handsome. I have missed you so much."

"Momma, your hair is up."

"Yes. It is. Let me look at you," he pulled back and put his hands on her cheeks. "You are so beautiful, Jacob. I prayed for you everyday."

"Momma…"

"Yes, honey."

"You look funny. Your clothes are funny."

"I will fix it soon. You do not like them?"

"I guess so. They just look funny… Momma?"

"Yes, Jacob?"

"We do not live here anymore."

"I am so glad. Where do we live now?"

"Up there. On the bluff. Papa heard you calling to him. We have been waiting for you."

Sarah's throat tightened, "I am so glad that you were. Thank you for coming back to get me."

"Papa said to wait by the river, but it was taking too long."

Sarah pressed his head down to her shoulder and rocked him back and forth. "Oh my baby." she whispered and breathed in the smell of his blanket of ebony hair. Sarah pulled him back to look at him again, "But a baby you are not. You have grown so!" She started walking back to the carriage with her son in her arms. "You have gotten heavy," she teased.

"I am almost grown," he giggled when she tickled his ribs.

"Jacob, I want you to meet my sister."

"Not Talking Bird?"

"No, this is *my* sister; Talking Bird is your father's sister. Her name is Katherine."

"She looks like you. She has skin like you."

Sarah laughed. It felt good to laugh. "Yes, she does." She turned his face to greet them and spoke in English, "Jacob, this is your Aunt Katherine and Uncle James."

He waved and spoke in perfect English. "Hello. My name is Jacob. It is nice to meet you."

Everyone laughed. "What? Did I say something wrong?" he asked.

"You said all the right things, my love." Jacob beamed. "And this... is your sister." Sarah introduced the new siblings. Little Feather crouched down so he could see her.

Sarah walked up to Katherine who finally climbed down from the carriage. She handed Sarah her letter box. "Here. You might need this... so ... you won't... forget me," Katherine said through her tears. "And here..." she reached around in her bag and pulled out a fat envelope. "A new letter for you. The children all wrote one, too." Katherine opened the lid and tucked it inside.

"Oh, sister, I will never, *could* ever, forget you. You are so special to me. I love you. This is not easy. But you can see. I belong here. Tell me you can see that."

Katherine nodded. "I can see it. Your family is wonderful." Katherine leaned in and whispered in her ear, "Are all Indian men so... open with their affection?"

Sarah tipped her head back and laughed. "They do not hide their emotions well. All of the people are pretty affectionate, but I got the best one."

"It is obvious that he loves you. I couldn't leave you, otherwise."

"Katherine, we will see each other again."

"I will hold you to that sister." They embraced again.

"I will have Johnson unload the wagon just inside the tree area... is that alright with you?" James asked.

"Yes, that would be wonderful. Thank you, James." She walked over to his side of the carriage. He climbed down, looking over to Little Feather almost looking for permission. Little Feather nodded, very much to James' relief. He embraced his sister-in-law. "You are always welcome at our home. But I wish you the very best of luck."

"Thank you, James. But I think I'll be alright."

He nodded and hugged her again, "It looks like you'll be in good hands."

She smiled, "I think so. Thank you for all that you have done for me and Emma."

"I have known you almost your whole life. You will always be family to me."

Little Feather came over to stand beside his wife. James stiffened at his presence

"I owe you much thanks," Little Feather spoke in broken English, "I am happy to have my wife return home." He nodded to James, and James nervously nodded in return.

Sarah took Little Feather's hand and went back around to attempt to make her final good-byes to her sister. She looked on while Katherine listened as Jacob chattered on.

She stood when she saw Sarah and Little Feather watching. "I guess you are waiting for me to give her back," Katherine stuttered. With her arms wrapped around Emma, she leaned down to kiss her niece one last time. She handed Emma over to Sarah, and then crouched back down to be face to face with Jacob. "You are quite a wonderful young man. I am so happy to have met you." She reached out and ran her fingers on his hair. "May I give you a hug?"

Jacob smiled and let his aunt envelope him into an embrace. "You are pretty. Just like my mother."

"Well thank you. I think you are very handsome." She ruffled his long, unkept hair. "Help your mother to take care of your new sister."

"Yes ma'am, I will."

Katherine stood and patted Jacob again and he ran over to cling to his mother's leg. The tears came again as Katherine looked at this... perfect family standing in front of her. She saw no color, just a loving family. Sarah was right; it is possible to be color-blind.

Sarah stepped forward, "Katherine, there are no words." Sarah tried to speak as the words got caught in her throat.

"None are necessary," Katherine smiled. "Just know that I love you." They embraced once more and Sarah stepped back again to stand beside her husband.

Little Feather stepped forward and helped Katherine into her seat in the carriage. James clicked at the horses to turn the carriage around. Sarah and Katherine waved and looked to each other until they were only dots on the landscape.

When the carriage was out of sight, Little Feather turned to his wife and wiped away her tears. "Are you going to be alright?" he asked. She nodded. "Let me take you home," he whispered and leaned down to kiss the new tears away.

"Do we have a home?" she asked.

He just laughed.

"How did you escape?" she asked, "Is everyone okay? What happened?"

"Wife. We have the rest of our lives together. Can these questions wait until tomorrow?"

She smiled up at him and nodded.

"What is all of that out there?"

"A taste of the other world," she smiled.

"No more leaving us again?"

"Never. Never again."

The End

Elizabeth Bourgeret

Epilogue

After the long hike to their new home, which was a beautiful flat wooded area atop the cliff, she was told the tale of the massacre.

Little Feather had taken her horse to the village and they were going back that night to take Natayah from the army. He was unaware that she was already gone. Little Feather fell asleep before the raid and the words of Wild Dog came back to him. "You had better hide your families because the white man is coming to kill them."

It woke him up with a start. He looked over to his son lying close beside him.

"Son, wake up. Come with me. Grab your blankets and things."

Jacob followed his father's directions without saying a word.

Little Feather took him over to Talking Bird and Two Spear. "I am sorry to wake you. I am here early. But I feel we must get as many as who will follow and move them to a safe place. What if there is truth in what Wild Dog says?"

"You would believe anything that he would say?" Two Spear asked.

"I do not want to take any chances. Talking Bird, please, if it is safe, I will come and bring you home tomorrow."

"I will go, but where?" she asked, her concern growing.

"To the caves of the bluff. Can you make it

in the dark?"

"Yes, but who will go with me?"

"Get as many as possible. I will go to Chief Black Elk now to persuade him to go with you."

"I am staying here," Grieving Mother said.

"No, mother, you need to go to with Talking Bird and the children."

"No. I will stay here. I am too old to climb the bluff. I will stay and wait for Natayah. I have things I want to tell her."

"Mother."

"Son. I have spoken on this matter."

The plan was put into action but only one fourth of the tribe was convinced to go. Black Elk was among those who stayed, and died.

As soon as the families were safely across the river, Little Feather, and Two Spear went after Sarah. Everyone else went back to bed.

The two men snuck all the way around to the half built barricade where they saw Clara, Natayah's horse come.

The army base was quiet with the exception of a few guards near the front and rear entrances. The two warriors took care of the two soldiers that were standing in their way in the rear. The frame of the base was made up of the buildings that housed the soldiers. The center was filled with the white tents waiting for the barracks to be completed.

"Which door?" Two Spear asked.

Little Feather shrugged and they went to the first window on the left. The bed was empty. They went to the next window; the bed was empty. The sun was just coming up over the horizon. A wave of fear ran through the men, they stepped to the next door and opened it. There was no one there.

"Where is everyone? Do you think it is a trap?" Two Spear asked, his heart beginning to race.

"I do not know. The place looks empty," Little Feather looked around confused.

Two Spear couldn't pass up the opportunity to boast, "They are hiding. Your wife told them of our bravery and our fierce warrior ways and they have fled from us."

Little Feather couldn't help but laugh, as he shook his head, but it did not calm his fears.

"We must go. The sun is almost up."

"Where is she?" Little Feather felt defeated.

They sneaked back out the same way they came in and rested when they made it to the tree line.

"Maybe we should stay and watch to see what and where they are this early in the morning. I am sure they will show her to us," Two Spear reassured.

Little Feather was about to agree when gunshots and screams filled the otherwise silent sunrise.

*****

Natayah kept her promise and stayed with her tribe until her death. She and Little Feather went on to have three more children and became respected leaders of the small group. Little Feather took on the duties of chief and was much loved and respected.

Natayah went on with her Bible studies but also offered reading and writing and speaking of the English language to the children and whatever adults that might be interested. She was convinced that it would help her people to get along with the growing number of white people that took over the area beneath them. Natayah would go to the edge of the cliff and look down at what was once the Seapaugh village. Sorrow filled her heart as she watched endless numbers of people, wagon trains, horses, oxen, tear through the calm forests and pastures without regard to the history that was there before them. Every once in a while a child or one of the pioneers would catch her peeking down at them and she would disappear into the mists and the trees before they could catch a second glance. It left them wondering if she was there at all.

The tribe grew in number and was able to stay hidden on their bluff for many years. The white man offered their small tribe safety on a reservation just across the river, but Little Feather was adamant that his people be allowed to grow up and grow old on their land.

The tribe suffered greatly when the white man's illness invaded their people killing many. Little Feather was one. He was buried in the Christian way, underground on the bluffs overlooking the beautiful river. With everyone looking to Natayah for direction, she led them into the reservation in Illinois.

They combined with many other tribes and lived in peace with some modern conveniences such as running water and gas lamps. The Seapaugh tribe eventually blended away, and there are very few of us left.

Natayah was given a schoolhouse to continue her teachings.

All of her children grew to adulthood and she was able to see each of them begin their own

Captive Heart

families.

Because of the location of the reservation and the more modern roadways, Natayah was able to see her sister again and often. She and her children learned to walk comfortably through both worlds. The white man, and the Indian, lived among each other... peacefully. Natayah's dream, always.

Some say, when the sun is shining bright and you look up to the edge of the cliff, an outline of a woman can still be seen. They say she stands near the edge, watching what goes on below. Staying close to her bluff and river and the village she came to love.

This was the story of my mother, as it was told to me over the years. She is gone now, but her spirit lives on through the lives that she touched, spreading God's word to a simple people and living a life of courage and love. She showed God's love and trusted God's will in the most trying of times.

Sarah Natayah died of natural causes and a longing to be with my father. She was buried beside my father on the bluff.

Sarah Natayah was my mother. I am Jacob Blue Eyes.

Elizabeth Bourgeret

Acknowledgements

While these names below may not mean a lot to the average reader, they mean the world to me.

Always, always, I thank my mother who has supported me through everything... and I mean everything. She has seen me at my best and at my worst and has encouraged me every step of the way.

My beautiful, wonderful children. They have been my biggest fans but have also been honest giving me support and critiques along the way. They were patient when I had to spend hours in front of the computer even gently reminding me to get my computer time in on a regular basis. They were happy to entertain themselves while I would spend hours writing in the shadows of my beloved Bluff feeding from the energy of the "magic tree". My Sarah and Katherynn, you are the beat of my heart. I love you with every fiber of my being.

Thank you to my readers of early (barely discernable) story ideas and outlines and my editors who make it make sense.

To my family. I love each and every one of you so very much. I am just happy that you are a part of my life. I love being your sister, mother, grandmother, aunt, and child. Thank you for not giving up on me completely, and for second chances.

To my friends who put up with me as I stress out about every little detail and offer advice and encouragement on everything from outfits, to life choices, to just... being there. And no, just because this book is finished, I will not "return" to a sense of "normal". There are more books to be written.

To Bob Caldwell, for so, so many things, but especially for coffee ice cream.

To my Tonya Hopkins, who made sure I didn't starve and who has been my friend through thick and thin and still manages to love me anyway.

To my Christina Walz and my Dorothy Nichole Luster, who have taken (shoved) me out of my "comfort box" to see a bit more of the world and all it has to offer.

And to my Eric Rowlett, who teaches me that loving unconditionally is not always an easy choice to make, but it is always the right choice.

And I thank God for using me as His vessel to put this story out there and for allowing me to find out who I was meant to be. And for surrounding me with the people who came to be a part of my life even if for a brief moment, that helped me get to this; This exact coordinate on my life's path. I am so very blessed and I am so very grateful to be forgiven.

Made in the USA
Charleston, SC
21 May 2014